THE
TENTH CIRCLE

THE
TENTH CIRCLE

A BLAINE McCRACKEN NOVEL

JON LAND

OPEN ROAD

INTEGRATED MEDIA

NEW YORK

Copyright © 2013 by Jon Land

Cover design by Mauricio Díaz

ISBN 978-1-4804-1479-2

Published in 2013 by Open Road Integrated Media, Inc.
345 Hudson Street
New York, NY 10014
www.openroadmedia.com

For the men and women of the United States Special Forces
De Oppresso Liber
Then, now, always.

ACKNOWLEDGMENTS

We meet again; you, me, Blaine, and Johnny back together for another adventure, thanks to the vision and dedication of the whole team at Open Road Integrated Media. That team is headed by the great Jane Friedman who provided me the ability to work with wonderful professionals like Pete Beatty, Libby Jordan, Rachel Chou, and Nina Lassam. I'm especially grateful to my agent Bob Diforio for bringing us together and, even more, to the one holdover from so many pages like this, my amazing and brilliant editor, Natalia Aponte. I'd hate to think where this or any of my books would be without her pushing me to be better each time out—not always an easy task when a series enters its eleventh book. Before moving on to hopefully greener pastures, Stephanie Gorton really helped bring this one over the finish line and I can't think of anyone I trust more to help push me along the home stretch than Jeff Ayers.

Because here's the thing, the delivery mechanism for books

ACKNOWLEDGMENTS

like this might have changed, but one thing hasn't: a great story is a great story no matter how you read it, and I've done my best to deliver just that here. While you're sitting where you are, and I'm sitting where I am, I can picture you turning the page and predict you won't stop reading until the final one is flipped.

Only one way to find out if I'm right or not. (You can let me know at www.jonlandbooks.com!) So I'm going to shut up now so you can get started.

THE
TENTH CIRCLE

A hero is no braver than an ordinary man,
but he is braver five minutes longer.
Ralph Waldo Emerson

PROLOGUE: LOST

Roanoke Island, North Carolina: August, 1590

"Where could they have gone?" Governor John White asked, his voice quivering as he paced about the abandoned camp in the fetid summer heat. "What could have become of them, in the name of all that is holy?"

White knelt to smooth the land, as if it might yield some clue as to the whereabouts of the entire colony under his command, the ground mist hiding the trembling of his hands. The overcast sky and thick canopy of tree cover had bled the light from the clearing, the grayness of the scene befitting his mood. White's fear, apprehension, and building grief knew no bounds, since his own daughter and granddaughter had been among the colonists.

Now among the missing.

The fort the colonists had occupied was gone, leaving behind only earth berms and rotted logs where cabins and structures had once stood. As if a vast storm had swept in and swallowed everything in its path, including the men, women, and children who had lived here.

"No trace, no trace at all," he said out loud to himself, as the others who had accompanied him from the ship watched him wipe the tears from his eyes. They had arrived at dusk, the shadows of the coming night making the overgrown brush look like spectral monsters snapping at the air with their leaf-like teeth. The only other hints of the fort's existence were some still-standing posts and beams, forming the shell of the exterior wall. The land was overgrown with weeds and dead brush, and a sour, spoiled odor hung in the thick air rich with the hum of black flies and mosquitoes typical of August this far south in the new land. This was actually the second colony to be based on Roanoke Island off the coast of North Carolina, the first having been abandoned due to insufficient supplies and incessant battles with the local native tribes who proved less than hospitable. White had resolved to avoid both of those maladies this time, as evidenced by the fact that his own daughter and son-in-law were included among the colonists. They'd had a child shortly before his ill-timed return to England, a daughter: White's grandchild, Virginia Dare, a fact that left his insides knotted and gnarled like a bad cramp.

"No sign of any of them, Governor," noted Thomas Glanville, captain of a privateering expedition who had ferried White here from England for a considerable price.

"My granddaughter," said White softly, sadly, "the first English child born in the Americas. I left her here along with the other one hundred fourteen colonists three years ago with a promise to return in no more than one. I left them to their deaths. This is my fault."

"We don't know they're dead, sir, not for sure."

"Today would have been her third birthday," White said, his expression grim and spine stiff as he lingered over the remnants of the well the colonists had dug to supply them with water.

With the camp so close to Albemarle Sound, a tributary of the Chesapeake Bay, they were able to find water just a dozen feet down. But it must have gone dry or soured, because a replacement well had been dug farther up a rise on a natural earth berm. "We must find what became of her," he continued. "We must find what became of all of them."

Life had proved so harsh here that the colonists had convinced White to journey to England to plead for them to be able to come home. His long-delayed return sprang from a winding journey full of false starts and aborted voyages that had waylaid his plans to make it back sooner. He had dreaded giving his people the unfortunate news that their request had been turned down, and now he dreaded something much worse.

"No sign of the signal you described, sir," a sailor whose name White had forgotten reported, returning after a careful survey of the area. White noted that the man had trimmed off the sleeves of his thick canvas shirt and rolled up the legs of his woolen britches to his knees. The other three sailors who'd accompanied White and Glanville to the colony had done the same, perhaps regretting it since their exposed flesh sent the buzzing insects into a feeding frenzy.

"Signal?" asked Glanville.

"If anything befell the colonists," White told him, "my instructions were to leave a Maltese cross on a tree. The fact that there's none can only mean . . ." He let the remainder of his thought dangle in the air amid the hot, misty breath trailing each word from his mouth. "Whatever happened here," he finished finally, "must have happened very fast."

"Well, I did find something else, sir," the sailor resumed, leading White toward the southwest corner of the camp.

While the other sailors continued their check of the perimeter, White found himself before a still-standing post of the fort with the word *Croatoan* carved into its surface.

"What is it?" Glanville wondered.

"An island nearby."

"Could it be that the colonists sought refuge there, Governor?"

"Possibly," White said, feeling a flicker of hope rise in him, "but it could also be a reference to the local native tribe known to be friendlier than the others."

White ran his fingers over the etching, hoping the depth and condition might yield some clue as to how long ago it had been carved. He had known natives of this new land who could discern such things, but for him it was just conjecture further complicated by the sky darkening ahead in promise of a storm, a big one judging by the feel of the air.

The governor turned his gaze that way, addressing Glanville as he did. "How bad a blow are we looking at, Captain?"

"Bad, sir." Glanville seemed to sniff the air. "Very bad."

White nodded, his expression turning even grimmer as the color washed from his face. "Then we have little time to continue the search, to—"

He stopped suddenly, something about the ground between this tree and the replacement well grabbing his attention. White retraced their path, stopping over a slightly raised mound. He knelt and smoothed his hand over the earth.

"We must go," he said, rising stiffly. "Our decision is made. No more lives can be placed at risk."

"You paid me to do a job, Governor," Glanville started. "I'd prefer to see it done."

"It is done, Captain. The colony is lost. Hope was lost long ago. They're dead, each and every one of them, my family included."

"You don't know—"

"Yes, I do." White inhaled deeply and blew out more breath caked with steaming mist. "Now we must be gone from here. And fast."

"You speak as if we're in danger, sir."

"Because we are. Whatever killed my people is still about, Captain, still hungry for more death. I feel that in my bones too."

The sky rumbled with the first hint of thunder. The wind shifted to the northeast, blowing in a swatch of fog from the nearby sound.

"Feel *what*, Governor? I've never backed down from a fight and those natives you mention will get more of a battle from my men than any fifty you left behind."

"It wasn't natives, Captain. The fate that befell my people was the work of no man."

"What then?"

White looked away, swinging about in the rain that had begun to dapple the air. "It will all be in my report, along with a warning to Sir Walter Raleigh and the crown itself."

"Governor?"

"That no Englishman ever set foot on this cursed land again. And we must get back to your ship before we join the colonists in the same fate."

Glanville held White's stare as best he could through the thickening fog that stole from him sight of the sailors still patrolling through the weeds and overgrowth.

"What is it you see, sir?"

"Not what I see, Captain, so much as what I don't."

That's when the first gurgling scream sounded, followed by a second, and a third. Then gasps from the sailors lost to the fog at the camp's outer perimeter.

Then nothing.

Glanville went for his sword, but White jammed a hand down on the hilt.

"It won't help. Trust me. We must run."

"I can't leave my men! I can't—"

But White grasped his exposed forearm and yanked Glanville into motion, away from where the screams had come.

"Now, Captain, now! Before it's too late, before there's no one left to tell the tale!"

Glanville gave up on his sword and fell into stride alongside White. Lightning bursts cut through the fog, illuminating their path as branches and brambles scratched at their faces and tore at their clothes, the Roanoke Colony lost behind them.

Bay of Gibraltar, Atlantic Ocean: 1872

"I know that ship," said Captain John Moorehouse, his voice stiff with concern, as he lowered the spyglass from his eye and turned to his mate. "She's the *Mary Celeste*."

The *Dei Gratia*'s second-in-command, Abner Devereaux, joined Moorehouse at the foredeck under a crystal-clear sky and calm winds. They'd never sailed together before, Devereaux having joined the crew as a last-minute replacement for the regular mate who'd fallen ill suddenly. Devereaux had heavy-lidded, hooded eyes and, during the voyage across the Atlantic from New York, had been prone to keeping to himself, in contrast with the gregarious Moorehouse's penchant for staying close to his men.

"Her captain, Benjamin Spooner Briggs, and I had dinner the night before we both set sail from New York," Moorehouse continued, having first spotted the *Mary Celeste* yawing. Now he watched her come into the wind and then fall off, the currents having steered her into the Bay of Gibraltar between Portugal and the Azores. "She's floundering, out of control."

"Where's she bound?" Devereaux asked.

"Genoa with seventeen hundred barrels of American alcohol in her holds," Moorehouse told him, comparing that to the *Dei Gratia*'s cargo of an almost identical number of barrels filled with petroleum.

"I see no distress signal," said Devereaux, squinting and shielding his eyes from the bright afternoon sunlight.

"What say we see if she responds to our call?"

"Aye, sir," the mate said, and grabbed a silver hailing trumpet, heavy and large at eighteen inches in length, from a nearby hook. Reflexively, he wiped its mouthpiece prior to raising the instrument to his lips and blew hard three times to blast a signal. Devereaux waited for a response and when none came he tried again with the same result.

"What say we board her," said Moorehouse, "and see what we can see?"

"She's abandoned for sure," Devereaux reported after supervising a search below deck of the three-hundred-ton brigantine's cabins. "No sign anywhere of the captain and crew."

Standing on the deck of the ghostship, Moorehouse stiffened. "Benjamin Briggs had his wife and little girl with him. His mate, Albert Richardson, is as good a seaman as I've known."

"Well, they left in a hurry, sir. Fast enough to leave their oilskin boots and pipes beyond."

"Pirates, then," Moorehouse groused.

"I think not. Her holds are intact, the cargo undisturbed. I did find this."

Devereaux handed Moorehouse a tattered, leather-encased ledger.

"The captain's log," Moorehouse noted. "This should tell us something anyway."

"You said she was bound for Genoa."

"I did."

"Strange then that the course the captain had laid out was bound for England, a port not far from Chislehurst."

"That makes no sense," from Moorehouse, his discomfort worn in something between a scowl and a frown, the hot sun carving fresh fissures in his already-leathery skin.

Moorehouse gazed about the abandoned deck of the ghost-ship, eerie in its desolation, every yaw and creak exaggerated by the silence.

"Mutiny perhaps," suggested Devereaux.

"You find any trace of liquor on board?"

"None, besides what leaked out of a cracked barrel in one of the holds I checked."

"Because Briggs forbade it, a God-fearing man who never touched the drink and chose his crews from among men of a like mind. I've never known a mutiny not fueled by the spirits."

"What then, Captain?"

"Rig the ship for tow. We'll string her to port with us."

"There's something you're not saying, sir."

Moorehouse had hoped his mate wouldn't see the new sense of hopelessness he felt flashing in his gaze. "No captain would leave his logbook behind upon abandoning ship. I believe he and the others were taken or . . ."

"Or *what*, in the name of Christ?"

"Something made them vanish, chief mate, vanish into thin air."

Chislehurst, England: 1872

Louis-Napoléon Bonaparte, better known as Napoléon III, was bedridden when his dour-faced visitor, Henri Jaubert, arrived. Since being released from a German prison in the wake of France's disastrous defeat in the war with Prussia, his health had deteriorated sharply. That war had been waged at his urging and under his command. So its miserable failure had not only branded him first a prisoner of war and then an exile, but had also marked the end of the Second French Empire. A new republic had now replaced it, adding to Napoléon III's misery, further exacerbated by a chronic lung infection and a knifing pain riddling his extremities for which doctors had yet to find the proper treatment. He alternated between terrible bouts of sweating and equally racking chills, and was given to fits of delirium that left him lost in the illusion he still ruled his beloved France. But that condition now threatened to forestall his plans to seize back the crown with the help of the actual cargo of a ship that was now two weeks late in arriving at port here.

A cargo that could change the balance of power in the world and, more importantly, France's place in it.

"Is there any news of the ship?" Napoléon III asked Jaubert, who stood at the foot of his bed, his lean frame still enough to block the sun pouring in through the window. In contrast to Jaubert's woolen, tailored suit that was shiny enough to look wet, Napoléon wore a nightshirt that stank of rot and spoilage, the odors rising from his own flesh worsening more and more as the days went on.

"There is, but not good. Things did not go as planned. I'm afraid unforeseen circumstances intervened."

With considerable effort, Napoléon III forced himself upright in bed. "Just tell me the barrels are still intact. Tell me that much."

Jaubert cleared his throat. "Intact, yes, but they ended up in Gibraltar."

"Gibraltar?"

"It seems we may have outsmarted ourselves. They'd been off-loaded before my contacts arrived in the port, Your Excellence. My men were unable to trace what became of them. But given time—"

"Time? There is no time. Not for me, not for France."

"We must find another way, Your Excellence."

"Another way to take my throne back? Another means with the power of those barrels' true contents? Don't be a fool, Henri. Our British friends put this opportunity before us for a considerable sum we now risk squandering. There can never be another opportunity like it."

"But if what you say is true . . ."

Napoléon III stifled a fresh cough. "Someone will open those barrels, Henri. Someone will open them and unleash something they won't comprehend and cannot control."

Henri Jaubert crossed himself. "May God have mercy on their souls."

"And what of our souls, what of France's soul?" This time Napoléon III was overcome by a coughing spasm that left him gasping for air, his face purpled with blood vessels leaking red onto the whites of his eyes. "Your men are still in Gibraltar?"

"Of course, Your Excellence."

"Get word to them. Have them retrieve those barrels at all costs, while there's still hope."

"And if it's too late?"

A wet, wheezy sloshing sound heaved from Napoléon III's lungs. "Then may God have mercy on our souls too."

PART ONE:
UP CLOSE AND PERSONAL

CHAPTER 1

The Negev Desert, Israel: The present

"We have incoming, General! Anti-missile batteries are responding!"

General Yitzak Berman focused his gaze on the desperate scenario unfolding in amazingly realistic animation on the huge screen before him. Eight missiles fired from Iran sped toward all major population centers of Israel in a perfect geometric pattern, about to give the nation's anti-missile system, Arrow, its greatest test yet.

"Sir," reported the head of the analysts squeezed into the underground bunker from which Israel maintained command and control, "initial specs indicate the size, weight, and sourcing of the missiles . . ."

"Proceed," the general said when the analyst stopped to swallow hard.

"They're nuclear, sir, in the fifty-kiloton range."

"Targets?"

Another young man picked up from there. "Jerusalem, Tel Aviv, Haifa, the Mediterranean coast, the Sinai, our primary airfields . . ." He looked back toward Berman. "And *here*, sir."

"Anti-missile batteries are launching!" a new voice blared through the strangely dim lighting that seemed to flutter as the missiles drew closer.

And Berman watched the animated simulation of dozens and dozens of Israeli Arrow rockets, along with larger American Patriots, shooting upward in line with the incoming missiles. Four hits were scored in the maelstrom of animated smoke bursts, more rockets launched to chase down the remaining four nukes that had survived the fist salvo.

"We have two more confirmed downed!" yet another young voice rang out.

But the bunker fell silent as the sophisticated animation continued to follow two surviving Iranian missiles as they streaked toward Tel Aviv and Haifa.

"*Schmai Israel, hallileh hoseh,*" one of the young voices began, reciting the prayer softly as the missiles' arcs turned downward, on direct courses to their targets with nothing left to stop their flight.

"Order our fighters holding at their fail-safe positions to launch their attacks," instructed Berman. "Destroy Iran."

He'd barely finished when two flashes burst out from the animated screen, bright enough to force several of those squeezed into the bunker to shield their eyes. As those flashes faded amid the stunned silence and odor of stale perspiration hanging in the air, the bunker's regular lighting snapped back on.

"*This concludes the simulation,*" a mechanical voice droned. "*Repeat, this concludes the simulation.*"

With that, a bevy of Israeli officials, both civilian and military, emerged from the rear-most corner of the bunker, all wearing dour expressions.

Israel's female defense minister stepped forward ahead of the others. "Your point is made, General," she said to Berman. "Not that we needed any further convincing."

"I'm glad we all agree that the Iranian nuclear threat can no longer be tolerated," Berman, the highest-ranking member of the Israeli military left alive who'd fought in the Six-Day War, told them. "We've been over all this before. The difference is we're now certain our defenses cannot withstand an Iranian attack, leaving us with casualty estimates of up to a million dead and two million wounded, many of them gravely. Fifty simulations, all with results similar to the ones you have just witnessed." He hesitated, eyes hardened through two generations of war boring into the defense minister's. "I want your formal authorization."

"For what?"

"To destroy the Iranian nuclear complex at Natanz."

Israel's defense minister started to smile, then simply shook her head. "We've been over this before, a hundred times. Our army can't do it, our air force can't do it, our commandos can't do it, and the Americans are saying the very same thing from their end. You want my authorization to do the impossible? You've got it. Just don't expect any backup, extraction, or political cover."

Yitzak Berman returned his gaze to the wall-sized screen where the animated versions of Tel Aviv and Haifa had turned dark. "The man I have in mind won't need of any of that."

"Did you say *man?*"

CHAPTER 2

Natanz, Iran

"We are descending through a million tons of solid rock," the Islamic Republic of Iran's Minister of Energy, Ali Akbar Hosseini, told the filmmaker squeezed in the elevator with both his equipment and the trio of Revolutionary Guardsmen. "A technological achievement in its own right. You understand the great task you've been entrusted to perform."

"Just as you must understand I'm the best at my job, just like your scientists are at theirs," said the bearded, award-winning filmmaker Hosseini knew as Hakeem Najjar. Najjar's appearance was exactly as depicted in photographs, save for the scar through his left eyebrow the minister did not recall. He was dressed casually in dark cargo pants and a long-sleeve cotton shirt rolled up at the sleeves, bulky clothing that hid what was clearly a V-shaped, well-muscled frame beneath. "I was told I'd be given total access to the facility."

"And you will, at least those parts deemed appropriate by me."

"That wasn't part of the deal. It never is with my work."

"This is a different kind of opportunity."

The elevator started to slow.

"Then you should have gotten a filmmaker more adept at wedding videos," Najjar snapped. "Perhaps we've both made a mistake."

"You are about to see what few men ever have," Hosseini continued, wearing a fashionable suit instead of a military uniform. "And it will be your blessed privilege to chronicle it for the world to see when the time is right. You call that a mistake?"

"You chose me because I'm the best. I ask only that you treat me that way."

"I could have retained a simple videographer for this assignment," Hosseini said, his shoulders stiffening. "I chose you because I wanted something that would stand the test of history. This will be my legacy, my contribution to our glorious Republic, and I want it to be celebrated, not just appreciated, a century from now. I want anyone who watches to see not just a place, but a point in history that changed the world forever. An awesome responsibility I'm entrusting you with."

"I look forward to exceeding your expectations."

Hosseini's eyes fell on the bulky equipment lying at the filmmaker's feet: a camera, portable lights, and a quartet of shoe box–sized rechargeable batteries to supply power. "Others I've worked with have turned to much smaller cameras for video, even ones that look like they only take pictures."

"And how did their work turn out?" asked the filmmaker, his tone still biting.

"Acceptable, but not impressive. This assignment clearly required something more, a case I had to make to the Council's finance board to justify your fee."

"If you aren't satisfied with what I produce for you, you owe nothing. I'll return my fee to the Council personally."

"Both of us know that will not be necessary. Both of us know you will produce something that will stand the test of time through the ages and serve both of us well," Hosseini said to the man he'd personally selected for the job.

"I value your regard and the confidence you have in me," Najjar said more humbly in Farsi.

Then he slung the camera over his shoulder and scooped up the batteries and portable lights in his grasp, beckoning the minister to exit ahead of him.

"After you," said Blaine McCracken.

CHAPTER 3

Washington, DC: Two months earlier

"You're kidding, right?" Blaine McCracken said after the Israeli he knew only as "David" finished.

"You come highly recommended, Mr. McCracken. Back home you're considered a legend."

"Another word for *dinosaur*."

"But far from extinct. And my American friends tell me you're the only one they believe can get this done."

"Meaning I'd have to succeed where two governments have failed."

David shrugged, the gesture further exaggerating the size of his neck, which seemed a stubby extension of his shoulders and trapezius muscles. He wasn't a tall man but was unnaturally broad through the upper body. McCracken couldn't make out his eyes well in the darkness, but imagined them to be furtive and noncommittal.

They'd met at the Observation Deck of the Washington

Monument. It was closed to the public for repairs indefinitely, but still accessible by workmen, though not at night, always McCracken's favorite time to view Washington. He liked imagining what was going on in offices where lights still burned, what plans were being hatched and fates determined. There was so much about the city he hated, but plenty from which he couldn't detach himself. In the vast majority of those offices, officials were trying to do good; at least, they believed they were.

McCracken found himself wondering which of those offices David had come here from; it would have been State or Defense in the old days, across the river in Langley just as often. These days it was Homeland Security, the catchall and watchword that got people nodding in silence; with its offices spread out all over the city proper, it was responsible for an untold number of the lights that still burned.

A few work lamps provided the only illumination inside the gutted Observation Deck, riddled with a musty basement-like smell of old, stale concrete and wood rot mixed with the fresh lumber and sawdust that covered the exposed floor like a floating rug. David had sneezed a few times upon first entering, passing it off as allergies.

"It's not that we've failed," David told him, "it's that all the plans we've considered have been rejected out of hand. We've come to you for something nontraditional, something no one expects."

"You've got a lot of faith in me."

"If anyone can do it, it's you. Otherwise, we will have no choice but to try something that is doomed to fail and perhaps even make things worse. But our hands are tied. With Iran so close to getting their bomb, the choice is gone."

"Your name's not really David, is it?" McCracken asked the Israeli.

"Why would you think that?"

"Because the last few times I've worked with your country, my contacts were named David too. A reference to David and Goliath maybe?"

A flicker of a smile crossed the Israeli's lips. "I'm told you had a plan."

"No, what I've got is an *idea*. It's risky, dangerous, and I haven't even broached it to the powers at be here."

"Because you don't think they'd be interested?"

"Because they haven't asked." McCracken looked out through the window at the twinkling office lights again, already fewer of them than just a few minutes before, imagining the kind of things being discussed after office hours had concluded. "The only time my phone rings these days is when the SEALs or Delta have already passed on the mission, with good reason this time."

"We're asking you," said David, "not them. And we'll provide you with the right resources, *any* resources you require."

McCracken gave David a longer look, the younger man's thick nest of curly hair making him seem vulnerable and innocent at the same time though neither was true. "Tell me you're ready to fight fire with fire. Tell me that's what you meant about making the right *resources* available."

David seemed to grasp his meaning immediately. "And if we are?"

Blaine smiled.

CHAPTER 4

Natanz, Iran: The present

McCracken lugged the equipment from the elevator, careful to show strain and exertion on his features to avoid raising any suspicions in Hosseini. The hall before them was brightly lit, as clean and sterile as a hospital's. The air smelled of nothing—not antiseptic, not solvent, not fresh tile. Nothing. The lighting looked unbalanced, harsh in some places and dull in others.

The new Iranian president, Hassan Rouhani's successor, had made no secret of his desire to chronicle Iran's greatest technological achievement ever. When the time was right, he wanted the world to see the true scope of his country's accomplishment, so long hidden behind innuendo and subterfuge.

The true Hakeem Najjar, the award-winning Iranian filmmaker chosen for that task, was virtually the same height and weight as McCracken and the two men bore more than a passing resemblance to each other, right up to the scruffiness of their tightly trimmed beards. Of course, the plan was not without its flaws. Most notably, McCracken had no idea when Najjar would be summoned to capture the Natanz facility in all its glory. Based on the current timetable for the Iranians' ability to generate enough fissionable material from the refuse of their vast centrifuges, though, he guessed no more than six months.

It turned out to be only two.

The filmmaker Najjar was already under twenty-four-hour surveillance by Israeli Mossad agents long entrenched within Iranian society. Barely an hour after the filmmaker was contacted by Minister Hosseini's office on extremely short notice, McCracken boarded a private jet with a makeup specialist on board to finish the job of matching his appearance as closely as possible to Najjar's. The result, after a laborious process that took much of the flight, exceeded even his expectations. The lone oversight had been not to disguise the scar through McCracken's left eyebrow from a wayward bullet decades before. Although Minister Hosseini had clearly noticed it, he seemed unbothered by its presence.

While Najjar waited in his apartment for his government car to arrive, a fresh Mossad team, just in the country, entered his apartment by using a key fit to the specifications of his lock based on the serial number. The filmmaker, who was still packing, was unconscious in seconds, with McCracken ready in his stead, equipment in hand, as soon as the car arrived for the first leg of his journey.

Once out of the elevator, McCracken knew he was about to encounter plenty not mentioned in David's reports on the structure and its schematics. Israel's intelligence on the Natanz facility was an amalgamation of satellite reconnaissance; prisoner and defector interrogations; and four separate brilliantly crafted infiltrations. Each of these had provided the particulars of at least a section of the facility, but even taken in sum, they didn't offer a thorough rendering of all of it.

The assembled intelligence did reveal a sprawling single-level underground facility. The original plans had called for multiple levels, but this had proven too onerous from both construction and security standpoints. Natanz had been chosen for the site of the plant specifically because of the heavy layers of limestone and shale beneath which it would be contained, along with an under-layer of nearly impenetrable volcanic rock formed in prehistoric times. Contrary to conventional wisdom, the nuclear generating plant that sat at ground level was not positioned directly over the underground facility at all; rather, it served as effective camouflage for the vast tunneling efforts that had forged Natanz from the side instead of from above. The facility was laid out roughly in a square, the size of six football fields placed next to one another, and featured the sophisticated technology required to enrich uranium along with the centrifuges responsible for generating it, a process that undoubtedly included the massive pumps and water systems required for cooling.

But the very features that made Natanz impenetrable to an attack from above made it vulnerable to what McCracken was planning from within.

David versus Goliath indeed.

"One more thing before we get started," Hosseini said, opening a door McCracken hadn't noticed before. "If you'd join me inside here . . ."

It was a locker room, more or less, each open cubicle featuring an orange radiation suit and wrist monitor hanging from a hook inside.

"Standard procedure," the minister explained. "The lightest weight suit manufactured anywhere. You slip it on right over your clothes," he continued, starting to do just that himself.

McCracken followed in step. Modern, sophisticated nuclear

plants like this were hardly prone to leaks, so the donning of such protective material could only mean Hosseini meant what he said about assembling a complete picture of one of the world's most secret facilities.

"Come," the minister beckoned, "let us witness the means by which we will destroy Israel."

CHAPTER 5

Natanz, Iran: The present

"We will begin shooting here," said Minister Hosseini, after they exited the changing room, the trio of Revolutionary Guardsmen having donned the radiation suits and wrist monitors as well.

"I'd prefer to decide where to begin shooting."

"I was told you were impetuous, even arrogant."

"I take my job seriously, Minister."

"So do I. And I have very specific instructions from the president, which *both of us* must follow. His orders are to capture the scope of the facility while stressing its magnificent self-contained nature. I stress that nothing will be off-limits to make sure the historical record you are fashioning is complete. You are about to ensure that history will know things very, very few men have seen before. Does that satisfy you?"

"I haven't decided yet. Would you mind?" McCracken asked

Hosseini, extending portable lights toward the Republican Guardsmen.

The minister nodded and the soldiers shifted their weapons in order to hold the lights as the filmmaker instructed. McCracken made sure they were connected to one of the portable batteries and then hoisted the Canon XL-10 up to his shoulder. It belonged to the real Najjar and was known to be his camera of choice, enabling McCracken to practice with an identical model back home to master at least the rudimentary mechanics. An Israeli documentary filmmaker had spent hours teaching him to hold, wield, and steady the Canon just as a professional would, specifically Najjar.

"You assured me I'd have unlimited access to the facility."

"And you will," said Hosseini, "only under my guidance and supervision. Any room or section we avoid is the result of that area's contents not bearing the merit to help tell the story your film record will."

"I don't like being told not to use any sound or narration."

"The narration will be added later, along with interviews with the esteemed scientists and officials most responsible for bringing this project to fruition, all for the historical record."

McCracken pretended to be busy checking his camera to spare himself a response.

"Follow me," Hosseini directed, "and we will begin." The minister stopped and looked back at him. "You don't mind following me, do you?"

"So long as we can get started," said McCracken.

They entered the VIP elevator. The video tour of the facility would commence just down the hall in a large but sprawling security area featuring a bank of six elevators, on which workers arrived for their shifts that ran nonstop throughout the week. Since the facility was perpetually under some form of construction, Hosseini explained that the workers were divided between the builders and the technicians actually responsible for getting Natanz on line and for supervising the complex enrichment process.

"For security reasons," Hosseini elaborated, "we can't have our workers commuting in a traditional fashion. So their living quarters rest in cleverly disguised areas in the facility above us. They need only walk down a single hallway and press a button to arrive here. For reasons of privacy, those living quarters will not be included in the historical record you are making. But all you see before you here will be."

That included a bevy of armed Revolutionary Guardsmen who checked the workers through security after scanning their badges and radiation wrist monitors. The badges, dangling from neck lanyards, were color-coded according to the various areas of the complex each worker was permitted to access. Based on what McCracken saw, he could safely estimate the facility likely employed from 750 to 1,000 workers in total. The men looked nervous and McCracken noticed they didn't tote lunches or anything else along with them, since bringing anything in from the outside was strictly prohibited.

From here, the vast bulk of the workers entered a changing area complete with banks of open lockers where they dressed into the proper radiation suits, some emerging with helmets outfitted with respirators as well. Attempting to enter an unauthorized area by any of them would automatically trigger an alarm. McCracken played director by instructing the soldiers accompanying him to aim the lights appropriately and shot the arrival scenes from several different angles, just as the Israeli filmmaker who was well acquainted with Najjar's award-winning work, had taught him. Interesting how so much of his career had been about learning how to wield various weapons. For this mission, it was a camera instead.

"Let's move on," Hosseini said, tightening his shoulders and starting to fidget impatiently when the process of shooting the parade of arriving workers drew on too long for him.

"I'm not finished."

"This isn't important."

McCracken kept shooting. "I'll decide what's important."

Hosseini covered the lens with his palm. "There are scheduling concerns you aren't privy to. I'd ask you to respect that."

McCracken lowered the camera and then continued the process, as instructed, with shots of banks of offices manned by analysts and technicians busy monitoring and collating data from their respective departments. Again, McCracken could feel Hosseini getting antsy, impatient through Blaine's painstaking process of capturing the more mundane areas of the facility that he explained could be edited out later. The minister led him past the huge pumping station lined with layer upon layer of piping connected to massive vats of constantly recycled water used in the cooling process so crucial to any nuclear facility.

"The temperature of the gases contained in the centrifuges," Hosseini explained, "could easily reach several thousand degrees, a recipe for explosion if the cooling mechanisms ever failed."

"You should consider doing the narration yourself, Minister," said McCracken.

Hosseini started to smile, then caught the sarcastic gleam in the filmmaker's eyes, and did not bother to add that previous efforts to destroy or destabilize Natanz had targeted either the cooling systems or computer controls themselves, both via highly sophisticated computer viruses, including the infamous STUXNET. But the effects of those attempts had been negligible at best, as well as temporary. The facility was state of the art and then some, far beyond what the best intelligence reported, as if Iran had been laying low the whole time, wanting the world to think they were constructing something second rate. On the contrary, Iranian nuclear scientists and physicists had clearly borrowed, or stolen, the best nuclear technology available, a fact further confirmed at the next stop on the historical record.

"Our crowning achievement," the minister announced proudly. "The centrifuges. Truly a gift from Allah," he added, almost reverently, as they reached a thick glass wall that looked down into a huge sunken space filled with an equally endless chain of finely polished centrifuges. "Behold what has allowed us to enrich more U-235 than the world could possibly realize."

McCracken could hardly estimate how many there were of the standing, interconnected cylindrical machines outfitted with thick spaghetti-like strands of hosing that joined up with a sophisticated network of overhead piping. Technicians wearing the most advanced of the radiation suits walked the floor holding iPad-sized electronic notebooks, on which they constantly added readings gleaned from computerized readouts over each grouping. McCracken had seen all the various estimates of how close Iran was to actually being able to build a bomb. He was no expert, but he didn't have to be to know all those estimates could be thrown out the window since, if this particular part of the facility was an accurate indicator, the enrichment process was proceeding at a staggering clip.

He continued to film through the glass, as Hosseini smiled smugly.

"The Americans thought they were setting us back with their computer virus," Hosseini said contemptuously. "But while they were attacking our software, we were perfecting our hardware. This facility has a benchmark of fifty percent purity, but we have been achieving sixty. Sixty! Can you believe it? And it is impregnable, beyond the reach of even their most advanced bunker-busting bombs. Your video is capturing a change in the world's balance of power that will endure for lifetimes."

McCracken glanced at the minister briefly, then just kept shooting.

"Make sure you miss nothing," the minister ordered.

"Please don't tell me how to do my job."

"Consider it constructive advice, so you may record for history what only a handful of men will ever see for themselves. . . ."

Hosseini continued to drone on, leaving McCracken to understand one thing with perfect clarity.

After hearing so much, there was no way he was getting out of there alive.

CHAPTER 6

Natanz, Iran: The present

The next stop on the tour featured the most terrifying part of the process: extraction and storage of the super-enriched, bomb-ready uranium. It was done in a room sealed behind foot-thick steel walls, by men working remotely in isolation suits with gloved hands that maneuvered robotic pincers in six-inch-thick glass enclosures. The same kind of high-tech machines used in the most complex microsurgical procedures. The nature of this last stage of the process was painstaking, maddening. Only relatively small amounts of the uranium were produced from each extraction, but over time—and not very much of it at all—those small amounts would add up to more than enough to construct a dozen or more fissionable bombs that could change the balance of power in the world.

McCracken had already done plenty of imagining of what a single one of those bombs could do in the hands of a terrorist organization, or in an all-out war with Israel, to the point where he found himself wondering if he was witnessing the end of the world through a view plate. Especially since Iran had done a surprisingly effective job at subterfuge, leading the world to believe their nuclear technology was woefully outdated.

"You are pleased with the shots?" Hosseini asked him.

"I'm starting to be."

"Good, because I've saved the best for last," said Hosseini.

They approached an ultrahigh security area behind what looked to be a wall formed of lead and steel, accessible through a single door guarded by a half-dozen Revolutionary Guardsmen standing rigid and purposeful. Warnings that included NO FURTHER ADMITTANCE and EXTREME RADIATION DANGER in both English and Farsi lined the walls, although McCracken doubted anyone who worked in the Natanz facility would venture this far without proper clearance.

Prior to being permitted entry, both he and Hosseini donned thicker radiation suits that included helmets complete with respirators and faceplates. The suit, with the texture and heft of an astronaut's, came complete with a separate radiation monitor, which was currently reading in the green.

"You will leave the batteries and lights behind," the minister instructed. "Take only your camera from this point."

They moved toward the single entry to the high-security area where guards checked Hosseini's identification and subjected him to a pupil scan. Once cleared, both the minister and McCracken submitted to a thorough pat-down that included a careful inspection of McCracken's Canon camera. From there, one of the guardsmen used a metal access card dangling from a chain strung from his neck to open a sliding door that vanished inside the wall McCracken could now see was upwards of a foot thick.

The door accessed a second security area where Hosseini placed his palm against a wall scanner under the watch of yet two more Revolutionary Guardsmen. A light flashed green and a second steel door slid open to reveal a clear wall that looked like glass but was more likely some acrylic polymer.

"Here is where the world will change forever," the minister announced proudly.

And McCracken found himself watching what could only be the final step in the process of turning the uranium harvested from the centrifuges into the final ingredient required to actually build a nuclear bomb.

"Your camera," Hosseini prompted.

"I'm sorry," McCracken said through his faceplate, raising the Canon to his now thickly padded shoulder. "I was . . ."

"I understand," the minister said, smiling through the plastic. "Even the objective artist cannot help but be impressed by such moments. It's starting to look like this was all worth it, yes?"

"I believe it just might be."

McCracken began recording, focusing on the process unfolding through the lens. Calcium was being added to the uranium hexafluoride gas to create highly enriched uranium metal by an army of workers working at individually sealed stations inaccessible from one another. The calcium would react with the fluoride to create a salt, forming the pure-uranium metal that would turn Iran into a nuclear power in a mere few months, if not weeks. McCracken knew the warheads would be assembled here or, perhaps, in another secret area located below this one, regardless of Hosseini's claims to the contrary.

"Make sure you get everything," Hosseini was saying. "History is unfolding before our eyes."

Back outside the high-security area, McCracken stripped off his more secure radiation suit, noticing that his Revolutionary Guard escorts remained while his lights and batteries were nowhere to be seen.

"They will be returned to you later," the minister explained. "Decontamination procedures, you understand." His eyes fell on the camera now resting at McCracken's feet. "We will need to keep your camera with us as well."

"I was never informed of this."

"You've done your job. Now you must let us do ours."

"My equipment is sacred!" McCracken protested, his entire body stiffening.

"This is for your own good."

"I won't leave here without my camera."

Hosseini stepped forward and laid a hand gently on his shoulder in an unusual show of deference. "I understand, my friend. You have done wondrous work here today and you have the gratitude of the entire Republic for your efforts. I am truly sorry for the inconvenience."

"But what am I to do about my edit?" Blaine asked, conceding. "Any filmmaker knows therein lies the true art."

"In time, in time. All to be covered in due course," Hosseini said, suddenly reluctant to meet his eyes. "These men will escort you back up to ground level and see you safely back to Tehran. Go with Allah and know that the Republic will always hold you in the greatest respect and reverence."

And then McCracken felt a guardsman grasp him at either arm just forcefully enough, steering him back down the hallway as Minister Hosseini forced a smile and wave his way.

CHAPTER 7

Natanz, Iran

McCracken checked his watch as the soldiers ushered him into the same elevator that had brought him down from the above-ground facility. Four of them, two on either side, believing they were about to execute a simple filmmaker.

The compartment doors slid closed. One of the Revolutionary Guardsmen pressed the proper button.

Tick, tick, tick started the clock in McCracken's head as he doubled over, pretending to be sick, perhaps terrified in recognition of what was transpiring.

"Please," he said in Farsi, his voice shaky and body trembling, as the guards nearest him crouched on either side. "Please," he begged again.

McCracken felt one of them touch his shoulder, whether in feigned reassurance or as a firm show of authority, he wasn't sure.

And it didn't matter.

McCracken looped his left arm around the soldier's, straightening it and then slamming it upward so it snapped at the elbow. Then he jerked the man downward toward him and smashed the ridge of his hand into the man's throat, shattering the cartilage. The man's gasp had barely sounded before Blaine was behind him, the soldier's MPT-9 submachine gun, manufactured by Heckler & Koch, pinned between them.

Fourteen seconds, four more to go before the elevator reached the surface . . .

So McCracken went for the man's pistol instead, a PC-9 that was an unlicensed variant of the SIG P226 with which he was eminently familiar. No safety, just a decocking mechanism to ensure that a round was always chambered and ready to fire.

Blaine fired through the holster by jerking it upright. His first bullet took out the elevator's security camera, while two of the remaining three soldiers were still struggling to right their submachine guns, clumsy weapons for such a confined space, when his barrage of nine-millimeter shells *thwacked* into them.

Eleven seconds . . .

The fourth soldier either never tried or quickly gave up trying to get his MPT-9 around. Just barreled into his wheezing comrade from the side, forcing McCracken up against the elevator wall. Pinning him there while the soldier fought to free his own pistol.

No way Blaine could find the now-writhing man's holster again or free his submachine gun in time, at least not all of it. But the angle of impact had left the butt riding high above his shoulder, just the angle McCracken needed to employ both hands to jam it forward, striking the final soldier in the forehead the same moment the man's pistol cleared its holster.

Five seconds . . .

He got off one shot and then another, the first missing McCracken's left ear by mere inches and the second clanging into the ceiling. Blaine, meanwhile, kept the butt pressed against the fourth man's shattered nose and shoved forward, the writhing soldier still pressed between them when the final man's head slammed into the far compartment wall. An instant was all McCracken needed—to draw the submachine gun butt backward and resteady it for a blow straight on—with enough practiced force for the man's nose to explode bone backward into his brain.

Two seconds . . .

The mental clock in his head nearly exhausted, Blaine jerked that MPT-9 from the shoulder of the solider still pressed against him, letting him crumple. The elevator doors opening as he stripped a second MPT-9 from the body of the slumped soldier whose face was only a memory. Both weapons in hand when he burst out into the security area manned by soldiers caught between motions, the echoing din of gunshots having already reached them.

McCracken opened up with both submachine guns, catching all of them by surprise. He felt the surge from the steady pulse of fire kicking up superheated air into his face, his teeth rattling in rhythm with the steady clacking of the twin weapons. His ears first stung, then seemed to bubble with air. Blaine was only vaguely conscious of the bodies toppling around him, most suspended between breaths and actions. A few at the outside of his firing arc managed to free their weapons, even find the triggers before McCracken's fire cut them down with neatly stitched bullet lines across their torsos. He'd heard battle described any number of ways over the years, as a fog, a dream, even as a razor-sharp reality. Today, with a dozen men felled before any could get off a decent shot, it seemed a combination of all three.

McCracken discarded the empty submachine guns, the air rich with the smells of oil and gun smoke. The clock in his head had started up again, telling him he needed thirty more seconds to execute the final stage of his plan. Cutting it close, then, even closer than he thought when he caught the sound of helicopters approaching overhead.

CHAPTER 8

Natanz, Iran

Blaine knew the choppers couldn't possibly have been responding to an emergency call, not this fast. They must have been carrying replacements as opposed to reinforcements. Still, the two dozen or so troops likely to be inside the old Russian MI-8 helicopters would learn in mere moments what was transpiring and would surge from inside their cabins ready to join the battle.

That left him with no choice other than to rush through the doors leading into the facility, waving his arms frantically to signal the choppers. In that moment, the side doors on both MI-8s jerked open, the troops ferried here already poised on the starting blocks with weapons steadied before them.

McCracken backed away, pretending to be warding off debris kicked up by the rotor wash when his real intention was to reach the garbage truck currently emptying the first of several dumpsters lined up one after the other. The truck had turned up innocuously in several satellite reconnaissance photos, enough to give him an idea of where to find the last thing his plan required.

A means of escape.

"What do you mean he's gone?" Minister Hosseini demanded of the Revolutionary Guard major in charge of security for the aboveground installation. "He can't be *gone!*"

"We've searched everywhere," the major insisted.

"But you sealed off the grounds. We're in the middle of nowhere here with an electrified fence surrounding the complex. Keep looking, Major."

"But—"

"You have your orders," said Hosseini. "Now follow them."

The garbage truck rumbled down the last stretch of highway before the rendezvous point, just moments away now.

"Gotta hand it to you, boss," said Sal Belamo from behind the wheel. An ex-middleweight boxer who'd once fought Carlos Monzón for the crown, Belamo had the scars to prove it and experience dating back to the heyday of the Cold War where he specialized in close, professional-style enemy executions. A generation before, he'd actually been assigned to take out McCracken, but opted to join forces with him instead, which began a relationship that had endured ever since. "You outdid yourself this time. You ask me, anybody thinks you're too old for this shit better throw away their watch."

"You agree, Indian?" McCracken asked the hulking, seven-foot figure squeezed against the door on the other side of him.

"I've never owned a watch, Blainey," said Johnny Wareagle, his oldest friend, who'd fought by his side in Vietnam and in pretty much every war since, mostly the ones nobody ever heard about. "I determined long ago that the passage of time has nothing to do with minutes and seconds."

"Guess we're living proof of that, aren't we?"

Sal Belamo braked the truck and eased it off the main road toward the rendezvous point with the Israeli team who'd be escorting the three of them out of Iran. "This is a Mercedes, you know. Goddamn Mercedes garbage truck."

McCracken could only hope that the dumpster in which he'd taken refuge while Sal and Johnny completed the real drivers' rounds contained no radioactive material.

"I ever tell you I was supposed to be part of the whole Desert One fiasco back in 1980?" Belamo continued.

"What happened?"

"I got pulled after telling the suits in charge the plan was for shit. They took offense to that. Wasn't one of my better days."

"Just like this isn't going to be one of Iran's better ones," McCracken said, turning to Wareagle. "Got that satellite phone, Indian?"

"Where could he have gone?" Hosseini demanded of the Revolutionary Guard major, after still no trace of the filmmaker had been found twenty minutes later.

"Perhaps you're asking the wrong question, Minister. Perhaps you should concern yourself with what he was doing here."

"Isn't it obvious, you fool?"

A subordinate rushed over, extending a satellite phone toward Hosseini, who clutched it to his ear. "Speak!"

"We found the real Hakeem Najjar bound and gagged in his apartment," the secret policeman he'd dispatched reported. "Shaken, but otherwise fine."

"Find out everything he knows, especially about the man who impersonated him, and then make sure he disappears for good."

"Understood, Minister."

Hosseini ended the call and handed the satellite phone back to his subordinate, turning to find the major still standing there.

"Isn't there something you'd be better off doing? Like finding the man who infiltrated this complex, perhaps?"

"I was just wondering how anyone could have pulled off something so elaborate. And why?"

"He saw everything the complex has to offer. He knows *everything*! Isn't that enough for you?"

"Oh, it's enough," agreed the major. "I'm just not certain that it's *all*."

"What else could there be?"

"His equipment," the major said, innocently enough. "I assume you confiscated all of it prior to his dismissal."

"Of course. The camera itself, along with the portable lights he used and the batteries that supplied power. All were inspected and X-rayed two different times in accordance with security protocols."

"These batteries would've had a lead casing," noted the major. "I assume your inspection team considered that in their protocol."

Hosseini felt himself grow cold. "In the name of Allah . . . No, it can't be . . ."

And then he was rushing back for the elevator, which was still slick with drying blood.

The Natanz facility was totally off-line, no way to make contact in or out other than via satellite phone. No cellular or Internet service was available or accessible whatsoever. Had workers dared risk their jobs or worse by bringing in cellular devices with them, they'd find all signals blocked by sophisticated jamming devices that prevented any from getting in or out.

So McCracken took the satellite phone from Johnny War-eagle and began entering a number.

"The camera equipment!" Hosseini blared to the Revolutionary Guard captain in charge of security for the underground facility. "Where is it?"

"Placed just as you instructed."

"*Where?*"

The captain led him down the hall to a single narrow door and opened it to reveal shelves of military ordnance. A single shelf against the far wall that had been empty now held the fake filmmaker's confiscated equipment.

"See," the captain reported, "everything but the camera itself, also as you instructed."

Hosseini hurried to the shelf, reaching it just as the captain flicked on a light that spotlighted all four of the portable camera batteries, each about the size of a shoe box.

McCracken wasn't sure who had handled the conversion process, knew only that the plan he presented to David was to take three relatively low-yield tactical nuclear warheads in the five- to ten-megaton range and convert them from missile deployment to ground-based explosives. Originally these smaller warheads had been called Special Atomic Demolition Munitions and included models like the W48 that could be loaded into a 155-millimeter nuclear artillery shell. The warhead in the even older W33 would work just as nicely, although in a more crude fashion, but for his money, McCracken was betting the United States had supplied Israel with W45 warheads lifted from the deactivated line of MGR-3 Little John missiles for the mission.

McCracken didn't know whether it was Israeli or American scientists who'd handled the complex chore of refashioning three of his four Canon BP-975 battery packs into nuclear weapons with ground-based detonation capabilities. It couldn't have been easy trying to squeeze all that ordnance and technology into a prepackaged size, each with a combined yield many times greater than the much larger bombs used on Hiroshima and Nagasaki. The filmmaker Najjar actually used a smaller battery pack, with too small of a casing to use to hide a bomb, so this was the one liberty McCracken took with the man's process, prepared to explain the anomaly to Hosseini had he been challenged.

The four portable camera batteries, three of which had been converted to nuclear bombs, had been waiting for him when he reached Tehran. The fourth was all he needed to work the lights, the others purportedly there for backup power on the chance it was needed.

He came to the final number and paused briefly before pressing it.

"Boom," he said softly.

Hosseini and the Revolutionary Guard captain were halfway back to the elevator, each lugging two of the portable batteries, when a buzzing sounded. The men detected it in their ears but couldn't determine its source, until they cast their eyes downward in the last moment before the three flashes erupted together. The blast wave spread outward in a millisecond, consuming everything it reached in the last instants before the secondary blast sent fiery heat reaching a million degrees a mile in every direction underground.

Sal Belamo had just reached the rendezvous point a dozen miles away when McCracken felt the earth rumble. It wasn't so much beneath as all around him, the world itself quaking. There was no sense of a primary or secondary blast, no air burst that flushed heat into the atmosphere. Instead there was only a vast cloud of dirt and debris coughed into the air, not in the shape of the traditional mushroom cloud so much as a smoke storm kicked up from an oil fire.

McCracken continued to feel the rumbling for several more seconds in the pit of his stomach, wondering whether it was his imagination at work or if this part of the world was literally shaking itself apart. Then it subsided, slowly, leaving Belamo to let out a hefty sigh.

"Now that was some ride," he uttered. "You ask me, even Disneyland's got nothing to match it."

"I might head there myself, now that this is over," McCracken grinned, noticing Belamo exchange a wary glance with Johnny Wareagle. "Uh-oh, what am I missing here?"

"It's not good, boss," Belamo told him.

"The Hellfire reborn, Blainey," Wareagle elaborated, using the term he'd coined way back in Vietnam. "Only in our own country."

"And this time it hit close to home, boss," added Belamo grimly. "Up close and personal."

CHAPTER 9

Missouri River

McCracken stood on the shore just short of the cordoned-off east-bound span of the Daniel Boone Bridge that had been blown up by placing explosives strategically in line with the aging supports. The entire span had ruptured, plunging more than sixty vehicles into the waters below the previous morning while he was still in Iran.

He ran his eyes past the assortment of uniformed and other investigative personnel identified by the initials on their jackets, stopping on a civilian who viewed the scene with feigned detachment. Blaine made his way toward him, watching rescue and search efforts that had continued unabated for twenty-four straight hours now.

He reached the civilian standing apart from all the others and flashed an ID he hadn't used in years, still enough to make the man's eyebrows flicker and to study Blaine's face closer.

"I read you as the kind of man who goes after the shitheads who pull of shit like this," the stranger said.

"Likewise."

"Di Oppresso Liber," the man said, quoting the Special Forces motto: To Free the Oppressed. "Wish I was still in that game. Rather be pulling grenade pins than strings."

" 'Nam?"

The man didn't nod, didn't have to. "We got two hundred in the water. A man like you shows up on a scene like this, I'm guessing it's about one of them."

The whole trip here, McCracken had been replaying a visit he'd had from an old friend twenty-five years ago. There hadn't been a lot of lovers in his life, and Henri Dejourner came with news about one of them.

"She died two months ago."

"You haven't come here to inform me I was mentioned in her will."

"In a sense, I have. Lauren Ericson is survived by a son. He's yours." Dejourner had a memo pad out and was reading from it. "The boy's name is Matthew. He's three months past twelve and is enrolled in the third form at the Reading School in Reading, England. He is, at present, a boarder at the school after having lived the rest of his life in the village of Hambleden twenty-five minutes away."

"How did Lauren die?"

"Traffic accident."

"Does the boy . . ."

"No, *mon ami.* He has no knowledge of you. Lauren told him his father deserted them."

"Then he does have some knowledge of me."

Matthew had turned out not to be his son at all, but that hadn't stopped Blaine from treating him like one through the rest of the boy's youth, never prouder than when the young man was admitted into Britain's Special Air Service. Matthew had had a son out of wedlock, but had ultimately married the woman who later ran off, leaving Matthew to raise Andrew Ericson by himself. Blaine had met the boy once, years before, but had no idea he was in the United States for the year on a student exchange program until Johnny and Sal broke the news of the terrorist attack in which Andrew been caught.

Matthew, meanwhile, was on a mission somewhere, the Middle East probably. He couldn't be reached, and Blaine didn't want him getting this kind of news from some mountain messenger when he'd never leave his squad anyway. That left the task at hand to him. McCracken had let himself hope it wouldn't be this bad. That the drop wouldn't be as long or the waters as cold and deep. But he'd been on scenes like this often enough to know the odds of a successful rescue diminished by the hour under these conditions, and the grim expression worn by the man by his side pretty much said it all.

"Sixty rescued so far with a bunch of those not expected to make it," the man continued.

"How deep's the water?"

"Averages seventy-five feet. Temperature's just under forty degrees. You want a reason for hope? Bodies will be washing up on the shoreline as far as fifty miles away for the next two days and a few of them will still be alive. A few."

"Sounds like you've been here before," McCracken told him.

"Haven't we all?"

"It's different when it's personal."

The man slid closer to him, took his hands out of his pockets as if about to comfort Blaine with a touch to his shoulder, but then just left them there dangling. "My advice? Don't get involved."

McCracken gazed back at the remnants of the classic cantilever bridge built way back in 1932. Ironically, construction of a replacement span was already nearing completion. Blaine took his phone from his pocket to snap some pictures, but it slipped from his grasp to the cold ground.

The stranger retrieved the phone and handed it back to him. "My second piece of advice: Keep this handy in case you need to call 9-1-1."

"I am 9-1-1," McCracken told him.

The man stuffed his hands back into his pockets. "Then I guess it's unfortunate you were too late to help that kid."

CHAPTER 10

Washington, DC

"Washington's on lockdown," said Henry Folsom, gazing across the table at McCracken. "The whole country's on lockdown. Can you believe this shit?"

"I came straight to meet you from the airport."

"Not like you to initiate contact."

"I made an exception."

"What changed?"

"Keep talking, Hank."

"Forty-eight hours ago, terrorists firebombed a church in Ohio. Over a hundred casualties. Just over twenty-four hours ago, they blew up a bridge in Missouri. Those two attacks came in the wake of two gunmen shooting up a restaurant and an explosion on a subway train. They're hitting us coast to coast, going after infrastructure as well as innocents."

"Like 9/11, every goddamn day." Blaine nodded.

Folsom studied McCracken closer. "But at least there's some

good news. I hear Iran's nuclear enrichment plant in Natanz nuked itself yesterday."

"Did it now?"

"Yes, sir. No further details available. But you didn't come straight from landing back in country to see me."

"No, I came from Missouri, the Daniel Boone Bridge specifically, where bodies are still being pulled from the water."

They'd met the same place they had the first time circumstances had brought them together: the F Street Bistro in the State Plaza Hotel, a pleasant enough venue with cheery light and a slate of windows overlooking the street that Blaine instinctively avoided. Today, that street was crammed with police and a few National Guardsmen sprinkled in for good measure. On alert, assault rifles not far from their grasps.

McCracken had arrived first, as was his custom, and staked out a table as close to a darkened corner as the place had to offer. He'd used this location in the past because of its status as one of Washington's best-kept secrets. But the last time he was here, the room had filled up around him, every table occupied within minutes with an army of waiters scurrying between them. McCracken found himself missing that kind of bustle today. Theirs was the only table occupied. Washington looked to be staying home for the day, along with the rest of the country, in the wake of four terrorist attacks in little more than a week.

Folsom leaned back in his chair. He had the look of a man born in a button-down shirt. Hair neatly slicked back, horn-rimmed glasses, and youthful features that would make him appear forty forever. The Department of Homeland Security probably had a thousand just like him.

"Soft targets all," Folsom elaborated. "Civilians, infrastructure . . . Like the Missouri attack. You telling me that's what brought you here? What the hell for?"

"Because somebody important to me was on that bridge when it blew."

Folsom remained silent for several long moments once McCracken was done.

"Saved me the trouble of calling you in on this, I guess," he said finally.

"Well, here I am."

Folsom leaned across the table, looking almost relieved. "That bridge and all the other attacks were carried out by Islamic extremist groups, because of one man's crusade against them."

"And who's that?"

"A man who doesn't care if this country burns, McCracken."

CHAPTER 11

Tampa, Florida

"When I see a Muslim, I turn away," the Reverend Jeremiah Rule said to all those gathered around the fire pit.

His faithful applauded.

"If he does not turn away, I shove him aside!"

His faithful cheered.

"And if he is still there, I spit in his face!"

His faithful cried out their agreement, deafening Rule to all other noise. Many pounded the air with their fists. Others held their hands high toward the sky. Still more dropped to their knees in reverence to him; those who followed the reverend from stop to stop, place to place, seeing in him the one true spokesman for their most deep-seated feelings and hatred.

I speak for you, he thought as the cheering, unrestrained and cathartic, continued. *I speak for all those who've lost their voices or been silenced by others who would betray this country.*

Then Rule looked down at the flames rising from the pit the

closest of his devoted had dug just that morning in the ground of Tampa's Al Lopez Park, within view of a beautiful pond well stocked for fishing. The "cleansing service," as he called it, had been scheduled to take place in a different park, but had been moved here at the last minute when his permit was rescinded. There'd been no time to arrange permission for the fire now raging, and Rule welcomed any attempt by Tampa authorities to make their way through the five hundred faithful gathered for the service to shut him down for violating some ordinance he didn't even know existed.

Five hundred, Rule thought reverently. There'd been times, not too long ago, when he'd preached these very same words to no more than five and only as many as fifty on his very best day. Then he came to the realization that actions spoke far louder and better than words. That was the day he'd doused a copy of the Koran in gasoline and lit it on fire before an audience of twenty-five faithful followers. One of those twenty-five recorded the burning with his phone and put it up on YouTube, where it went viral. The Islamic world exploded with violence and vengeance, ravaging American consulates as they took to the streets like crazed, rabid animals that revealed them, in Rule's mind anyway, as the heathens and barbarians they were. His actions had exposed their true faces to the world, and the reverend ratcheted up his efforts to bring that truth further into the light so the world might know them in their true form.

"But this is your service, not mine, my brothers and sisters!" he blared into the microphone to the faithful who'd greeted him in Tampa, feedback sent screeching out the outdoor speakers. "This is your time to lash out and be heard. For I give you a voice when everyone else ignores your words. So come forth now and offer a token to the flames so you might be cleansed. Come forth with whatever symbols you bring of the cursed people who would infest our land with the ugliness of their word and unholy nature of their purpose, the sin of their very being, brothers and sisters!"

It was cool for January in central Florida, but Rule's face glowed with a light sheen of sweat from his proximity to the fire pit dug six feet down, his feet flirting precariously with the edge. He was a big, husky man with skin the texture of leather from spending years selling Bibles door to door. His long graying hair was gnarled together in snakelike strands that flapped side to side with each twist of his head. His thick mustache curled upward at the end, wet with sweat and snot from his own wild rants that had whipped him, as well as the crowd, into a frenzy.

"Come forward!" he urged again. "Who will be the first to offer a symbol of all that must burn in the eternal fire of damnation!"

A young boy, eleven or twelve maybe, slid out of the crowd holding a small rolled-up carpet. Rule's heart skipped a beat. The boy seemed to glide, not walk, his steps making no imprint in the park grass.

It couldn't be . . .

The boy, appearing to float now, smiled at Rule with reverence.

A ghost from his long forgotten past . . .

The boy mocked him with his big blue eyes, still coming forward.

Be gone with you, demon! Rule wanted to shout. *Get thee back to damnation!*

The boy extended the rolled-up rug out to him now. Only it wasn't a rug anymore, it was the body of a dog, stiff and dead.

Because the boy was dead too, drying blood caked up on his skull and brow, the tears and splits made in flesh and bone by the reverend's own hands.

A long time ago.

CHAPTER 12

Alabama: The past

How many years ago had it been?

More than the man who'd then been known simply as "J. D. Rule" wished to count. He'd been driving the Alabama country-side in a beat-up van that stank of sweat and beer, complete with a moth-eaten mattress, on which he slept in rest stops or parking lots after another failed day of trying to sell Christian Bibles door to door. An especially bad day, an especially hot day, finishing in a thunderstorm that soaked him to the gills in the walk back to his van from a farmhouse where the residents hadn't had the courtesy to even open the door. Then, halfway to his van, an ugly square shape of dog, all muscle and jaw, lunged out at him.

Rule's sample Bible went flying off into the mud, and the dog lunged at him again when he stooped to retrieve it. Rule took the good book in hand and smashed the dog's snout with it. And when the animal yelped, he struck at it again, missing but driving the dog backward toward the oak tree to which it was chained. Some kind of mangy, bony hound, ugly and scarred. He'd kicked at it, loving the sound and feel of his work boot mashing flesh and ribs through fur. The dog cowered and wailed as he kicked it again and again, then smashed it with his ruined sample Bible until it wailed no more.

Rule was nearly out of breath when he turned to find a blond-haired boy, ten or eleven maybe, staring at him in wide-eyed despair and horror.

"You killed my dog, mister! You killed my dog!"

Rule came toward him, realizing the dog's blood had splattered his clothes.

"No, I . . . I . . . er—"

The boy turned and ran back for the house.

"Hey. Hey!"

Rule caught him just short of the steps, intending to just get the boy quiet, settle him down a bit. But he wouldn't stop his screaming and in that moment all of Rule's anger and bitterness over the lot he'd been cast spilled over. First slapping the boy, then striking him with closed fists until his knuckles split and bled, and the screaming became a whimper and then a strange airless gurgle that left the boy's blue eyes bulging and sightless.

God, forgive me . . .

Rule stumbled up off the dead kid, covered in more blood, along with muck and rain and urine from where the boy had pissed through his jeans. Leaving the body there, he hightailed it back to his van, speeding off on bald tires with his weak windshield wipers barely able to slap the rain away and his shredded, swollen hands fiery with pain.

"Oh Lord, how I have failed you," he sobbed as he drove, the van whipsawing back and forth across the two-lane road. His hands hurt so much from striking the boy's skull and face, he could barely close them on the wheel. "I carry your word in books but not in my heart. And all these weeks I've sold not a single one, because I am not pure enough to know your word. But I resolve to change that. Here and now, I promise to be your faithful servant spreading your word through more than just the good book. If you'll have me in your kingdom, I swear on all that is holy that I will be worthy of your grace."

That was it. He'd dedicated his life to God then and there, resolved to commit himself to the service of the Lord to avoid eternal damnation. Not selling Bibles, but buying back broken souls like his own. Showing them that the error of their ways was through no fault of their own, that there were others to blame who must be vanquished so their very beings could be free. Killing the boy had been the making of his own transition to spiritual completion, committing the ultimate sin so he could know how to help those guilty of smaller ones.

The key was to give them something to rally against, something to make the true nature of their beings and moralities rise to the surface to bury all else beneath it. It wasn't enough to have faith.

They needed something to hate.

And Rule found the answer to what in his own heart, a heart that had forever detested Muslims and their cursed religion from his days selling Bibles door to door. He'd found himself in a neighborhood devoted to Islam once, and to this day he could not get the hateful stares cast his way and doors slammed in his face out of his mind. Undeterred, he'd gone to a local mosque and presented a Bible to the imam, who promptly tossed it in the trash and lit it on fire as Rule watched.

That memory resurfaced when the epiphany to burn Korans struck him in the wake of a Muslim being elected president of the United States. Regardless of all the protestations otherwise, Rule knew that to be the truth. He could see it in the man's eyes and hear it in his voice, could sense the secret agenda he'd brought with him to the White House.

The time had come to make a stand, to set the whole country on fire if that's what it took to make people wake up and know the truth as he did.

Set the whole country on fire . . .

An image he came back to again and again in his mind. Because it was more than a prophecy.

Because it was coming.

CHAPTER 13

Tampa, Florida: The present

But now, here today in Tampa, it was the image of the boy that was back, except his hair wasn't matted down by the rain and, on second glance, was black instead of blond. And his face wasn't beaten and battered to a pulp. Approaching Rule now with a smile, full of life, taunting him with an offering.

The reverend looked down, half expecting to see his knuckles swollen and bloodied.

Haven't I done enough in your service? he demanded of God in his mind. *Have I not redeemed myself before your blessed eye yet?*

Rule believed with all his heart that killing that boy had been part of some greater cosmic plan to set him on the road he needed to be on, the road that had brought him here to Tampa today. Doing the Lord's work, spreading His word about the nature of true evil in the world. Because to fight that evil, to fully understand it, Rule needed to know the evil in his own heart. And in beating that boy to a pulp, in feeling his life drain away in gasps and spasms to the pounding of his fists, he had achieved that well enough to recognize it held some higher purpose for him. Not that day, surely, not even the following week or month. He kept his heart and mind open, waiting to learn how he was to serve Him.

"Here you are, Reverend," the dark-haired boy said, in a voice distinctly different from the one Jeremiah Daniel Rule remembered so well, as he extended the rolled-up rug further.

"You killed my dog, mister! You killed my dog!"

So Rule shook off the illusion, the memory, and took the rug in his grasp. "And what have we here, son?"

"It's a prayer rug," the boy said, big eyed and grinning. "My daddy took it off one of them when he was in Afghanistan. After he shot him."

"Praise be to your daddy, son." Then, turning to his faithful, he said, "Praise be to this lad's daddy!"

"My daddy's dead, Reverend. Killed dead by those folk after he volunteered to go back for another tour. I wish they was all dead too."

Rule touched the boy's shoulder. "Your daddy's a hero, son, a warrior in the service of the one true God—our Lord, not that of the heathens." He eased the rolled-up rug back into the boy's grasp. "I want you to do the deed, son. I want you to burn the offering so you might fan the flames of your late father's love and know salvation. Do it, son. Feel His heat and His love."

With that, the boy tossed the rug toward the flames, watching it unfurl on the way down before disappearing into ash embers that floated up toward the sky.

Rule clamped a hand tighter on the boy's shoulder, all memory of his likeness to the boy he had slain at his becoming now vanquished. "Know this boy in your hearts, my brothers and sisters! Know this boy for the love he represents and the hatred we must all rid from the world! We will do it one object at a time, one offering at a time, and for each life of another brother or sister they take, the door to eternal damnation for all of their kind will open that much wider. We will push them through that door, my brothers and sisters, each and every one! Let them riot and loot, let them come to our shores and attack us in desperate retribution. We have smoked out the heathens and infidels, and their days of walking this blessed Earth will soon be done, as our Lord unleashes all of His wrath and fury upon their multitudes who walk with sickness in their souls."

The crowd parted to allow a young woman to come forward, taking the boy's place before Jeremiah Rule.

"I have nothing to offer!" she cried out, sinking to her knees and wrapping her arms tightly around his legs. "I have nothing to offer but my sin and my failure!"

The reverend stroked her hair tenderly. "Speak, my child. Free your soul."

"I've been corrupted, Reverend," the young woman said, squeezing his legs tighter. "I turned away from the Lord when I married one of them, turned away from my faith to theirs. And I'm sorry for it, Reverend, I'm so sorry, so lost." Her face, soft and beautiful, looked up him pleadingly. "Can you help me, Reverend? Is there any hope for me at all?"

Rule separated himself from the young woman and backed away. "Rise, my child."

He watched her long, dark hair tumbling past her shoulders, tossed about by the breeze as she climbed back to her feet.

"Can we save this child, my brothers and sisters?"

"Yes!"

"Can we save her?"

"*Yes!*"

"I say again: *Can we save her?*"

"YES!"

The applause, hoots, and cheers picked up again, rising through the crowd to a deafening crescendo that sounded like thunder booming in the sky with the portent of a storm in the offing.

"Be saved, child!" he screamed into the microphone, touching the young woman's head. "Be saved!"

And she dropped back to her knees, sobbing.

"But my work is not done, child," he said, speaking only to her with the microphone held away. "Come to my church, so it might be completed and you may know full salvation." Then, to the crowd again, *"Praise the Lord, she is saved!"*

And they exploded in deafening cheers again, everything Jeremiah Rule had set into motion the day he killed the boy and his dog coming to a crescendo as well.

"Be warned," he continued, "there's a storm coming, my brothers and sisters, a storm that will sweep away all those who do not see the world for what it is and have defied the Lord's word. Find safe harbor from that storm with me, so when it comes, you will be spared its fury! For we will not stop, will not cease, will not relent, will not weaken until the last of their kind is rid from this earth with the pestilence that is their word and their very being! Because it is our mission, my brothers and sisters. And we will not rest until we see it done, until every Muslim on Earth has returned to the dirt that spawned them. Let them know our strength!"

"Amen!"

"Let them know our wrath!"

"Amen!"

"Let them know we shall not weaken in the face of their onslaught . . ."

"Amen!"

". . . and for each of our lives they strike down, they shall pay a millionfold!"

"Amen!"

"Because their time has passed, my brothers and sisters, while ours fast approaches!" Rule finished, smiling smugly at the prophecy to be realized in a mere five days' time, when the storm of his making finally arrived.

Five days . . .

When it had taken even God one day more than that to create the world.

CHAPTER 14

Washington, DC

"The Reverend Jeremiah Rule," Folsom finished.

"Never heard of him," Blaine said, having expected to hear something else entirely.

"It's not surprising; he's not exactly a household name, just a damn dangerous one, out there burning Korans and every other symbol of Islam. He's gathered a million signatures on a petition to have all American Muslims declared enemy combatants and placed in internment camps or deported. That means he's got followers, lots of them of the same mind, and that's ended up unifying the Islamic radical world. They've activated all their sleeper cells and utilized every means they can find to infiltrate the country. It's all-out war, McCracken. They're pulling out all the stops, which means we must too."

"That normally means me."

Folsom didn't nod or respond at all. "Glad you see my point."

"Why not just arrest the whack job?"

"Rule hasn't broken any laws."

"How about accessory to murder?"

"We prefer to handle this internally. Outside the system."

"That normally means me, too. But this vengeance thing is new to me."

"Then don't look at it that way, McCracken."

"You got a better idea?"

The men fell silent, the remark hanging in the air between them until Folsom leaned back.

"You took out Natanz to save lives down the line, maybe millions of them."

"What's your point, Hank?"

"Same thing here. Jeremiah Rule is a walking nuclear bomb. He doesn't go quietly into the night, lots more innocent folks get dropped into rivers and the body count keeps climbing."

The remark stung McCracken, Folsom surprising him with such uncharacteristic directness. Then again, the situation called for it.

"I'm just not sure being a bigot with a big mouth makes a man worthy of assassination," Blaine said finally.

"Tell that to this kid you know who fell into the Missouri River. Check the calendar, McCracken. These days a man can do a lot more damage with a bullhorn than a bullet. Jeremiah Rule lobs words as if they were bombs, and they're taking out innocent people every time they land." Folsom stopped to await a response, resuming when none came. "I know I don't have to draw you a picture, because you've already seen it up close and personal."

McCracken rose to his feet. "I've got lots of frequent-flier miles to use up, Hank. Just tell me where I can find Jeremiah Rule and forward the intel on."

Folsom stood up, rattling the table slightly as he joined him. The two of them looked out the nearest window toward a street that should have been crammed with lunch-hour pedestrian and vehicular traffic. But cars buzzed on without much delay and figures bundled up against the harsh winter winds passed outside only sporadically. Washington, and most everywhere else in the country, was paralyzed with fear over where and when the next attack would come. Sheltering in place.

Then a sputtering car's backfiring sent some pedestrians lunging for cover and others fleeing in all directions. Cars swerved wildly, brakes squealing, the sickening crunch of metal on metal signaling a chain collision had occurred just beyond McCracken's view. Sirens, incredibly, were already sounding, rushing to respond to nothing at all.

Folsom's phone buzzed and he looked down to check the text message, his expression paling and then turning grim. "Better make it fast, McCracken."

CHAPTER 15

San Francisco: Twenty minutes earlier

The Golden Gate Bridge was a mess. In both directions. Accidents everywhere, the worst of which had happened at virtually the same moment at the ends of both the east and west spans to keep commuters sitting just as they were. An average of 120,000 cars crossed the bridge every day and at that moment it seemed they were all stuck at once.

No one going anywhere. Because there was nowhere to go.

Even when an SUV centered on the eastern span and a minivan centered on the western one opened their doors to allow a half-dozen gunmen to spill out of each. Sheathed in masks, helmeted visors, black commando gear, and heavy body armor, they looked more like robots than men. Their assault rifles shined in the morning sun, the cacophony of their automatic fire disturbing the quiet breached moments before only by car horns. There were plenty of screams too, desperate and horrible, along with the screech of metal on metal as panicked commuters accelerated with no room to maneuver. Some shoved other vehicles forward with them. Others got nowhere at all before their windows were pierced by fusillades that were terrifying in their randomness and devastating in their destruction.

The gunmen ejected spent clips, exchanging fresh ones in their place while missing nary a beat in their relentless fire. Their targets were anything and everything their bullets could hit, picking up their pace only to cut down those commuters trying to flee on foot. All the blood made for a strange contrast with the orange of the steel girders and supports, its smell strangely like the bridge's ever-present rust as it dried quickly in the sun.

When it was over, the gunmen shed their armor and gear to melt into the throngs fleeing in panic. A strange and uneasy silence, broken only by sobs, whimpers, and cries for help, settled over the bridge until the wail of sirens began. The sounds of those sirens bled into one another, even as the sun streamed through the pockmarked windshields, dappling the dashboards through the bullet holes and splaying onto the victims trapped behind their wheels.

CHAPTER 16

Istanbul

Zarrin's fingers flew across the keyboard, in rhythm with the air and the world beneath the huge concert hall's golden lighting that reminded her of the setting sun. In moments like this, she surrendered herself to the music, so much bigger than any one artist whose job was not to play the notes but to channel them. Do justice to the composer.

Today's performance featured Tchaikovsky's Piano Concerto no. 1, among the most famous and greatest piano concertos ever composed. An immensely challenging piece given that it had been played and tried by every great pianist in history. The bar, then, was set understandably high, which suited Zarrin just fine.

Located along the shores of the Golden Horn, the Haliç Congress Center in the middle of Istanbul had long been one of her favorite venues in which to perform. Zarrin had arrived for her performance right around sunset, in time to see the sun's rays reflect off the Horn's waters in a way that cast the world in a golden glow. Parks and promenades rimmed the center on its other three sides, creating the perfect setting in which to let the beautiful music take possession of her. Surrender to it so that all else in the world seemed insignificant by comparison. So few were blessed enough to be a master of a single craft, never mind one as challenging and exacting as a concert pianist.

But Zarrin was actually master of two.

A smartphone rested in her lap, tuned to a video broadcasting an image of the road D.885 from Syria to Sanliurfa, Turkey, fifty miles north of the border. A group of rebel leaders had set out in a convoy after dark to attend a secret meeting concerning a final assault on Damascus at Urfa Castle. They were coming to plead with their Western allies for air support.

But they were never going to get there. Earlier that day, Zarrin had installed a speed-lowering rubber rumble strip across the road approaching the checkpoint at Akçakale. The thin layer of rubber concealed fifty pounds of plastic explosives she'd packed inside the hollowed-out rumble strip. And an application installed on her phone would tell her the speed of the convoy as it passed the camera she'd set up a half mile short of that spot. From there Zarrin needed only to calculate how many seconds it would take for the vehicles to get there, before pressing another key on her phone to trigger the explosives.

All routine, as was playing the concerto.

But then Zarrin's hands betrayed her, unfortunately routine recently as well. She pictured the keys her fingers needed to grace, but was unable to move them as she needed. The sense, in that ever so anxious moment, was of a painless cramp that turned into a spasm. Her hands going off on their own against her mental instructions to the contrary. To play at this level meant that action needed to flow ahead of thought. Thinking about what you were doing meant you weren't doing it, weren't surrendering to the music and letting it dictate all. But even Tchaikovsky could not dictate to fingers suddenly twitching and caught in spasm. The audience seemed not to notice as Zarrin's rhythm with the keys sputtered and slowed—just an infinitesimal change, yes, but one that separated the music from her being and left her playing it instead of it playing her.

Her cell phone beeped softly, the rear of the convoy passing before the camera by the time she glanced down. The number 105 was flashing on screen, giving her the convoy's speed in kilometers, the calculation of the trigger point in her mind coming dangerously slow, slow enough to risk the entire operation.

Zarrin felt her fingers begin flowing smoothly again, enough in that moment to restore her full concentration, her training and experience doing the rest. At 105 kilometers per hour, she estimated it would take twenty-eight seconds to travel the half mile to the explosive-laden rumble strip.

The clock in her mind told Zarrin seventeen seconds had already past. Her right fingers were twitching madly and left had gone rigid by the time she reached the final sequence of the concerto. Her phone was programmed with voice commands, so she let the seconds count down in her mind until she reached three.

"Activate," she said downward, as her fingers struggled across the keyboard, finally managing to complete the concerto's finale at the very same moment her explosives should have destroyed the convoy and killed the rebel leaders.

The standing-room-only crowd erupted in applause, lurching to their collective feet, the hall rumbling and quaking as she stood and bowed with hands clasped tight behind her. In her heart, Zarrin felt the rhythm and beat of the concerto still pulsing. In her mind, she saw the bodies of the Syrian rebel leaders strewn in pieces across the road to Sanliurfa.

Before her, the standing ovation continued and Zarrin took another bow.

CHAPTER 17

Istanbul

She opened her dressing room door to more applause, two broad-shouldered figures standing over a third smaller one seated on the bench set before the piano placed here to facilitate her preparations.

"Bravo!" the smaller man said, rising to his feet. "Bravo! Your performance was brilliant tonight, truly masterful."

"Thank you, Colonel Kosh."

Kosh stopped clapping and tapped at the keys to produce a harmonic drivel. He had a large round head, much too large for his small frame, clean-shaven so it looked like a basketball. "I always wanted to learn how to play. Perhaps you could give me a lesson."

"I'm too expensive for you, Colonel."

Kosh tapped two different keys at the same time, listening to the contrast between their respective sounds. "Money can be no object if you wish to work with the best."

As head of Iran's Ministry of Intelligence and National Security, also known as VEVAK, Kosh had long provided Zarrin with an endless stream of missions, for which she was paid exorbitantly well. She tightly clenched the fingers of both her hands to keep them from trembling, as he tried to string his tapping into an actual melody.

"It's not as easy as it looks," he reflected.

"Few things are. Being the best at anything requires an extraordinary amount of practice and commitment."

"So you think I'd be wasting my time with lessons."

"I do."

"But someone taught you, didn't they?"

"I was different."

"And why is that, Zarrin?"

"Because I pursue perfection, not mediocrity."

"A fact much in evidence tonight," Kosh complimented. "Here, as well as in Syria. Congratulations are in order."

"You normally don't stop by to give them personally, Colonel."

"As I said, I was thinking about taking lessons."

"Why don't you try some Tchaikovsky, Colonel?"

Kosh laughed. "A bit beyond my skill level, I'm afraid."

"Would you like to know the primary reason why? There's almost no rest at all in his concertos, like the one I played tonight. But it's become too much even for me, given that I'm not as young as I used to be."

"But equally skilled, I trust. Just more selective with your performances. Amazing the things you can learn growing up in a Palestinian refugee camp."

"Where the closest thing we had to a musical instrument was a stick banging against tin cans," Zarrin said, stiffening at the memories. "Except for a single legless piano."

"On which you learned while being raised there as an

orphan after witnessing the Israelis murder both your parents," Kosh continued. "Rescued and trained by a legendary Palestinian intelligence official, trained himself by the Soviets at the height of their power. The legendary Zarrin, specialist in every weapon, but renowned for making use of objects that aren't weapons at all, allowing for close-in kills utterly impossible for all others who practice your trade. Then, of course, there is your expertise with explosives, thanks to which the Syrian rebels are now looking for new leaders and Iran's interests there will remain secure, at least for the time being."

"What do you want, Colonel?"

"I have another job for you."

Zarrin flexed her hands, pushing the blood back into them and hoping Kosh wouldn't notice, lest she appear vulnerable in any way. "I'm not interested."

"You haven't heard about the job yet," Kosh said, extracting a picture from his pocket and unfolding it. "You are familiar with this man?"

Zarrin regarded the picture without taking it in hand. Something changed in her expression. "Blaine McCracken. I thought he was dead."

"Then it must have been a ghost who destroyed Natanz and our country's dreams along with it."

Zarrin moved to her dressing table and eased both her hands into ice-laden, frigid water. The agony waned quickly, leaving her hands numb and still. Every day a bit worse than the day before.

"Name your price, Zarrin."

"I already said I was too expensive for you."

"An example must be set," Kosh told her, thin shoulders stiffening. "Otherwise we stand for nothing."

"Then that will be price for McCracken: nothing."

Kosh's eyes narrowed. "What's the catch?"

"How many of your operatives did I kill all those years ago on behalf of the Iraqis?"

"I lost count."

"Sixteen. I want a million dollars for each of them. Consider McCracken a bonus."

"And what would an artist like yourself do with so much money?"

Zarrin finished her mental count to thirty and yanked her hands from the ice bath. She dried them with a fresh white towel and looked back at Kosh.

"Maybe I'll buy a villa in the Mediterranean."

"Why not your own private island, Zarrin? But then who would you perform before?"

"Myself, Colonel. In the end, that's the most important person to please."

"I'm sure Blaine McCracken feels the same way."

"Not for long," Zarrin told him.

CHAPTER 18

Mobile, Alabama

"Brothers and sisters," the Reverend Jeremiah Rule greeted, his voice booming over the crowd of 750 gathered around the fire pit in Crawford Park, "welcome to your future. Welcome to salvation by renouncing the heathens among us, who have infiltrated our culture to besmirch His word. They would try to weaken us by slaying the innocent, but their efforts only make us stronger, toughening our resolve."

McCracken watched and listened to the service from the adjoining road, high up in the bucket of a utility truck, an unfamiliar feeling tugging at his insides and leaving them knotted. He couldn't look at Jeremiah Rule without thinking of Andrew Ericson, as close to a grandson as he'd ever have, missing in the frigid waters of the Missouri River in the wake of the terrorist bombing inspired by this madman's rants. Blaine kept imagining he'd spotted Andrew in the crowd, only to shake off the vision as cold sweat rose to the surface of his skin.

He wanted to kill Jeremiah Rule so much that he could feel his hands clenching and unclenching, the same way they did in the moments before he readied fire with an assault rifle. Wanted to do that so bad now he could feel himself quivering. An altogether foreign feeling.

McCracken rotated a smaller version of standard binoculars to better view the festivities and had come equipped with a laser microphone rigged to an earpiece to better listen to them. He'd chosen this spot mostly for the vantage point it provided the sniper rifle that looked, at first and second glance, like a sophisticated camera equipped with telephoto lens. It fired not a bullet, but a tiny dart loaded with a potassium-rich toxin that would bring on a heart attack within minutes to an hour.

A chilly drizzle was falling, accompanied by a shrill winter wind beneath a gray sky soaked thick with clouds. The wind and cold combined to cast Rule's wild gray hair into a matted mess that looked like thick, stringy clumps of dust and dirt balls. The clumps flew wildly from side to side with each frequent shift of his head, as he sought to meet the collective gaze of all who'd gathered in a circle around him.

McCracken noted the presence of Alabama highway patrolmen posted just far enough away, and casually dressed, broad-shouldered men who stood inside the circle facing the crowd instead of the reverend. He would have pegged them as professional private-security personnel even before noticing the wireless buds coiling from their ears and neat pistol bulges beneath their jackets. The cut of their clothes and hair, the way their eyes moved and scanned the crowd, told McCracken they were ex-military for sure, perhaps even special ops. Just a sense he was getting from the way they'd positioned themselves, the careful proximity of one to another.

So how, McCracken thought, *did a man like the Reverend Rule end up with that kind of security?*

Rule's rally, revival, service, or whatever you wanted to call it was being held in Crawford Park, a municipal facility located on the city's outskirts where suburban homes began to dot the landscape with increasing frequency amid wooded patches. McCracken arrived in the unseasonably cold and damp weather for Alabama in January, just as a backhoe had completed the task of digging what would become a fire pit, laying the mound of excavated earth carefully to the side so the ground could be restored to its former condition. Municipal employees had handled that chore, though under the supervision of Reverend Jeremiah Rule himself.

McCracken had known enough fanatics in his time to be keenly aware that they feasted on incidents sparked by their own ill-conceived and self-serving proclamations. That was the thing that was most striking about men like Rule; they may have claimed to serve a higher power when all they really cared about was furthering their own. More akin to cult leaders, they thrived on chaos of their own causing, reveling in it, creating a moral cesspit of low-thinking humanity willing to soak in the stink it spread. So many had died senselessly in service to men like the reverend. McCracken had known them in countless countries, speaking in countless languages to countless numbers of the wide-eyed impressionable who knew no better and accepted their word as convenient, ready dogma. He'd once heard it called drive-thru religion and couldn't agree more after seeing the damage it had done on every continent he and Johnny Wareagle had fought. The lives they'd seen squandered for causes that were thinly disguised shams, cult-like in their singular notion of fanaticism. Rule was no different; he was just better at it.

And now, soon, he'd be dead.

With that thought, McCracken raised the camera-like sniper rifle up to his eye. It was remarkably light and one twist of its lens brought the madman so clearly into focus, Blaine thought he could reach out and touch him. A simple touch of the same button normally used to snap a picture was all it would take to silence the Reverend Jeremiah Rule once and for all. Blaine kept him in focus as he edged a finger into position, ready to press, starting to apply the necessary pressure. Pictured the man dropping dead, just as he deserved.

But then he stopped and moved his finger away. Because one of the reverend's security guards had slid into the edge of the frame, making the part of McCracken's mind that wasn't focused on Andrew Ericson once more wonder where the man had come from. Who was paying him and the others for their services?

Those questions gave Blaine enough pause to make him swap the sniper weapon for his binoculars again. If there was someone behind Jeremiah Rule, someone backing him with the resources and contacts required to arrange for a security detail composed of special-ops veterans, then assassinating the reverend here and now was unlikely to achieve its desired effects. Sure, it would eliminate Rule, but not those perhaps equally responsible for the bridge bombing that may have claimed Andrew Ericson's life.

Someone was supporting Rule, someone was helping enable him to inflame the entire Muslim world and unleash the Islamic radicals now unified in their holy war against the United States.

Beyond that, it was even possible that Rule's assassination would unleash his venomous followers, which included any number of white supremacist and militia groups, creating even more chaos in the name of ending it. There were literally millions of armed crazies who fit that bill, many of them of the survivalist mode who hated government and were convinced the black helicopters were hovering over their homes even now. McCracken had known enough of them in his time to be as frightened of their convictions and capabilities as those of any terrorist. He needed to get closer to Rule right now, to feel the energy and anger of the crowd. It was much easier to judge a man up close than through binoculars and listening devices, and Blaine would get a better look at his private security detail from that vantage point as well.

Blaine moved to the bucket's controls and lowered it. He wanted to see Jeremiah Rule up close and personal. If nothing changed, he'd approach to shake Rule's hand at the end of the service and jab the potassium-rich dart into his wrist. Feel him go cold, just the way it had been for Andrew when he hit the frigid waters of the Missouri River.

"Every man's fate is his own to control," he heard Rule clamor, as the bucket thumped to a halt just short of the ground. "And every man must accept the consequences of that."

Couldn't have said it any better myself, McCracken thought.

CHAPTER 19

Mobile, Alabama

"Soon we will accept your offerings to the flames, your symbolic rejection of the teachings of heathens who have infested and corrupted our culture and that of the world. For a time, a long time," the reverend continued, his booming voice rising through the chill mist as he moved about the circle, backlit by the flames, which cast him in an almost surreal glow, "I was lost in a wasteland of confusion and quandary. Of not grasping the true origins of those who must be vanquished or the purpose they provide for the rest of us, the test they provide every day. But then a beautiful light burned bright before me through the dark decay, and I saw the truth. I saw a truth, brothers and sisters, I will now share with you."

God won't be able to help you if you got Andrew killed, McCracken thought, approaching across the grass.

He watched Rule stop and look down, more at the ground than the flames rising from the pit. It had started to drizzle ahead of an approaching storm, seeming to quell the flames briefly before a stiff wind fanned them further. Two fronts were about to collide, unseasonably warm air flooding the region with the portent of powerful thunderstorms and even scattered tornadoes through the Mobile area. As he approached across the park through the steady drizzle, McCracken thought he saw the reverend's lips moving, perhaps in silent prayer, his face scrunched up tightly enough to wrap the folds of his skin around each other. Then his eyes opened again, narrow and wild in their intensity.

"Dante wrote that there are nine circles of Hell. The circles are concentric, my bothers and sisters, representing the gradual increase in wickedness and evil, and culminating at the center of the earth, where the Devil himself reigns. Each circle's sinners are punished in a fashion befitting their crimes. Each sinner is afflicted for all of eternity by the chief sin he committed. People who sinned but sought forgiveness and absolution through prayer before their deaths are found not in Hell but in Purgatory, where they labor to be free of their sins. Those in Hell, who inhabit one of the nine circles, are people who tried to justify their sins and seek no penance."

A clap of thunder boomed, as if to echo the message of his words. The wind picked up to a steady, howling gust. The drizzle became a light rain that left the attendees reaching for the hoods on their jackets or sweatshirts. But their wide eyes never left Rule, waiting to scream and shout their affirmations of his word.

Rule stopped and rotated his gaze about the crowd that had refused to budge, undeterred by the elements. True to form, the crowd had gone utterly silent, hanging on his next words, many with hands raised high for the heavens. Only the reverend's professional security personnel stood out, their expressionless visages rotating from left to right and back again, the intentions held in their eyes hidden behind dark sunglasses.

"But then, one day, I realized. I realized, brothers and sisters, that the craven heathens who would besmirch and defame the word of the one true God have a circle of Hell all to themselves where they live for eternity among others just as vile and without compassion or regard for human life. A residence reserved for the most damned who seek nothing but death and destruction during their wasted time as interlopers in the world of our Lord.

"The tenth circle," Rule finished to the wild cheers and impassioned cries from the crowd. "Home to the hopeless!"

The crowd's blustering response bubbled McCracken's ears.

You think you know what hell is? McCracken thought to himself. *Not even close. . . .*

"Residence of the reviled!"

The response grew louder.

"Destination of the damned!"

Louder still, so loud it nearly swallowed the next clap of thunder that sounded like a tree splitting.

"Brothers and sisters," Rule continued, as the fervor approached a crescendo, McCracken feeling it like an electronic wave or pulse charged with energy that radiated from person to person, "let those who have brought offerings to the pit come forward so they may be returned to the tenth circle, where they belong, for eternity. Let us begin with the cursed word that has justified so much wanton death and destruction!"

And with that the reverend yanked a tattered book from inside his jacket. The rain intensified, drenching his hair and clothes, making him look even more wild in the bluster of a storm that rivaled his own. McCracken couldn't see the book from where he was standing, but knew it could only be a copy of the Koran, watching Rule raise it high for all to see before dropping it into the flames before them. Close enough to tempt their reach. Much of the crowd now sank to their knees as they hooted and hollered and cheered amid the spiraling winds and quaking trees. More Islamic radicals about to be inflamed and inspired, this man of hateful rhetoric not caring at all about the loss of more innocent lives like Andrew Ericson's.

The body hasn't been found yet, McCracken reminded himself. *The boy's not dead. There's still hope. . . .*

Another clap of thunder roared, followed by something else.

Pop, pop, pop . . .

Even amid the deafening roar, McCracken knew gunshots the moment he heard them. And he could tell Rule's professional security detail recognized the sound too, converging on the reverend with their own pistols already drawn. One of the guards went down and then another to more gunshots, Rule himself never wavering from standing shrouded by and aglow in the flames, hands held high with eyes closed as if to welcome his fate until his security detail tackled him to the ground.

McCracken heard another pop, louder this time, and a woman just a few feet in front of him went down. He had his SIG Sauer palmed in the next moment, eyes sweeping the crowd as panic finally set in, the highway patrolmen starting to rush in as well.

"There he is!" someone screamed. "It's him!"

It took a full instant for McCracken to realize arms and fingers were being thrust his way, identifying him as the shooter, the guilty party.

"Somebody stop him!"

In that moment, McCracken saw Rule's remaining guards aiming pistols his way through widening slivers in the fleeing crowd. Pictured them seeing him with SIG steadied in his hand, pistols ready in theirs as well.

They were going to shoot; two of them, sighting in even now. McCracken had no choice and, even if he had, instinct and experience overruled it.

He readied himself to fire. But then . . .

Pop, pop, pop, pop . . .

Again, the SIG held cold and unfired in his hand. The guards were there, standing and about to fire themselves, and then they weren't. When the crowd parted next, he saw two more downed bodies on the damp ground not far from where others had toppled the Reverend Rule and continued to protectively cover him.

The skies opened, unleashing a windswept downpour that engulfed the scene. Thunder boomed and a bolt of lighting seemed to arc downward directly over Rule's toppled frame.

McCracken lit into motion through the torrents, instinct again taking charge. He caught up to the thickest swatch of the fleeing throng and melted into it, knees bent to reduce his size and thus target, gun camouflaged against his hip. Felt the mass shift as highway patrolmen pierced it, likely on his trail. But they were quickly swallowed up, and McCracken centered his attention on a grove of trees and thick brush rimming the park where he could elude them across Straight Street near a basketball court.

The storm proved a blessing now, providing camouflage he could never have concocted on his own. Making every soaked form separating from the swell of the crowd to flee the area look the same. McCracken might have to abandon his rental vehicle, still a small price to pay for getting away.

"There he Is! Over there!" a voice cried out.

"Somebody, stop him!"

"Shoot him! Shoot him!"

And McCracken saw fingers thrust his way ahead of the gunshots.

CHAPTER 20

Mobile, Alabama

The members of the crowd fighting for a fix on him in their sights surged forward, toppling a laggard segment of elderly attendees and causing a mass pileup of bodies that looked like a chain collision on the interstate. McCracken had just veered left when an older woman hit the ground hard not far from him, crying out in pain and panic.

He never hesitated, swooped in and scooped her off the drenched ground that had gone soggy under the canopy of the wooded area of the park. With no other alternative, he carried the woman forward through what now felt like hail in search of a place to gently lay her down where she might be swiftly found and tended to. The hailstones pelted him and he heard the distinctive rattle and clacking of their impact against trees, brush, and ground. McCracken felt hail pellets crunch underfoot, some almost as big as golf balls spit from the sky. He tightened his grasp of the old woman, canting his body to shield her from the torrents as best he could. Remarkably enough, that had the unintended effect of providing him the ideal cover, for who would expect a potential target or fleeing assassin to delay his escape to rescue a fallen senior citizen?

Soaked to the bone himself, McCracken kept his head down and his grasp of the woman's moaning form tight as he neared the street where a phalanx of additional highway patrol cars were tearing onto the scene. Certain the arriving officers had no clear sense of what was happening or whom they were actually after, McCracken moved straight up to the line of cars and laid the woman down on the soft grass near a pair of patrolmen yanking on their flak jackets.

"This woman needs help!" he called.

"Not our problem," one smirked casually, listening to his walkie-talkie clack off a description of the suspect as a big man with a beard.

The officers' stares froze on him, their hands starting for their holstered pistols, when McCracken pounced. An elbow to the face shattered the nose of one and a heavy palm-heel blow under the second man's chin sent him slamming backward into his squad car and then slumping down it.

The next instant found Blaine lurching behind the wheel and tearing off down the road, past a fresh armada of arriving vehicles. He watched them spinning around wildly in his rearview mirror to give chase, others joining in as McCracken clamped down harder on the accelerator.

His eyes were still cheating looking toward the mirror when a roadblock formed by two squad cars parked nose to nose appeared directly before him across the road.

CHAPTER 21

Mobile, Alabama

"What the hell happened down there?" Hank Folsom demanded, once McCracken finally managed to reach him.

"I see you've heard."

"Heard? It's on every network. Please tell me that wasn't you who crashed through a police barricade. Jesus Christ, what was I thinking giving you the Go on this?"

"That you were fortunate I volunteered for the job. Now you should be thinking that I had nothing to do with what happened, because I didn't."

"You're supposed to be a professional."

"Are you listening to what I'm saying? I was set up. They knew I was coming."

"That's ridiculous!"

"Wake up and smell the way the world works, Hank. Someone's always watching you and somebody else is always watching the watcher. Somebody got wind you were sending me down here and that somebody's the one who set me up."

"I have no idea what you're talking about."

"Okay, let me put it this way: There's a leak smack dab in the Homeland office you're talking to me from right now that could only have originated on your end. Means this probably isn't a secure line," McCracken added, from beneath an empty, covered bus stop being hammered with hailstones atop its glass roof in downtown Mobile. "So get to one and call me back in twenty minutes at this number."

"They've got your picture somehow, identified you as a suspected covert government operative," Folsom told him, upon calling McCracken back nearly thirty minutes later instead.

"You believe me now about the setup, Hank?" McCracken asked from beneath another bus stop overhang. The rain was still pounding the streets, but the wind had abated and thunderclaps sounded only distantly.

"For what it's worth, I'm sorry."

"For being a fool or an idiot?"

"Take your pick."

"We need to meet, Hank. We need to sort this out."

"Just name the time and place, McCracken."

"Something else. Get in touch with whoever Homeland has inside Rule's entourage."

Silence filled the other end of the line, making McCracken figured he'd been cut off.

"Hank?" he prodded.

"I don't know what you're talking about."

"Yes, you do. You told me Rule's been on Homeland's radar for a while. You know stuff about him you couldn't get out of news reports or religious pamphlets. That means Homeland must have had someone on the inside feeding you information."

A deep sigh filled the line. "You make me feel like a fool *and* an idiot, McCracken."

"You're neither, Hank, just an amateur. In over your head, and now you've dragged me along for the ride, and I was dumb enough to follow."

"I just thought—"

"Forget what you thought. Too much thinking gets you into trouble. Just have your man meet me at the Greyhound bus station on Government Boulevard. Tell him to come prepared to tell me everything he knows about the Reverend Rule, so I can figure out why a two-bit preacher has the kind of security a million bucks wouldn't buy."

"That means my man in Rule's organization will have to risk exposure."

"Execution's the alternative. He's on borrowed time already. Take your pick, Hank."

"Better you come in from the proverbial cold, McCracken. I'm sorry about this boy in Missouri, but you're not being objective, not thinking straight. I didn't even think the personal existed for you."

"Neither did I, but the fact is Rule's only a part of what's going on, and if you want to stop more bodies from plunging off bridges, you'll do what I tell you."

CHAPTER 22

Mobile, Alabama

McCracken was watching the bus station from a nearby local version of Starbucks an hour out from the time of his planned rendezvous. The plan was for Homeland Security's unnamed plant in Rule's camp to wear an Alabama Crimson Tide football hat so Blaine would recognize him. Since he'd started watching the station, though, no man wearing any such hat had passed through the doors.

McCracken entered the bus station at the designated hour anyway and searched the waiting crowd for the man in question. Spotted him wearing a baseball cap that read ROLL TIDE!, seated alone in a bank of four chairs divided by a built-in, table-like platform for resting coffee cups or magazines. A small tote bag, nice touch for the further cover it provided, rested on the floor at his feet. McCracken moved toward the man and took the seat next to him.

Younger than Blaine had expected, of an age to still be able to wear his hair long enough to push out from beneath the ROLL TIDE! cap's confines. Thirty years old maybe, with a tan bred of spending lots of time at outdoor rallies, services, or whatever you wanted to call gatherings like the one held earlier in Crawford Park.

McCracken kept his eyes fixed forward, sleeve held in a way to disguise the fact he was speaking. "I've got your ticket right here. We'll talk on the bus. Ninety-minute ride to—"

He stopped when he realized the man was utterly unresponsive, hadn't even looked or glanced his way.

Blaine jostled him slightly at the shoulder. "Hey . . ."

The younger man slumped sideways, ROLL TIDE! cap falling off to reveal a thick patch of matted blood on the right side of his head soaking through his hair, evidence of a small caliber bullet.

McCracken stood up as casually as he could manage, pretending to stretch while paying the slumped figure no heed. Prepared to just walk off, leery of the same killer laying in wait for him, aware the young man must have come here to meet someone.

He started to back away, stopped when he glimpsed what looked like a magazine that had fallen to the floor when he'd ruffled the man's shoulder. McCracken stooped and retrieved it innocently enough, noticing immediately it was open to a page featuring a crossword puzzle with only a few of the boxes filled, incorrectly by all measure since a sequence of numbers and letters moved across the page.

4271FH121

And running down the page, coming up short of filling all the required boxes for that entry, was a single word:

CROATOAN.

CHAPTER 23

Mobile, Alabama

McCracken held his ground, fighting against the urge to simply bolt the area. The murdered man's killers were almost surely still on site. They'd be mixed among the crowds both inside the terminal and waiting to board buses in the departure area outside.

His eyes swept one way, then the other, then back again.

Nothing.

Damn!

Whoever they were had melted away, taken up positions concealed from his vantage point, perhaps with him zeroed in their crosshairs.

Come out, come out, wherever you are. . . .

Easier said than done. They wouldn't show themselves, so Blaine needed to make them. Strip the advantage from them and turn it to him.

Also easier said than done. These men were well-trained professionals; anyone brazen enough to murder a man in full view of dozens of witnesses had to be. But they wouldn't know who he was in all probability, and right now that was the best thing he had going for him.

McCracken tried to gauge their thinking, starting with the fact that they'd let the Homeland plant get this far to see if he was meeting with someone. So long as Blaine didn't act rashly, they couldn't be sure he was that man, at least not sure enough to risk exposure by starting a gunfight that would undoubtedly claim plenty of bystanders in its path here and now.

Which gave him time.

"Atlanta bus boarding now. The two o'clock bus for Atlanta is boarding now."

The booming voice's announcement was met with a large exodus from the terminal area, forty or so people rising to clutch their suitcases or loop their carry-ons and laptops over their shoulder. McCracken rose with them, grasping the dead man's tote bag for cover. He pretended to glance at his phone for the time, when in fact he was using it as a mirror to check behind him, see if there was any activity of note coming his way.

Nothing he could detect. So far.

McCracken joined the flow of bodies exiting the terminal. He felt for any disturbance in the mass, a sudden buckling or jostling indicative of men forcing their way forward. Nothing there either and, outside, McCracken found himself waiting in line before the Atlanta-bound bus while the driver collected tickets just short of the open door. With no intention of actually boarding the bus, Blaine would have to make a move soon. The terminal lot was cluttered with buses squeezed against one another with barely enough room for anyone to pass between them. Dozens lined up all the way to the road where a big John Deere front loader was hoisting the refuse of ongoing reconstruction into a dump truck.

Just before his turn came in line, McCracken veered away from the bus and sliced behind it, entering the tight confines separating it from the next. The buses were parked two, and in some places three, deep all the way to a fence that paralleled the street just short of the sidewalk. Blaine hit the ground and rolled under one bus and then another, a plan forming in his mind even as he caught the first signs of pursuit in the form of heavy footsteps and the soft garble of voices.

"I lost him, Red. You got anything?"

"Sorry, Blue. Nothing on my flank."

"This is Green, boys. Man just disappeared into the pavement. Fucking shapeshifter."

"He's moving for the street, using the buses," said Red. "We need to take him before he gets there."

"This is White. I'm on it."

"White, circle round and enter the maze halfway down. Brown, you read me?"

"Loud and clear."

"You circle into the maze from street side and work your way back toward us."

"Roger that, Red."

"Blue and Green, you know the drill. Now let's go bag this son of a bitch and find a wall to mount the trophy."

McCracken heard bits and pieces of the chatter, enough to discern presence though not plan. Five men, he guessed, maybe six. Talking like operatives who knew their way around a bus terminal, but not necessarily a battlefield. He needed to bait them, make them look where he wanted them to instead of where he intended to be.

*   *   *

"This is Blue, Red, I'm middle in. I just saw someone roll under a bus."

"Roger that, Red," from Green. "I'm middle out. He just rolled under the next bus in line here. I'm closing."

"This is White. I'm dead center. No glimpse of the bitch yet."

"He's going for the street for sure," said Red. "Close in on center of the maze grid, eyes peeled downward, weapons hot. Brown, you hold your position. I'm coming in."

As soon as he found a clear aisle, McCracken rose and hoisted himself atop a bus just past the center of the stacked-together assemblage of steel. Hardly a difficult feat, but one that proved taxing to his body, which needed a bit of coaxing to respond to what had once been simple tasks not given a moment's thought, nonetheless. Intense gym workouts, hours stretching out, could make it all doable at his age, but they couldn't make it easy.

Fortunately, the close spacing of the buses left leaping from one roof to the next just that simple, the biggest challenge being to land lightly without alerting any of the patrolling gunmen of his presence. Especially with their eyes aimed low, figuring he was still rolling his way under one chassis through to the next.

The fence was coming fast and, beyond it, the next phase of his plan.

"Anybody, got anything?" Brown said from the fence line. "Got nothing here, no sign whatso—"

"Brown, this is Red Leader. Say again."

Nothing.

"Repeat, say again."

Still nothing.

"Anybody have eyes on Brown?"

"Negative," from White.

"Nada," from Blue.

"That's a negative," from Green.

"Move for the street, people. Repeat, move for the street."

The men heard a screech, followed by a clanging and the sound of a rippling crash.

"What the hell was that?" Red demanded. "Anybody got eyes on anything?"

"Holy shit," one of the men said.

McCracken crashed through the fence, the big John Deere front loader he'd commandeered from the construction site obliterating the chain link without even slowing. The driver had been surprised to see him approaching the cab, even more surprised when Blaine climbed up, tossed him to the shredded concrete below, and replaced him behind the controls.

He wasn't sure what he was about to try would work, not sure he'd be able to gather enough speed to build the momentum he needed. In fretting over that, though, he'd forgotten about how powerful this particular John Deere 644K hybrid wheel loader was. Twenty tons of unstoppable power under his control.

McCracken got the shovel up and leveled just before he hit the last bus parked in the endless line of them stacked all the way to the terminal building. He felt the shovel teeth shred the bus's thin side steel, his intention to tip this bus into the one next to it, and so on, to create a domino effect that would trap his pursuers amid the jammed together mash of steel.

Instead, though, the massive power of the John Deere slammed the last bus in line into the one immediately next to it. He felt both start to move, crunching together, and McCracken responded by giving the loader more gas and working its gears to continue the process it had started on its own. Bus glass shattered and flew everywhere. The squeal and grind of metal tearing sent a flutter through his eardrums, as the buses folded up tight like an accordion instead of dominos.

"This is Red Leader! Everyone, get your asses out of there. Report! I want statuses!"

"Green here."

"Blue here."

"White reporting!" a different voice chimed in, bus tires exploding around him. "Tight squeeze, but I'm almost out. Jesus Christ, who the fuck is this g—"

A gasp followed, a thump, then nothing.

PART TWO:
CROATOAN

CHAPTER 24

Blountstown, Florida

Jeremiah Rule was praying when the door to his ramshackle church, built with the hands and funds of his own parishioners, opened and closed just as quickly. Rule was conscious of a brief shaft of light, followed by the sound of quick footsteps coming his way.

"Colonel Turwell, you have a measured step, but your thoughts give you away."

"Do they now?" said Turwell, stopping in the shaft of light streaming through the church skylight that leaked in bad storms. The sun slipped behind a cloud, the result being to make his cocoa-colored skin seem almost as dark as his black sport jacket worn over a black turtleneck. His neatly trimmed Afro was sprinkled with gray and he wore thin, wire-rimmed glasses. His chest looked overly large, its size further exaggerated by the fact that he held himself so far forward that it seemed pumped full of air. "And what about your thoughts? How are you holding up after this morning?"

"I pray for the brave souls who died in my service and protection." Rule turned from where he was kneeling on the raised dais at the front of the church, covered in a thin carpet that was still damp and rancid after the last hard rain had soaked it.

"You mean *my* men, don't you?"

"Who were serving me at the time. Who died for nothing less than devotion to the cause and my protection."

"Sacrifices to a greater cause to which they gave their lives."

"I wish no more to perish in service to me. I have the Lord to protect me, Colonel. If His plan is for the next attack to succeed, then so be it. I want your men gone. I will not have the peace of my sanctuary or my faithful disturbed by such distractions."

"My job is to keep you safe, Reverend, so our plan can reach fruition, so the country can be saved. We're just days from the finish now. You should keep that in mind."

Rule had adopted Blountstown, nestled within Florida's northern Panhandle, as his home because it felt right. He liked the fact that it was bracketed by water, rivers specifically, with the Chipola to the west and the Apalachicola to the east. So too it featured majestic limestone bluffs that he saw as sentinels standing brave and strong to ward off evil, to shield the town from the miseries of the outside world. Blountstown actually boasted its own rich history and tradition, including the Panhandle Pioneer Settlement, an impressive collection of original and replica structures featuring nineteenth-century log cabins, a farmhouse, and a school. There was also a working farm on the grounds that produced its own sugar cane and syrup. And the settlement's annual quilt shows and peanut boils took Rule back to simpler times long before he'd kicked a dog and beaten a boy to death to complete his transformation and begin his true mission. So enamored was he by the settlement's ambiance that he'd had his church constructed to jibe perfectly with the nearby settlement, its leaks, uneven flooring, and patchwork roof replicating olden times perhaps a bit too much.

Turwell took another step forward, stopping even with the front pews that wobbled a bit thanks to the church's uneven settling.

"You lost men in Afghanistan, too," Rule said, still not regarding him.

"As necessary then as it was today, Reverend."

"Your superiors didn't see it that way, though, did they, Colonel? You faced an Article Thirty-Two hearing and accepted what was termed a 'non-judicial punishment' once you agreed to resign your commission."

Turwell came all the way around and stepped upon the dais, placing himself between Rule and the altar. "And are you without sin?"

"Any man who claims to be stands as a liar."

"Three convictions for fraud," Turwell continued, "taking money from your followers under false pretenses."

Rule stiffened and finally met Turwell's gaze. "I was a different man then."

"Two, apparently, based upon the names under which you were convicted. I believe the second time involved you convincing the gravely ill to change you to the beneficiary of their life insurance policies in return for entrance into Heaven. That is what you promised them, isn't it?"

"They were sorely in need of spiritual guidance, Colonel. I was doing the work of the Lord, following His word."

"Just like I was doing the work of my country in Kandahar Province, Reverend."

"The very work we are both doing today."

"Then we are both imperfect men joined together by pursuit of the same goal. I'd recommend we leave things there."

"It's not that simple, Colonel. That's what I wanted to talk with you about. I need to *see*."

"See what?"

"The means by which we will inflict the tenth circle of Hell onto the world."

Turwell stiffened just enough for Rule to notice. "That's not your concern."

"The Lord feels otherwise. He wishes to see the great weapon of change through His servant's eyes. He instructs that I must *see* what I am praying for. He who has walked in the darkness has seen a great light. Show me that light, Colonel, or He may choose a new path for me, separate from the one you walk."

"Tomorrow," Turwell relented, "I'll take you to see our weapon tomorrow."

"Then leave me now," Rule said, easing himself back into position of prayer before the altar, "so I may pray my eyes are ready for what they are to behold."

Rule waited until he was sure Turwell was gone before rising and moving toward his private office placed at the church's rear. "You can come out now," he called. "It's safe."

CHAPTER 25

Blountstown, Florida

The young woman who'd come to him at the Tampa service that very day emerged from his office, trembling with arms wrapped about herself.

"Come, child, let God warm you."

Rule took her hand and led her up onto the altar with him. The dim overhead bulbs cast her face in a mixture of shadows and light that only added to her beauty. Her unwashed hair had turned stringy, smelling of must and oil, but still framed her face in a way that made her look sad and hopeful at the same time.

"I don't know how to thank you, Reverend," she said, lips quivering. "I've got nowhere else to go."

"God's house is home to all."

"I converted to Islam to marry my husband, Reverend. I'm a traitor."

"There are no traitors here, only those who seek His love."

"Can you help me?"

"Only He can. I'm merely His vessel."

"I could never leave the house without my head covered, like I was hiding myself, my true faith. How could I not see it, Reverend?"

Rule wrapped a tender arm around her shoulder. "Because you were deceived, my child. I shall call you Rachel, she too a victim of deception, as the Bible tells us, when she was supposed to marry Jacob. They are born deceivers, these people who welcomed you only to trick you into betraying your faith and God."

She fell against him, hugging Rule tightly through her sobs, her tears dampening his shirt. "I did betray Him, I know I did!"

"You can still be saved, Rachel."

She eased herself away from him, still clutching Rule by the elbows. "How, Reverend? I'll do *anything*."

"Your sin lies in your tongue, in the words you spoke against the Lord and your true faith. Salvation comes with a price."

"I told you, *anything*! I'll pay the price. Just tell me!"

"The object of your sin must be excised, sliced away so it can betray you no more."

Rachel opened her mouth as if to speak, but no words emerged.

Rule extracted a knife from a sheath clipped to his belt and extended it out to her.

"Cut it out."

Rachel took the knife, turned it around from one side to the other, watching the blade struggling to glint in the naked light of the church.

"Cut it out, my child."

She looked back at Rule.

"Slice the tongue from your mouth, so it may never betray you again and find yourself welcomed back to the house of the Lord."

He watched Rachel start the knife up slowly in a trembling hand.

"In pain there is salvation. In sacrifice there is hope."

The knife stopped, then started again. She opened her mouth.

"I'm with you, Rachel. God is with you. Prove yourself to Him. Return to His graces."

The tip of the blade disappeared between her lips, then the rest of it, the young woman's eyes never leaving Rule's.

He nodded placidly. Closed his eyes, then opened them. Nodded again. Giving her as much time as she needed, as much as time as it took.

The woman he'd named Rachel jerked the knife up and to the side.

The screaming began.

CHAPTER 26

Point Pleasant Beach, New Jersey

"Right on time, Hank," McCracken said, coming up alongside the man from Homeland Security, the wind blowing harder off the nearby water in the chilly early morning air.

Folsom shivered and took his gloved hands from the pockets of his topcoat. "Why here, McCracken? Why not just meet at the North Pole?"

"Because I didn't want to bother Santa Claus. See, this used to be a nice town with good people, until Superstorm Sandy hit Whole area's been condemned now. Even the former residents are still prohibited from returning after all this time. Fitting, don't you think?"

"Why?"

"Because they knew a storm was coming. It was inevitable. They just didn't know when. Like what happened to me yesterday, getting set up to take the fall for trying to kill the Reverend

Rule and gunning down four of his guards instead. I'm wondering if you were a part of that."

"Is that the real reason why we're here?"

"I'm still wondering, Hank."

"I'm the least of your problems, McCracken. Even local law-enforcement agencies have access to sophisticated facial recognition software these days. And your face showed up in some places even I didn't know about. Disney World, for example. And San Antonio just after what they still call the Second Battle of the Alamo. Colonial Williamsburg where you fought it out with those Omicron soldiers."

"Right, the good old days . . ."

"This isn't funny."

"I'm not laughing. Andrew Ericson still hasn't been found."

McCracken started walking along what had been a beach-front promenade but was now a seldom-traveled, sand-covered path. Closer to the water, at what had been the shoreline, foundations and pilings were all that remained of buildings that had stood strong for decades. No one was about nearby and no one would be until the rebuilding effort reached this far down, if that ever came. The ravaged houses that still stood in varying forms were awaiting demolition and the burnt-out shells of several further down the shore had perished to gas fires that had burned out of control when impassable roads kept firefighters from responding.

"This Rule thing's been your baby from the beginning, right, Hank? That was your man I found dead in the bus station."

Folsom swallowed hard. "Chase Samuels. He had a wife and young son. He was thirty-three, a top undercover, who came over to Homeland from ATF."

"Andrew Ericson, age fifteen. As close to real family as I've got. You want to continue swapping stories?"

"No. I'm sorry."

"I only met the kid once. If it wasn't for Christmas cards, I wouldn't even know what he looks like. Good thing I won't have to identify the body, Hank, because he's still alive. You hear me? He's still alive."

"I hear you," Folsom said softly. "Just tell me what the next step is."

"Word *Croatoan* mean anything to you?"

"Outside of the fact Chase Samuels left it as some kind of message for us, no."

"A British relief party found it carved into a tree at the Roanoke Colony in the late sixteenth century," McCracken told him, as the wind picked up again, whipping the sand into a funnel cloud.

"The one where all the settlers vanished?"

"The very same."

"Sorry," Folsom said, looking as flustered as he did anxious and frustrated. "I've never heard the word before today."

"How about the other note in the crossword puzzle? Four-two-seven-one-F-H-one-two-one."

"We're still running it."

"We?"

"Analysts. Bottom of the food chain, but the best Homeland's got."

"Well, that's a relief."

"This is already hard enough, McCracken."

"I'm the one who's the object of a manhunt, Hank, not you."

Folsom stopped, eyes suddenly sweeping about the beach. "We're not alone, are we?"

"What do you think?"

"I think maybe I shouldn't have come."

"Johnny and Sal are here for your own protection, Hank."

"*My* protection?"

"In case somebody followed you here from Washington."

"You were hoping that would be the case, weren't you? You used me as bait."

"I wanted someone to have a little chat with. Sal Belamo was an interrogator with the CIA for a stretch. Very old school. Likes to use pliers and power outlets. I was hoping to get the chance to see him work."

"You think someone in Homeland is dirty?"

"I think that just begins to describe what we're facing here. What went down in Mobile yesterday wasn't the work of a backwoods preacher and neither was the security he had around him. Somebody's backing the Reverend Rule, somebody who's got him doing their bidding whether he realizes it or not. And since Homeland was the agency that sent me down there, you do the math."

"So you're blaming me."

"Only for being stupid and running a lousy operation on Rule. My guess is they made your undercover sometime ago and were just stringing the two of you along. That's why it's been so long since he provided any actionable intelligence."

Folsom looked suddenly wary, suspicious. "I never told you that."

"You didn't have to." McCracken hesitated to let his point sink in. "You're right, Rule's a dangerous man, but he's not acting alone, and I need to figure out who's pulling his strings."

Blaine heard Folsom's smartphone buzz and watched him lift it from his pocket, the look on his face saying it all.

"What is it, Hank?"

Folsom's face was blank, no expression or emotion whatsoever. "Looks like the people on that bridge in Missouri just got some more company."

CHAPTER 27

O'Hare Airport, Chicago: Twenty minutes earlier

"One of those days," air traffic controller Jane Plezak said, chewing on a straw.

"When is it not one of those days here?" her shift supervisor, Gus Kincannon, grinned from behind her.

"I don't know, today seems especially . . ."

"Especially what?" Kincannon asked when Plezak let her remark drift off.

"I don't know."

"Last time you said that, the baggage handlers walked out."

"That's right."

"And the time before, a 747 clipped a commuter plane during taxi."

"I remember."

"So what's it going to be today, Jane?"

Her hourly five-minute break over, Plezak returned all her attention to her screen filled with countless blips over a dark circular depiction of the skies above O'Hare. A maddening assemblage of icons with associated flight numbers that was mind-boggling in its congestion and complexity. Plezak had learned to get past that by disciplining herself to focus on her grid and her grid only, and the ability to segment the screen before her was all that kept her sane through her shift on difficult days like this.

"Jesus Christ," Kincannon mumbled.

"What?"

"Down on the tarmac, looks like a fuel truck racing an Airbus."

"Must be Bob Semple," Plezak said, mouthpiece covered but eyes still locked on her screen. "Man's committed to breaking the record for most planes refueled in a day."

"I'm glad I fly out of Midway," Kincannon told her, referring to the smaller airport on the other side of the city.

Down on the tarmac, Bob Semple had just topped off a United Dreamliner and was rushing to do the same for one of the airline's commuter fleet. Traffic backup, bad even by O'Hare standards, had left dozens of fully loaded planes stuck at their gates, with engines still running to keep the passengers inside warm on the frigid January day. His dashboard-mounted gauges indicated he still had three-quarters of his tank.

Semple was just starting to turn toward the line of planes parked at their gates, angling for the ninety-seater, when he heard, more like felt, a gurgle. At first, he thought it might be his own stomach rumbling, then passed it off as too much air gathered in his pump line. Nothing of concern.

Until the flash came.

Gus Kincannon saw it from the O'Hare tower, but Jane Plezak noticed nothing amiss until the air burst accompanying the explosion that hit the glass with the power of a hurricane-force wind. The whole tower seemed to buckle, its occupants too far away from the explosion to hear its fury, although all could feel it and see the flames blowing outward into the air, swallowing everything in their path.

Bob Semple's truck ruptured into a thousand flaming projectiles rocketing everywhere, badly damaging the planes farthest out and catching the nearer ones on fire. The fuel tanks of the two parked at the nearest gates exploded in secondary blasts, flames seeming to spread forward from the tails until each was totally consumed.

As his controllers frantically rerouted their planes circling in anticipation of landing, Gus Kincannon couldn't take his eyes off what looked like a jagged trench dug across the tarmac, spreading outward from a cylindrical crater carved by the initial explosion and disabling three major runways. The scene, awash in black smoke that clung to the air like tar, was catastrophic, impossible to imagine, much less witness. Surreal, unreal. The product of a nightmare.

One of those days, he remembered Jane Plezak saying just a few moments before.

CHAPTER 28

London

Zarrin wasn't surprised when the big man took the stool next to her in the Heathrow bar, because she'd spotted him watching for her as soon as she entered the airport's international terminal.

"Tell me something," she greeted, not bothering to turn the big man's way, "are all Israelis named David?"

"You know the routine," the man smirked, his experience showing in coarse hair that was as much salt as pepper.

She had spent the minutes waiting for his expected appearance studying herself in the bar's mirror behind the shelves of bar and high-end brands. Her long, wavy black hair looked more limp than she was accustomed, sprinkled with strands of gray near the temples that the dim lighting of the bar concealed. So too it disguised the fatigue present in her eyes. Still bright and vital, but droopy, as if she was always ready for a nap. The concert the night before had taken a lot of energy and, nearing forty now, Zarrin needed more time to fully recover. Her other chosen avocation, one she excelled in just as much, was a young person's game. Even this particular David was growing too old for it, but the Israelis stayed active in the field longer. Life treated hunters easier.

Zarrin finally glanced at him, up toward his face looming over her. "Except you look more like Goliath."

"That's why they sent me. So we could have this discussion in an airport terminal free of weapons."

"But I'm never free of weapons, David, am I?"

The Israeli smirked again. "As long as I can see your hands . . ."

"I can see yours too," she told him. "And I know how good you are with them."

"Another reason why they sent me. Figured that might even out the odds a bit." David checked her drink, watery with melted ice now in a tall glass.

Squeezing an icy glass alternately with her left hand and right had become a ritual for her as of late, because it helped control her symptoms. She would do it on the plane every hour, or at least every other, as well.

"We can't let you go to the United States."

"Maybe I have a concert to perform, or a personal appearance to keep."

"We checked. You don't. McCracken's been a great friend to Israel. He's off-limits."

"I'll keep that in mind."

"When you think about it, I'm actually doing you a favor."

"How's that?"

"Saving your life. Something to thank me for. You think you're the first to go after Blaine McCracken? He's left behind a trail of bodies longer than the road to Damascus."

"He's a relic, a dinosaur. Old now, past his prime."

David turned on his stool all the way to face her. "You need to go home. I can't let you get on that plane. Go back to your piano. Live out your life to standing ovations and rave reviews. Take your bows and early retirement as someone who has something to retire to. Live to play another day, Zarrin."

Zarrin shrugged and reached for her glass, ended up knocking it over to the floor where it smashed, spraying chips of ice and glass shards across the floor.

"See what I mean," David smirked.

Zarrin eased herself off the stool with napkin in hand, stooping to collect the fragments. Her hands rebelled at first. But, as she had when playing Tchaikovsky the night before, she pushed her very will into them, controlling her fingers along some jerry-rigged neuro-network of her own making.

She looked up at David. "I'm going to ask you to simply leave and forget we had this conversation."

"I can't do that."

Zarrin rose from her crouch, retaking her stool. "I suppose I couldn't either."

Before David could respond, she jerked her hand out sideways, burying a dagger-sharp shard of glass she'd broken off into his windpipe. There was very little blood, no spray at all, and Zarrin twisted the shard around a bit to make sure the job was done, clamping a hand on the big man's shoulder to hold him in place as he wheezed, quickly bleeding out internally.

But then her hand locked up, wouldn't let go. Seemed to hold there for an eternal moment before her mind regained control and willed the fingers to open, enabling her to slide her hand away and ease David downward so his face was resting on the bar's wooden surface. His chest moved in shallow jerks, lungs stealing what little air they could grab, the time between motions already lengthening.

She slid away, careful to keep her face angled downward so the bartender wouldn't notice. It had been too close this time, much too close to suit her psyche or make her fit for such conditions to engage a man as deadly proficient as Blaine McCracken.

David had known that just as much as she did. *But he didn't know everything, not even close*, Zarrin thought, not realizing her cell phone was ringing.

CHAPTER 29

Sunnyside Yard, Queens, New York

"Don't piss me off, MacNuts, or I may turn you in for the reward money," Captain Seven said, his voice turned raspy by the heavy dose of smoke he'd just sucked into his lungs.

"There's a reward?"

"Figure of speech," the captain winked, inhaling another long drag off the marijuana blunt rolled into a cigar wrapper that smelled of cinnamon and grape as it burned.

His gray hair dangled well past his shoulders, hanging in tangles and ringlets left to the whims of nature, as if he used the rain as a washbasin. The captain wore a Grateful Dead tie-dyed T-shirt under an old leather vest that was fraying at the edges and missing all three of its buttons. So faded that the sun made it look gray in some patches and white in others. His eyes, a bit sleepy and almost drunken, had a playful glint about them. And when he uncrossed his arms with the still-smoking marijuana blunt in hand, McCracken noticed his

T-shirt featured a peace sign with MAKE LOVE above it and NOT WAR below.

"You said it was important, MacNuts," said Captain Seven. "You didn't say it was this important."

"I don't remember saying anything."

"Eyes are the window to the soul, man, window to the soul. And yours look about as pained as I've seen anyone not bright enough to improve their mood with some high-end hydro."

"There's not a drug in the world that can manage that right now, Captain."

McCracken had no idea what the captain's real name was, only that he had gotten this one thanks to behavior, eccentricities, and intelligence that had led one military commander to call the eccentric tech whiz a visitor from the seventh planet from a distant galaxy. *Captain*, accordingly, wasn't a real military rank. Even though he'd never spent a day in boot camp or wearing a uniform, his efforts along with his scientific knowledge and creativity had saved countless lives. Captain Seven had been one of those on the forefront of using technology as a prime weapon against opponents of all levels, starting in Vietnam where he'd been assigned to further the efforts of McCracken and others in Operation Phoenix.

To reach the captain's "home," McCracken had made his way through the tight cluster of train cars packed into Amtrak's Sunnyside Yard that ran along the lower length of Queens. Constructed in 1910, it had once been the largest locomotive storage yard in the world, occupying almost two hundred acres at one point. Today, it featured an amalgamation of mothballed engines and passenger cars overgrown with weeds sprouting from beneath their track beds and still-active train cars awaiting use when overflow or repairs demanded. Many, if not most, of the cars stored there might never leave the yard again, including two interconnected rusted-out relics located just short of an overpass and perched against a heavy steel fence, beyond which stood a ten-story self-storage facility.

Blaine had found the captain not in those cars in which he lived, but in an area of Sunnyside Yard hidden behind both a curve and an assortment of rusted steel corpses of train cars stacked off the tracks. The area looked utterly innocuous, perfect staging ground for the many experiments Captain Seven continued to carry out either on his or the military's behalf.

Today, those experiments seem to involve what McCracken had first thought was a swarm of bees, but now realized was something else entirely.

"Mini-drones," the captain said, flailing at the air briefly before snatching one for Blaine to see. "That's what I call them."

"Surveillance?" McCracken asked, holding the light, bee-like device up for closer inspection.

"Not quite. Allow me to demonstrate." With that, Captain Seven hit a single button on a small remote, pointing the device toward a clothesline assemblage layered over the worst-dressed scarecrow ever. "Time to let my bug-thing go."

" 'Bug-thing'?"

"Haven't come up with a fancier name yet."

McCracken opened his fingers and the marble-sized bug-thing took off like a jet, straight for Captain Seven's horribly attired scarecrow. Impact came with a blast powerful enough for McCracken to feel the aftershock ripple from even forty feet away. When the smoke cleared, there was nothing left of the scarecrow except for a few stray patches of an old denim jacket.

"Vintage Levi's, MacNuts," the captain proclaimed, approaching to better view the effects of the blast. "Always like to see my old shit go to a worthwhile end."

"Miniature flying bombs," McCracken said, shaking his head in amazement.

"I like that. Think I'll call them 'bug bombs' instead. They key on temperature so I made sure to heat up the scarecrow to a comfortable 98.6."

"Why didn't the bug bomb just zero on me?"

"Ah, you noticed!"

"I'm still standing here, aren't I?"

"Proximity," the captain explained. "My bug bombs don't arm until they're twenty feet from whoever's wielding them, the controller. So as long as you don't move much and the target, or targets, are a reasonable difference away, just cover your ears."

"Targets plural?"

"Artificial intelligence, MacNuts. My bug bombs automatically veer to the next available target when they read another on a course identical to theirs. Pretty simple shit, actually."

"For you anyway."

Captain Seven gave him a longer look. "And what about for you?"

"You remember my kind-of-son Matthew?"

"I remember he's got a son of his own now," the captain said, as if seeing something in Blaine's eyes.

"Hopefully," Blaine said, leaving it there.

"What brings you here again?" the captain managed and took another hit from his blunt.

"The word *Croatoan* mean anything to you?"

"Holy shit," Captain Seven said, coughing the smoke out.

CHAPTER 30

Sunnyside Yard, Queens, New York

"Welcome to my humble abode, MacNuts," Captain Seven said, arm extended to beckon McCracken to enter the train car that served as his home.

He lived among the yard's relics. His heat and power came courtesy of underground propane tanks, the track on which his cars were perched taken off-line years before when he took up residence with the full acquiescence of the government in exchange for his work in the field of unique weapons development.

They slithered through a narrow break between a pair of engines parked nose to nose to reach the two passenger cars that formed the captain's home, shielded by a minefield of strung-together passenger cars, some of which looked as if they dated back to the time of the yard's opening.

"I'm sorry about the kid," he said once they were inside, sucking in a deep hit off his tightly wrapped cigar blunt and exhaling a fresh cloud of smoke.

"Am I crazy for believing he might still be alive?"

"You're crazy for still doing the shit you do, but not for that. Strange, inexplicable stuff happens every day; I'm living proof of that."

"You mean like miracles?"

"I can only name about a thousand. Look around you."

They'd entered the trailing car that contained the captain's workshop. A collection of machines and half-completed experiments resting amid stacks of beakers, burners, chips, and diodes, and objects salvaged from here or there waiting to be tested or employed in one jerry-rigged weapon or another.

"Good thing you played to my soft side," the captain said, " 'cause otherwise I'd still be retired."

"Since when?"

"Since I got your call. My mind was so messed up after our last adventure, I had to give up drugs a while, and I do not intend to go through that hell again."

"You're serious," McCracken realized.

"As a heart attack—something else I narrowly avoided thanks to you."

"I'm sure you have plans."

"Thinking about starting up an old-age home for new-age folks like me. You know, where the elderly get to choose which cannabis to smoke, instead of fighting for the shuffleboard court. Rogue agents need not apply."

"But since I played to your soft side . . ."

"I am definitely intrigued, MacNuts." Captain Seven took another deep drag off his blunt and let it out slowly.

His wild hair, twisted into ringlets, shifted from side to side as he shook his head. "Croatoan . . . Only one of the greatest remaining unsolved mysteries known to man. How almost one hundred twenty settlers on Roanoke Island off the North Carolina coast simply vanished from the face of the earth. Except they didn't."

"Didn't what?"

"Disappear. In fact, they never even left the fortress encampment where the colony was built."

McCracken took a step closer to him. "You been reading a different history book than me on the subject?"

"Funny you should ask," Captain Seven said and lifted an old, worn leather journal from a stack on his shelf. He eased it from inside the kind of perma-seal bag favored by archaeologists, flashing the front cover long enough for McCracken to see THE JOURNAL OF GOVERNOR JOHN WHITE scrawled in faded gold print upon the tattered leather. "Because something killed those colonists, MacNuts. Something really, really, really deadly. Call it an original version of a weapon of mass destruction, maybe the first one in existence, unless you count the meteor that killed the dinosaurs."

"And you think whoever's behind what I'm facing this time figured out what it was?"

"Nope, worse—I'm worried that they found it."

CHAPTER 31

Roanoke Island: 1590

I make these entries from my cabin on board Captain Glanville's ship in full knowledge they may serve as my epitaph should this journal ever be found at all.

I fear it will not. I fear my return to the site of the island colony once in my charge will see my death, as it saw the deaths of so many I was responsible for, including my own dear grand-daughter. So perhaps I do this for Virginia, whose life was snuffed out much too young. Perhaps I do it because I cannot let her death go unanswered and unpunished.

Captain Glanville has resisted my overtures, my insistence about returning to the camp. He says we must pull up anchor and be gone from this cursed place as soon as the fog and the storm clear. He does not understand we cannot leave this unfinished, especially if my greatest fears turn out to be true. For if we dare flee as frightened, cowering men, we risk sentencing others to the same fate.

But I have kept the truth of my suspicions from the good captain. He is a simple man who knows war and must know his enemy at the sharp end of his blade. I will let him believe Indians were responsible for the fate of the colonists. I will let him believe we return as a war party to seek them out, that there will be a large bounty waiting for the savages' skins when we return home. I cannot share the complete truth with Glanville because I am not aware of it myself. I only know with dread certainty, first, that the colonists are all dead and, second, that the Natives had nothing to do with it. There was no evidence of an attack because there was no attack; indeed, the signal for such in the form of a Maltese cross was nowhere to be found where it otherwise would have been near CROATOAN *as carved into a still-standing post.*

But no colonist carved it; I see that in the clarity that distance brings, the same clarity that tells me I must return once the storm passes. I suppose the word could be easily passed off as something geographical or some indication from the local tribe of Natives. But the word Croatoan, *I have learned, has another meaning, one of dire impact and portent that makes the placement of the word not an announcement at all.*

But a warning.

Of what exactly I do not know; at least, am not totally sure. What I do know is whatever befell the colonists, including my own family, struck them all at once, in a mere instant. It struck them down as they stood or slept, with a malevolence never seen before. I remain a God-fearing man, but in recent years have not seen fit to make time for religion or church. My duty became so all-consuming that it swallowed my faith and bastardized my beliefs. Perhaps, if things had been different, I would have a better understanding of the nature of the evil that struck the colony I now must return to confront and destroy as best I can.

That evil had lain dormant for years, for centuries, waiting for our coming to serve up victims to its ultimate contentment. And then it still lay in wait for the proper time when the colony was least prepared. I commissioned the building of the fort myself, personally supervised the crafting of its walls and fortifications to be able to repel any attack, even if it came from a vastly superior force. So, too, the plans I left in place assured sufficient stores of food and water to withstand a long siege. I sailed from the colony lo those three years ago secure in the notion my people were safe from any attack from the outside.

I never considered the need to protect them from an attack from within.

So tomorrow I return to the colony, my colony, with Captain Glanville and those of his men who know what it is to see death and dispense it themselves. But I fear even their trained and practiced eyes are ill prepared for what we will find. And I fear, too, their weapons will be useless against the enemy that resides there.

Glanville wants revenge for the two men he lost to the evil; perhaps he wasn't as hard to convince as he let on, making me dangle bounty before him as an added incentive. But such bounty is worthless to any man dead before he can claim it. And if we are not careful, that will be the fate that awaits us all.

So take these words, if you are reading them, as warning to make sure no one ever sails the waters with Roanoke Island as their destination. Strike it from the maps of shipping lanes, nautical charts, and the knowledge of this New World that bears with it dangers and the grim reality that we never should have ventured here.

33333333

CHAPTER 32

Sunnyside Yard, Queens, New York

"Are we finished now?" Captain Seven asked, after McCracken was done reading.

"You sure this is authentic?"

"I matched the writing against White's signature on a number of requisition orders that survived the era. Door's over there. You can let yourself out."

"Only White survived and returned to England, didn't he?"

"Spent the rest of his life at odds with Sir Walter Raleigh, doing everything he could to steer future expeditions away from the New World. Lots of people thought he'd lost his mind. Maybe that's why I relate to him so well, MacNuts," the captain said, taking a glass-blown bong from a nearby shelf and packing it with the contents of a Ziploc bag. "Invented it myself," he explained. "Noncombustible. No match or lighter required. Simple oxygen supplies the required spark. Cleanest high you'll ever experience."

"Not for me, Captain."

"Come on, make believe you're back in the 'Nam world."

"Didn't smoke there either."

"No? And me thinking you hung out with that big Indian on account of him being a whiz with homegrown. You know, Indians were the original weed farmers. Shit, why do you think the pilgrims had such a good time that first Thanksgiving? Hint: it wasn't the turkey."

"Since White survived, why are there no more entries in his journal?"

"Must've had so much to say he started a new one. Makes sense, considering there aren't a lot of pages left in this volume. It was discovered a few months back among the possessions of a collector, the only White journal found there or anywhere else for that matter."

"So whatever I'm looking for . . ."

"Only one place I can think of to find it."

"Think I'll head down to North Carolina to check out a certain island."

The captain bounced up out of his seat. "Sounds good to me."

"I thought you were retired."

"Nope, just thinking about it. Who else is gonna hold your hand, lest you end up unleashing a shit storm on the world."

"How's that exactly?"

Captain Seven grabbed a small tote bag and began stuffing in all manner of bowls and bongs, along with three Ziploc bags of pot. "Because whatever killed the colonists might still be there."

CHAPTER 33

Steubenville, Ohio

Zarrin moved purposefully about the law-enforcement personnel inside the cordoned-off crime scene where a bomb had laid waste to a church four days ago. Her ID badge dangled from her neck, identifying her as an agent for one of the various investigative agencies on the scene—so many that it was easy to fit in and hide in utterly plain sight. She had many such IDs for intelligence and investigative services all over the world, an invaluable resource when it came to the kind of close access to the scene her detailed planning required.

She spotted a group of Alcohol, Tobacco, and Firearms agents conferring off to the side, two of them showcasing objects in their hands sheathed in plastic evidence-gathering gloves. Zarrin approached and stopped just short of them, making sure they could see her badge.

"Is that the trigger?" she asked a female agent holding a small twisted and charred metal object.

The woman checked her dangling ID, clearly impressed as she nodded. "You know your shit, don't you?"

"I've been around a bombing site or two," Zarrin told her.

The call she'd gotten at Heathrow was from Colonel Kosh.

"You should have told me," he accused. "Now you have placed my mission at risk."

"Colonel?"

"You think I wouldn't have realized? That church bombing in Ohio has your trademark all over it. How could you not tell me of your involvement?"

"Because there wasn't any."

"Don't take me for a fool, Zarrin. Your return to the United States is hardly advisable at this time. Somebody may have seen you, be able to identify you, in which case you'd be in a position to identify me. The Republic of Iran does not need that right now."

And Colonel Kosh terminated the call before Zarrin could respond.

Ohio, he'd said, a church bombing.

. . . has your trademark all over it . . .

The ATF woman held the twisted husk of metal out but didn't hand it over. "Well, what we've got here is the classic two-chain trigger. Minor amount of explosive to ignite a much larger amount of accelerant consistent with exactly what happened here."

"You mind if I take a look?" Zarrin asked the female ATF agent, pulling plastic gloves over her hands.

The woman passed the trigger over. Zarrin felt its familiar heft and raised it toward her nose to sniff.

"What has your investigation revealed so far about the bombing itself?"

"The perpetrators soaked the floor in a chemical compound we've identified as an offshoot of kerosene," another of the ATF agents explained. "We believe they were in the guise of a cleaning crew on the premises without prior authorization. No security cameras, though. They might as well have been invisible."

Just as she'd once done in Istanbul, to the letter, and more than enough to arouse Colonel Kosh's suspicions of her involvement.

"Survivors all describe a massive flame burst," the female agent picked up. "What the perpetrators essentially did was turn the entire church into a fuel-air bomb."

Istanbul again, as well an office building in Amman. A signature of hers, almost certain to be matched up to this bombing. Meaning that she was about to become a suspect.

But why would someone go through so much trouble to implicate her? And since she wasn't responsible for this bombing, who was?

"Thanks for your help," Zarrin said, disciplining herself to keep her English measured and perfect, as she walked away.

Zarrin had her cell phone out and at her ear by then, waited until she neared the jagged facade riddled with blast debris to press out a number.

"I need to see you," she said, after a beep sounded prior to a single ring. "Please make time immediately. I'm on my way."

CHAPTER 34

Blountstown, Florida

Jeremiah Rule took Rachel from behind to avoid having to look at her face and the horrible swelling from the wound that remained bloody and unhealed. He needed to bed her tonight because she was ripe and ready, a blessed opportunity not to be squandered. He took her in his stiflingly hot bedroom, the windows all closed to shut out the sound of the rain while leaving the air fetid and stale.

Rule lived on the same grounds as his church in a simple one-story modular home that was actually composed of several prefabricated modules joined together. He had retreated there to join the young woman once his prayers were done, but only after draining the buckets collecting the spill from another January storm.

"All men have demons, child," he said out loud, as he continued to ease himself in and out of Rachel, listening to her whimpers and sobs as the blood dribbling from her mouth soaked his pillows and sheets. "They can never be vanquished, but they can be controlled. The strongest among us are capable of that. I was not always counted among that number, yet my weakness has painful roots all its own that help to explain my helplessness, my yielding to temptation. I offer the truth of my past not as excuse, only so you understand the path that brought me to a terrible place that could have been my end had not light shined bright and found me in its glow."

Rule's thrusts quickened. He pushed himself deeper inside her.

"I was orphaned as a young boy, abandoned actually by my parents and forced to live in a boys' home. The orphanage was a cold place in the mountains of North Carolina. An ugly place surrounded by beauty, which made no sense to me, even as a boy. I remember it seemed cold all the time, except in the summer where the cottages—that's what we called them—were like ovens. In winter, the cottages were heated by steam pipes, which were strung overhead like something out of a science-fiction movie. They'd hiss and clack and drip hot water on you as you slept."

Rule felt the passion, the moment, building inside him.

"I learned my religion there. Mass every day of the week with the longest saved for Sundays. I learned to love God because I hated everything else. Had these older kids, late teens or early twenties maybe, watching us, called counselors. One day, one of them lost a five-dollar bill and accused us nine-year-olds of stealing it. When nobody confessed, the counselors made us hang from the steam pipes until our hands began to blister. Each time a boy finally let go and fell off, he was beaten. I was the last to fall and they beat me worst of anyone. Then this fat kid who smelled bad confessed and gave back the five dollars, but I was the one forced to suffer for his sins more than anyone else."

Almost there now, the moment of bliss that would beget an even greater plan nearly upon him. Rule pounded Rachel more feverishly, yanking back on her hair and fighting for his own breath, not caring how much she sobbed or whimpered beneath him.

"I had God back then," he gasped. "God was all I had, and I promised, I promised to serve Him all my days if He saved me from that awful place. Every morning I'd pray to get through that day and every night I'd pray to get through the next. And since the Lord delivered for me, I figured the least I could do was deliver for Him. So I got that job selling Bibles, feeling even then He had some bigger plans for me and I guess I was right, wasn't I? *Wasn't I?*"

And with that he exploded, hard and fast, holding Rachel by the hips until he'd emptied himself inside her.

Rule had just pulled out of her when he heard a heavy knocking on the door and pushed himself back to his feet. The pounding had grown loud enough to rattle whole front of his house by the time he had pulled his clothes back on and moved to answer the door. He opened it to find Colonel Alvin Turwell standing there silhouetted by the sun.

"You wanted to see how we're going to change the future, Reverend. I've got a plane standing by."

CHAPTER 35

Roanoke Island

"Forget about where they take the tourists, this is the actual site of the colony . . . and the original weapon of mass destruction," Captain Seven said, breath misting before his face in the chilly, dank air. The temperature was dropping fast in advance of an approaching storm forecast to spread a mix of rain and snow through the mainland. Powerful gusty winds and lots of precipitation were fast approaching, further darkening a cloudy day lit in splotchy fashion by the stray light able to sift through the forest's thin, bare canopy. "This is where John White must have found his people when he returned with Captain Glanville and his men the day after he made that entry in his journal."

"Hold on—the colonists were never found."

"That's what history says, and technically it's accurate, since White didn't find them alive."

"Graves," McCracken realized. Prior to making the trip, he'd done his best to change his appearance, including shaving his

beard for the first time since his first tour in Vietnam and comb-
ing his hair straight back. "You're talking about graves. . . ."

The captain nodded. "Lined up one after the other, all one
hundred eighteen of the colonists, including White's own family.
One grave for each settler dug by members of the Croatan Indian
tribe that lived nearby. Hence that one word carved into a tree as
a signal to alert anyone who showed up who'd buried the bodies.
See, the colonists were killed all right, but not in an attack. Nope,
those poor bastards didn't fall to hostile action at all. They fell to
something much worse and much more dangerous."

"Any idea exactly what?" McCracken asked the captain, after
exchanging a glance with Johnny Wareagle, who'd joined them
for the trip.

"I'm almost there, MacNuts, but not quite. It all comes down
to isolating a weapon that could kill so many people so fast way
back in 1590. White figured out the disturbances he spotted in
the ground and topsoil to be graves, dozens and dozens of them.
He came back the next day to set fire to the very ground we're
standing on to erase any trace of their presence and, hopefully,
whatever it was that killed them."

Wareagle knelt and smoothed the grass, as if it might yield
some further clues.

"Johnny?" Blaine prompted.

"There was a legend in these parts even before the first settlers arrived prior to the doomed Roanoke party, Blainey. A
legend of an invisible force, violent and wild, that rises when
conditions are right to wreak havoc on the land and its residents. Each of the tribes had their own version, along with their
own name in their own language. But the legend's the same.
Always something monstrous and malevolent."

"Big fella's more than right," Captain Seven echoed. "Makes
me think he's been lying to us all these years about having his
own private patch of homegrown, because that kind of percep-

tion does not come without some chemical enhancement, I shit you not. See, a few days before his death, and following a disappearance that remains unexplained to this day, Edgar Allan Poe was brought to his deathbed in a state of delirium whispering the word *Croatoan*. The same word was found in other places at other times: scribbled in the journal of Amelia Earhart after her disappearance in 1937, carved into the post of the last bed that the celebrated horror author Ambrose Bierce slept in before he vanished in Mexico in 1913, and scratched on the wall of the cell that the notorious stagecoach robber Black Bart inhabited before he was released from prison in 1888, never to be seen again. And, most disturbingly of all, written on the last page of the logbook of the ship *Carroll A. Deering* when it ran aground with no one aboard on Cape Hatteras in 1921."

"What's your point, Captain?"

"More of an observation, MacNuts, that maybe we're not the first to figure out that something big and bad got loose here."

McCracken moved his gaze back to Wareagle. "Tell me more about these conditions you mentioned."

"Fog, mist, the air sometimes hot and sometimes cold. Always in the midst of a storm or just in advance of one, Blainey."

Captain Seven whistled. "Yup, real dark and stormy night shit, I'd say. The point being something killed these colonists in the blink of an eye, and I'll bet you my stash it's not done yet."

CHAPTER 36

Roanoke Island

"Talk to me about this weapon of mass destruction, Captain," McCracken said in the center of the brush-riddled clearing amid the increasing chill and darkening sky.

"Already told you, I haven't figured that part out yet."

"But you wouldn't be here if you didn't have some idea."

"I've had *some* idea for a long time, but I'm just beginning to figure out I've been right all along. Should've known better than to doubt myself."

"About what exactly?"

"Go back to what the big fella said about weather conditions."

"Mist, fog, a storm coming or already there."

Captain Seven grinned. "See, you know this shit as well as I do."

"Not really."

"Atmospheric conditions, MacNuts, specifically low barometric pressure. Whatever killed the colonists feeds on that, at least thrives on it. The two sailors Captain Glanville lost in his first trip ashore with John White died in the fog as a storm approached. Yup, it all adds up."

"To what?"

"To something we need to consider on an entirely different plane of understanding, and I mean a plane even beyond what ganja can do for you." The captain stopped, getting his bearings of the camp as it had been over four hundred years ago. "Remember the cartoon that had the WABAC machine in it? Sherman and his dog Mr. Peabrain or something?"

"I think it was Mr. Peabody, Captain."

"Whatever. Anyway, imagine you and me climbing into that WABAC machine and going back to 1590 right where we're standing. What do you think we'd find?"

"Living colonists, if we picked the date right."

"I'm talking about in nature."

"Why don't you just enlighten me? Nature's been your specialty for as long as I've been digging foxholes in it."

"Well, the fact of the matter is, at the time of the Roanoke Colony, this land was pretty much unspoiled, even untouched for a million years or so. No development, no building, no exploration. Even the Indian tribes stuck to a pretty small area, maybe because all the legends about the danger in these woods led them to steer clear of this very site. Might also explain why they proved so inhospitable to the colonists, since they were afraid of them unleashing whatever had laid claim to this land. Comes down to the fact that sometimes when you start digging to build a world, you end up unearthing the kind of stuff that goes bump in the night."

"You think that's what the colonists did?"

"I think they were exposed to something never introduced into the world before, something that exists under a set of bio-

chemical rules they understood no more than they could possibly understand what was killing them."

"*What*, as opposed to *who*. Care to elaborate?"

"Uh-uh. I'm not nearly stoned enough to manage the effort."

"Something that powerful doesn't just go away. So tell me
what happened to your original weapon of mass destruction
after the colonists let it out."

The question seemed to ruffle Captain Seven, his big, crazed
eyes suddenly narrowing, looking uncharacteristically unsure.
"It went back into hiding, an inert state until the right conditions arose to trigger it again, at which point—"

He stopped when he saw McCracken twist suddenly toward
Johnny Wareagle. "What is it, Indian?"

Wareagle's eyes were sweeping left to right, focused on the
woods. "Someone's watching us, Blainey."

CHAPTER 37

Dearborn, Michigan

"I'm sorry to bother you, Colonel," Zarrin said to the man bouncing the toddler on his knee amid a birthday party raging around him in Chuck E. Cheese's.

"Your message said it was an emergency."

Zarrin looked around at the festivities for one of her mentor's older grandchildren. "You don't look happy to see me."

"I'm not," said Nabril al-Asi, a resident of Dearborn for nearly a decade, along with the rest of his family, since he'd fled Palestine. "Your presence here endangers my family. I do not wish to be seen with you. I'm an American citizen now."

"I had nothing to do with the church bombing in Ohio."

"The evidence indicates otherwise."

"What about my word?"

Zarrin could see al-Asi's mind working, the colonel virtually unchanged from the first time she'd spotted him walking

JON LAND

through the Palestinian refugee camp where she'd grown up. "Then someone went through a lot of trouble to cast you with the blame."

"That's why I came to you, Colonel. To find out who."

"That could be a very long list, Zarrin. You have many imitators. Your work is admired throughout the world you helped create."

"I was never a terrorist, any more than you were."

"No," al-Asi said, with a twinge of irony in his voice, "for us it was always about politics. At least that's what we told ourselves."

"You think differently now?"

"Perspective changes with the years, and I choose to look toward what's ahead of me, not behind."

As al-Asi finished, a ball plucked from a ball pit closed for repairs jetted straight for his grandson's face, only to be snatched out of the air by Zarrin in the instant it crossed her line of vision.

"Nice to see you've kept up with your practice, Zarrin."

"A master always does, Colonel."

Nabril al-Asi eased his two-year-old grandson from his left knee to the right, the one reconstructed at an Israeli hospital in a time where a flirtation with peace elevated him to one of the most powerful positions in the Palestinian Authority. As head of the Palestinian Protective Security Service, al-Asi had presided over what began as Yasir Arafat's secret police, but under his tutelage morphed into a sophisticated security agency. In large part, this was due to the force of his own personality and the fact that al-Asi had the support of his competing agencies in Israel, unthinkable now but attainable in the mid-1990s after the signing of the Oslo Accords.

"It seems so long ago now, doesn't it, Colonel?" Zarrin asked, as if reading his mind.

"Because it was. And I'm not a colonel anymore. Just a grandfather and a father living without fear or headaches. Until

154

this new wave of attacks brought new scrutiny down on all Muslims."

"And what have you done about it?"

"Planned my grandson's birthday party."

"This coming from the spymaster whose Protective Security Service kept the opposition groups in check and held the fragile and fractured politics of Palestine together almost on its own. . . ."

"I don't know that man anymore."

"Too bad, because he's needed again, now more than ever."

Al-Asi stared at her for several long moments. "I used to buy all your recordings," he said suddenly, thoughts veering. "Now I download them, starting with the *Live at Lincoln Center* performance. My eight-year-old granddaughter showed me how. That's one of a thousand things I enjoy about my new life here. That's the man I am now."

Al-Asi stopped bouncing his grandson, eyes suddenly scanning the Chuck E. Cheese's in search of another family member to take the toddler off his hands. He gestured toward his daughter as Zarrin realized his hair and mustache were just sprinkled with black now, gray having claimed the rest. The colonel's daughter approached and took the toddler from his grasp.

"I still remember the first time I saw you strolling through that refugee camp," Zarrin said when she was gone.

"I saw you first."

"You looked like you were shopping."

"And I found what I was looking for."

She slid her chair closer to his and placed her free hand atop al-Asi's. "I've never really thanked you, not adequately anyway."

Al-Asi's gaze turned sad, reflective. "Then why didn't you tell me?"

"Tell you what?"

"That you have Parkinson's disease."

CHAPTER 38

Roanoke Island

Wareagle emerged from the woods, big hunting knife newly wedged into his belt and holding a teenage boy by the scruff of the neck. An Indian boy with wavy black hair that dangled well past his shoulders, wearing boots, jeans, and a beat-up leather jacket. Indignant scowl plastered across his anomalously soft features that didn't mix well with a patchwork of bruises across his cheeks at various stages of healing. The middle of his nose looked a little like Sal Belamo's, although broken on only a single occasion as opposed to several.

"I could've killed you, you know," he spat, drawing closer to McCracken and Captain Seven, "all of you."

McCracken watched Wareagle open a worn leather pouch he'd confiscated from the boy and remove a pair of oblong, home-made grenades complete with fusing strung from thin holes in their centers.

Blaine could smell the black powder through the cold air. "Why the firepower, kid?"

"Never know when you're gonna run into a few assholes.

"Homemade grenades? Really?"

"Hey, I didn't know if you were friendly or not. I still don't."

"So, if we weren't, you planned on blowing us up?"

"Maybe just scare you off."

McCracken watched Johnny return the homemade grenades to the pouch. "You don't use a weapon like this to scare somebody. Or that knife my friend here took off you."

"Okay, so maybe I had other plans. Just in case."

"Just in case?" McCracken gave the bruises a longer gaze, let the kid see him doing it. "Somebody else you tried to scare off do that to you?"

"None of your fucking business," the boy said, trying to sound tough, but his eyes had lost their resolve and harshness. He looked young and frightened, his gaze turning furtive and restive at the same time.

"Why were you watching us?"

"I'm not answering any of your questions," the boy said stridently, blowing some of the stray hair from his face. "I'll answer his," he added, cocking his gaze back at Johnny Wareagle. "What tribe are you?"

"Oglala Sioux."

"I'm a Croatan. Native to this place for maybe a million years. But we're called Lumbee now. All that's left of the Croatan tribe, and I still call myself a Croatan."

"An offshoot of the Carolina Algonquian tribe, related to the great Algonquian tribes of the north," Wareagle noted.

The boy looked closer at Johnny. "Wish I had some Sioux in me. That warrior tradition might help out now and then."

"Right," McCracken said, again eyeing the boy's bruises, a few of which were still yellow with healing, "I see your point. What's your name?"

The kid smirked, looked back toward Wareagle again.

"Answer him," Johnny ordered.

"You'll laugh if I tell you," the boy said.

"Why?"

"Because it's the same as the kid from the *Twilight* movies."

"*Twilight* movies?"

"You know," said the boy, "the werewolf."

"Sorry, kid, I *don't* know."

The boy rolled his eyes. "Jacob, all right? My name is Jacob. There, you can laugh now."

None of them did.

"Okay, Twilight," McCracken picked up, "why were you watching us?"

"Don't call me that."

"What?"

"Twilight. It's lame. I told you my name."

"Why were you watching us, Jacob?" McCracken relented.

The boy looked back at Wareagle again instead of responding. "I've heard Sioux warriors are plenty badass. You a badass?"

"Ask him how old he is, Indian."

"Fifteen," Jacob told Wareagle before he had the chance. "And I'm sorry I was sneaking around, watching you like that. I wasn't sure, that's all."

"Sure about what?"

"Whose side you were on. If you were one of them."

McCracken and Wareagle exchanged a wary glance.

"One of who?" from Wareagle.

"Been a long time since anybody figured this for the real site of the lost colony, as opposed to the place they pack the tourists into. Then, all of a sudden, people start showing up, at night mostly. This is still Croatan land—well, kind of anyway. That makes it trespassing."

"You saw them?" McCracken posed.

"Another kid did first. He came back to watch them another night and nobody's seen him since. Everybody thought he was a bad kid, figured he'd run away. But he wasn't a bad kid and he'd never run away. He was my friend."

"And you thought we were the same guys he was watching."

"Maybe. I wasn't sure. I think they killed him and buried him somewhere nearby. I see him in my dreams sometimes and know he's not alive anymore." Jacob looked back at Wareagle again. "You see stuff in your dreams too?"

"All the time," Wareagle told him.

The boy looked about the lifeless clearing. "You ever see what really happened here, what it is about this place that makes it cursed?"

"No."

"Because I know we're different tribes, but I just figured there might be a connection somewhere."

Wareagle shook his head. "I'm sorry."

"When did your friend disappear?" McCracken asked.

"Eight months ago, maybe nine now."

"And you've been watching this place ever since?"

"Croatans have been watching this place for over four hundred years, just in case it comes back."

"In case *what* comes back?"

"Whatever killed the original colonists. It's kind of a legend in these parts. Some believe it, some don't."

"Do you?"

"I didn't," Jacob said, blowing more hair from his face. "I do now. Ever since they killed my friend."

McCracken thought of Andrew Ericson, holding out hope

the boy was still alive in frigid waters seventy-five feet deep. "You can't know he's dead."

The boy reached up to touch Wareagle's shoulder. "Tell him."

"He can know, Blainey."

"Blainey?" The kid chuckled. "What kind of name is that?"

"One you won't find in any movie, Twilight."

Jacob looked from McCracken to Wareagle and back to McCracken again. "You're looking for the same thing they were, aren't you?"

"We're not exactly sure what we're looking for."

"Good, because it's gone. And it's been gone for, like, one hundred fifty years now."

"What's been gone for one hundred fifty years?"

Jacob rolled his eyes. "Don't you guys know anything?"

"We're here, aren't we?"

"Well, my, like, great-great-great-great-great-great-great-great-great-great-grandfather was chief of the Croatan tribe back in 1590. He led the party that found the colonists' bodies after he heard their screams in a dream." Then, with his gaze fixed on Johnny Wareagle, he said, "Guess he had the gift too. Anyway, he and the rest of the party buried the bodies as best they could, hoping that would be the end of it, but knowing it wasn't. Ever since, the story's been passed down through the generations, with the firstborn of each chief in the lineage responsible to stand vigil in case the dying starts again."

"You?"

"Me," the boy said meekly as he blew the stray hair from his face again.

"You knew we'd be here," noted Wareagle.

"I knew somebody would. That's why my family's been running the tribe for so long, 'cause we got this gift. Just lucky I guess," Jacob said.

The wind picked up, whipping larger snowflakes through

the air, the fall becoming steady as the storm intensified off the water.

"You'd best be off this island before it starts blowing big and bad," Jacob warned.

"Was there a storm the day the colonists were killed?"

"Yes, but it was rain, a real soaker that turned the land to mud. The Croatans had to wait until it passed before setting out to the colony where they ended up burying the bodies. Wasn't the first time it happened either, just the first time with people. Before it was always just animals. Explains why the woods around here are so quiet, since they never came back. Maybe they're smarter than we are, smart enough to know to avoid it."

"Avoid what?"

"The White Death."

CHAPTER 39

Dearborn, Michigan

"How did you know?" Zarrin asked him.

Al-Asi glanced down and laid a hand over Zarrin's. "You've been filling prescriptions for Sinemet. Different pharmacies, scripts written by different doctors, even filled in different names." Al-Asi's gaze relaxed, the color of his eyes seeming to change from gray to blue. His touch felt cool, but tender and reassuring at the same time. "Sinemet is composed of levodopa and another drug called carbidopa. Levodopa enters the brain and is converted to dopamine while cardidopa increases its effectiveness while lessening the side effects."

Zarrin's gaze drifted out a nearby window toward a lone man seated at a picnic table, trying to appear not to be looking inside. He'd been there when she'd first pulled into the parking lot, doing the very same thing.

"You've done a great job of hiding your secret from the world, but not from me," al-Asi continued after a pause that exaggerated the sounds of children cackling, laughing, and blowing noisemakers. "Did you really expect I wouldn't find out?"

"Keeping tabs on all your former agents, Colonel?"

"Just you, Zarrin."

"What about the operatives who accompanied you here, settled in Dearborn just like you? American citizens too, aren't they? Your personal security force trained by Mossad and Israeli Special Forces."

Al-Asi couldn't help but smile, in that moment very much his old self. "Who is keeping tabs on whom?" His smile vanished, as he glanced down at Zarrin's hands. "You've sought out all the medical opinions, I'm sure."

"And then some. The treatment retards and controls the disease to a degree, but the future is inevitable."

Al-Asi stopped just short of a laugh, the gesture seeming to relax him. "The future is always inevitable."

"Not to people like you, who managed to control it."

"Something else you must have learned from me."

"Colonel?"

"You think I don't know where a great deal of your fortune has gone? All the schools you've funded, all the medical supplies that exist in the camps only because of your efforts. The teachers, the doctors, too many to count, drawing compensation from foundations set up by you."

"It wasn't supposed to be so easy to discern."

"It wasn't," al-Asi said slyly. His eyes flashed their former spry gleam, playful and dangerous at the same time. "I remember the first time I saw you in the refugee camp, the way others looked at you. You walked through the camp without fear, even as a child. First time I had seen anybody do that. It's what attracted me to you immediately, how I knew I'd found what I came for."

"I watched my parents die, Colonel. Nothing could ever

scare me after that until now. I'm scared for our people. These attacks on innocent Americans are a setup. How many more are we to be blamed for before innocent Muslims, both here and at home, pay a terrible price?"

"This is my home," al-Asi reminded her.

"All the more reason for you to help me uncover who's really responsible for the wave of attacks." Zarrin regarded the children charging about around her, tomato sauce from the just-served pizza dribbling down their chins and staining their cheeks like paint smears. "Otherwise, days like this may be few and far between, even for you."

Al-Asi rose with a sigh, not speaking until Zarrin joined him on her feet. "I can't help you, Zarrin. I'm not that man anymore. It's time for others to fight this war." He waited for a response, surprised at the one that came. "Why are you smiling?"

"I was thinking of my father, how much you remind me of him. He taught me the piano as a young girl, but I did my best learning inside that camp. From an old man on a legless piano salvaged from a trash dump."

"Kazim," al-Asi nodded.

"You knew?"

"I sent him to you," al-Asi told her softly. "As a test, to see how well you could learn what you loved."

Zarrin's gaze turned out the window toward the man she'd been watching, who was now straddling the concrete and grass strip that rimmed the parking lot. A phone at his ear.

"With maybe another test about to come," she muttered.

"Pardon me?"

"Nothing, Colonel," Zarrin said, still eyeing the man. "Not yet, anyway."

CHAPTER 40

Roanoke Island

"White Death," McCracken repeated.

Jacob nodded. "The Indian word is *pakenappeh*. Came from the old days when there was this ice fog in the winter. But my ancestors had a whole other reason for calling what killed the colonists and haunted the land that."

"Which was?"

"Nobody ever saw it."

"Hold on," said Captain Seven with eyes squeezed closed and fingers pressed hard against his temples, "I'm having a moment here, a genuine quickening." His eyes opened, the lids fluttering. "Yup, I think I know what wiped out the Roanoke Colony. Nailed it dead solid perfect."

"Please continue, Captain."

Captain Seven moved to the center of the former encampment, standing atop one of the natural berms. "It was right about here, mentioned in White's original journal. I should know better than to doubt myself. See what happens when you pull me away from my daily allotment of ganja, MacNuts?"

"What'd you miss from White's journal, Captain?"

"The original well the colonists dug had run dry, something White discovered when he returned here to find them all missing. He also found the recently dug replacement well about right here on this natural berm, if I've got my bearings straight."

"The replacement well," McCracken repeated.

"That's where whatever killed the Roanoke colonists came from. Starts with the fact that water wasn't the only thing they found when they dug that new well right where you see this depression."

McCracken exchanged a wary glance with Wareagle. "You've got our attention."

"Then try this: Know what you're standing on?"

"Ground?"

"Try a volcanic plain. Sure, the nearest known volcanos are Virginia's Mole Hill and Trimble Knob, and, sure, their last eruptions were forty-seven million and thirty-five million years ago, respectively. But this island formed essentially over waters that were crater lakes that burned hot with occasional lava flow back when T. rexes and velociraptors ruled the land. And I don't have to tell you how stubborn that kind of shit can be."

"Yes, you do, Captain."

"Oh yeah, I forgot. Not much for the science books, are you?"

"Why bother when I've got you?"

"Good point."

"And what's the one you're getting at with lava and volcano plains?"

"About four hundred fifty years ago, around the time the Roanoke colonists dug their fateful well, the tectonic plates on the seafloor beneath this island weren't where they are now. And what was there must have included a pocket of magma—that's a mixture of molten and semi-molten rock mostly. Now magma leaks good ol' carbon dioxide, lots and lots of it, into the waters it settles in, turning that ordinary $H2O$ into something called carbonic acid. You with me so far?"

"Enough to know anything with the word *acid* in it can't be good," McCracken told him.

"Especially in this case, because what happened here around 1590 was unprecedented on this continent. Would have been goddamn exciting if it wasn't so goddamn scary."

"If *what* wasn't?"

"The water became a bomb, MacNuts. It goddamn exploded," said Captain Seven.

"I don't mean literally," he said after a pause that felt longer than it really was. "More a figure of speech that comes from the notion of exploding lakes, which are actually limnic eruptions. Natural disasters of true epic proportions that don't get more attention because, thankfully, they don't happen all that often. Now 'limnic eruption' is just a fancy term for what happens when dissolved carbon dioxide, or carbonic acid, stages an escape from the waters in which it's contained, normally under intense pressure."

"So when the colonists dug this new well . . ."

"They pierced a thermal layer and gave all that carbonic acid its escape route. Chances are, and this is just me talking here, that the barometric pressure was really low, a storm coming or already there, because that would create the perfect atmospheric conditions for what happened next."

"Lake Nyos," Johnny Wareagle said, before Captain Seven had a chance to continue.

The captain's eyes bulged as he grinned at Wareagle approvingly. "Maybe you should spend more time around the big fella here, MacNuts, so his smarts might finally rub off on you."

"I've heard of Lake Nyos too, Captain."

"Really? Then you know it's a deep lake high on the flank of an inactive volcano in the Oku region of Cameroon in Africa, complete with that pocket of magma leaking carbon dioxide into the water. You getting the picture here?"

But McCracken had turned his attention to Jacob, who'd grown suddenly antsy, sweeping his gaze from left to right and back again. "What is it, kid?"

"I don't know. I get these feelings sometimes. Like . . ."

"What?"

The boy turned away from the woods beyond. "Nothing."

"Anybody mind if we get back to business?" said Captain Seven. "I'm losing my train of thought here and it's been way too long since I last smoked up."

"Proceed, Captain."

"Smoking?"

"Explaining."

Captain Seven hummed a few bars of *The Twilight Zone* theme song. "In August of 1986, what happened in this very spot, to a smaller degree, happened in Lake Nyos, to a much larger one."

"Don't tell me; the lake exploded."

"So to speak. A large cloud of carbon dioxide in the form of carbonic acid burst out of the water and suffocated around seventeen hundred people in nearby towns and villages. Spread for miles. No one in range was spared. How's that for White Death?"

"Did you say *suffocated*?"

"As in asphyxiated, MacNuts. Guess I need to draw you a simpler picture that includes the four thousand or so heads of livestock that got killed that day too."

"You're saying that's what killed the Roanoke colonists," said McCracken, not yet struck by the fact that Captain Seven had just solved one of history's greatest mysteries.

"Quickly and horribly, or horribly and quickly. Take your pick. Based on what Twilight here is saying, my guess is the magma pool that spawned the carbonic acid rose just short of ground level. Means the contents of the entire well were contaminated, meaning weaponized."

"But the colonists lived here for years without incident."

"Until they dug that replacement well, effectively allowing this White Death to mix with the air, oxygen. Then—*boom!*—you've got Lake Nyos on a smaller scale."

"What happened to the well?" McCracken asked him.

The captain shrugged. "Can't say for sure. Twilight's ancestors probably covered it up when they buried the bodies, hid all trace anyone had ever been here. Which brings me to this . . ."

Captain Seven whipped out a thick pen-like object and pulled on a slot carved into its top. The insides of the object spiraled outward, narrowing at the tip when it reached a yard or so in length. The metal was finished in an absorbent, felt-like material. The captain dropped to his knees and sunk the object into the ground depression where he'd identified the position of the replacement well to be. Then he eased it back out and ran a hand down its length and then up again.

"Just like I thought."

"What'd you think?"

"Feel for yourself." Captain Seven resumed, as Blaine did just that. "Barely moist and crusted with dirt. That tells me the ground still holds remnants of the White Death, but the supply that killed the colonists must have been drained."

"Maybe by those guys lurking about the premises a few months back," McCracken thought out loud, "the ones who killed Twilight's friend."

"It wasn't them," Jacob interjected, continuing when they all turned toward him. "It was somebody else. A long time ago, back when my great-grandfather was—"

The boy stopped, noticing Wareagle's gaze lock on something no one else could see in the woods beyond them. He seemed to be sniffing the air.

"The boy was right, Blainey. We're not alone," he said, in the last instant before the gunshots sounded.

CHAPTER 41

Dearborn, Michigan

Zarrin watched the birthday party at Chuck E. Cheese's finally winding down. From her strategically chosen parking place in the lot, she could see parents starting to fetch their children's coats, extending them toward tiny arms.

The man who'd been seated at the picnic table when she'd first arrived remained standing, totally on the grass now with his cell phone pocketed. Zarrin kept watching him, as her mind drifted back to the Palestinian refugee camp where she'd spent much of her youth before Colonel al-Asi's people came for her.

And the first man she'd ever killed.

The West Bank, 1988

"What do they call themselves, this gang that runs the camp?" she asked her piano teacher.

"Concentrate on your studies," Kazim instructed.

"This is important too."

"Why?"

"Because I like to know who my enemies are." The then-fourteen-year-old Zarrin looked at him closer. "And because of the way they treat good people like you."

Kazim nodded grudgingly, certain there would be no more teaching of music today until the most gifted student he'd ever had was satisfied. "They are called *Hamsa*, after a palm-shaped amulet thought by many to symbolize the hand of God."

He went on to explain how Hamsa controlled distribution of clean water, food, even medicine, appropriating the vast bulk of supplies that came into the camp courtesy of the Red Cross or supportive nations.

"Like the antibiotics you need," Zarrin concluded for herself, "because of your diabetes."

Kazim looked down at the stumps that ended where his knees should have been, infections having cost him both legs. "That isn't a problem now."

"But it will be. What then?"

"Worry about perfecting your playing, not me."

"I can worry about both."

"Not today."

It was a week later when Kazim's fever spiked to 103. He tried desperately to get Hamsa to provide him with antibiotics as they had in the past, but this time he had nothing left to trade other than the similarly legless piano on which he taught Zarrin to play. He was sweating badly, struck alternately by bouts of being horribly hot and terribly cold. She tried to comfort him as best she could with blankets and whatever water she could scavenge, but his condition continued to worsen by the hour.

Zarrin knew she had no choice. She held only vague memories of the off-target Israeli air strike that had killed her parents, still clear enough to resolve she would never stand helpless again while someone important to her died. So that night, Zarrin shadowed one of Hamsa's soldiers in his nightly run through the camp dispensing goods to those with the money or goods to exchange for them. She waited until he emerged from a ramshackle shack in the darkest section she could find. Then she pounced, coiling a knife stolen from a Red Cross commissary around his neck.

She was going to make him give her the antibiotics, threaten him with death unless he dropped his satchel. But the man was stronger than he looked and started to fight her. Zarrin could feel him starting to twist, the advantage soon to be his, a beating or even death at his hands the likely upshot. The men of Hamsa walked the camp like gods; no one dared accost or threaten, never mind kill, one. But Zarrin had no choice. She felt herself draw the blade sideways, slicing the man's jugular. She'd stripped the satchel holding medical supplies from his shoulder and fled, while he lay writhing toward death amid the muck of the street.

"I convinced Hamsa to change their mind," she told her teacher.

Kazim showed improvement after the first dosage of the antibiotics Zarrin had stolen, distributing the remaining medicines to those most in need. Within two days, he was able to get around again in his wheelchair or on crutches. But on the third, when she went to his shack for her piano lesson, she found him lying on the floor amid the shattered remnants of his piano, badly beaten with blood and drool dribbling from his mouth.

"No, no!" she cried, cradling Kazim in her arms, willing him not to die and refusing to acknowledge it when he took his last breath.

The memories of her parents' deaths struck her in that instant with crystal clarity, to the point where she thought she could hear the rumble of the Israeli jets overhead. Somehow, though, feeling Kazim die in her arms was worse. Maybe because she was older. Or maybe because, this time, she could not live with the pain that cut through her insides like a knife and do nothing.

Zarrin pictured herself killing Hamsa's murderous leader, who was also one of the most wanted terrorists in the world. She would do it soon, as early as the next day, thoughts of her own survival irrelevant. She would sacrifice her own life to get close enough to do it with the same knife with which she'd cut the throat of his soldier. Prayed only that she'd live long enough to watch the fear in his eyes as the animal realized death was coming.

"For you, my teacher," she whispered into Kazim's ear. "I do this for you."

Zarrin had tucked the knife inside her belt under her shirt, intending to approach the Hamsa leader with a basket of flowers she managed to collect. She'd hand him one, a gesture of respect and subservience to his power, and when he reached for it or moved to thank her, she would stab him in the throat and tear at it with her blade until his men struck her down.

She was moving for the section of the camp Hamsa occupied, flower basket in hand and knife at the ready, when men she'd never seen before intercepted her. They dragged her, literally kicking and screaming, away. Zarrin's first thought was that they must be from Hamsa, dispatched to deter and detain her. Or much worse.

But instead of doing to her what they'd been rumored to have done to so many other young girls, these men spirited her to another section of the camp and into the rear of a van that waited with its engine still idling.

"Who are you?" she demanded, as bravely as she could manage. "Where are you taking me?"

The men didn't answer her, just smiled. Until the van pulled away and one said, simply, "We are taking you to school."

Her training had begun almost immediately, first at another camp that would later be labeled a terrorist training ground and raided by Israeli defense forces. By then, though, Zarrin had already been sent to Russia, where she completed her training at the hands of experts.

Experts in killing.

They made Zarrin into the legendary assassin she'd eventually become, finishing the work that had begun when she slit the throat of the Hamsa soldier to save Kazim's life.

Zarrin's mind was jerked back to the present when a dark SUV turned into the parking lot, circled once, then backed into a slot on the opposite side of the restaurant from her.

Zarrin gunned her already warm engine.

The front doors of the SUV opened at the same time, a pair of men wearing long, dark overcoats and dark gloves climbing out. She could tell by the way one hitched up his shoulder that he wore a submachine gun dangling from it, cold steel concealed by the heavy fabric.

Zarrin shifted into gear and sped forward, braking just enough to make sure there was no screech when she twisted round the corner at the building's edge. She'd timed the move perfectly, the two men positioned in the middle of parking lot's single big lane, halfway between their SUV and the restaurant entrance.

Zarrin accelerated at the last second, the screech she now wanted to sound freezing the men long enough to swing toward her in the last instant before the bumper slammed into them. She hit one of the men square on, flush, the other with a more glancing blow that nonetheless spun him to the side and pitched him airborne. His jacket separated, offering Zarrin a glimpse of the submachine gun dangling from a shoulder strap. Meanwhile, she'd felt the bones of the man she'd hit square on crunch on impact as he flew up and over the roof, hitting her stolen car's trunk before bouncing to the pavement below.

The spotter made a run for his car, fumbling a cell phone from his pocket when Zarrin aimed her pistol out the window and fired twice. The man jerked to a halt, as if being halted by a leash. Then he crumpled to the concrete.

Zarrin eyed the parking lot exit, screeched toward it only to jam on the brakes. Because she'd remembered something.

The ball pit, closed for repairs on the day of Colonel al-Asi's grandchild's party. But what could break in a ball pit?

And then she was bringing the car around, twisting and tearing forward straight for the glass wall. Crashed through it to send shards and fragments spraying in all directions, narrowly avoiding adults pulling children's arms into their coats. Screams, wails, and cries flirted with the outskirts of her hearing, Colonel al-Asi lurching her way, still trying to make sense of what had transpired in the parking lot.

But Zarrin was ready when the two figures burst up from the ball pit, submachine guns in hand. Their disorientation cost them the next moment, left it all to her. And that was all Zarrin needed to empty the remainder of her magazine into the two men, bullets divided equally between them until they pitched downward to be swallowed anew by the colored balls. Sinking slowly until they disappeared, by which time al-Asi had reached the hood of her rental car, staring at her in abject shock.

"Get in, Colonel!" she yelled at him. "Get in!"

He rode stiff in the passenger seat, clutching the dashboard before him so tightly Zarrin could see the fingertip impressions.

"Thank you," he said finally.

"They came for you, Colonel. Anticipated my actions perfectly and waited until they thought I was gone to move."

"You saved my family, Zarrin, saved everything."

"I noticed the spotter. I got lucky."

"Training, not luck. And experience. I now owe you a debt I can never repay."

"Then help me find them, Colonel. Help me stop this before it's too late."

He nodded deliberately, sneering, the calm and confidence in his expression replaced by resolve. "Consider it done."

"And answer a question for me."

"Anything."

"Back in that refugee camp, did you order the death of Kazim, my music teacher, so I'd be free to do your bidding?"

"You think I'd do such a thing?" he challenged, genuinely miffed.

"Yes, if it suited your purpose."

"You disappoint me, Zarrin."

"You still haven't answered the question, Colonel."

"No," al-Asi insisted finally, "but I did stop you from retaliating. Wouldn't want to waste such exceptional skills, especially after I'd witnessed your work firsthand."

"I don't understand."

"The Hamsa soldier you killed. I saw a recording of that."

"You were watching me even then. . . ."

"Of course I was. Waiting until you proved yourself more than a just a survivor. I saw it in your eyes when I toured the camp, but I needed to see it in action."

"And now, thanks to me, you're still alive to enjoy your grandchildren. Whoever was behind setting me up was watching you because you'd already been deemed a threat. And they'll be back, Colonel."

Something changed in al-Asi's tone, familiar in memory but distant in time. "Then I guess we have some work to do."

CHAPTER 42

Roanoke Island

"They came back," Jacob muttered, face pressed against the hard damp ground with McCracken holding a hand on his back.

"A dozen men, Blainey, maybe more," said Johnny Wareagle.

"Waiting for our asses," managed Captain Seven.

McCracken thought quickly, eyes moving to the pouch from which Wareangle had pulled Jacob's homemade grenades. "Those things really work, kid?"

"Oh yeah. For sure."

Then, to Captain Seven, "You said there's still some White Death left in the ground."

"Traces anyway."

"Then give me the laces from your Vans."

"Huh?"

"Both of them, Captain," McCracken said, as fresh hails of automatic fire hummed over their heads.

*   *   *

Jacob and Captain Seven crawled off, staying low to be as far out of sight as possible. Wareagle made a show of returning fire with his pistol to hold the enemy at bay, certain now that a dozen was likely a low-range estimate.

"There are more of them beyond the tree line, Blainey, laying a trap to the south."

"Very direction the kid and Seven are headed."

"The boy will sense them too. He'll know."

There were three homemade grenades in Jacob's pouch, little more than black powder sifted from high-powered firecrackers mixed with small roofing nails inside a cast-iron ball that looked like part of the base for some piece of heavy machinery. Each had short fusing poking out from their tops, and Blaine tied Captain Seven's Vans laces to two of them.

Eighteen inches, about a second to burn down for each inch, meaning he'd be cutting very close.

While McCracken worked to string the laces to the exposed fusing of two of Jacob's homemade grenades, Wareagle twisted a third open and sifted the black powder into his palm, turning it moist with spit. Then he spread the paste-like compound along the length of one shoelace, rubbing hard to make it meld with the fibers.

Once Johnny had gone to work on the second, McCracken pushed the first grenade down into the ground directly over the replacement well the Roanoke colonists had dug in 1590, leaving only the tip of Captain Seven's Vans lace over the surface. Then he repeated the process with the second, while Johnny continued to return fire to hold the enemy gunmen at bay.

"This doesn't work, it's gonna be a long night, Indian."

"Maybe not long enough."

Wareagle handed him the lighter from Jacob's pouch.

"Not much changes, does it?"

"Let's find out, Blainey."

And with that, McCracken flicked the lighter to life and touched the flame to one lace tip and then the other. The sizzling hisses started up immediately and the next moment found McCracken and Wareagle rushing through the former encampment, returning fire in token fashion as they ran, counting down the seconds the whole time.

They caught only glimpses of the men crashing into the clearing before darting into the woods on the opposite side, hitting the ground hard at a safe distance away from what they hoped was coming. Torrents of gunfire traced over their heads at the fifteen-second mark.

The grenades ignited a breath apart from each other at sixteen. Then the screams started, just as described in Governor John White's journal, only much, much louder given how many more men had been trapped in the clearing when the same noxious cloud that had killed the Roanoke colonists claimed its next victims.

The screams became rasps, then horrible gasping sounds as the gunmen heaved for air before crumpling over the makeshift graves of the original colonists, leaving an eerie quiet in the cold air rich with snowflakes now. The stench of burned gunpowder dominated the scene, drowning all other smells out, as smoke wafted over the victims, thinning to the point it all but disappeared.

McCracken and Wareagle lurched back to their feet, both realizing they'd involuntarily held their breath until that moment. They surged into motion, toward the south, ready to confront whoever lay in wait to spring the trap. Only that part of the assault team was gone, having fled at the sound of the terrible screams that had come at the hands of exposure to the White Death. Blaine and Johnny found Jacob and Captain Seven still hidden under the makeshift cover of leaves and brush.

McCracken jerked the boy to his feet, startling him.

"I told you they'd work," Jacob said proudly.

"Finish what you were saying before, about what happened when somebody came back for the White Death."

Jacob jerked free of his grasp. "It wasn't them," the boy said, looking back toward the camp.

"Who, then?" McCracken demanded. "And when?"

Jacob started to back off, brushing himself off as he turned for the path. "You want the answers, you'll have to come with me. The rest of the story is best told by somebody who was there when it happened."

CHAPTER 43

West Virginia

"You asked to see the means by which we will open the tenth circle of Hell, Reverend," Colonel Alvin Turwell told Jeremiah Rule. "And you are about to bear witness personally."

The upward bank of the ground was rich with tangled roots and brush, looking untouched by human step. Around them the foliage had browned for winter but still looked somehow rustic and lush. Other than a rock face shiny with morning dew, there seemed to be nothing ahead on the mountain path that sliced through the Allegheny range of White Sulphur Springs, West Virginia. Just a few miles away stood "the Bunker," the once-secret government location constructed to house the country's leaders in the event of a devastating attack on the country. The infamous Greenbrier mountain facility was open to the public for tours, a Cold War relic now a living testament to history.

Other lesser-known bunkers had been erected amid the

mountains as well, their intended use to house supplies and ordnance to make sure America maintained the capacity to both fight back against whomever had attacked the country and to rebuild. Those bunkers, too, had been emptied, abandoned, and forgotten except by someone like Turwell, who'd never lost sight of their original purpose.

He led Rule off to the right, toward a steep rock face that extended upward like a natural obelisk. "This bunker contains the means to complete our work, Reverend. To wake this country up once and for all. The final attack."

"It is God's work, Colonel," said Rule, huffing slightly for breath from the exertion of the climb. "We are merely the instruments of His will."

They'd taken a private jet from Florida to the nearest private airport where a car waited, already warming, on the tarmac. And now, an hour's drive later, Turwell felt about the sheer face for a notch, pulling downward when his fingers found it to reveal a numerical keypad. He pressed out a series of four numbers and a hidden door, less shiny than the rest of the mountain face around it, slid open.

"Follow me," he said.

It was like a mammoth self-storage facility, football-field lengths separating the doors beyond which enough weapons to fight a war and defend a nation had once rested. The two men's steps echoed off the floor tile that had remained clean and antiseptic in spite of the facility's mothballed state.

Turwell stopped at a set of doors halfway down, an alphabetical keypad on the wall adjacent to it this time. Again he keyed in the proper code and again a heavy door formed of solid steel slid open.

"Behold," he said dramatically, stepping aside so Jeremiah Rule could see beyond him. " 'The night is nearly over,' " Turwell recited from Romans, " 'the day is almost here. So let us put aside the deeds of darkness and put on the armor of light.' "

"Praise the Lord," Rule said, voice cracking with excitement at the sight of what was stacked high before him for as far as his eyes could see into the darkness beyond.

"Just four more days, Reverend, four more days before the government falls and the people of this nation wake up to a whole new world."

CHAPTER 44

Roanoke Island

Jacob's entire family lived in a three-story tenement house. His grandfather had died in Vietnam, but his great-grandfather was still alive, still relatively spry and in possession of all his faculties at the age of somewhere between ninety-eight and a hundred and two, as Jacob put it. The old man had fought in World War II and displayed his medals proudly in his first-floor bedroom. He walked with a cane he pretended not to need, his expression perking up and growing almost whimsical when told what had befallen the group earlier in the day, especially the part about how they'd managed to survive.

"The White Death," he muttered between suddenly trembling lips. "At least it finally did some good." He stopped and settled himself as best he could with a deep breath. "Call me Red Lake. The *red* stands for blood," he said, focusing on Blaine and Johnny. "See, I been where you've been."

"Is it that easy to spot?" McCracken asked him.

"Sometimes I need the voices in my head to tell me. Not today. Today my eyes told me what I needed to know. You saved my great-grandson's life."

"Actually, it was closer to the other way around."

Now Red Lake's gaze locked on Wareagle alone. "You hold the wisdom of many years and many battles."

"Different enemies," Johnny told him, "yet always the same."

"The only thing that changes with evil is what it calls itself from one age to the next."

"Sometimes one day to the next."

Unlike much, if not most of Roanoke Island, the village of Wanchese was no tourist trap. It was the same fishing village it had always been, long before the Washington Baum Bridge linked the Outer Banks to the island. Wanchese occupied the southern end of Roanoke where the Algonquin Indians were probably the first to discover the bountiful supplies of shellfish there. For centuries, a huge mound of empty shells rose near a place that had won the name "Thicket Lump" as a result. Although that mound was long gone, Wanchese remained an insular fishing village populated almost exclusively by hard-scrabble locals with faces turned wrinkled and leathery by the sun and hands scraped and scarred by handling fishing nets with the texture of razor wire.

The two-lane roads that wound through Wanchese were dotted with what looked like an uneasy mix of mobile homes, farmhouses, cottages more resembling shacks, and newer modern homes built to take advantage of the proximity to the water. Some of the older homes had rowboats decorating the front yard or larger boats stored for the season beneath covers in the driveway. There were no chain stores, no high-end restaurants, no motels other than a single bed and breakfast. Besides the docks that dominated the town's shoreline, the biggest sign of modernity was the Wanchese Seafood Industrial Park devoted to storing, building, or repairing boats and to processing the thousands of tons of seafood caught annually in the nearby waters. Many of Jacob's relatives, including Red Lake, had worked there at one time or another, but the boy professed to have no interest in the business whatsoever.

"We'd like to hear about the day the men came back for the White Death," McCracken said to the old chief.

"I will tell you everything I know in the hope it serves your cause," Red Lake continued. "I only ask one favor in return: You must help Jacob."

"Grandpa!" the boy started to protest.

"You notice his bruises?"

"We did," McCracken acknowledged. "He wouldn't tell us where they came from."

"From the bar where he worked until recently. They don't like Indians, so they fired him. I'd like him to get his job back. I'd like you to get it back for him."

"Our pleasure," promised Wareagle, who filled out the entire doorway.

Red Lake moved toward him, his cane tapping the floor in rhythm with his step. "Good. Let's go. I haven't been out of the house for a while. I'll tell you the tale when we get there."

"Just one question, Chief," McCracken said, as Red Lake's cane continued tapping away. "Why bother getting the boy his job back at a place like that?"

"So he can quit," the old man said, winking.

CHAPTER 45

Roanoke Island

"What is troubling you?" Red Lake asked McCracken while they covered the short distance from the family home to the Ebb Tide bar.

"Isn't it obvious?"

"No, that's why I asked."

Wareagle smirked in the passenger seat next to McCracken, while Captain Seven rolled a joint in the back.

"Whoever's behind all this hurt somebody important to me," Blaine told the old chief.

"Somebody close?"

"Hard to say."

"It shouldn't be."

"Close by association."

"You hedge your terms," Red Lake told him.

Captain Seven licked the rolling paper and tightened it over the finely milled weed. "Man's got a point, MacNuts."

"MacNuts?" from Red Lake.

"Short for McCrackenballs, what people call me from time to time."

"How did you come by it?"

"I was working in England when a plane got taken over by terrorists at Heathrow Airport. We, the British Special Air Service and I, wanted to stage a rescue, but bureaucracy took hold and one hundred fifty people ended up dying for no reason at all."

"Bet you were pissed," said Jacob.

"I went to Parliament Square and machine-gunned the statue of Winston Churchill there. His private parts specifically. Earned me the name McCrackenballs."

True to form, the Ebb Tide didn't do much to advertise its presence, save for a simple sign carved out of what looked like driftwood, backlit by a small light array that had lost several of its bulbs. The sign flapped in the stiff breeze coming off the water, stiffer now that the sun had gone down, while snow continued to fall in a light curtain of white.

McCracken pulled into a space directly across the street from the Ebb Tide, the vehicle silent as Johnny Wareagle stepped out into the night and beckoned Jacob to follow. The two of them walked across the street, lost to the shadows briefly before they disappeared inside.

"Tell me about what happened in those woods all those years ago, Chief," McCracken said to Red Lake.

Roanoke Island, 1872

"My tribe had clung to a small stretch of land along the same road that led to the remnants of the original fortified settlement. One morning the tribe was awoken just past dawn by a heavy rumbling. Turned out the source of that rumbling was a large British landing party rolling across the land in a convoy of wagons stocked with wooden kegs of the kind normally associated with storing spirits. My own grandfather, hardly more than a boy himself at the time, mixed easily with the sailors and American laborers who'd met the ship at the island's docks. They were friendly to him, but proved less than willing to share the nature of their task, mostly because they weren't aware of all the details themselves. Something about a pumping operation to pull something out of a long-dormant well with some huge machine, the disassembled parts carried by a trio of wagons nearest the front.

"Upon reaching the former colony, those parts were assembled into what my grandfather recognized as an innovative steam engine, far advanced from the Corliss variety, the four-valve counterflow version more common for the time. This engine, a boisterous engineer explained to my grandfather, was of the compound variety. Very advanced and known for exhausting steam in successively larger cylinders to accommodate the higher volumes at reduced pressures, providing far greater efficiency with what he called 'expansion technology.' My grandfather only pretended to understand."

Captain Seven raised a lighter toward the finished joint held between his lips. But McCracken reached into the backseat and snatched it from his mouth, crushed the joint in his hand, and dumped the remains into the captain's palm.

"Hey!" he protested.

"Sue me," said Blaine.

Through the open driver's window, meanwhile, they all heard a muffled thud coming from inside the Ebb Tide. The falling temperatures accompanying the cold front had fogged up with the bar's front windows with condensation, making it difficult to see anything inside, especially from across the street.

More thuds, like heavy bumps, reached them though the

open window and the three of them looked toward the frosty windows that gave up only brief glimpses of splotchy, sudden movements inside the bar. McCracken thought he heard something like glass breaking.

"Sorry for the interruption, Chief," he told Red Lake. "What happened next?"

Roanoke Island, 1872

"My grandfather watched the biggest and thickest hose he had ever seen being strung from the steam engine pump down a fresh hole dug along the sunken perimeter of the well the colony had dug to replace the one that had gone dry. It was a long process that relied on the barrels of water they'd brought with them flowing into the boiler portion of the engine and heated to produce the steam that drove the massive pistons of the pumping apparatus in a churning fashion to pull the water from under the ground.

"The hose began to expand, the rotating action of the steam engine pumping the contents from deep within the colony's well into the first of the barrels. The process went on through the entire day and much of the night until the well ran dry, the hundreds and hundreds of barrels filled and loaded back onto the wagons that now sagged considerably under the added weight."

Red Lake stopped when more motion flashed through the clouded windows, visible in variances of the light inside, accompanied by heavier thuds and additional breaking glass. The remnants of a chair crashed through one of the Ebb Tide's frosted glass windows. Some fixtures must have broken, because the lighting suddenly took on a strobe effect, capturing shapes and shadows in splotchy, uneven motion concentrated in the same area as before.

The loud bang of a single gunshot rang out accompanied

by a flash that seemed to linger briefly like an echo. Then the frame of a writhing man followed the path of the chair out the window, taking more of the glass with him.

"You were saying, Chief," McCracken prodded.

Roanoke Island, 1872

"The sun had risen the following day before the process was finally complete, slowed and waylaid further by equipment breakdown in the form of seized engine parts and broken wagon wheels among others. The workers were uniformly filthy and cussing up a storm by the time it was done with the last of the barrels loaded, the big steam engine disassembled for transport north in the wagons, all the way to the Port of New York."

" 'They'll be ready for us in port,' " my grandfather overheard one of the men say in a thick Cockney accent. " 'Extra barrels won't make a tuppence worth of difference to a brigantine the size of the *Mary Celeste*.' "

Movement flashed inside the Ebb Tide. Large shapes hurtling this way and that, as if launched into the air, each followed by the thwack or crash of impact with something. Suddenly, the lone entry door opened and Johnny Wareagle emerged, looking as calm and unruffled as he did when he entered. Jacob walked alongside him, staring up in dazed wonder and awe. McCracken watched for someone bursting out after them with his pistol held at the ready, but no one emerged.

"Did you say the *Mary Celeste*?" he asked Red Lake.

"I see the ship means something to you."

"It's only one of the great maritime mysteries of all time. The *Mary Celeste* was found abandoned at sea in the Bay of Gibraltar. No trace of her captain, crew, or passengers; they were never heard from again. She was supposed to be carrying alcohol."

"Apparently not," said Captain Seven, working to roll a fresh joint using the crushed refuse of the first.

Wareagle reached the SUV and opened the door for Jacob to climb in ahead of him into the silence.

"The boy's been rehired," was all he said.

McCracken's phone rang.

"Hello, Hank," he greeted Hank Folsom.

"How'd you know it was me?"

"Because no one else has the number you just dialed."

"How soon can you get to Washington?"

"Depends on the reason, Hank."

"Make it fast, McCracken, because I've deciphered the message you found in that crossword puzzle," Folsom told him, "and we haven't got much time."

PART THREE:
THE WHITE DEATH

CHAPTER 46

Washington, DC

Alvin Turwell fastened the knee brace into place over his right leg, keenly aware of the younger man alongside him watching the whole time. They had the gymnasium all to themselves. The air inside it felt cold, but was still rife with the scent of stale sweat, and only the lights strung over the half of the court they'd be using had been switched on.

"Sprained ligament, sir?" Congressman David Forlani asked.

"Torn ACL. Happened on a parachute jump. Training mission. Too many young greens like you I had to keep my eye on, make sure their chutes opened."

"You're sadly missed in the House, sir."

Turwell finished strapping on the brace, getting to the point now. "I'm glad to hear that, my boy, glad to hear it. I take that to mean the boycott of the president's State of the Union speech this Tuesday that you've undertaken on my behalf is going well."

Forlani swallowed hard, realized he could hear the rhythmic tapping of his Nike hightops echoing in the emptiness of the gym. "No, sir, it's not."

Turwell took the basketball resting between them and bounced it once, squeezing it in his big hands, discolored from burn scars. "We're trying to save the country here. You tell me they can't see that?"

"They're afraid of the optics."

"Optics? This country's at war for all intents and purposes, and they care about optics. Do you think any of them can tell me how many were killed in that Ohio church bombing, how many *children*?" With that, Turwell snapped a chest pass Forlani's way, the younger man just managing to catch it before it slammed his face. "I sent a dozen men to their deaths in Afghanistan," Turwell continued, the lights making his skin gleam as if it had been painted on. "But I took the objective and rejoiced afterwards because I thought it would take twice that many. No great victory comes without great sacrifice, and only a true hero is willing to accept that sacrifice in view of the greater picture."

"I was a Ranger, Colonel. Please spare me the lecture."

Turwell finally realized what Forlani was getting at, feeling as hot and winded as he might have after a full game. "You already signed on to this. You stood by my side with the planning. You helped with the recruitment, for Christ's sake, because you know where this country's headed if action, drastic action, isn't taken. You're either with me or against me, my boy—there's nothing in the middle."

"You've gone too far, just like you did in Afghanistan when you sent those men to their deaths." Forlani whipped the ball back toward Turwell, who snatched it effortlessly out of the air. "This isn't what I signed on for. End it before it goes any further, or I'll end it for you."

"I thought you were a hero, son, but you're just another coward."

Forlani moved forward, getting right up in Turwell's face. "Do you want to play or not, Colonel?"

Turwell opened his hands and let the ball drop to the floor. "Oh, most certainly."

He drove the knife he'd slipped from the pocket of his warmup pants under Forlani's thorax, deep and then slicing across from left to right. Continued jerking the blade until Forlani stiffened and started to drop, shocked eyes starting to glaze.

"Game over, Congressman," the colonel told him before he died.

CHAPTER 47

Blountsville, Florida

Kneeling in the root cellar-like basement where he'd constructed his personal altar, Jeremiah Rule couldn't get the wondrous sight of the contents of the storage hold in West Virginia out of his mind. The means to cleanse the country, to achieve the mission he'd been chosen to fulfill, at last before him. The mere thought brought tears to his eyes.

And yet he felt unworthy. In this glorious moment of his greatest achievement, of his word being heard and followed, he was struck by emptiness. An unclean part of his soul and spirit that no amount of scrubbing seemed to relieve. He had failed the Lord horribly once, and now, in the moment of his ultimate redemption, he found himself fearing terribly that he'd fail Him again.

Oh Lord, show me the way. . . .

The fear threatened to consume Rule, left him steeped in sweat in the squalid, festering heat. He'd prayed as he had as a child until his knees throbbed and skin stuck tightly to the wood, peeling off when he finally rose. His shirt was sodden with perspiration, reeking so much from the nightmares that had spawned it that the odor had roused the reverend from his sleep just before dawn and sent him down to his personal sanctuary. Growing worse the more he prayed, more fetid the more he remembered.

Rule's sample Bible went flying off into the mud, and the dog lunged at him again when he stooped to retrieve it. Rule took the good book in hand and smashed the dog's snout with it.

Could he not vanquish the memory of that horrible day from his mind and memory? Was it destined to haunt him for the rest of his days and deny him entry into the Kingdom of Heaven, no matter how much of the Lord's work he did?

"You killed my dog, mister! You killed my dog!"

How was he to repent if no deed was good enough? How was he to find his way back into God's good graces with such an unpardonable sin marring his past?

Rule caught him just short of the steps, intending to just get him quiet, settle the boy down a bit.

And then it struck him. Light shining amid the murkiness of his basement.

First slapping the boy, then striking him with closed fists until his knuckles split and bled, and the wailing became a whimper and then a strange airless gurgle that left his blue eyes bulging and sightless.

Only now, with his eyes closed, the boy's broken, battered, and bloodied face appeared whole to him again. He looked at Rule not in recrimination, but with love, and Rule wondered if this was the boy's ghost or a vision of him from before the beating, before he'd staggered away covered in mud and sprayed blood, feeling the boy's urine soaking through his own pants. And in that realization Rule's eyes snapped open with a vision of what he had to do. Snapping alert with a jolt, his voice dry and hoarse as he resumed his praying, he sank back to his knees as motion scuffled amid the dank darkness behind him, accompanied by a sound like wounded animals whimpering in the woods.

"Oh Lord, I see how I can never be redeemed, but I see too how I must prove to you that I've changed. That I'm a different man now, having learned to follow your word above everything else." Rule's heart hammered against his chest, starting to steal his breath. His vision narrowed, the scope of the world shrinking before him. "I thank you, Lord, I thank you for showing me the way, for giving me this test I must pass in order to prove myself worthy of your graces."

He rose with his heart pounding, as excited as he could ever remember when he turned to the rear of his basement carved from the earth itself.

"I'll be back soon, my children."

CHAPTER 48

Panama City, Florida

Back upstairs in the steaming heat, Rule bolted the hatch and slid the carpet back into place to conceal it, then set about on a mission that had suddenly become his one and only concern.

He went out and scoured used-car lots and salvage yards until he found a near perfect replica of the Dodge Ram van he'd driven in those dark, cursed times. The rear hold emptied of all else but space for his boxes of Bibles and his meager possessions and sleeping bag, so he might wallow away the nights to the static-riddled sound of a transistor radio and smell of his own stink. He hadn't seen then how his unclean body was just a metaphor for his unclean soul. But he was a different man now, a changed man, and had to prove it the only way he knew how.

The used 1981 van, its under panels little more than a patchwork of rust and steel worn thin enough to stick a finger through, came with the same 225-cubic-inch Slant Six engine. Same bald tires, even missing a hubcap from the same rear wheel. It had once been burgundy in shade, now faded to a pinkish red with rust bubbles all over the hood and roof, whereas the original had been olive green. Its engine, though, started and sounded exactly the same. It smelled of the same mold-ridden upholstery and stale plastic, duct tape holding the driver's seat together.

Rule bought it for five hundred dollars in cash, filled the tank, and drove off to prove once and for all he was past the anger and hatred that had left him staring down at the young boy he'd just killed, his eyes frozen open. Looked like a doll's, all that had been human robbed by his pounding fists, now aching and bloodied, the knuckles swollen and torn.

The Reverend Jeremiah Rule took to the Panhandle roads he knew so well, letting God and instinct direct him to the freeway leading out of Blountstown. Staying on it until just outside Panama City, where he was guided to the Countryside Estates Mobile Home on the corner of Boatrace and South Gay.

"Estates" was hardly an apt description and neither was "Countryside" for this place. A nestling of one-level homes perched on concrete slabs mixed among the iron husks of RVs. Even though it was winter, Rule saw lots of open water and power connections, what passed for the best locations sitting in rare shaded spots spared by the recent scourge of storms. Rule didn't know what he was looking for, only that it was here and he'd find it.

A dog's incessant barking grabbed his ear through the ancient Dodge Ram's open window. He realized he'd been sweating up a storm ever since spotting the entrance to the mobile home park from across the road, his heart thudding against his rib cage with enough force to turn his breathing shallow and raspy. The sweat wedged him to the old vinyl and duct tape like glue. Trying to peel his trousers free made a squishing sound and the sticking grew only worse when he settled down again. The heat of the sun was relentless, burning off the light-colored and steel roofs and turning the Countryside Estates into a vast steaming pit.

Rule stopped the van in the lee of some shade trees nestled in the back rear corner, a choice spot that featured a pit bull chained to a steel pole rising out of the ground no longer supporting whatever it once had. The reverend remained inside the Ram, feeling nothing, none of the terrible impulses from that fateful day returning.

He was certain the evil inside him that defined his unworthiness was vanquished, but Rule had to prove it to God, so he opened the door with a whining creak and climbed down to prove himself worthy.

The dog's crystal-blue eyes followed his approach, repetitive barks seeming to merge into one as drool flew from its lips.

"Easy there, fella."

The dog snarled, growled.

"Easy, I just wanna make friends."

The dog bared its teeth.

"Good boy, good boy," Rule said, crouching closer to the animal, feeling in his pockets in the hope of finding some stray bit of candy or something.

The dog lunged, taking all the chain would give. Rule rocked backwards, falling over and hitting his head on the rock-infested ground. Then he lurched back to his feet with the biggest rock of all clutched in his grasp, starting to come upward. Pictured it splitting the dog's skull in two.

"Don't hurt my dog, mister."

Rule stopped, turned, saw a boy standing there just down from the mobile home's steps, half in and half out of the sun.

Dirty white tank top draped over tight blue jeans and bare feet. Fear in his eyes.

Just like the other boy. Could have been the other boy.

And the Reverend Jeremiah Rule felt the rock heating up in his grasp, saw it coming down on the dog and then the boy. Again and again.

And again.

CHAPTER 49

Washington, DC

"You're serious," Hank Folsom said, standing next to McCracken on the steps of the Lincoln Memorial.

Beyond the memorial, the sky had clouded up with the wind carrying a frigid bite and the promise of snow in the offing. From here, McCracken had a clear view of the Vietnam Memorial Wall that inevitably left a lump in his throat every time he was close by, intensified today by the strange desolation around him. Other than a smattering of tourists, the National Mall and all the attractions contained upon it were all but deserted, out of fear this would mark the ideal site for the next attack. In ironic counterpoint, Blaine actually thought he counted more Capitol police and National Guardsmen about than those they were protecting.

"That's right, Hank," he told Folsom. "The man you had inside the Reverend Jeremiah Rule's organization was trying to warn us that the Reverend Rule's after whatever it was that wiped out the lost Roanoke Colony. Those settlers didn't disappear, they didn't vanish into the ether, and they weren't murdered by Indians. They died within minutes of one another, maybe even quicker, died horribly in a single night."

"Who killed them?"

"Not who—what, something the local Indian tribes called the 'White Death,' " Blaine said, and then explained Captain Seven's theory.

"You'll have to do better than that, McCracken," Folsom said when he'd finished.

"Then try this. I think someone from Rule's camp was on Roanoke Island eight, nine months back. I think they killed a Croatan Indian boy who happened to be in the absolute worst place at the absolute worst time. Friend of the kid said the tribe figures he ran away. But if you check the area carefully enough, you'll find him buried probably not too far from where his ancestors buried the colonists before Governor John White returned to burn the remnants of the camp."

"You have any idea how crazy all this sounds?"

"No crazier than plenty of the other shit I've been dealing with since you were in diapers, Folsom."

"Make your point, McCracken."

"I thought I just did, Hank," Blaine said. He felt himself stiffen, noticed Folsom recoil slightly at the slight gesture. "The Reverend Rule and whoever's behind him may have their hands on whatever wiped out Roanoke."

"Back in 1590. This 'White Death.' "

"That's the assumption so far."

"All this because my undercover wrote *Croatoan* in a crossword puzzle."

"Not quite," McCracken told him. "I saw it in action myself. The White Death helped me take out part of the contingent that probably killed that Indian boy and it seems a safe bet there's plenty more where they came from." McCracken shifted about until Lincoln's statue was positioned between him and Folsom. "Your undercover—Samuels—was an experienced field agent, right?"

"Of course."

"He'd know he was in danger. He'd know he'd uncovered something that might be about to cost him his life. My presence, the meeting, just accelerated things. He needed to get out of Dodge, report in on his suspicions."

"Keep going."

"Assumptions, Hank. Your man was killed for what he'd figured out. It had nothing to do with the fact that he was about to meet with me. My presence was just icing on the cake. You put that together with Captain Seven's conclusions and you've got your answer, Hank."

"A crazy man with a super weapon."

"And somebody, or some*bodies*, not so crazy backing him. The question today being what they plan on doing with the White Death and how all this is connected to innocent victims of the terrorist attacks they've unleashed."

"Any word from Missouri on that kid?"

"Nothing."

Folsom tried very hard not to show what he was thinking. "Well, the answers you're looking for may be in Boston."

"Boston, Hank?"

"The likely site of the next attack, McCracken."

CHAPTER 50

Panama City, Florida

"You killed my dog, mister! You killed my dog!"

Rule heard the words, but the boy before him didn't speak them, his lips never moving. In his mind, he could squeeze the rock in his hand as if it were soft and spongy. In his mind, it was coming forward, the boy first this time and then the dog.

Oh my God, it's happening again!

"Mister?"

But Rule heard nothing. It was thirty years ago again and he was living out of the bug-infested rear of his van, sleeping in a sauna that became more like a steam bake by dawn that found him drenched in his own sweat with even his boxer shorts soaked through. Frustrated, bitter, lost. That awful part of him he'd thought was gone forever was just dormant, waiting to be awoken. His true self, his true nature.

"Something wrong, mister?"

The voice was the same, everything was the same, even the

drool-infested snarls coughed his way by the boy's dog. The sounds bounced about his head, pangs of agony left behind that had to be quelled. Just one way to do it. The rock smashing bone, brain matter and skull fragments hurled mist-like into the air to be scattered by God's winds. The only way, the only way. Then as well as now.

The reverend started toward the boy, hiding the rock behind him. The dog gone crazy now, the clinking sound of the chain fully extended, stretched to its absolute limit just as Rule was.

Another step, then another, the boy starting to retreat, back up the stairs, losing his balance and grabbing a rusty railing to regain it.

Just one lunge away now, time having sped backward, the color washed out of the world so there were only sepia tones that vibrated in the super-heated air.

Rock starting forward.

The door jerking open to reveal a massive shape, too big to emerge without ducking under the jamb.

"Dad," the boy said.

The dog stopped barking.

"What the . . ." The shape in the doorway's voice froze there. His heavy work boots hammered the steel stairs until they stopped at the bottom, eyes narrowing with recognition as the sun hit his bald head, rife with tattoos. "Wait a sec, I know you. . . ."

Rule stood there speechless, the rock gone from his grasp to *thump* against the parched earth.

"You're that reverend, the one hates all the damn Muslims."

Addressing him like one of the faithful. Rule could see it in his eyes, which the sun couldn't make squint, hear it in the giant's voice. He'd never seen a man this big and layered so heavy with muscle.

"That I am," he managed, "that I am."

"I heard of you, I heard all about you."

The man stopped there, his expression opening into a smile. A few of the teeth Rule glimpsed were chipped, the residue of bar fights perhaps, except the reverend couldn't imagine anyone mixing it up with this guy, at least not doing so and coming away to talk about it. He towered over the world, stretching nearly to the size of the mobile home minus the concrete slabs on which it was perched. Black leather biker vest worn right over his flesh, cutting off some of the tattoos layered over his torso. Those tattoos stretched across his shoulders and deltoids too. Up and down both arms as if there was a story in them somewhere, a beginning and end to follow along some ink-laden trail that looked wet in the sunlight.

The giant took another step forward and Rule felt his bowels turn to ice. His hands looked like slabs of dry, crusty meat, warped and scarred at the knuckles. The reverend started to take in some breath but stopped short of completing the effort.

"Been meaning to get to one of your services, Reverend," the giant said. "Like where you're coming from, I surely do, but God and me, we never have gotten along so good."

"My services give back what you bring to them, no matter what that is," Rule managed.

The giant straightened a bit, seeming to grow even taller. "I killed my share of Arabs, back in the real Gulf War, the one where we got to let loose and fight. Stuff went on over there nobody ever heard about, on account if they did, they'd never let us do it again."

The giant winked, flashing his chip-toothed grin.

"Name's Boyd Fowler," he continued, extending one of those meat slab hands. "This here's my boy Jimmy."

Rule eased his hand forward, felt it utterly swallowed by Boyd Fowler's. "How many Muslims you figure you killed, sir?"

Fowler scratched at his scalp. "Can't rightly say. I lost count after the first dozen, most after the war had officially ended but that didn't stop the 5th Armored Cavalry when those sand jockeys took some potshots at us."

"And have you killed any since?"

"Reverend?"

"Since you've been back, here in the States."

Fowler twisted his neck toward Jimmy, making Rule think an uncoiling snake tattooed across the top of his chest was about to strike. "Go inside, son."

Jimmy did as he was told, the door rattling closed behind him.

"I killed plenty since I been back, Reverend, mostly since I got out of prison, but no Muslims among them. I'm not saying I'm proud of what I've done, what I do, but they were mostly bad people and punching their tickets puts food on the table. Man's primary responsibility is to take care of his own, right?"

"It is indeed, Boyd. Can I call you Boyd?" Rule asked, the light dawning on him growing brighter.

"You sure can, Rev."

"It's the very same thing I do in my work, Boyd. I take care of my own. God's children. I take care of them all when they come to hear me speak His word. He speaks to everyone who stands before me in my voice."

Rule took a step forward, shrinking the distance between them. He could feel the heat radiating off Boyd Fowler and pricking at the air. It was like standing near a bakery oven.

"You know, Boyd, I had a spat of trouble the other day."

"I heard about that on the news."

"I need someone willing to stand up against the heathens who want to silence my voice. I need someone to guard God's word so it may continue to be spoken through me."

Now it was Fowler who took a step forward, close enough to Rule for him to feel something like static electricity leaping off the giant, the two of them trapped in a dark patch by the shade trees.

"I might be the just the man for the job, Rev," the giant grinned, those chipped teeth flashing again. "And I can bring others of the same mind."

"A blessing, Boyd," Rule grinned back, realizing that the Lord had directed him here to Countryside Estates for an entirely different purpose altogether. "Just one question: What was it you were jailed for in the first place?"

"Treason, Reverend. Trying to do right by this country."

CHAPTER 51

Dearborn, Michigan

"What exactly are you looking for, Zarrin?" Nabril al-Asi asked her in the private office space he occupied on Dearborn's Warren Avenue.

The colonel had purchased the three-story office building shortly after settling in the city a decade before. Office suites on the first two floors were occupied by a staid combination of lawyers and accountants, the third taken up entirely by businesses maintained by his family members and the Palestinian Progressive Foundation he'd founded shortly after immigrating.

"I'm not sure exactly," she told him. She worked the laptop atop his desk to rewind the digital recording from the surveillance cameras on the Golden Gate Bridge and watched it again, this time in slow motion. "Did you isolate the pictures like I asked?"

"On another flash drive, yes."

Al-Asi inserted the other flash drive and keyed up the faces in question.

"There," he told her.

Zarrin clicked on each of the individual pictures, none of which were either familiar to her or could be matched up with any database, and stored them in a single file. The nationalities and ethnicities were clearly varied, including Middle Eastern and African. But, grouped alongside one another, there was something about them that bothered her, the hair and beard styles too similar.

"What are you up to, Zarrin?"

"Whoever's behind this must've managed to erase any individual pictures of the perpetrators, turning them into ghosts. Now that we've expanded our selection, let's see if they managed to do the same thing with any group shots that might have been taken. How good's your software?"

"I still have the codes for the government servers."

"Which government?"

Al-Asi couldn't help but smile. "All of them."

"This can't be," al-Asi said, even after checking the results a second and third time, after the server's work was complete. "There must be some mistake."

"Ours, Colonel, for not realizing it earlier."

"It makes no sense, Zarrin, none at all."

"It makes plenty."

"They'll never believe us."

"One man will, and you need to help me find him."

CHAPTER 52

Boston, Massachusetts

McCracken stood across Congress Street, flush with the statue of Samuel Adams centered amid the three long rectangular slabs of buildings that made up Fanueil Hall.

"We think it's code for a meeting, the where and when. Four-two-seven-one-F-H-one-two-one," Folsom had told him earlier that morning, repeating the sequence of numbers and letters Blaine had found filled in down a row of boxes in the crossword puzzle. "The first four numbers are longitude-latitude designations for the city of Boston. One-two-one is January twenty-first, today's date."

"And F-H?"

"We believe that's 'Faneuil Hall,' a combination indoor/outdoor shopping and restaurant complex. Prime tourist attraction, especially during the lunchtime rush."

"Which makes it a prime target for terrorists, ideal choice for the next attack."

"I don't buy it, McCracken."

"Why's that?"

"Because how could my undercover agent have learned that from inside Rule's camp?"

"Good question."

"I assume you've got an answer."

"Not yet, Hank. But if I'm right, this is our shot to catch them in the act. Get the Indian and me a plane and have the cavalry standing by when we call."

The one-hour flight passed mostly in silence, save for one stretch where Blaine's thoughts got the better of him, taking him back to the trip he'd made to Crazy Horse, South Dakota, where Johnny had been holed up for months on his latest mission. Not reconnaissance, rescue, or extraction, but the completion of a monument to the greatest Sioux warrior of all time, Chief Crazy Horse.

Once completed, it would be the largest sculpture in the world: a granite portrait of the famed warrior on horseback, carved, blown, and whittled out of the imposing Black Hills. In scale as well as complexity, the final product would dwarf even the collection of presidential profiles on nearby Mount Rushmore, the portrait's nose alone stretching to twenty-seven feet. Construction had actually started way back in 1948, subject over the years to endless financial and political setbacks before suffering further stagnation in recent years, despite eighty-five full-time staff members dedicated to its construction.

Wareagle's involvement originated in the lack of an accurate rendering of what Crazy Horse actually looked like. Descended from a long line of Sioux warriors, Johnny had been the beneficiary of old drawings picturing subjects from his own warrior lineage standing with the legend himself—

his great-grandfather and great-great-great-grandfather, if memory served McCracken correctly. These were deemed the most accurate of any Crazy Horse portraits. But the level of Wareagle's contribution changed as soon as he visited the site and proclaimed he could not, would not leave until he saw the portrait out of granite completed.

"Remember when I came and rescued you from that mountain in South Dakota last year, where you were chiseling away at the monument, Indian?" he asked suddenly.

"Not exactly my recollection, Blainey, but yes, I do."

"You weren't wearing a safety harness."

Wareagle looked at him, a bit befuddled by McCracken's stating the obvious.

"That's the way I feel right now," he continued, getting to the point. "Like I just stepped off the ledge with nothing to keep me from falling."

"This is about the missing boy."

"We can hope he's only missing."

"And therein lies the problem, Blainey," Wareagle said in his typical, sage-like fashion, the cold wind blowing hairs that escaped his ponytail about his face. "You have never been one to hope, always one to believe instead. It's what has kept you—us—going so long."

"You think I've adopted a defeatist attitude, Indian?"

"No, I think you've come to question your invincibility."

"I never considered myself invincible, just lucky more than my share of times."

"You miss my point, Blainey. You were invincible because nobody could hurt you emotionally, the greatest strength both you and I possess. It's why we live alone, apart, why I chose to spend time pounding away at a granite face, because it made me feel connected to something other than the fleeting causes we serve. That statue of Crazy Horse carved out of the mountain won't be fleeting. It will survive for centuries and ages, beyond our lifetimes and many to come."

"I'm still missing the point, Indian."

Wareagle responded without missing a beat. "When you stood next to me on that mountain, could you see the face I was toiling before?"

"No."

"Why?"

"We were too close to it."

"Exactly. To see it in its entirety, we'd need to step back, change our perspective. This boy's disappearance in an attack at the hands of the enemy we now face changed your perspective the same way. It left you too close, so you couldn't see the entire picture."

"His last name," McCracken said suddenly.

"Blainey?"

"I was looking at what was left of the bridge, standing next to this Homeland Security spook, and I couldn't remember Andrew's last name. It's Ericson, but I stood there then unable to remember it."

"This worries you?"

"Because maybe I didn't want to remember, maybe I'd blocked it out. Just like you said, so it couldn't hurt me. But it still did."

"That's not all I said. On the mountain, you see everything from too close up because you have no choice. Once off it, the choice of how much to see and feel is yours to make. That's why you told Folsom to let us handle this instead of shutting the site down."

"Indian?"

"You want to know who did this to the boy. You want to see the faces of your enemy."

"Spirits have anything to say about whether Andrew Ericson is still alive?"

Wareagle shrugged his huge shoulders. "Sometimes they see the future more clearly than the present, Blainey."

It was closing in on lunchtime now, Wareagle having entered Faneuil Hall ahead of McCracken to scout the scene. While waiting for him to return, McCracken busied himself with a review of what he knew about Faneuil Hall itself, a model for other developments like it all across the country, combining strong historic elements with modern shopping convenience. The colonial buildings, restored to their original beauty, housed a variety of shops ranging from food and clothing to electronics and touristy knickknacks sold from open-air pushcarts that operated through all seasons, though today with considerably less bustling traffic. The central Quincy Market was separated from its twin parallel appendages by walkways stretching maybe three hundred yards in length and running about thirty yards in width. McCracken's mind inevitably transposed everything into such logistical concerns, adding windows that would make the best shooting perches and other areas offering potential concealment.

He spotted Johnny crossing Congress Street toward him, still a dozen feet away when Blaine caught the look on his face: resolve, resignation, and surprise all mixed together.

"Indian?"

"Twelve men, Blainey, scattered between the two levels, all with concealed heavy weaponry. Getting ready to launch an attack."

"Six Africans from Yemen or Somalia probably," Wareagle continued. "Four appear Middle Eastern. Two indeterminate."

"I've never known African and Middle Eastern terrorists to work together in the same group."

"Something's not right here, Blainey. Something doesn't fit. The problem is I can't put my finger on what."

"I think I can, and we're running out of time, Indian. Lunch hour's about to peak; Boston's as defiant as ever," he added, wishing in that moment that the city was sheltering in place, more like Washington.

"There's something else," Wareagle was saying. "Someone else inside. Someone who noticed me."

"Not a terrorist."

"A different agenda entirely. And skill set. I felt his eyes on me."

"We can't worry about that now."

McCracken put himself in the minds of the terrorist masterminds behind the attacks. With the country paying notice, changing their behavior and becoming willing prisoners in their homes, the availability of potential targets was substantially reduced. Settings like Faneuil Hall were the last gathering points still likely to draw crowds large enough to be thought of as legitimate soft targets. With each attack, that list would be reduced further to the point where, at least for a time, it would be whittled to practically nothing by attrition.

And then the terrorists would have won. But they weren't going to win today, not here.

"I'm calling Folsom," McCracken told Wareagle, phone already in hand. "Let Homeland Security hit the panic button with first responders."

He pressed Folsom's preprogrammed number, waited for the ring that never came.

"*The number you have reached is not in service at this time. Please check the number and—*"

McCracken pressed the end button, tried again as his stomach muscles began to knot, hearing the welcome click of the phone being picked up this time.

"State your name and designation," an unfamiliar voice droned.

"Who is this?"

"State your name and designation."

McCracken looked at the number still showing on his screen. "Is this Homeland Security?"

"State your name and—"

Blaine pressed END again. "Folsom's been taken out of the picture," he said, dialing 9-1-1. "Let's see if we can bring the cavalry on board ourselves. I've got to figure local authorities have heavily armed response teams standing by and ready to move."

But his call never went through, Blaine heard a dull hum in the background.

"The terrorists have taken the 9-1-1 system off the grid," he told Wareagle, turning his gaze back on Faneuil Hall. "Looks like it's just us, Indian."

CHAPTER 53

Boston, Massachusetts

Zarrin watched, waited. The appearance of the huge Native American, whom she recognized as Blaine McCracken's legendary right-hand man, had unnerved her, suggesting something awry and unexpected. Al-Asi's contact had said nothing about McCracken's purpose in coming to Boston, or the presence of Johnny Wareagle at all. But the way the big man had scouted the site clearly indicated their presence here to be far from innocuous.

Once, she watched him stiffen below her on the first floor and actually turn to gaze upward, almost directly at her position as if he'd felt her eyes upon him. Zarrin maintained the presence of mind not to dart or turn, nothing to give herself away.

So maybe the legends were true, after all, and if they were, she wanted to see whatever it was Wareagle had seen.

Zarrin had reconstructed his path through the two floors

of Quincy Market as best she could as soon as the big man had drifted out of sight. She was suffering from the dual ill effects of not enough rest and the connecting flights that had brought her to Boston. Once mere inconveniences that never would have even occurred to her. But now everything occurred to her. Everything when it came to movement and exertion that needed to be rationed and measured, the days stealing more and more normalcy from her at every turn.

Now she needed to steal as much of it back as she could.

All she'd endured at the KGB training camp in the remnants of the old Soviet Union seemed so distant and foreign now. Endless days of hunger, sleep deprivation, being tortured to make sure she could withstand the worst an enemy might do to her. Being matched up against fellow students in groups of four and sent into the woods with instructions that only one would continue in the program.

Zarrin was the only one to advance by incapacitating the other members of her team instead of killing them. Showing that she understood subtlety and restraint, that she could turn anything into a weapon, including the hands al-Asi ordered that she use to practice the piano to exhaustion when the other trainees were allowed to sleep. Frigid winter morphed into steaming hot summer. She lost track of the days first, then the weeks, and finally the months.

Her body became leaner, lines of sinewy bands of muscle strung to her five-foot-eight-inch frame. But she also learned quickness; not speed, her instructors were fast to say, but quickness. Her profession required being able to move in confined spaces, not large ones, cover small distances in blinding fashion. In winter, training for this covered leaping from boulder to boulder in a frigid mountain stream on the outskirts of Siberia. Only the speed of the water kept it from freezing and even then there were ample chunks of ice floating past her as she trained in bare feet, necessitating her jumps be immediate and fluid. Miss a boulder and she was likely to drown since her instructors were under strict orders to offer no respite for failure.

At the same time, she had become remarkably proficient behind the piano as well—to the point where it was difficult to tell which pursuit she excelled at more. They seemed to compliment each other, strides in one discipline leading to similar strides made in the other and vice versa. Feeding off each other, as they helped Zarrin achieve the perfect balance.

Continuing her work on the piano had the dual effect of keeping her original teacher, Kazim, close to her heart, always her mentor no matter how many Russian masters tried to take his place. And in remembering Kazim, she remembered Hamsa, its terrorist leader, and her vow to return to the refugee camp to finish the job Colonel al-Asi had interrupted.

Upon graduation from her training in the Soviet Union, the camp was the first stop she made, only to find al-Asi waiting for her. A tall, broad-shouldered man she took to be the colonel's bodyguard lurked in the shadows nearby.

"You must learn not to be so predictable, Zarrin," he greeted.

She stiffened. "I have business here."

"It's already done, completed just this morning."

"Interesting timing, Colonel."

"The Israelis decided they could wait no longer."

"The Israelis?"

"A man they sent, actually. A specialist in such things. Hamsa is no more. I made sure its leader's throat was cut. I thought that to be fitting, closing this particular circle."

Zarrin realized the man she'd taken for al-Asi's bodyguard was gone, as if he'd simply vanished. "Should I thank you?"

"Yes, for making sure you didn't squander all the progress your training has produced on a mission of vengeance."

"As an assassin or a pianist?"

"Both, Zarrin," the colonel had told her.

Zarrin counted ten men in retracing Wareagle's path, all heavily armed, but there were probably more, obviously here to stage the next attack, dispatched by the very same party who had made the church bombing look like her work.

She needed all her skills now, needed to be the same expertly trained killer who emerged from the KGB camp, not just the skilled operative who could plant explosives on roadways and detonate them from hundreds of miles away.

Make her body like fingers across the keyboard . . . Flowing and smooth without stiffness or stumbling.

Zarrin began to steady her breathing, employing the visualization technique that never failed her, using the lessons gleaned from one of her pursuits to support the other. This as she watched Blaine McCracken step through the glass entry doors on the floor below with Johnny Wareagle right by his side at the very moment the gunfire began.

CHAPTER 54

Boston, Massachusetts

McCracken registered the first shots as blisteringly loud reports that bred a bare moment of utter silence before the screams began. The moment froze in his mind, snapshots of the families, the children, the school groups, the baby carriages, the diners, and the strollers he'd glimpsed all ratcheting through his mind in rapid succession.

Outside, he and Johnny had made their way through the crowds gathered to watch street mimes, jugglers, and a man twisting balloon animals into various shapes in record time, all brought out by the sunlight and unseasonable January warmth. It had been much colder down in North Carolina, the seasons thrown out of whack along with everything else. McCracken even noted a man dressed in clown makeup folding paper and cardboard into colorful, tall hats that were then placed atop the heads of children gathered for what looked like a grouping of birthday parties in a heated outdoor section beneath a restaurant's glass overhang.

The Faneuil Hall crowd might have been larger than anyone could have anticipated under the current climate of fear, but the city of Boston had taken plenty of precautions in the form of a massive law-enforcement presence. In full riot gear. On horseback. Not afraid to showcase their assault rifles and ammo belts. The National Guard was present too, in full combat attire, including flak jackets.

It made people feel safe, but McCracken knew it was a false sense of security. Taken by surprise, in a single moment of unified violent assault, the posted security would be cut down. Not because they weren't brave or prepared, but because they were about to go up against men well practiced in killing. Men who'd done it before, and likely often. It was cowardice of the worst kind, but it defined the way the world worked today. Death had come to be treated too often like lost points in a video game.

With the 9-1-1 system disabled, trying to warn the police and National Guardsmen what was coming would only hasten the attack before McCracken and Wareagle were in place to do their best to thwart it. And how exactly would Blaine, currently a fugitive, announce himself? On whose authority was he here, when even he couldn't get the only government official who could attest to his involvement on the phone?

McCracken's plan was for Wareagle to take the second floor, crowded with lunchtime patrons in need of tables, while he'd handle the first floor cluttered with eating establishments of all varieties amid yet more tables. They entered Quincy Market, negotiating a path through an exiting throng when, through the nearest windows and wall-length glass frames, they glimpsed the mime, juggler, and balloon impresario tear weapons from beneath their jackets. Those machine pistols were spitting fire in the next moment, aimed for the exterior security detail that was caught totally by surprise.

Bystanders scurried for cover. Police and National Guardsmen struggled to steady their weapons before they were gunned down, then found themselves afraid to fire with so many rushing to flee in their sights. A riderless police horse charged by, changing directions in a flash at the sound of more gunfire ratcheting.

The interior crowd and noise hid both sound and sight of what was transpiring from the police and guardsmen inside long enough for the gunmen Johnny's reconnoiter had already identified to burst up with assault rifles blaring on full auto. Stitching a jagged line of blood, death, and panic across both levels that left McCracken and Wareagle frozen between enemy factions both inside and out.

"Indian, go!"

Johnny was already in motion, his huge bulk tumbling bodies aside to forge a path through the crowd for the stairs leading to the second floor. Their plan gone to shit, advantages turned to disadvantages. Bodies outfitted in both Boston Police blue and National Guard camouflage continued to fall, some of the first-floor terrorists starting to train their automatic fire toward the panicking crowd when . . .

Blam! Blam! Blam!

Single shots, measured as to be precise, pierced the din. McCracken saw one terrorist go down in mid-stream, then a second. He looked up toward the source of the bullets to find a lithe shape, more shadow than man, gliding away, slipping through narrow fissures in the chaos.

Except it wasn't a man.

That was McCracken's last thought before he whirled forward, SIG opening up on a terrorist who'd just shattered a bank of windows with a stitch of fire, the rest of his bullets finding fleeing patrons slowed by exits stuffed with swells of congestion. He wasn't sure how many shots he fired, only that the terrorist's shots turned the clutter into a mass pin-cushion, twisted around with each thumping impact, victims wheeling wildly like a marionettes manipulated by a drunken puppeteer. Then another terrorist went down to fresh fire from above, same cadence and caliber as before. Fired by a woman, McCracken in no position to consider her presence or identity. A phantom, a specter, an anomaly that made no sense.

A woman!

Could it be someone from law enforcement, off duty or working undercover at the Faneuil Hall complex? No, not a chance, given the accuracy and clear, practiced nature of her fire. This was something entirely different—more seasoned and professional—a woman who'd used her gun to kill before many, many times.

That thought crystallized as McCracken sighted in on two targets who'd reacted fast enough to the counterassault to take cover. Their mistake was continuing to target civilians, retraining their fire on convenient, fleeing targets instead of confronting their unexpected adversary. McCracken's biggest problem was finding a sight line and shooting angle through the Quincy Market patrons still swarming around him in panic.

He pushed his way against the grain, gun raised and stead-ied, ready to fire the moment a clear path to either of the two terrorist gunmen opened up. The first one did, enough of a sliver to glimpse the whole of a man's head over the assault rifle he was wielding. The sun was streaming down from the atrium skylights, seeming to cast him and him alone in its light. McCracken used three shots, unsure how many hit before the man crumpled, his rifle's strap catching on the toppled table behind which he'd taken cover and holding him up halfway to the floor.

The other gunman nearby spotted McCracken and jerked upright from behind the counter of a pizza restaurant. Instinct turned his attention away from his real targets to the unexpected threat who'd just gunned down a member of his team. The man fired a wild spray of automatic fire that cut down two more bystanders, while McCracken dove beneath it. Rolling amid the sea of churning shoes and sneakers until he came to a halt ready to fire. Four shots this time, two of them hits for sure.

Back on his feet now, McCracken felt the momentum of the crowd sweep him away, nearly lifting his weight off the floor. Based on Johnny's count there was only one gunman left on this level, Blaine stealing a gaze upward in search of the mystery shooter before pushing to free himself from the swell around him.

He was wrong.

Because there were two gunmen left, not one.

Each claimed strategic positions; one behind a candy display counter, shooting out through the now-shattered glass, and the other hidden by shelves of homemade sauce and various pastas featured at a popular Italian eatery boasting old-fashioned goodness. Both ready to fire, McCracken with neither angle nor shooting lane to claim for himself.

But that didn't stop the terrorists, who unleashed twin torrents of fire forward that cut down more victims between them and Blaine. He felt the heat of a bullet actually singe his scalp enough to flood his nostrils with the sickly stench of burned hair. The sensation forced him to twist away reflexively to the right, and the move spared him from another bullet's impact, resulting in a graze to his rib cage that felt hot and cold at the same time.

He wanted to shoot back, *needed* to shoot back, but there were still too many innocents between him and the terrorists. No way his bullets could find them without risking those lives as well, no way. He needed another weapon, something like, like . . .

McCracken spotted what he needed attached to a beam diagonally across the room and lit out for it, more enemy fire tracing him and felling more bystanders in his path.

CHAPTER 55

Boston, Massachusetts

Zarrin watched the big man, McCracken's Native American friend, work. He wielded twin Desert Eagle brushed-chrome semiautomatic pistols, the model XIX that used a .44 magnum load and took an 8-shot magazine. Zarrin had never seen a man capable of firing in two different directions at once, using his eyes to take a mental picture he then followed in his mind to fire. But Wareagle seemed equally adept at shooting what he could see as shooting what he couldn't. Even more amazingly, some inexplicable sixth sense, some primordial warning system, kept him from firing when someone crossed either of his Desert Eagles' shooting lanes, even when he was looking in the other direction.

Zarrin was flexing her hand, trying to push the blood, warmth, and life back into it after gunning down three of the enemy on the first floor herself. Maybe saving McCracken's life or, at the very least, sparing him the trouble and helping to even out the odds.

The carnage up here on the second level was less magnified than the first, and she tried not to imagine what either floor would look like had the terrorists only needed to deal with the police and additional personnel dressed like soldiers in uniforms much too stiff and clean. Could have stretched well past a hundred victims, given the firepower the terrorists had brought along and the frenzied chaos and clutter that created a fish-in-a-barrel scenario. The final number of casualties might well have eclipsed all the other attacks, had McCracken and Wareagle not shown up.

As for Zarrin, she tried to see Quincy Market as a piano, her body like her fingers skating across the keys. Lost in her music, always a step ahead of the pain and stiffness that otherwise plagued her. She needed to be able to move with the grace and precision more befitting the person she'd been several years ago. Doing replaced thinking and fixating. Once in motion, she was fine until she stopped, her mind tricking her body to turning fluidly and smoothly, gracefully negotiating the stuck swell of bodies hurtling downward. Propelled by absurd instinct since they were flowing straight into a shooting gallery in that direction as well.

Zarrin stayed in motion, the Parkinson's vanquished for now. Her mind moved from one concerto to another, snippets of each combined into a medley paced to fit the mood. She heard Mozart as she saw a stray gunman lurch out, from nowhere it seemed, righting her pistol on him. Then Brahms when she traced another terrorist's dash across the floor, ready to fire when she heard the distinctive boom of the Desert Eagle before she could pull her trigger. Zarrin swung to find Wareagle's gaze upon her, a world of bodies, wafting gun smoke, and the stench of panic between them before he rushed off again on another terrorist's trail.

That cleared enough of a path for her to see out the bank

of second-floor windows downward, where what barely passed as a gunfight on the concrete plaza and walkways continued. Barely passed, because the outnumbered costumed trio of terrorists utterly outmatched the police and those dressed clumsily as soldiers. Their weapons looked all wrong in their hands as they fired or tried to, while the juggler, the mime, and the man wearing a huge hat formed of balloons seemed as indestructible as the cartoon figures they resembled. Firing in nonstop streams or quick bursts, more bodies continuing to sprout from a corpse garden growing out of the asphalt thanks to their bullets.

But now the cartoon figures were retreating—maybe with their particular role complete or maybe because they had caught on to something going horribly wrong with the overall plan inside. The rhythm of the shooting, perhaps, or the lack of automatic fire that should have perpetrated a massacre of unprecedented proportions. For the cartoon figures, the front line of the attack, the feeling could be as jarring as a heavy wave in a calm sea or as subtle as a slight ripple in the current.

Either way they fled, still firing wildly about to clear their path, rushing toward big SUVs that looked as if they could seat a dozen. Three vehicles that must have just squealed to a halt on Congress Street blocking a lane of traffic.

They would escape, the rest of their team all dead behind them, the trail gone cold.

Unless Zarrin acted. Unless Zarrin found the speed she'd lost and agility she barely remembered.

The concerto playing in her head was Wagner now, booming beats driving her toward the emergency exit, beyond which lay the street.

And something else on which she had focused.

CHAPTER 56

Boston, Massachusetts

In the end, McCracken launched himself airborne and rolled the rest of the way to the fire hose coiled inside a steel container box attached to a thick wooden beam.

He had it out and unspooling even as he twisted the spigot. Held its powerful, snakelike form in both hands and felt the water explode outward in hissing burst.

He aimed for the shelves first, too much clamor and screaming to hear the rattle of homemade spaghetti sauce jars rattling against one another and thumping to the floor. He saw the terrorist who'd taken cover there shoved backward, the shelf keeling over at just enough of an angle to send the remnants of its contents raining onto him.

Which left the one poised behind the candy counter, assault rifle now protruding from the cracked glass, muzzle just starting to flare when McCracken hit the display case with the full force of his hose. He was ready with his pistol in the next instant, ready to fire. But the force of the water not only obliterated the remainder of the display case, it concentrated the collection of ruptured, nail-sized shards of glass into a single storm of deadly sharpness that obliterated the man's face like a million needles pricking at once.

The final man, meanwhile, jerked the collapsed shelving from him and, covered in red sauce, lurched upright to steady himself anew. McCracken had already dropped the hose by then, SIG held in its place. He pulled the trigger and felt bullets pouring out the barrel until the slide locked open, the magazine now expended and the sauce mixing with even darker blood as the terrorist slumped down the wall against which he'd slammed.

McCracken swung toward the door, where Quincy Market was still emptying in a steady stream. Bodies littered the clearing floor like stray clumps, several writhing and moaning, the awful carnage still only a fraction of what it could and would have been. He heard sirens wailing, the exaggerated nature of his immediate senses dissipating now, normal operation slowly being restored.

Then he spotted the juggler, the mime, and the balloon hat maker sprinting for one of several huge black SUVs that had made a parking lane for themselves on Congress Street.

McCracken sprinted for the door, bursting out into the unseasonably warm sunlight just as Johnny Wareagle rounded the corner through another exit door and the lead SUV tore out into traffic. The whole thing felt surreal, but in a nightmarish way. The spill of bodies everywhere was being tended to by brave bystanders with the approach of real help still minutes away. The air seemed to smell of gun oil and smoke, but McCracken knew this to be an illusion fostered by the scents now embedded in his nostrils. The scent of blood was real enough, strong and distinct, the stench of it evoking memories of both victories and defeats, of life and death.

Never pretty, McCracken knew, but this was about as ugly as it got. His rough estimate had the total number of dead at twenty, maybe, with somewhere around three or four times that number wounded. All in the space of little more than two minutes from start to finish—that was it, in stark contrast to the false assumption that bloody battles like this went on and on. Far from it. The worst and deadliest firefights often lasted even less.

"We're not alone, Blainey," Wareagle said, drawing even with him.

"Figured that out all by myself, Indian."

"Zarrin. . . . I recognized her."

They both heard the blare of a horn that sounded like a duck quacking and swung their gazes from the escaping SUVs to an awning strung over the street that read BOSTON DUCK TOURS, just as one of the boat-shaped vehicles tore toward them across the promenade with Zarrin behind the wheel.

CHAPTER 57

Boston, Massachusetts

"Hold on!" she yelled to McCracken and Wareagle after they'd climbed on board, voice raised about the wail of the approaching sirens.

Then Zarrin twisted the tour vehicle with BEANTOWN BETTY stenciled across its side into traffic, impervious to the squeal of brakes and grinding screech of metal on metal as vehicles swerved and braked to avoid it. Few realized these touristy amphibious vehicles, that normally included a cruise down the nearby Charles River as part of the attraction, actually enjoyed a rich military history going back to World War II. A vehicle that was half boat and half truck that could run on land and water. "Betty" herself was the first "DUCK," purchased twenty years ago without the expectation of being pressed back into this kind of service.

"Notice I haven't asked what you're doing here," McCracken said back to her, holding on to the rail separating him from Zarrin in the driver's seat.

"I was supposed to kill you."

"Why am I not surprised?"

"You should be happy I'm here."

"I'm sure you had your reasons."

"We're both being set up, McCracken. That means we're on the same side."

He looked toward Wareagle. "Lucky us, Indian."

Which drew a disapproving glance from Zarrin. "Why do you call him that?"

"Oh, jeez," McCracken muttered, shaking his head as *Beantown Betty*, a seventy-foot, open-air vehicle with seating for upwards of forty, barreled down Congress Street after the convoy of SUVs.

Zarrin's driving wasn't subtle, crashing the old girl through vehicles placed inconveniently between her and the fleeing SUVs containing the surviving makers of a massacre.

"Someone offered me a fortune to kill you," she resumed.

"Don't tell me; the Iranians."

"They tend to hold a grudge when you destroy their dreams."

"What changed your mind?"

"Nothing. I never had any intention of trying to kill you. But had I refused the assignment, Colonel Kosh would've sent someone else."

"Kosh? That little shit?"

"None other."

"So why go through all this trouble to save my life?" Blaine asked her.

Zarrin kept her eyes focused on the road ahead. "Because I owe you a debt I've been waiting to pay for years."

"Debt? We've never even met before."

"No, but our paths have crossed, McCracken. Once."

"Where?"

"The Palestinian refugee camp where I grew up, when I

returned from training with the KBG." She finally looked from the road to McCracken, matching his face to the man she'd taken for al-Asi's bodyguard all those years ago. "The day you wiped out the gang and terrorist leader who killed my piano teacher."

Beantown Betty slammed through orange barrels laid before a construction site and surged on.

CHAPTER 58

Boston, Massachusetts

"I remember now, a favor for Colonel al-Asi . . ."

"I saw you that day, McCracken. I knew you were the man who did it as soon as the colonel told me someone had done my work for me. I didn't know who you were then; I didn't learn that until years later. But you saved my career before it even began."

"Hope that means I did you a favor too, Zarrin."

Zarrin ignored a red light, slamming a pair of vehicles from *Beantown Betty*'s path, pinballing them aside. The SUV convoy dipped and darted along the Boston side streets approaching the revamped Southeast Expressway to avoid traffic congestion that had sprouted up out of nowhere. The loop took them down Milk Street and then veered *Betty* onto the much narrower India Street that left her scraping off side mirrors and ping-ponging off fenders with shaved and dented steel left in her wake.

If McCracken had his bearings right, the loop was taking them all the way around the rear of Faneuil Hall, the fleeing SUVs trying to avoid the patches of traffic further snarled by rescue and police vehicles tearing toward the complex from all directions. They trailed the SUVs down what had once been called Surface Road when it provided access to the Route 93 ramps, and was now a dug-out route perpetually under construction.

That road spilled out onto a fork breaking toward traffic stalls in both directions, the SUVs having squeezed their way to the front of the pack and just turning onto yet another street where movement came only in maddening fits and starts.

"We're gonna lose them," McCracken said, angling himself closer to the driver's seat as if intending to seize the wheel.

"No, we're not," Zarrin told him and twisted *Beantown Betty* up onto a sidewalk construction zone, squeezing her between a row of mothballed parking meters and a fenced construction site for a building waylaid by the stalled economy.

The move ended at a row of Jersey barriers lined to further cordon off the construction zone. No way *Betty* could find a way around those, but the SUVs were snared in an interminable traffic jam on the connecting street running perpendicular to this one.

"Indian," McCracken called.

"With you, Blainey," Wareagle said, already positioning himself to leap down from *Beantown Betty*.

"I know; don't call him that," McCracken said to Zarrin. "We'll be right back."

Zarrin watched them, the impossible unfolding, two men who were legends within the world she was lucky enough to still inhabit. Her own mind registered the logistical limitations, the absurdity of attacking through stalled traffic with no room to maneuver and minimal space to negotiate. Space was the actual key in such deadly encounters, something only those seasoned enough to have survived this long realized. Because, in a confined area lacking such space, even the best could find themselves trapped and vulnerable. Might as well be in closet.

Don't do it, Zarrin willed.

As if they could hear her thoughts, McCracken and Wareagle leaped atop vehicles as soon as they swung on to the adjoining street, one in each lane, and began charging toward the stalled SUVs, jumping from hood to trunk to roof in a crazed rhythm. The blaring of horns intensified, slammed by drivers perhaps jealous of the fact these men were moving.

When they were halfway to the SUVs, doors opened and gunmen spilled out. The mime and the juggler looked absurd with weapons blasting away in their hands, the balloon hat maker only slightly less so. The SUVs' drivers were firing as well, errant shots spider-webbing windshields with telltale pings or clanging off steel. Terrorists used to slaying innocents, their sensibilities softened by the ease of such kills in comparison to taking on professionals who'd been here before.

McCracken and Wareagle both fired as they dipped, darted, and leaped. Pistols flared in their hands, muzzle flashes incredibly flat and uniform, no different from firing from stationary positions. Their bullets dinged steel and showered glass up into the opposing force's eyes, making Zarrin wonder if that had been the purpose of the shots. Either way, their next twin volleys spun the enemy gunmen about, seeming to corkscrew them into the pavement. Zarrin's precise mind tried to impose order onto the sight, but chaos had seized her thinking along with the street now filled with panicked passengers and drivers fleeing their cars, a few holding cell phones at their ears or out to record what they were too afraid to stay and watch themselves.

For the last stretch, McCracken and Wareagle looked like dancers, floating through the refuse of their gun smoke. They seemed to move in slow motion in direct counterpoint to the ugly, dented roofs and hoods they left behind. Zarrin didn't know when the last enemy gunman fell, only that no more were standing, a realization accompanied by her hands twitching and spasming on *Beantown Betty*'s wheel. No more fooling or tricking her body, which had turned on her once again.

She worked to relax them, but her fingers locked up solid on the steering wheel, betraying her as well.

McCracken and Wareagle landed on the pavement in unison amid the panic of feet churning away from the area. Pistols trained downward now, since all members of the opposition were either dead on the pavement or soon would be. Several were propped up against a fender, bumper, or tire. A few still seemed to be breathing, but none were moving or brandishing weapons.

Blaine noticed the eyes of the terrorist disguised as the white-faced mime fidgeting wildly and crouched even with him, while Johnny checked the interior of the vehicles for a shooter potentially laying in wait.

"Do you speak English?"

Bloody froth bubbled from the man's mouth. He began quivering, shock setting in as a precursor to death.

"Talk to me and I'll save you!" McCracken followed, making a show of tearing the man's shirt open, as if he were about to commence CPR. "Talk to me and—"

Too late. A flood of air-rich froth from a lung hit dribbled between the man's lips, his eyes locking open and sightless. He slumped over to the left, exposing the shoulder that McCracken had already bared and the small but distinguishable tattoo all but lost to the blood.

75TH . . .

It couldn't be, yet it was.

And it all made perfect sense.

CHAPTER 59

Boston, Massachusetts

The Seventy-Fifth, McCracken thought, charging back toward *Beantown Betty*.

As in the famed Seventy-Fifth Ranger Regiment. As in headquartered at Fort Benning, Georgia. As in a crucial expeditionary force for J-SOC, the Joint Special Operations Command, former American soldiers in the guise of terrorists.

As in exactly what Blaine had expected as soon as Folsom had explained the message his undercover agent had left for them.

"Take the wheel!" Zarrin implored McCracken, as he and Wareagle lunged back upon *Beantown Betty*. "Listen to me, the terrorists, they're—"

"Americans," Blaine completed for her. "I figured that out all by myself."

He watched her fingers finally releasing their grasp, exertion tightening across her features, her hands looking like frozen claws when she finally got them free. He didn't argue, just replaced Zarrin behind the wheel and twisted *Betty*'s nose toward a gap between two parked cars parked on either side of the corner.

The gap proved slighter than he'd estimated, forcing *Beantown Betty* to slap the cars aside to slide between them in search of a hole in the stalled traffic. Word of the link behind what had just transpired here and what the attack at Faneuil Hall sent massive numbers of fresh police and National Guard vehicles converging on the area. McCracken knew their only chance for escape was a mere football field's length away, within clear sight if not reach.

So he steamed *Betty* forward diagonally across the street, snowplowing traffic-snarled vehicles out of his way, while the sirens grew louder and flashing lights clearer from all directions. A pair of police cars screeched to a halt nose to nose to block his path, but McCracken slammed right through them, too, the waters of the Charles River glimmering straight before him.

McCracken knew he needed a ramp to assure a smooth entry for *Beantown Betty*, but, short of that, braked the old girl and pulled back just as her nose crested over some barrier fencing. Over she went on a ten-foot drop, nose handling the rattling impact with surprising ease. The old girl leveled out quickly with barely a rattle, her engine sputtering before catching again, alone in the river waters.

McCracken drove *Beantown Betty* up on the meager shoreline on the other side of the Charles River, tapping the old girl's dashboard fondly before climbing up to street level with Zarrin and Johnny Wareagle. There, they melted into the pedestrian traffic crowding the sidewalk amid the parking lot of vehicles lining the Cambridge side of the river as well.

Everywhere, people's attention was riveted to their smartphones, following the news that continued to break in real time just across the Charles. McCracken separated himself from a throng and was searching for clearest route out when he collided with a Boston policeman.

The man recoiled, eyes meeting Blaine's as he jerked a hand for his gun belt. McCracken moved in, a single lunge, ready to stop him from drawing his pistol, when the cop drew a smartphone from his pocket instead.

"Can you believe this?" the cop asked him, flicking the screen to life.

Leaving McCracken to shake his head. "What's the goddamn world coming to?"

CHAPTER 60

Washington, DC

"It's a goddamn mess is what it is," Robert Carroll said to Colonel Alvin Turwell, who was seated stiffly next to him on a bench on the outskirts of the deserted mall.

"We both lost men, good men," Turwell told him. "Now we need to get past it."

"Am I missing something here or are you not getting that this whole mission of yours has gone to shit?"

Carroll was a bullet-shaped man whose narrow head, sitting atop a wide, thick frame, seemed to come to a peak. When he was angry—commonplace in a career spent mostly in hallways walked by few others, where fates and futures were determined—he arched his neck in a way that made the peak seem higher. "An even dozen casualties on that goddamn island and they're still adding up the tally in Boston. Cat's about to be let out of the bag, Colonel. That means it's getting close to the time to head for the hills."

"Boston's been contained."

"And I'm supposed to take your word for that?"

"Make the calls yourself. Bodies will be in friendly hands before anyone can get a whiff of something off."

"As in the truth, as in you trying to tread water in a shit storm."

"Then it's a good thing you're Homeland Security."

"I run the Gap," Carroll said in a slow southern drawl. "Security arm of Homeland that this rogue bastard McCracken you've unleashed used to work for."

"I unleashed him for a purpose. Seized an opportunity. It's called a mission protocol."

"But that purpose didn't pan out, did it? In fact, you even fucked that up royally and put our entire end game in jeopardy," Carroll said, making sure to stare Turwell right in the eye.

"I respectfully disagree," Turwell responded, trying not to sound as defensive as he felt. "It was just a setback and a minor one at that."

"Setback? *Minor*?" Carroll folded his arms, thick overcoat bagging at the sleeves. "McCracken's been pulling off shit like this since Vietnam. I imagine you've heard of that war, right?"

"Enough to know the rules of engagement beat what I experienced in Afghanistan," Turwell said, not bothering to disguise his bitterness.

Carroll shook his head. "Man, you are just full of all them fancy West Point terms, aren't you? Thing is, there's not a hard drive in the world that can hold all of McCracken's and his Indian buddy's exploits. Thanks to them, you got shit backing up in your toilet, and I'm the man with the plunger."

"You speaking for the others?" Turwell asked him, not particularly wanting to hear the answer.

"You rather speak to them yourself, Colonel? I'd advise against it, given they're even more pissed off at you than I am. Matter of fact, it wouldn't surprise me one bit if they were racing one another to the Justice Department to see who can nail himself an immunity deal first."

"Let's stick to the subject at hand," Turwell said, trying to sound calm and hoping Carroll didn't notice how fast his heart was beating or the sweat rising to his brow. "McCracken's not just a rogue, he's a wanted man with a dragnet thrown across the whole country. You telling me he can operate even in those conditions?"

Carroll just shook his head. "He was bred in those conditions, for Christ's sake. But it's a good thing you got me to hold your hand."

"What are you talking about?"

"I took some precautions of my own. Let me put it this way, son: since you can't handle McCracken, it's a good thing I can."

PART FOUR:
THE *MARY CELESTE*

CHAPTER 61

Boston, Massachusetts

"Nice trick," McCracken said to Zarrin, after she'd used her universal key card to access the room at the Airport Marriott.

"Works especially well at airport hotels because of the quick turnover," she said, closing the door behind him and Wareagle after one last check of the hall. "No better place to hide out with so many people coming and going."

"You already knew the terrorists were Americans, soldiers in all probability," McCracken said, within the relatively safe confines of their hotel room.

"Thanks to the security tapes taken of the attack on the Golden Gate Bridge," Zarrin explained. "First, with the way the gunmen were holding their weapons."

"No one else noticed, including me."

"Of course not, because you didn't train in the old Soviet Union like I did. Terrorist training camps still use the old Russian techniques to this day."

"How could I have missed that?"

"Because you've got something else bothering you."

"Is it that easy to spot?"

"It is, for me. Beyond the gun thing, somebody went through great pains to pin the blame for the Ohio church bombing on operatives with the same training I received."

"Jihadi terrorists again."

Zarrin nodded. "Someone very sophisticated and very concerned about planting a false trail was behind that. It was the only explanation and it changed the entire nature of what your country was truly facing, in my mind."

"What else?"

"I saved the best for last. I grouped the faces captured on the Golden Gate Bridge surveillance footage together and searched for a match that way instead of individually."

"What'd you come up with?"

"A single, grainy picture taken by an embedded journalist in Afghanistan of an American special-ops team on some black mission."

"I'm guessing there's more."

"No trace they ever served, no match with any military or intelligence database because they must've been scrubbed. I think those men made up one of the deep-cover teams responsible for the atrocities over there mostly confined to rumors. I think your army, or government, found out about it and stripped off their uniforms before they could cause any further embarrassment."

"Making them prime candidates to play pretend terrorists unleashed on a fake jihad."

"My thinking exactly."

"All that's missing is the end game, but not the means to bring it about. That's where the White Death comes in."

"White Death?"

*   *   *

Zarrin studied McCracken while he laid it all out for her. Eyes darting into every line and wrinkle on his face, before settling on the scar that ran through his left eyebrow.

"I was set up too," McCracken concluded. "To make the Reverend Jeremiah Rule seem even more a victim, to increase his following and strengthen his base at the same time."

"These staged terrorist attacks can't go on forever."

"No, because the country's being set up for something bigger at the hands of the White Death, and right now the only clue we've got as to what is the *Mary Celeste*."

"Ah, the famous ghostship . . ."

"You've heard the story?"

"Bits and pieces."

"Then let me get an expert on the phone so we can hear the whole thing."

"Sorry," Captain Seven said, once McCracken had reached him, "can't talk now. I'm in the midst of a much-deserved, weed-induced vacation. Twice as high as I am normally and that's pretty damn high."

"The *Mary Celeste*, Captain."

"*Beeeeeeeeep!* Please leave your message at the tone and I'll return your call when I damn well please."

"I had to leave for Boston before you could properly explain your theory."

"I'm trying to smoke here, MacNuts," the captain greeted over the speaker of McCracken's phone. "Can I call you back?"

"Multitask, Captain."

"According to its manifest, the *Mary Celeste* was carrying seventeen hundred barrels of commercial alcohol used for fortifying wines. When the ship was discovered abandoned at sea, the entire cargo was found intact, untampered with, and undamaged. Seems pretty obvious, though, that she was really carrying whatever those British seamen pulled out of the ground on Roanoke Island. And manifests are easily altered, manipulated. Especially when somebody wanted to hide something."

"Why?"

"Assume, thanks to what Chief Red Water, Red Sea, Red Lake, or whatever his name is, told us, that whoever showed up at the colony in 1872 had figured out the same thing we did. Assume they left with enough of the White Death loaded onto their wagons to head north and fill the cargo holds of the *Mary Celeste*, intending to use it in some war themselves."

"Like you said," McCracken noted, "the first weapon of mass destruction. But why wait so long to come get it if they already knew of the White Death's existence from John White's journal, Captain?"

"That's easy. Because until right around then, the technology to pump that much shit out of the ground didn't exist. The way Chief Water Log described it, sounds to me like that steam engine pumping apparatus was custom made. Somebody wanted that carbonic acid awfully bad and went through a lot of trouble to first haul it north to the Port of New York and then transport it across the ocean."

"But we're forgetting something, aren't we?" McCracken pointed out. "The same thugs we encountered didn't kill Jacob's friend in 1872; they killed the boy just a few months ago. Why do that if they already had the White Death in their possession?"

"Because they didn't, at least not yet. They were looking for clues just like we were."

Blaine thought for a moment. "What we do know about what happened after that other ship—"

"The *Dei Gratia*."

"—found the *Mary Celeste* abandoned at sea?"

"Here's what her ship's log has to say on the subject," Captain Seven said, reciting the rest from memory. " 'The day begins with fresh breeze and clear, sea still running heavy but wind moderating. Saw a sail to the East at two p.m. Saw she was under very short canvas, steering very wild and evidently in distress. Hauled up to speak to her and render assistance if necessary. At three p.m. hailed her and getting no answer and seeing no one on deck or on board, accompanied the mate and two men on board. Sea running high at the time. We boarded her without incident and found her to be the *Mary Celeste*, bound from New York for Genoa and abandoned with three feet of water in her hold.' That help at all, MacNuts?"

"Not one bit."

"Then let's back up a bit and assume the captain of the *Mary Celeste* knew the seventeen hundred barrels he was carrying didn't contain alcohol as advertised. His ship springs a leak, just a modest one, but scary as hell given what happens when the real contents of those barrels mix with water. So he goes to check those barrels and notices one or more of them was leaking too. With his own family on board, the captain decides he has no choice but to abandon ship before the same thing that happened to the Roanoke colonists happens to them too."

"But that doesn't explain why the ten people who climbed into that lifeboat were never seen again," Zarrin noted.

"Who's the babe talking?"

"A friend, Captain."

"She smoke?"

"I doubt it."

" 'Cause I've resolved to only trust people who smoke God's herb. Save me the trouble of getting my ass shot at on account of you anymore. And, to answer her question, the *Mary Celeste*'s crew and passengers showing up in a port would have posed a big problem for somebody. Imagine the story they had to tell, imagine the explanation they'd have to give the ship's owners, and the insurance company, for their actions. Nope, whoever those barrels containing the White Death were intended for," Captain Seven continued, "couldn't afford the truth coming out, a truth only the survivors could tell."

"Here's what I don't get," advanced Zarrin. "Why would anyone bother with these barrels today? Why not just create something in a lab somewhere that achieves the same effect?"

"What, you think it's so easy?" challenged Captain Seven, toking audibly on a joint. "Let me ask you a question, girlfriend. In spite of the devastation and death that happened at Lake Nyos, why has no one ever managed to successfully weaponize that event? Because water tends to swallow up anything you dump into it. You wanna know what I think? I think plenty of people have tried to artificially replicate carbonic acid and the effects it has in good old H_2O. But the formula, the mixture, is just too damn difficult, especially when you figure the presence of volcanic activity screwing up pH levels to an unfathomable degree. But, now, hear this, if the bad guys we're chasing really did get their hands on the White Death, you wanna be somewhere else far, far away when they unleash it."

"What's the equivalent amount that killed the colony, Captain?" McCracken asked him.

"Impossible to say, MacNuts, but best guess? Try a single barrel at most. For Lake Nyos, a much bigger body of water, I'd say a hundred barrels, maybe as many as two hundred."

"That event killed over three thousand people," Blaine recalled. "And our bad guys may have as many as seventeen hundred barrels of the White Death."

"Don't think number," said Captain Seven. "Think area. Even stuff this potent tends to dissipate in the air over a larger area. So with seventeen hundred barrels at the ready, I'd say you're looking at the size of a city maybe."

"New York or Washington?"

"Potentially."

"With a nearly one hundred percent mortality rate, asphyxiated the same way the people living around Lake Nyos were . . ."

"That's right."

"Then we need to find these barrels," said Zarrin. "Pick up the trail in Gibraltar, where the *Mary Celeste* ended up, and see where it leads. But something else is bothering me."

"Why didn't they die?" McCracken completed for her. "The crew and passengers on the *Mary Celeste*."

Zarrin nodded. "If they abandoned ship because one the barrels in their holds was leaking, the contents should have mixed with the water they'd been taking on and killed them all before they could abandon ship."

"Now, that's a quandary."

"One we can't solve here and now."

"Am I done?" Captain Seven wondered.

"For now."

"I'm changing my phone number, MacNuts. Don't bother calling back."

CHAPTER 62

Blountstown, Florida

Reverend Jeremiah Rule knelt before the altar in his church, listening to the plop of the rainwater leaking through the roof hitting the buckets below. No matter how much he patched, sometimes with his own hands, new leaks sprang up.

Rule had come to realize that the leak was an apt metaphor for life, God sending him a message.

Plop, plop, plop . . .

"I understand, Lord," he said out loud. "You have shown me the light, the way, the path away from indiscretion and temptation. I see this particular mission you sent me on is drawing to a close and a new one is dawning to replace it. I know I can speak to you as I can no man, because you alone understand the darkness that lurks within me. You know what I brought in my heart to that trailer park; you know the evil intentions that rose out of my soul. You put me in a place where I could relive my becoming, but then you set me on a path to a different salvation. And so I realize it must be for every man who in his nature and soul is neither good nor evil, but both."

Plop, plop, plop . . .

Rule realized his knees were beginning to ache badly, but refused to shift positions. The pain made him feel alive; God's way of reminding him how much work remained for him in this next phase.

"I wanted to blame the devil for the depravity I displayed in that terrible moment of weakness, but now I see the Devil is an excuse for that depravity, not an explanation for it. And if you had not intervened in that trailer park, I would have been lost forever. Sunk into a cesspool of my own sin, never to be brought back to the light. But now that light shines bright upon me and I see what I must do with it; yes, I see why you spared my soul and the bidding I must do on your behalf in return. Make me worthy, oh Lord. I beg of you to make me worthy!"

Plop, plop, plop . . .

Upon leaving the church, he found Boyd Fowler standing by his pickup truck with two other members of the Rock Machine motorcycle gang, ready to assume their duties taking over his personal security detail.

"I won't be needing you anymore," he told the guards assigned by Colonel Turwell. The two men looked at each other uncomfortably. "The Lord has seen fit to bestow upon me my own sentinels."

The men regarded the massive Fowler and the other two gang members again, now standing with arms crossed against the Ford Super Duty over which he towered, smirking.

"You have my gratitude and the Lord's for your service," Rule continued. "And you are always welcome to join me in worship. I believe you know the schedule, and I will make sure the website is continually updated."

He left them without another word. They were out of his life and, thus, out of his mind, and he moved straight for Boyd Fowler, whose tattoos looked shiny and wet in the fresh soak of the storm.

"I'm going to retire to the residence now," Rule informed the giant, "to do some things that need doing. I'll need you and your men to stand post, allow no one entry. Is that clear?"

Fowler moved his gaze to the reverend's former bodyguards, a wide grin stretching across his face. "It sure is, Rev. For starters, I'll make sure those boys vacate the premises." He started to move away, then stopped abruptly. "Oh, and one more thing. I think you may have a rat problem in your crawl space."

"Rat problem?"

"I heard scuffling under the floorboards. Sounded like a whole mess of the bastards."

"Let's leave them alone, Boyd," Rule said, forcing a smile. "All creatures have a right to be."

CHAPTER 63

Washington, DC

"Well, well, well, look who it is," H. J. Belgrade said, looking up from the bench placed amid the spacious grounds of the Armed Forces Retirement Home.

McCracken straightened the dark-blue scrubs he'd dressed in to look like an orderly. "Surprised to see me?"

"Surprised it took so long, given that the country's gone to hell."

"It's worse than you think."

Belgrade fed a handful of bread crumbs from the bag in his lap to birds that weren't there. "Then you'd better sit down. They always sit down when they're babysitting me. And they call me H. J. here, short for Henry John."

"Except John isn't your middle name."

"Adds to the mystique."

"And the fact that you want them to believe you're crazy."

"Helps keep the real crazies away."

"You mean like me, H. J.?"

Washington's Armed Forces Retirement Home was housed on three hundred acres in the very center of the nation's capitol, among the city's richest and most lush grounds within minutes of every seat of power the the city offered. This in addition to a nine-hole golf course, driving range, walking trails, fishing ponds, a computer center, and six-lane bowling alley. The AFRH-W, as it was generally called, was far more than just a senior-living residence; instead, it was essentially a self-contained and self-sufficient village where many of those who'd once fought the nation's wars, both known and unknown, lived within clear view of a majestic tower made of the same limestone as the Washington Monument.

"I was thinking more along the lines of my last visitor, just yesterday."

"And who was that?"

"Bastard by the name of Robert Carroll. Took over the Gap after I was deemed unfit for service. Not sure if they dumped me 'cause I knew where too many bodies were buried, or 'cause I'd forgotten."

Much of Belgrade's "deterioration" may have been a ruse, but age had not been especially kind to him either. McCracken's memories of him were of a raw-boned, thick-bodied, no-bullshit man with a set of shoulders as wide as a Cadillac. Big everywhere, especially through the neck and head, and bull-shaped. An imposing figure, to say the least, the perfect appearance to suit his ill-defined role in government. That role tended to be whatever he wanted to make it, but was normally confined to dealing with the dirtiest of the dirty work that tended to slip into the "gaps" between the more traditional organizations.

In contrast to all that, the Belgrade of today was a wizened figure with knobby bones poking through what had once been muscle. He'd cut his teeth as a mere boy in the wake of World War II with the likes of Bull Donovan and Allen Dulles, the true giants of the early intelligence apparatus. That would put him well into his eighties now, a far cry from the troubleshooter Blaine recalled from fifteen years ago when they used to meet regularly at the Lincoln Memorial.

"I assume Robert Carroll came looking for me."

"Right as rain, McCracken, and I'm guessing the reason he's after you is what brought you here."

"We're up against it this time, H. J.," McCracken told him.

"Aren't we always?" Belgrade asked him, stringy hair blowing in Brylcreem-dappled clumps from one side of his head to the other.

"This is different."

"Why?"

"Because someone's going to hit the country hard," McCracken told him. "The hardest we've ever been hit. The attack's coming from the inside, and you're the best hope I've got to help me stop it."

Belgrade smiled halfheartedly. "Maybe you should take a better look at who you're sitting with here. A broken-down, old man feeding invisible pigeons," he said, tossing more bread crumbs to the sidewalk before him.

"Who still has everyone's number in his Rolodex."

"I lost my Rolodex a long time ago. Replaced it with a cell phone, and then I lost that too." The old man looked at Blaine closer, as if seeing him for the first time. "And I heard you got your own problems."

"That explains why I'm here. I can't trust anyone else to do the right thing."

"Well, I still have the phone numbers, McCracken, but that doesn't mean the people on the other ends will pick up."

"You'll find a way to make them."

"I appreciate your faith."

"You may not feel that way when you hear the full story."

"Who's our opposition this time?"

"Ever heard of the Reverend Jeremiah Rule?"

"A little. Not much. Cult figures who like instigating turmoil don't always make my radar."

"This one should, because he's involved in a big way."

"Wait a minute, is this the nutcase who started out burning Korans?"

McCracken nodded. "And now he's intent on burning down the whole country."

"The wave of terrorist attacks?"

"Supposedly launched in response to his rants."

"Supposedly?"

"There are no terrorists, H. J.—just our own outcast soldiers following somebody's orders in carrying out the atrocities the Islamic radical groups are getting blamed for."

"Oh boy . . . Sounds like something they picked up from those Truthers who believe we were the ones who toppled the Twin Towers, not Al Qaeda."

"Only it *is* the truth this time."

"On *whose* orders exactly?"

"That's what I need you to help me figure out. I was working with a contact at Homeland before somebody slipped him off the grid when I started getting too close."

"Ah, your specialty . . ."

"These attacks are just the preliminaries, H. J. Something big and bad is coming, something we're not likely to recover from for a long time."

"Need one hell of a weapon to pull that off."

"The bad guys have one," Blaine told him, "believe me."

Belgrade turned away to spread some more bread crumbs for his imaginary flock. His gaze looked distant, dreamy, the harshness and power that had briefly flickered in his eyes vanquished again.

"We have to sing now."

"Huh?"

"I always sing with my gatekeepers. If I don't do it with you, whoever's watching will start to get suspicious."

McCracken glanced around subtly.

"Don't bother," Belgrade warned. "You won't see them or their damn cameras but they're sure as shit there. I can smell the bastards and I truly mean that. I spend the whole day watching Elmer Fudd and Daffy Duck cartoons to keep them from becoming any the wiser. Do you know 'The Wheels on the Bus'?"

"Not anymore."

"Words are sure to come back to you. Come on, just sing along. *The wheels on the bus go round and round, round and round, round and round*."

And then McCracken joined in, the two of them singing together. Badly.

"*The wheels on the bus go round and round, all through the town*."

"See," Belgrade said, pulling another handful of bread crumbs from his bag, "that wasn't too hard, was it?"

"The Viet Cong had worse tortures than listening to us sing." McCracken touched his old friend's shoulder lightly. "Your condition's not all a ruse, is it?"

Belgrade shrugged shoulders that had once been big and broad. "Not all of it, no. Not even most, some days."

"I'm sorry."

"Don't be. I had my run."

"And right now you're the only man I trust in this city."

Belgrade smiled at that and took a deep breath, letting it out slowly. "So what do you need?"

"For starters, recon on the Reverend Jeremiah Rule."

"Satellite?"

McCracken nodded. "Archival as well as present. I've got the specs."

A single pigeon landed and began pecking at the bread crumbs scattered across the walkway.

"Hey, look at that." Then Belgrade's eyes strayed suddenly to nurse's aide walking across the grounds in the narrowing distance, seeming to appear out of nowhere. "He's new."

"You don't recognize him?"

"Never saw him before in my life."

McCracken turned his gaze to follow Belgrade's, just as the man dressed as a nurse's aide raised his hand to speak into a wrist-mounted microphone. The coiled thin cord of an earpiece was tucked under his collar.

"We need to get inside," he said to Belgrade.

"What? You need to speak up."

"Inside, H. J.," Blaine said, helping him up. "Now."

CHAPTER 64

Washington, DC

The receptionist at the front desk looked up at McCracken, returning a phone receiver to its hook. "The phones aren't working," she said, mystified.

"I can't get any service on my cell either," said a second woman from nearby, holding up her Android phone.

Belgrade laid a knobby, arthritic hand on Blaine's shoulder. "How much time do we have?"

"Ten minutes tops," McCracken said, taking out his SIG Sauer.

"Must be coming for me. You can still get out," Belgrade told him. "There are no armed guards here, no guns. You can't fight them alone."

"I'm not going anywhere. And I'm not alone," Blaine added, with his eyes on the nearby rec room.

The men dressed as nurse's aides moved up to flanking positions across the shaded entryway of the building. Moments later a trio of ambulances streamed onto the grounds, with no sirens or flashing lights. They stopped immediately before the glass entry, their rear doors bursting open to allow black-clad commandos armed to the teeth to spill out and take up positions on either side of the door. The last group to exit was the first to enter, storming inside to find the reception desk empty and no one to be seen anywhere in the lobby.

All eleven fanned out immediately to secure the area, with four making straight for the third floor and H. J. Belgrade's room. Another trio remained in the lobby, aware something was clearly awry amid the empty silence, but sticking to the plan and their orders, while the remaining four headed off to secure the common areas and exits. All were attuned to the slightest sound or movement when the black eight ball rolled slowly across the pool table in the adjoining recreation room. The three commandos padded that way, M1A4 special-ops versions of the M16 held before them. Two twisted inside from either side of the open entrance.

And were met by the weighted end of pool cues slamming across their faces. Bones gave, noses bursting blood as the men sank to their knees, a pair of ex-marines joined by a pair of former navy men in lurching outward to attack the third man, unleashing a flurry of wild blows that left him toppled in a heap on the floor.

The four retirees, all battle tested many years before, looked at one another and exchanged a salute.

"Guess you navy boys ain't so bad, after all," said one of the marines.

Another pair of commandos reached the cafeteria, their orders to keep it secure it until the mission was complete.

But only a single table was occupied by a pair of World War II army veterans playing checkers in uniforms that sagged badly on them.

"King me," one said, reaching the other side of the game board.

"What?"

"I said, *king me!*"

"What?"

"Where is everyone?" one of the commandos asked, reaching the table.

"Who?" the old soldier waiting to be kinged asked him.

"The other residents."

"What'd he say?" the soldier across the table asked.

"He wants to know where everyone else is."

"Who?"

The commandos looked at each other, then toward the kitchen where a woman who'd served as a nurse in Vietnam emerged with a glass coffeepot in either hand. She looked unsteady on her feet, legs growing wobbly by the time she reached the one occupied table.

"Who wanted decaf?" she asked.

"What'd she say?" the hard-of-hearing veteran wondered.

The eyes of the commandos were still on him when Nurse Jacqueline French hurled the contents of both pots into their faces, driving both men to the floor screaming.

An old man wearing an American Legion ball cap wheeled himself feebly toward the commando posted at a first-floor exit at the other end of the hall. His wheelchair was vintage, as was everything else about him, including the tattered blanket covering legs he'd lost the use of thanks to arthritis instead of shrapnel.

"Hey, sonny, can you tie my shoes?"

The commando had crouched over to oblige when he noticed the man was wearing slip-ons and looked up just as the miniature baseball bat cracked him in the top of the skull. The bat, a souvenir from a Yankee–Red Sox game from sometime in the seventies, struck him two more times before he got a hand up to ward it off. And by that time he was already woozy, consciousness slipping away when a fourth blow slammed across his brow stole it altogether.

A commando watching the building's rear exit found an old man wearing pajamas collapsed in the middle of the floor.

"Mister? Hey, mister . . ."

He lowered a hand to rouse him and was met by a stiff, knobby hand brandishing a can of pepper spray the old man carried on his walks for fear of coyotes and cougars he was convinced were roaming the retirement home's grounds. Blinded, the commando lurched back to his feet and wheeled about wildly between two other old men lobbing lightweight bocce balls at him. One of the throws caught him in the groin and another square in the throat, doubling him over so the three Korean War veterans could pounce.

The final four commandos stepped out of the elevator on the third floor, one remaining just outside it with a foot planted over the sill to make sure the compartment remained in place. The duty desk up here was abandoned as well, no one and nothing to be seen save for empty wheelchairs and unoccupied walkers strewn about the hallway. The other three commandos continued on, leery of each open doorway they passed en route to the room occupied by H. J. Belgrade.

The fourth watched until they turned a corner and drifted out of sight, hearing the chime of the elevator alongside the one he was guarding sound. He slid sideways and positioned himself before the door to be ready when it opened, weapon raised just in case.

The doors started to part, a loud wail sounding from inside

before they'd separated all the way. The commando saw the wheelchair barreling toward him too late to do anything but feel its impact stagger him backwards, as two more wheelchair-bound veterans rolled out behind the first. The commando saw they both held something in their grasps, not identifying the objects as fire extinguishers until the twin sprays hit him broadside.

In that moment, the remaining commandos eased Hank Belgrade's door open with a creak and approached the bed where his shrunken form was tucked under the covers.

"Rise and shine, Mr. Belgrade," the leader said. "This is your wake-up call."

He flipped the light switch to no effect, the shades drawn to shroud most of the room in semi-darkness save for the light spilling in from the hallway.

The leader reached the bed and tried to rouse the old man's sleeping form.

"Let's go, Mr. Belgrade. Duty calls."

The shape finally stirred, turning over to reveal a much younger man.

"Sorry, wrong room," McCracken said as he drove himself upward, lunging at the speaker.

The leader crumpled under the force of a series of pummeling blows before the other two men could respond. And by the time they did, McCracken was ready, using the instant they'd wasted in trying for their weapons to his advantage. The man closest to Blaine was first in getting his pistol around until a strike to the windpipe sent him careening backward, both hands raised now instinctively in comfort before he passed out. The second man actually managed to find the trigger before McCracken got two fingers of his own wedged into the tight gap to prevent him from firing. He used a foot to take one of the man's knees out and then employed the butt of the man's own rifle to hammer him into unconsciousness.

Blaine then eased open the bathroom door to find H. J. Belgrade seated atop the closed toilet, snoring.

"Yo, H. J.," he called.

Belgrade came alert with a start, nearly toppling over to the bathroom floor. "Is it over? What'd I miss?"

"The good guys won."

Belgrade looked beyond McCracken toward the three bodies lying on the floor beyond. He flashed a grin, shaking his head.

"McCrackenballs . . . Some things never change."

"Like us, old friend."

"I'll bet you dollars to doughnuts those were Robert Carroll's men coming to pay their respects."

"And I'll keep that in mind when our paths eventually cross."

"Do that, please." Belgrade's eyes turned glassy, a whimsical smile spreading across his face. "You wanna sing with me again?"

McCracken had just left the grounds when his phone rang, a blocked number appearing in the caller ID window.

"Yeah?"

"You remember my voice?"

"Not off the top of my head."

"Maybe this will help: we met at the Daniel Boone Bridge a few days back. You remember me now?"

"I do."

"Five survivors of the bombing washed up on shore this morning. One of them's a teenage boy. I thought you should know."

Andrew Ericson, Blaine thought, recognizing the voice as that of the ex–Special Forces operative who was standing off to the side by himself when Blaine arrived, working out of Homeland Security now. The two of them viewing each other as kindred spirits.

"They were all taken to CenterPointe Hospital in Saint Charles," the man continued.

"Condition?"

"Alive. But I'd hurry if I were you."

CHAPTER 65

Blountstown, Florida

Alvin Turwell was already on his way to see Jeremiah Rule when the call came from the man he'd assigned to run the reverend's security detail.

"*What? When?* . . ."

Turwell drove faster, racing a storm building behind him that had already darkened the sky ahead. Big fat raindrops began dappling his windshield and Turwell switched on his windshield wipers. The world before him looked dark and angry, its scope shrunken by the reduced visibility. Being behind the wheel still felt strange to him, no driver handling the chore anymore while he worked the phone or planned strategy with his aides. He missed the days of being trailed by camera crews that used to hang on his every word, especially when vice-presidential rumors started springing up, but then died when his party opted for the safe choice just like they always did. He was no longer sought to provide his expert opinion on military or political issues, even on the friendly cable programs that used to love having him on air. Out of sight, out of mind, he guessed. Lose an election by a couple thousand votes and become persona non grata.

But that was about to change.

The night he'd lost his bid for reelection seemed to have dropped Turwell into some cosmic void. Today, his oft-repeated quotes had become the source of political ridicule and whimsy. Too abstract and out of the mainstream to be taken seriously because he spoke his mind. Spoke the truth that few wanted to hear because it scared them by upending their simple lives imprisoned between four walls of mediocrity and self-loathing. That was the America he hated and the America that had come to disregard him entirely.

And the America he would destroy in order to save it.

The Reverend Jeremiah Rule had become the centerpiece in his plan, the main cog in an operation undertaken with military precision. But ever since the attack on his life, Rule had begun behaving erratically, leaving Turwell to wonder if he'd pushed things too far, if there was something about the reverend he'd not yet fathomed. Dismissing the security assigned by him in favor of a motorcycle gang the reverend met in a trailer park made for the final straw.

Turwell got back on the phone, hitting redial on the number of his man overseeing the Rule's security.

"Where is he now, Sergeant?"

"Retired to his home, sir."

Turwell could hear thunder booming on the other end of the line and gazed ahead to see the storm clouds he was driving straight into.

"What's he doing inside?"

"We don't know, sir."

"I assume you've got eyes on the house."

"We do, sir. But there's no sign of him through the windows."

"It's a one-story house, Sergeant. Where the fuck could he be?"

"Unknown, sir."

"We may need to consider a breach."

"Sir, the reverend has that gorilla of his posted at the front door and three more almost as big patrolling the grounds. A breach could get messy."

"For God's sake . . ."

"What are our orders, sir?"

"Orders? Try this. Don't do a fucking thing until I get there."

CHAPTER 66

Blountstown, Florida

Jeremiah Rule was busy in his basement when he heard the pounding on his front door. He left the bucket he'd intended to dump down there and climbed back up the ladder, pulling himself through the hatch and storming toward the door. He threw it open to find Boyd Fowler looking down at him, a clearly pissed-off Alvin Turwell standing in his shadow.

"Man says he's got an appointment with you, Reverend."

"A *standing* appointment is what I said," Turwell corrected.

Fowler ignored him. "I know you said you weren't to be disturbed no matter what, but I figured the way this man was talking warranted an exception."

"You did right, Boyd," Rule said, afraid the stench from his basement had ridden with him back up here. He gazed toward Turwell, who looked hot and was struggling to steady his breathing from rapid huffs and heaves. Sweat had soaked through his sports shirt at the underarms and torso, and beads of it dappled his brow. "The colonel and I have some business to discuss."

Fowler turned sideways, holding a menacing gaze on the colonel as he passed by. Turwell didn't say another word until Jeremiah Rule had closed the door behind him with he and the colonel standing just inside the foyer.

"I was worried about you, Reverend."

And that's when Rule realized he'd forgotten to close the hatch. "Really? And why might that be?"

"My men told me you'd been behaving erratically. They were concerned the shooting the other day may have rattled you more than you're showing."

"It opened my eyes, Colonel," Rule said, aware only a sliver of the hatch was visible from this angle.

"To what?"

The reverend slid sideways, positioned to keep Turwell's eyes off it altogether. "To take more charge of my own destiny, not trust it in the hands of another who may not have my true interests at heart."

"Our interests are the same, Reverend," Turwell said, fighting not to show how agitated he was.

"And what if mine have changed?" Rule managed, still utterly distracted. "The Lord is sending me signs again, leading me to a place I haven't identified yet."

"Your safety is my responsibility, Reverend. That's why I need to inform you that you're taking too many chances, venturing out too much with so much at risk."

"The risk is well worth it. Everything is evolving, Colonel, nothing as it was yesterday or the day before. Even the last minute. It's gone, vanquished to the banks of history where it will likely be forgotten as most things are. But not His work. I see that now. His work alone endures and His word is the one true truth. The Lord and I had come to a crossroads, and I'm eternally in your debt for directing me which way to go."

"I don't believe I follow you, Reverend."

Thump.

"I am his vessel, his harbinger," Rule said, tensing at the sound coming through the open hatch, "and I will continue to speak the word of the one true God, serving my purpose to him with all my heart and soul. He delivered you onto me for a reason, Colonel. Our destinies are intertwined. Embrace that and rejoice in it."

Thump.

"I'm the man who brought you this far. That's something *you* should be embracing."

Thump.

"What was that?" Turwell asked, starting to turn.

Rule maneuvered to place himself between the colonel and the hatch, blocking the man's view. But Turwell kept trying to peer over Rule's shoulder in the direction from which the sound had come.

"I have a rat problem." Rule grasped the colonel's stare and held it. "Maybe a bigger one than I thought, because you don't truly believe, Colonel, not in your heart or your soul. You're a fraud, a charlatan. You've sought to use me, so lost in your own self-deception that you never saw I was the one using you, thanks to God. He brought you to me and now your purpose is done."

Rule detected fresh rage simmering over inside the colonel.

"You really don't get it, do you?" Turwell sneered.

"Why don't you shine the light brighter for me to see, Colonel?"

The *thump* sounded again, but this time Turwell seemed not to notice it.

"You're a cog in a much greater machine, Reverend, just like I am. You need to accept that and be thankful for it."

"Thankful for what exactly?"

"That you're still alive. You weren't supposed to survive Mobile. You were supposed to be martyred then and there to set up the final attack tomorrow."

Rule remained unruffled having still not broken his gaze off the colonel. "Well, then I suppose that proves the Lord has my back, even if you don't."

Turwell stood rigid, his lips quivering slightly as if regretting the words that had just slipped through them. "He may not have your back next time. You'd be wise to remember that and just do what's expected of you."

"Oh, that's exactly what I intend to do. Do exactly what's expected of me . . . by God."

"I'm warning you, Reverend."

"Actually, I believe you are threatening me. And when you threaten me, you threaten God. My survival in Mobile only confirms I'm serving His plan, not yours. And nothing you or these others can do is going to change that. See, you're the one who doesn't get it. Your purpose has been fulfilled. The rest is up to me."

"And what does that mean exactly?" Turwell asked him.

"God's final plan, Colonel. Growing clear to me even now. Boyd," he called loudly. And then, when the giant jerked the big door open again, "Please escort the colonel out," he said, still speaking to Fowler as he rooted his gaze on Turwell. "We have more important work before us."

Thump.

"You should really get that problem taken care of, Reverend," Turwell said, as calmly as he could manage. "The thing about pests is that they never clean up the shit they leave behind."

CHAPTER 67

Saint Charles, Missouri

The man from Homeland Security was waiting at the entrance to intensive care at Saint Charles's CenterPointe Hospital when McCracken arrived. Both the reception and waiting areas were still packed to the brim with relatives awaiting the latest word on the conditions of their family members injured in the terrorist attack. It was a scene Blaine had experienced countless times in his life, always hoping the next would be the last. But it never was.

"Four bodies made it here," the man he'd first met upon arriving at the Daniel Boone Bridge reported flatly.

McCracken felt a shudder ripple through him. "Except five were found alive on shore."

"That's right. One of them is unaccounted for. Care to guess which?"

"The kid I'm looking for."

"Hell of a world we inhabit, isn't it?" the man said, his tone unchanged even when he continued. "For what it's worth, I'm sorry."

"No, you're not."

The abruptness of McCracken's remark seemed to unsettle the man ever so slightly.

"See, I never said anything about the person I was looking for being a kid."

The man just looked at him.

"I'm guessing you're Gap, that you serve under an asshole named Robert Carroll. That tells me you were at that bridge waiting for me to show up, expecting me to. I need to keep going?"

"Rest is obvious," the man shrugged.

"The kid was targeted. The Daniel Boone Bridge wasn't a random target," McCracken said, fitting the pieces together for himself as well.

"In my experience, there's no such thing."

"They really find him washed up onshore alive?"

"I wouldn't know. What I do know is that you're going to stand down. Another forty-eight hours and then the kid gets returned to you. And the same goes for your Indian friend and that old fossil with the broken nose."

"Forty-eight hours . . ."

"That's what I said."

"I gotta figure you didn't just pull that number out of the air. Which tells me we're coming to the end of this," Blaine said, thinking of the White Death.

"That info is way above my pay grade."

"I could put you into early retirement here and now."

"But we both know you won't, McCracken. You're not holding any cards, so you've got no choice other to play it the way I tell you, or you start getting pieces of the kid sent to you via FedEx." A pause. "You related or something?"

"Something." McCracken held the man's stare and watched him smirk, confident of the upper hand he was holding. "You made another mistake," Blaine said then.

"Huh?"

McCracken took the phone from his pocket and flashed it. "Remember this? Back at the bridge, when we first met, I dropped it and you picked it up for me."

"You going somewhere with this?"

"You should have worn gloves, Mr. Edward J. Harm. Nice last name by the way, very fitting."

Harm's brow crinkled, his mask starting to crack.

"Right now, that old fossil with the broken nose is visiting with your family. Wife and two kids. Twins, age ten. You made the same mistake I did. You gave yourself something to lose."

CHAPTER 68

Asheville, North Carolina

The Reverend Jeremiah Rule hit the road as soon as Colonel Turwell was gone, heading north along interstates deep into the heart of North Carolina and his own past. His time of transition was coming, everything he'd been born to do was coming, but Rule still felt the old demons haunting him, refusing to leave him be.

And so he'd taken this second trip into his past, only much further back to his youth growing up with other orphans amid the scents of rust, sweat, and urine. He needed to know himself anew, to confront the parts of his life that had spawned the man he was today, the parts that needed to be excised once and for all.

The orphanage, the only home Jeremiah Rule remembered from his childhood, was nestled in the mountains outside of Asheville, North Carolina, a rustically serene setting that belied the evil that festered like mold. For Rule, the three-story school building that also held a chapel was like a steel hangar; frigid in winter and oven-like in summer with the other seasons irrelevant. It was enclosed on three sides by the various residential cottages barely suitable for human habitation. All structures on the spacious grounds had been painted a gunmetal shade of gray that had darkened in his years there until it appeared black as night even during the day. For that reason Beacher House, as the facility was called, became more commonly known as "Bleak House" after the Dickens novel, and then, even more fittingly, "Black House."

For the reverend himself, that was a metaphor for the color of virtually every soul that made it out of here, no matter the shade of it when they'd come in. The perimeter of Black House was surrounded by an imposing wrought-iron fence twice the size of the boys gaping up at it. The escapees were always the athletes, the climbers who could scale the iron without impaling themselves on the spiked spokes that topped each rail. But they were always caught and returned to the home where punishment was summarily enforced.

As Rule recalled, Black House fell under the domain of a particularly punitive Jesuit order that could not be bothered with the needs of homeless boys or dispensing sanction on the wildings that dared try breaching the walls and fence. No, that punishment was instead dolled out by the same kind of counselors who had made him hang from the steam pipes that heated the cottages in winter as a boy. The Jesuit brothers involved themselves only in the most serious of cases involving repeat offenders.

Through the dark days of his early youth, Rule recalled seeing some boys walking with pronounced limps and thought nothing of it given the terrible backgrounds from which many of Black House's residents hailed. Only in his latter years in the home did he realize the limps belonged to repeat offenders who, after their third failed escape attempt, would be tied to their mildew-ridden cot and have their leg bent back until their hamstring snapped. It would heal well enough, but never entirely the same, the modern equivalent of "laming" runaway slaves on farms and plantations not at all far from Black House.

The reverend needed to walk those cold, dark floors again, needed to know himself as he was then so he might know himself better now. He'd taken the old van on the trip, listening to it sputter and clank, the heater struggling to push any heat out at all, its musty interior smelling of stale cigarettes, spoiled food rotted under the seats, and the flatulence of its previous owners collecting like clouds near the broken dome light. The smells, the farts especially, rekindled memories of Black House, sleepless nights spent sobbing while boys alternated passing wind in the blessed sleep that eluded Rule.

He needed to know those cottages again, the creaky bed frames and moth-eaten mattresses. His recollection of those years brought with them not a single happy memory, not one. There was never anything to look forward to—not holidays, or birthdays, or friendship, or sports, or toys, or games. Nothing. There was only the stink and the pain that left sleep as the sole solace on the nights it would come unbroken for any length at all.

After an eight-hour drive, just past dusk, Rule arrived at Black House to find much of the steel fence collapsed or stolen away for scrap, and not a single building untouched by vandalism. Some of the residential cottages had collapsed under the weight of snow and ice. Still more had been upended by the savage storms that occasionally came ashore to wreak havoc on the North Carolina countryside. The same storms had uprooted trees that smelled sour and dead. No one had removed them, just as no one had removed the refuse of the cottages, or done anything about the dark shell of the main building, most of the windows long boarded up with the remainder missing and exposing the interior to the ravaging elements.

The reverend entered the grounds through a chasm where Black House's huge, heavy iron gate had once stood. Much of the fence, though, still remained, save for jagged gaps missing steel harvested for salvage. He walked the grounds with only a cheap flashlight purchased at a rest stop where he'd also grabbed some Little Debbie snacks. Recollection of the paths now strewn with brush and muck returned with surprising clarity, as if he had never left these grounds at all. He continued about the overgrown, untended grounds, praying silently for guidance in his journey, reaching a cracked and fractured window of a dilapidated cottage that froze him in his tracks.

I lived here once. . . .

And that's when Jeremiah Rule glimpsed the face of a boy staring back at him from inside.

CHAPTER 69

Asheville, North Carolina

But it wasn't a boy at all, just a trick of the moonlight's reflection in the falling night. He was looking at his own face, the features warped and distorted by the broken glass. All the same, the illusion sent his heart racing, down now to just a splotchy flutter as Rule approached the cottage entrance.

This was the very cottage in which he'd been forced to hang from the steam pipes, the cottage he'd returned to in later years as a counselor himself. The big heavy door had splintered away, just chunks left at the hinges where it looked kicked in, probably by local kids out for an adventure or adults in search of more to salvage and pawn. Rule entered out of the chilled air into something even more cold and dank. Because there was something for him here at Black House, in this very cottage; something he needed to know, something he had left behind that was a mystery even at this point of the journey.

His cheap flashlight made enough of a dent in the darkness for Rule to see the cottage as it had been fifty years ago. He looked up through the collected dust and cobwebs to find the steam pipes, from which he'd once hung by his fingers, were gone, torn from the walls so their generally worthless steel might be salvaged for something. The irony of trying to find any value in this place was striking. Rule took a deep breath and the air flooding his lungs felt rank and spoiled.

Suddenly, he smelled the sweat of unwashed bodies and urine festering on underwear that went weeks without being laundered. Rule shined his flashlight upward to find the steam pipes suddenly restored amid the dull glow. More than that, he saw a young boy hanging from one, gritting his teeth against the inevitability of falling. Beneath him stood a glowering, grinning counselor, poking at the boy with what looked like a garden stake found amid the tended areas of the grounds.

Poke, poke, poke . . .

The boy grimacing each time the stake left him swaying again, the blisters on his hands starting to pucker and pop. It was hard for Rule to watch, even in his mind, hard to watch himself suffer as he had so all those years ago.

Only the vision conjured by his mind wasn't of him at all. The boy starting to lose his purchase on the steamy tin had light hair, while his had been dark. A straw-colored mop of waves, with tangles and cowlicks sticking up this way and that. Being prodded and poked with a stick by a counselor with hair cropped military close on the sides and bunched tight on top.

And then the younger boy fell, in motion so slow that Jeremiah Rule could now see the iron bed frame against which his head slammed. The crunch was sickening and by the time the boy hit the floor, his eyes were rolling back in his head and he was making guttural wheezing sounds that ceased in the midst of a final exhale. His features locking blankly in realization, resignation, and perhaps relief. Dead.

The smell of urine became more potent, that of something like old, stale farts added to it.

"You don't remember."

Rule swung about in search of the voice, a boy's voice, taunting him. Then turned back to watch the counselor shed his garden stake and grasp the boy by the shoulders, shaking them in a futile attempt to revive him. The counselor swung Rule's way, seeming to regard him, to plead for help through timelines stitched together. The reverend recognized the counselor, knew him all too well.

Because it was *him.* As a teenager. A battered boy turned batterer. It was the way Black House worked and thrived.

"Come on, I'll show you."

Rule followed the boy's voice back outside, trudging along an overgrown path. He'd known those paths so well back then, knew them that well again now. And when he looked down, he was wearing cracked and torn sneakers instead of shoes, the dead boy now grasped in his arms growing stiff as foul air fled his anus. Rule shook the illusion aside, but the path remained, a destination programmed into his mind.

"It ain't too much further now."

He didn't even know how far he'd walked. But there was a thicket of brush shrouded by dead elm trees, their leaves all shed to show only skeletal branches frozen over the scene. Rule looked down to see hands caked with mud and blood from cuts in the flesh and one nail mangled from digging.

"Here I am, right here."

The ground had been soft that night, Rule shoveling his hands through it to forge a hole deep enough to pass as a grave. The dead boy would be reported missing, a token search conducted while proper reports were made out to the police. They'd pass his picture around for a time, maybe staple his likeness to the walls of a few local businesses, and then everyone would forget. His bunk would be taken by another from the waiting list who would sleep on the same stale and dirty sheets.

Rule didn't need his cheap flashlight to see the world before him anymore. He closed his eyes and smelled the fetid mud, felt it churning through his hands until an occasional rock blocked his fingers and bent them backward. Felt his nail crack and splinter on one of the rocks.

The body was stiff and cold, sightless eyes still open, when Rule finally lowered the boy into the hole and covered him in the piles of dirt, replacing it as best he could.

"It was just an accident."

The dead boy's voice again, only now his ghost was standing by Rule's side gazing down at the resting place for his remains.

"You didn't mean to kill me no more than you meant to kill that other boy. But you didn't bury him like you buried me."

Rule wanted to speak, wanted to respond, but there were no words and barely enough breath to form them anyway.

"Come on."

Rule looked down to see the ghost had taken his hand in fingers draped in mud that left Rule's cold and matted together. No way to get all that mud off no matter how much he washed and rinsed, as he'd learned as a counselor just short of his sixteenth birthday forty years before.

"I'm still there. Nobody done ever found me. Hey, did you ever find my coloring book? I could sure use it to help pass the time. And a couple crayons if you think of it."

Rule's mouth dropped but no words, not even any air, emerged.

"I know about that other boy you killed. Maybe did him a favor as much as you did me. Not much hope in life for either of us. Life ain't about much else and you more than made up for it."

"I have?"

"For sure, yes. All them people you helped. Gave them what nobody could ever give me or that other dead boy."

"Hope?"

"Yup."

"What's ahead? Can you show me that?"

"You don't need me to show you nothing anyway. You already know what's down that road. Just gotta open your eyes to see it, like you're seeing me. Killing me helped make you who you are, just like killing that other boy did. But if you don't do the right thing now, we'll both be stinking up the ground for nothing."

"I've preached the Lord's word, invited Him to speak through me so others may know Him too."

"It's not about what you said as much as what you gotta do, what you gotta finish. And don't ask me what it is either, 'cause I don't know. Just know there's something."

The boy took his hand again and Rule shuddered.

"And you know what that something is as sure as sure be. I'm in the ground now 'cause of what you were becoming even back then. Now the reason for that's getting clear as day."

Rule realized the boy wasn't holding his hand anymore, starting to drift away.

"Don't leave."

"Got to."

"Please."

The boy kept drifting.

"Let me, let me . . ."

"What, Reverend?"

"Let me take you with me."

"You mean it?"

Rule nodded and looked down at his hands, wondered what they might find after all these years if they churned through the soft ground of the boy's makeshift grave anew.

"There's a way," he told the ghost.

CHAPTER 70

Branson, Missouri

The steel and brick carcass of Celebration City amusement park rose on the outskirts of Branson like a ghost town. It had been conceived and built as a kind of mini–Disney World to celebrate Americana with elegantly reconstructed small-town streets layered between rides like a log flume and vintage wooden roller coaster. Over thirty of them that could be enjoyed through the day, then topped on a nightly basis seasonally with a laser and fireworks show. But the developers' ambitions greatly exceeded the demand for such an attraction in rural Missouri and the park had gone belly up just a few years after it was christened.

"I want the boy, Eddie," McCracken had said to Edward Harm back at CenterPointe Hospital in Saint Charles. "Simple as that."

"It's never that simple and you know it."

"Whatever Carroll and the others are up to, whatever they're planning, ends here and now."

"And what does Mr. Carroll get for such a generous gesture on your part?"

"He gets to live. That good enough for you?"

"It's not up to me."

"Then get the man it is up to on the phone."

McCracken was talking to Robert Carroll on Harm's cell phone in the hospital lobby minutes later.

"You are one goddamn pain in the ass, McCracken."

"Something works for me, I stick with it."

"Seems like we got ourselves a dilemma, doesn't it?"

"Well, you do—that's for sure."

"But I also got this kid you want so badly."

"How do I even know he's really alive, Mr. Carroll?"

"Guess we have to meet up face-to-face."

"Guess we do."

"Hash the rest of this out like the professionals we are."

"Suits me just fine."

"Leave that big Indian of yours home."

"Exactly my intention." McCracken paused long enough for Carroll to take his next breath. "That way, if this goes bad, you'll know that you and whoever else is involved won't be long for this world."

"Have you ever actually listened to yourself, son?"

"No, Mr. Carroll, I haven't. But you better."

And now here Blaine was, entering the debris-riddled mausoleum that was Celebration City through what was left of the steel gate. He could smell rust and rotting wood. The rides still towered over the scene, some stripped bare of iron and copper, while others creaked in the wind, looking ready to topple under the force of the next gust.

He turned right down a once-elegant recreation of an old-fashioned, small-town street from a simpler time, neatly paved and complete with the rusted husks of ancient cars stripped of tires and rims with bird nests sprouting from where their upholstery had once been. The elm and oak trees rising out of the smoothly layered sidewalks were still alive in stark contrast to the boarded-up windows of the movie house, emporium, and general store that once sold souvenirs, its empty shelves filled only with dust.

McCracken stopped halfway down the street and looked back over his shoulder to see two men armed with submachine guns had stepped out behind him. Before him, meanwhile, another pair accompanied Robert Carroll from inside the fabricated town hall set in the glistening sun. A third man pushed a wheelchair with the dazed form of Andrew Ericson slumped in it. His hair was disheveled and he looked dazed, but alive. Looking at the boy made Blaine think of Andrew's father, the first time he'd seen him playing rugby at the Reading School at a point he still believed Matthew Ericson to be his son.

Blaine found the boy just as a teammate gave him a perfect pass on the run and Matthew Ericson streaked down the far sideline like a champion thoroughbred. A deft stutter step stranded one opponent in his tracks, and a fake pass to the side left him with a clear path to the goal line. The boy ran with graceful, loping strides, propelled by a high leg kick that tossed mud behind him off his soggy cleats. His hair was straight and longish, curled at the ends now from the dampness.

Andrew was a spitting his image of his father from that day; he was even wearing a rugby shirt that looked sodden and soiled. One blanket covered him at the shoulders in the cold air, another draped over his legs.

Blaine started walking again, conscious not only of the pair of men at his rear falling in step, but also of eyes sighting down on him from the second- and third-story windows overlooking the imitation Main Street. A dozen at least, probably more.

Robert Carroll was taking no chances.

Almost to the town hall, one of Carroll's men signaled him to stop while another came forward and performed a cursory frisk, lingering briefly on the pouch wound through Blaine's belt and then shaking his head Carroll's way when he found no weapon.

"You've made a hell of a mess, McCracken," Carroll told him from just fifteen feet away.

"I've heard that before."

"And yet you keep doing it, long after most have hung up their guns."

"Unlike men like you, who just have other people pulling the trigger for them."

"It's a new world, McCracken."

"Hardly. Men like you just want to think that it is to justify the kind of shit you're trying to pull now."

"I'm pulling the plug, that's what I'm pulling, if it's any comfort to you."

"It's not," Blaine said, his gaze dipping to meet the boy's, which looked dazed and terrified. "How long have you had him?"

"Since EMTs pulled him off the bridge after the blast. The car he was in never even went into the water."

"Neat trick."

"It pays to think ahead, in this case to your potential involvement."

"I scare you that much?"

"Because you can't be reasoned with."

"You mean controlled, Carroll, don't you?"

Carroll backed off. "Take the kid and get out of here."

"That simple?"

Carroll shrugged.

"Because it occurs to me having to maneuver a dazed boy in a wheelchair would make it a lot harder for me to deal with those gunmen you've got covering the whole street from the windows."

Carroll said nothing.

"Ever get your own hands dirty?" Blaine asked him. "Ever served or seen combat yourself?"

"Never had the opportunity."

"Is that what you call it? Maybe if you had served yourself, you'd think differently about the way you do business, how you view life and death."

Carroll stiffened, looked up at the windows lining both sides of Main Street. "Make a move on me and you'll be dead before you take a second step."

"As opposed to waiting a few minutes more, when I've got a kid in a wheelchair to get out of here with me."

Carroll smirked. "Free passage, McCracken. I told you, the plug on this is getting pulled."

"Something go wrong, Carroll? Something in your grand scheme to murder innocent people in the name of whatever it is you're trying to accomplish?"

"You mean, save this country from itself? No worries; I'll just find another way, while you go about yours. Maybe next time you'll choose the right side. Now, take the kid and get out of my sight."

The man at the rear of Andrew's wheelchair shoved it forward. McCracken stopped it with his foot and came slowly around to take the handholds.

"Have your men throw down your weapons, Mr. Carroll, the ones in those windows included. Then tell me who else I need to pay a visit to and you get to walk away from this. Free passage."

Carroll frowned, the expression morphing quickly into a grin. "Man, you really are a piece of work, aren't you? How is it we've never met before?"

"Guess I'm just lucky. You should keep that in mind."

Carroll grinned again and shook his head. "A damn shame, McCracken. We're really not as different as you think."

"Yes, we are. Last chance, Carroll. Make your choice."

The man just stood there.

"Don't say I didn't warn you," Blaine said, squeezed the boy's shoulder tenderly and started the wheelchair down Main Street.

CHAPTER 71

Port of Gibraltar

"This is about the *Mary Celeste*, no doubt," Fernán Andrade said to Zarrin from the window that overlooked the sprawling Port of Gibraltar from the breakwater on the north side.

"Educated guess?"

"The only thing that truly brings people my way," Andrade told her, slapping his hefty stomach forcefully with both palms. He had a thick shock of white hair and icy-blue eyes that glistened in the light.

Zarrin gazed about his elegant office, focusing on wood-paneled walls papered with any number of nautical charts, as well as photographs and drawings tracing the port's growth and development. "And yet you were the longest-serving Captain of the Port in history."

"And I'd still be if politics hadn't intervened, the damn Brits. Replaced me with a goddamn bureaucrat, they did. Let me keep the office like I'm on display in a museum. Anyone with a historical inquiry is directed to me and those inquiries, invariably it seems, involve the *Mary Celeste*. I feel like the Flying Dutchman, doomed to repeat the same stories forever."

"Not today," said Zarrin.

Located at a crossroads of Mediterranean and Atlantic shipping lanes, on a strait traversed by over seventy thousand vessels per year, the Port of Gibraltar had become a stopover for any number of commercial, shipping, leisure, and even private craft. The local airport, into which Zarrin had flown, was located a few minutes from the harbor, the story of which was elegantly told by the pictures hanging from Fernán Andrade's walls. The early eighteenth century had seen the port as little more than a British garrison. But the opening of shipping lanes to the West and back as the decades wore on cast its strategic location in an entirely new light.

Andrade bypassed his elegant collection of photographs in favor of a detailed schematic of the port and surrounding waters from the late nineteenth century. "The *Mary Celeste* was found in the Bay of Gibraltar," he said, pointing to a spot on the drawing southeast of the port. "Right about here, where she was taken under tow by a nearby twin brigantine called the *Dei Gratia* and brought to a spot not more than a hundred yards from where we stand right now."

"What if I told you I know what happened to the crew, why they abandoned the ship for no explicable reason?"

Andrade looked utterly unimpressed. His massive jowls wobbled. "And which theory would you be fronting? Thievery by pirates gone wrong? The captain being double-crossed by someone to whom he'd agreed to sell the ship's cargo of valuable alcohol for spirits? Another ship the *Mary Celeste* had stopped to help, only to be seized herself? The British government smuggling something on board the captain caught wind of and wanted no part in? Which will it be?"

"How about none of the above?"

Andrade looked as if he didn't know what to make of Zarrin's answer or of her. "And what is it you know about the *Mary Celeste* that has escaped history this many a year?"

"That the answers I'm looking for can't be found on her decks or in her cargo holds. They lie somewhere else entirely."

"And where's that?"

"Another ship," Zarrin told him.

CHAPTER 72

Branson, Missouri

McCracken could feel Carroll's eyes still boring into him from back near the town hall, the bright sun glistening off the light-colored pavement now riddled with cracks and fissures. The elm and oak trees swayed gently in the breeze on either side of the street, their shadows splayed against windows behind which Carroll's gunmen were perched.

They'd wait until he was halfway down, whatever hesitation McCracken felt lost in that certainty along with the fact that the boy's life would be claimed as well. Which meant nothing to men like Carroll, of course, who'd now firmly moved from I-know-best-what-the-country-needs mode to cover-his-ass mode.

Meet the new breed, same as the old breed. Like the song says. Kind of.

"Can you hear me, Andrew?" Blaine asked, sweeping his gaze from side-to-side as he eased the wheelchair on slowly. "Andrew?"

The boy remained dazed, drugged as well probably, and didn't so much as stir. The sun burned into McCracken, making him feel even warmer in the cool air, and he hoped it would ease Andrew's trembling in the wheelchair. They had targeted the boy to insure his involvement, to better set him up.

Targeted a kid.

They deserved what was coming to them, what he was about to unleash while the gunmen felt safe and secure behind the windows above, ready to let go with a cross-fire fusillade that would cut him and Andrew apart. Carroll playing his final card, knowing McCracken well but not well enough.

Blaine glanced back at him, glimpsed Carroll and his men backing away, toward the protective cover of the once-pristine town hall, now marred with faded trim and peeling paint. Carroll reached the shade of the portico, almost lost to sight.

McCracken reached into the pouch threaded through his belt, its contents having escaped the pat-down just as he expected. He came out with a handful of what looked no more threatening than black marbles maybe the size of a quarter in diameter. He knew the shooting wouldn't start until he was dead center in the street, not until Carroll was safely back inside the town hall. With that point fast approaching, Blaine opened his hand and tossed the marbles forward, the motion probably not even registering with those sighting him in their crosshairs.

Except they weren't marbles at all. And, as soon as Blaine released them, metallic wings sprouted from both sides of each and they flew off, in all directions at once.

Captain Seven's bug bombs, identical to the one Blaine had seen tested back in Sunnyside Yard, sped through the air like crazed bumblebees, working even better than advertised in utilizing their artificial intelligence technology to speed toward the positions currently held by Carroll's shooters. Before those men could register anything amiss, the bug bombs pierced the windows. Honing in on targets their software had claimed and zeroed.

And then the blasts started, one after another, melding into one seamless, explosive stream, almost surreal in its impact and results. McCracken had seen what mines could do in the battlefield and what IEDs could do on roadsides.

But neither of those was anything compared to this.

The screams, the ones that had time to come anyway, didn't last very long and the blood, bone matter, and body parts bursting through the glass was like nothing he'd ever seen before. Filling the air and showering down through the smoke that hid them for a time. The bitter, coppery stench of blood claimed Main Street's air, Americana gone to hell. And, yet strangely, whatever Captain Seven had packed into his tiny killing machines seemed to have no blast residue odor at all. Blaine smelled only burned wood and scorched steel, realized his own ears were rippling toward momentary deafness from the percussions, even as he shoved Andrew's wheelchair across the square, shielding the boy as best he could.

McCracken managed to scoop up an assault rifle coughed from a window amid chunks of its former wielder without missing a step. He recorded the fact that the fifteen bug bombs he'd unleashed had all done their damage short of the town hall, meaning Carroll and three of his men remained to be dealt with.

Blaine crashed through a door leading into what had once been an apothecary shop recreated from times long past, dragging Andrew's wheelchair inside behind him. The boy had still not stirred, but his eyes sought McCracken's out, full of shock and terror. He smoothed Andrew's hair, laying a hand as tenderly as he could manage on his shoulder.

"I'm a friend of your father's," he said.

CHAPTER 73

Port of Gibraltar

"The *Dei Gratia*," Zarrin finished.

Fernán Andrade poured each of them a glass of port wine from a crystal carafe. "Got this all figured out, have you? More of the crazy talk I've been hearing all my life now."

"I don't think so."

The office he had kept after being relieved of service as captain of the port offered a near-total view of the facility. The sun streamed through the windows facing the sea, reflecting off Andrade's baby-like face, which looked as though it had been pumped with air.

"You can't buy this in any store in the world," Andrade proclaimed proudly, as he tilted the glass to his lips and savored a sip. "It's made truly special by the addition of Aragonez, or Tinta Roriz, from northern Portugal."

Zarrin joined him. Alcohol intensified the symptoms of her Parkinson's, particularly in the hands, and didn't mix well with her medications, so she seldom drank at all. But she needed to make an exception today. The wine tasted sweet and fruity, too sweet at first, until her pallet adjusted and she found herself longing for her next sip.

"You like it," beamed Andrade. "I can tell. It's of the Alentejo vintage, produced from thick, dark-skinned berries."

Zarrin took another zip.

Andrade raised his glass in the semblance of a toast. "To the *Dei Gratia* and whatever fool's errand that brought you here."

"Captain Briggs of the *Mary Celeste* abandoned ship because he thought he was carrying something deadly in his cargo holds, something that was leaking from a few of the barrels that had ruptured."

"Did he now?"

"He was trying to save his crew from something that wasn't there."

"You're saying the ship wasn't carrying seventeen hundred barrels of alcohol?"

"No, that's exactly what she was carrying: as a decoy, to draw attention away from the ship that really had a deadly cargo stocked in her holds."

"The *Dei Gratia*."

"Sailing from New York just a few days after the *Mary Celeste*."

"With a comparable number of barrels loaded with petroleum in her holds," Andrade nodded, as if impatient with her telling of the tale. "I've heard much of this before and so has the world."

"Neither you nor the world has heard everything."

"And what's that."

"It starts with the lost colony of Roanoke. . . ."

"That's quite a story," Andrade said, when Zarrin had finished, refilling his glass of port. "Another?" he said holding up the carafe.

She realized she'd nearly finished hers as well, checking her hands to find them still steady. "No more for me, thank you."

"I can't say I've ever heard anything like it, and I've heard just about everything. The *Mary Celeste* nothing more than a decoy? Some secret weapon carried in the hold of a sister ship?"

"And you don't believe a word of it."

Andrade smirked and started to pour another glass, then realized he'd already done so. "Well, there were rumors from around this time of the British being in league with Napoléon III to take the throne back in France. He may have had more friends in the Commonwealth than he had back home, and imagine the British salivating at the prospects of having a voice eminently friendly toward their interests running France."

"The problem is Napoléon III was sick, dying, by the time both the *Mary Celeste* and *Dei Gratia* set sail," Zarrin pointed out.

"Sick, yes, but he didn't know he was dying. And a man who'd lived his life with that name and so much power would never believe he could be felled by anything as mundane as illness. He would do anything necessary to regain his crown, and that includes this plan to use a legendary weapon to help his cause." Andrade clapped his hands. "Bravo. Congratulations are in order."

Zarrin felt her hands trembling, but when she looked down they were still. She ran her tongue around the inside of her mouth that seemed coated in chalk.

"For what?"

"Coming closer to the truth than anyone who's ever come to Gibraltar. You've done it, my good woman, solved the mystery. Unfortunately for you, that comes with a price, not a prize."

Andrade's words reached her only in splotches with brief gaps of emptiness between the syllables. It felt as if she was nodding off for one second, only to reawaken in the next before darkness claimed her altogether.

CHAPTER 74

Branson, Missouri

The only gunmen who remained would be holed up down Celebration City's Main Street inside the town hall. Andrew Ericson was under no danger from any of Carroll's other shooters— Captain Seven's bug bombs had seen to that. So Blaine need only concern himself with these final three gunmen and used the heavy smoke still drifting with the wind down Main Street for camouflage.

He drew no fire from inside the building at the edge of the square until the smoke cleared thirty feet away and pistol fire burned the air toward him. Difficult shots to manage under any conditions, much less on a moving target with the carnage left behind in McCracken's wake crystallizing in view through the dissipating smoke.

He neutralized their assault with three-shot bursts fired from the assault rifle he'd salvaged from the street strategically toward the first-floor door and second-story windows where it had originated. Then instinct took over, his experience in battle having imbued Blaine with almost a sixth sense for survival. He didn't think, didn't reason, didn't plan. Just moved into the flow, letting the moment guide him. No one survived this many, or even any, gunfights by thinking. Thinking meant delays and delays provided the space and time the shooters needed to right themselves and their aim. Thinking was for preparation and training, not battle.

Battle belonged to the moment.

McCracken crashed through the cracked open door from the side, assault rifle twisting on the gunman's exact position and hitting him with a quick burst that plastered the man to the wall and left him slumping down it. Along with thinking, emotion had vanished. These were men who were about to shamelessly kill a young boy, already party to untold harm done to the country. They were targets and nothing more, a means to an end.

And that end was Robert Carroll.

In that moment, McCracken was glad he had no bug bombs left. This was the way he wanted it, the way he did it the best. Up close and personal, as all wars from time immemorial ended one way or another. Boots on the ground. The surreal nature of a firefight when the senses of hearing and sight vanish behind a haze that grew impossible to describe as soon as it passed. Blaine felt that haze envelop him, entered it.

He rushed up the stairs, firing strategically to force motion and when it came he shot it down as if the bodies were no more than air to be superheated and pierced with rounds that were essentially miniature bombs themselves. Wreaking havoc with the body once they entered. He leaped over one with a stitch of gore carved in his midsection and then another with bloody holes up his spine, having taken the fire when he turned to run. McCracken surged to the only closed door along the hall, stopping short of twisting inside it.

Bursting through the open door immediately across the hall from it instead.

Robert Carroll managed to get off one harmless shot before McCracken knocked the pistol from his hand with the assault rifle's barrel and then rammed the stock just hard enough into his face to shatter his nose. A torrent of blood burst from both nostrils and the head of the Gap slammed backward against the wall, suspended there with knees bent.

"Fuck you, McCracken!" he wailed, both hands held to his face.

"That the best you can do?"

"You think you've won? You think this means anything?"

"What I think is you're part of a plot that's already killed a whole lot of innocent Americans. I think you got your hands on the kind of soldiers who use Afghanis and other civilians as target practice and painted bull's-eyes all over our own country. And I think the worst is yet to come."

Carroll slumped the rest of the way down the wall, eyeing McCracken hatefully and blowing thick wads of matted blood from his nose. "You're fighting for the wrong side. One day you'll wake up and realize things stopped being black and white a long time ago, back when dinosaurs like you still roamed the earth. It's gray out there now, and the sooner you realize that, the sooner you'll actually be able to able to do some good that lasts."

"There are a whole lot more than three shades to the world, Carroll."

"How many do you remember from Vietnam, son? How many did you assassinate in Operation Phoenix toward no end that mattered? How many others did you knock off since? Where'd that get you?"

"Here."

"Go to hell, McCracken."

"Not before you."

"It's called the Ozark Wildcat," McCracken said, straddling the wooden rails of Celebration City's wooden, retro roller coaster to which he'd just finished tying Robert Carroll on a straight-away that flattened out after the first drop. "Funny thing about coasters like this. They work almost entirely on gravity. Get the cars rolling and off they go, plenty of juice to get them this far anyway."

Carroll looked over Blaine's shoulder, as if expecting to see the cars cresting over the nearest rise. "I already told you I'm pulling the plug on this, son, already gave you the name of the asshole you need to visit. What else do you want?"

"You to get what you deserve."

"The great McCrackenballs doesn't kill helpless innocents."

"You're not helpless, Carroll, and you're anything but inno-cent. You went too far, crossed the proverbial line. You made your choice and you'll make the same one again down the road, given the chance I'm not going to give you."

Carroll's expression tightened in panic that quickly turned to resolve. "How am I supposed to clean up this mess if you leave me here to freeze, you son of a bitch?"

McCracken grinned down at him. "Oh, you won't freeze; I promise. And this mess is mine to clean up now."

There was just enough juice left in the backup batteries to get the cars still stacked at the Ozark Wildcat's starting line mov-ing. McCracken watched them fly down the first drop, picking up enough momentum to coast up the spiraling rise and then disappear over it, gathering speed as they hit the straight stretch on which he'd tied Robert Carroll.

Blaine was already heading for the apothecary shop where he'd left Andrew Ericson when he heard a single languishing scream followed by the thud of impact and crash of cars tumbling off the tracks.

CHAPTER 75

Costa del Sol, Spain

"Do you know where you are?"

Zarrin came awake to the sight of a bear-like mustachioed man looking down at her. His friendly grin showcased a single gold tooth that glistened in the airy room lit only by sunlight. One of man's eyes looked frozen, Zarrin figuring it must be made of glass.

"A vulnerable woman really must take better care of herself in a foreign country. Alas, even Gibraltar is not safe from cutthroats and heathens."

She was seated in a stiff wooden chair, hands bound by rope before her. Two other men, who looked like younger versions of the speaker, stood on either side of him, each with a cutdown double-barrel shotgun held nimbly, but unthreateningly, in hand. They were grinning too, wearing baggy pants that billowed outward at the thighs like britches better fit for another century. Their skin was dark, eyes more black than brown.

Gypsies, Zarrin realized. Her hands were still numb from the effects of whatever drug Fernán Andrade had given her back in the Port of Gibraltar. She busied herself with careful scrutiny of the logistics. The angle of the sun and depth of the breeze told her this place was well up on a hillside, the sounds of vehicles and activity indicating it to be a populated refuge, not an isolated compound.

"You are in Costa del Sol in the south of Spain. You will answer my questions or face pain at the hands of my sons who enjoy dispensing it far too much. Perhaps I have not raised them so well," the bear-like Gypsy smirked, looking from one of the younger men at his side to the other. "My name is Matias Bajão. In times long past, I would be called King of the Gypsies. Tell me how you came to know so much about the *Mary Celeste* and the *Dei Gratia*."

"You mean that the *Dei Gratia* was carrying the actual cargo the British were selling to Napoléon III. My theory's right, isn't it?"

Bajão grinned. "Why else would you be here? Andrade lacks my curiosity, turned you over to me simply so I could dispose of you."

"So I talk and *then* you dispose of me?"

"I haven't decided yet. I don't believe you came by all this information by yourself, which means others are involved, others who will follow you here. I'd like to know what I'm facing."

"What's your interest in all this, Matias?"

"You seem so calm."

"I'm not scared."

"You should be. You're facing a man who holds your fate in his hands."

"Then humor me. Tell me how a Gypsy gets caught up in one of the great historical mysteries of all time."

Bajão leaned forward in his chair, tilting his head as if to see Zarrin differently, perhaps growing more suspicious of her. But then he simply smiled, as if this was a game he enjoyed playing.

"Back in the nineteenth century, Gypsies were associated with any number of pirate networks that spanned the globe, operating mostly in docks and harbors since that was where the best bounty inevitably passed through. That network, scattered through the world's greatest ports, learned that something of great value was coming into the Port of New York, in November of 1872, something contained in cast wooden barrels, for transport to Europe. Originally they were to be loaded onto the *Mary Celeste*, but our people learned she was just a decoy and they were actually to be loaded into the holds of a sister ship, the *Dei Gratia*."

"Headed for Portugal where Gypsies would be waiting," Zarrin assumed. "But then something changed, didn't it? The *Mary Celeste*'s crew abandoning her put a big crimp in the plans of your ancestors. The *Dei Gratia* sailing into Gibraltar instead of Portugal with her in tow, taking all that attention."

"You're right. It set my ancestors scrambling, but they were still able to off-load the barrels from the ship while the inquiry took place over the course of six or seven days. The *Dei Gratia* crew was paid off, including the mate and the captain."

"They thought they were selling you petroleum."

"Of course they did. Valuable enough in its own right not to arouse their suspicions. They had no idea what their ship was really carrying. The hoax that another ship, the *Mary Celeste*, was transporting the barrels was insisted upon by Napoléon III himself. He trusted no one, including the Brits who'd joined in the conspiracy with him."

"And when did your ancestors realize the truth?" Zarrin asked him. "When did they realize those barrels carried something deadly and dangerous?"

Bajão leaned backwards, stiffening as he stole a glance at his two sons. "It would seem I've underestimated you."

"I'm after those barrels, Matias," Zarrin said, her hands quivering slightly but otherwise fully functional again. "You don't have to die today and neither do your sons."

The big Gypsy's face straightened into stone, then broke out into laughter. He was quickly joined by his sons, the three of them going red-faced.

"What he told me about you doesn't do you justice," Bajão said.

"What who told you?"

"Me," announced Colonel Kosh, stepping through a beaded curtain from the next room.

CHAPTER 76

Fairfax, Virginia

Alvin Turwell was staring out the windows of his house, moving from one to another, trying to spot the guards posted in his yard. His calls to Robert Carroll were going straight to voice mail, Jeremiah Rule was missing, and all he could do was try and figure out how to salvage something from a tactical plan years in the making as he parted a drape to peer outward.

"Four men," a voice said, suddenly behind him.

Turwell swung, going for the pistol he realized he'd left on the foyer table.

"A bit under the weather tonight, it seems," Blaine McCracken continued. "Johnny Wareagle sent them home early."

"McCracken . . ."

Blaine had taken Andrew Ericson to CenterPointe Hospital for observation, remaining there until operatives sent by H. J. Belgrade arrived to spell him. "I see my reputation proceeds me. Robert Carroll sends his regards, by the way. Called you an asshole."

"He said that?"

"Actually, I think he said '*fucking* asshole.' Apparently, he blames you for me ending his career in public service."

"I told him targeting that kid was a bad idea."

"Too bad he didn't listen. I'm guessing they've found his body by now. Poor guy got himself run over by a roller coaster."

"You . . ."

"I did what I had to do, Colonel, just like I'm doing now. See, Carroll didn't know where the barrels containing the White Death are hidden. You do."

"White Death?"

"What the Indians called the contents of those barrels you've got stashed away somewhere."

Turwell stood there motionless, not even seeming to breathe.

"It's over," McCracken continued. "Your term as the mayor of Whacko City has expired."

Turwell shook his head. "I expected more of you, McCracken."

"Really? And why's that?"

"Because unlike the rest of these fools, you're a soldier. Just like me."

"I'm a soldier. Nothing like you."

"You're on the wrong side of this."

McCracken grinned. "Your friend Robert Carroll said pretty much the same thing before I tied him to the tracks." He took a step forward, close enough to Turwell now to catch the faint smell of perspiration mixing with talcum powder. "You're going to take me to the White Death, Colonel. We're leaving now."

"You know what I'm doing is right and you're afraid to admit it."

"Right, keep telling yourself that. I've spent my life fighting people like you, only in foreign countries. What scares me the most is that you've come home to roost. And if there are more out there, like you say, I'll find them too."

"You are a piece of work, McCracken truly a piece of work. You talk like you're invincible, indestructible, but we've all got a clock running on us, and yours is going to run out just like everyone else's."

"Got it all figured out, don't you? Figure you know what's best for everyone else, that anyone who disagrees with you is wrong. That's called fanaticism."

"It used to be called leadership. The courage to do the difficult thing."

"You mean courage as in ordering a bunch of kids to their deaths in Afghanistan?" McCracken felt heat building under his skin, as if his blood was simmering to a boil. "Tell me something, Colonel. Where were you when those boys died? Leading them in an advancing position or hanging back where it was safe?"

Turwell bristled. "How many did you kill in Vietnam, McCracken?"

"None of my own. I don't know what's scarier: the fact people actually believe you or that you believe the bullshit you spout yourself. You talk like you're the only one who knows what's best for the country, the only one willing to make the hard choices that really aren't so hard at all because they end up serving your own ends. Interesting how the threats used to come from outside the country, but now they seem to come just as much from the inside."

Turwell just shook his head, looking more annoyed and disappointed than angry. "You should really listen to yourself, McCracken."

"And what would I hear?"

"Someone who has bought into all of the bullshit, hook, line, and sinker. You've been hung out to dry more times than last week's laundry and you still keep coming back for more. Well, there are millions out there like me who are done with all that. We see where this country's going, and we intend to change that path whatever it takes."

"And, what, that would be the ten-or-so percent of the country who believe in armed insurrection? We already fought this thing called the Civil War, Colonel. That was supposed to settle things on that note, but the people you speak for would rather fight it again. Or maybe they never stopped fighting it." McCracken studied Turwell closer, as if seeing him for the first time. "You know, my enemies used to make up a pretty exclusive club. Now anyone with a laptop and an Internet connection can try to start World War III."

A smirk bubbled over on Alvin Turwell's expression. "And you think you can get all of us?"

"There's only one more that matters right now, and he's my next stop. After you've taken me to those barrels of the White Death, Colonel."

CHAPTER 77

Costa del Sol, Spain

Kosh stepped all the way into the room, accompanied by the two hulking bodyguards Zarrin recalled from her dressing room at the Haliç Center in Istanbul. "It would seem we travel in the same circles," he grinned.

And then she realized. "You came for the barrels, not me."

"We've been hiding them this long because no one was willing to match our price," said Matias Bajão. "Your friend here changed that."

"What choice did I have?" Kosh added. "After Blaine McCracken wiped out our nuclear enrichment facility. You remember Blaine McCracken, don't you? The man I hired you to kill but who you've now, apparently, joined forces with?" He shook his round, bowling bowl–like head. "Full of surprises, aren't you, Zarrin? Like letting yourself be drugged so you'd be taken here. Tell me, have you already managed to get the rope free?"

Zarrin raised her hands still bound by the rope. "But the joke's on you, Colonel," she said to him, as Kosh's two guards came up on either side of her with guns drawn, close but not too close. "Because the barrels are gone from wherever these Gypsies hid them."

"My sons checked on the barrels just last month," Bajão insisted, "as they check on them every month. A responsibility passed down through the ages since we took possession of them in 1872."

"You're wrong, Matias." Zarrin looked back at Kosh. "And you came here for nothing."

He smiled at her with, his tobacco-stained teeth looking even darker in the room's thin light. "But I found you, didn't I?"

CHAPTER 78

West Virginia

The helicopter arranged by H. J. Belgrade got them as close to the secret mountain storage facility as possible, a big SUV with one of Belgrade's former right-hand men behind the wheel to take McCracken and Turwell the rest of the way.

"I'm not doing this for me," Turwell explained, breaking the silence he'd committed himself to for the bulk of the journey. "I'm doing it because of Rule. He betrayed me. He can open his tenth circle of Hell on somebody else's dime."

"Wait a minute, you're telling me Rule knew about the barrels, what they can do?"

"He made me take him here a few days ago. Insisted on seeing them for himself."

McCracken had heard of secret storage facilities like this one contained in the Allegheny Mountains, but had never actually been inside one until today. The endless hallways set beyond big titanium bay doors were dimly lit and musty, filled with an odor of stale air and disuse. The walls and floor felt chalky and the air, when the thin light caught it right, swirled with dust. Blaine felt that dust paint his clothes and face with a layer of grit that caught in his lungs as well, making him want to cough.

They reached the massive double-bay doors beyond which lay the chamber where the barrels had been stored. As Turwell approached the keypad, McCracken pictured the convoy of trucks it must have taken to haul all seventeen hundred barrels up the winding mountain roads where they had ultimately been off-loaded and stacked here. He imagined the deadly contents had been transferred into more secure storage barrels first for reasons of safety and preservation. Any way you looked at it, a daunting task requiring lots of men and equipment, including forklifts and bucket loaders.

Turwell punched in the code, looking back at McCracken as if he had something to say before hitting the last number. But then he simply sneered and pressed it slowly. A dull hum sounded, and the mechanical double-bay doors began to slide open.

"No," muttered Turwell, as he looked inside.

CHAPTER 79

Blountstown, Florida

"You won't be sorry for this," the Reverend Jeremiah Rule said to Boyd Fowler over the phone. "The end of this road holds great things for you and your boy."

Fowler was on that road now squeezed behind the wheel of one of the trucks owned by another member of the Rock Machine. That truck was part of a Virginia-based fleet normally used for moving all manner of contraband in the form of drugs, cigarettes, alcohol, or weapons, a fleet appropriated today for a much holier purpose.

"I'm coming into Washington now and the others aren't far behind. I'm just happy to be of service to God and you, Reverend," Fowler said, hands tightening on the wheel. "Feels a bit strange to be doing His work, though. Then again, like they say, the Lord does work in mysterious ways."

"He does indeed," grinned Rule.

"When you gonna join us up here?"

"I'll be leaving to meet up with you shortly. Just one last thing I need to finish."

The reverend had shown up excited and near breathless at Boyd Fowler's trailer just before dawn, having driven straight through from North Carolina.

"You okay, Reverend? Something wrong?"

Rule had forgotten how dirty he was, his clothes grubby and face streaked with grime. "I need your help, Boyd."

"Anything, Reverend, just name it."

"We need to get some men together. And trucks."

"Trucks?"

"Big ones. To carry the weight of the future."

Rule had given Fowler precise directions and instructions, the big man more than capable of handling the rest on his own while the reverend remained behind to complete one final task before joining him in Washington. From what he'd been told, the loading process had been finished just after dawn, all based on a vision that had come to Jeremiah Rule back on the grounds of Black House in North Carolina. Asking the old van for more speed than it could give him, the ghost of the boy he'd killed all those years ago next to him the whole time.

"I must confess something," Rule told the ghost, when they crossed into Blountstown.

"It's good for the soul."

"I . . . I don't remember your name."

"It's Jimmy."

"Jimmy," Rule repeated.

"James, actually. Named after my father and his before him."

"And how did you come to reside in Black House?"

"My parents gave me up to the state, Reverend. Said with six other kids they couldn't afford me no more. Promised me

they'd come back someday and take me home. Guess they never got the chance."

"I'm sorry, son."

"Don't fret on it, Reverend. They was never coming back anyway. I hadn't even heard from them for six months before that night you made me hang from the steam pipe, so maybe you ended up just sparing me a whole lot of pain." The ghost paused, seeming to fade out in that brief instant to reveal the faded and tattered car seat beneath him. *"I know why you did it."*

Rule tried to see the ghost more clearly and swallowed hard.

"Because somebody did the same thing to you. I saw it in your face then and I feel it inside you now. So where we going?"

Jeremiah Rule pushed the rancid stench that filled the van from his consciousness. The mud that had dried into paste on his hands seemed to glue them to the wheel. It was everywhere now, having seeped into the driver's seat where it had dried into a stench-riddled film.

"I'm gonna take you home, son," he told the ghost. "And then I'm gonna open the tenth circle of Hell."

CHAPTER 80

West Virginia

"A motorcycle gang?" McCracken raised, after Turwell had laid it all out for him.

"Reverend Rule's personal army of God," the colonel said.

Before them, the storage hold was empty. The tracks of the loaders that had removed the barrels and loaded them on to what must have been a convoy of trucks were evident, along with a number of large footprints left in the dust.

"The man has gone totally around the bend," Turwell continued.

"Territory you know all too well. What was the target, Colonel? What were you intending to hit with the White Death?"

"Looks like we're all fucked, doesn't it?" Turwell smirked, instead of responding. "Damn shame too, since this country was on a path to a fresh start, a whole new beginning, after tonight."

"Tonight?" Blaine asked, suddenly chilled by more than just the air-conditioning.

"Think about it, McCracken."

"Oh shit," Blaine said, realizing. "The president's State of the Union address."

"Our plan was to blow up the private Capitol subway with the barrels loaded on board," Turwell said, almost boasting as he walked ahead of McCracken into the storage chamber, gazing about in almost nostalgic fashion. His voice echoed amid the empty confines. "Rupture the walls and flood the tunnel, exposing it to the contents of the barrels halfway into the president's speech. But all the praying in the world won't help Rule pull that off."

"You a man of prayer yourself?" McCracken asked, backing up until he was flush with the entrance to the chamber.

"What's the difference?"

"Because of you're going to have plenty of time for it now," Blaine told him, stepping back into the corridor. "Rest in peace, Colonel."

And he hit the button to seal the chamber behind him.

The sound of Turwell's banging on the heavy doors grew fainter before dissipating altogether by the time McCracken got H. J. Belgrade on the phone just short of the exit.

"You say a motorcycle gang, son?" he asked before Blaine had finished.

"I did. They're part of a gang called the Rock Machine out of Canada where they're known for drugs and not much more. Down here they're known for something else."

"Got a feeling I'm not gonna like this."

"No, you're not. Several members of that biker gang the good reverend has enlisted spent time in federal prison for plotting to blow up the United States Capitol Building."

"And now they've got the White Death . . ."

"But this all still ends once Jeremiah Rule is out of the picture. It's ten a.m. The Indian and I will try to have him in chains by lunchtime."

"Then there's one more thing you need to know," Belgrade said. "That satellite recon I ordered for you turned up something underneath the Reverend Rule's house."

CHAPTER 81

Gibraltar

"This way," Bajão said, leading the group forward along the thin path so damp that it felt as slick as ice.

Zarrin followed next, flanked on either side by Kosh's bodyguards, her hands still bound before her. The colonel himself struggled to keep pace. She could hear the huffing of his breath, the rustling of his feet each time he almost lost his footing just ahead of Bajão's sons, who brought up the rear with shotguns slung by straps behind their shoulders.

"We're almost there," the Gypsy continued, and Zarrin heard Kosh sigh with relief.

The imposing shape of the Rock of Gibraltar was as impressive today as it had always been. Over four hundred feet tall at its highest point, the jaggedly shaped structure formed a peninsula that jutted out into the strait that bore its name, angling for the southern tip of Spain. Still a prime tourist attraction, the rock's limestone structure helped to account for the nearly 150 caves that had formed naturally over time. Those which had openings to the outside world would have made for perfect shelters, or storage holds, in times long past.

Or maybe not so long, as it turned out.

The group moved slowly, the fog, mist, and chill making traverse of the rock so precarious a single misstep could lead to severe accident or death.

"You're wrong, you know," Bajão said, turning suddenly toward Zarrin. "And I look forward to proving it when you see the barrels are still where they have been for well over a century."

"Tell me something, Bajão. Why did your people hold onto the barrels for so long?" Zarrin couldn't help but ask.

"Because British authorities scoured Gibraltar in search of them. We knew the Brits were up to something but never imagined it would reach the level it did. Trying to sell the barrels as common merchandise, even ordnance, would have led to our destruction, having drawn the wrath of an entire government. We'd be hunted down, jailed, or more likely executed on the spot. So we hid the barrels here, camouflaged and sealed the entrance to the cave, all the evidence of them removed from the world. We came back regularly to transfer their contents into fresh barrels, not as often once steel ones replaced the wooden variety around World War II." Bajão seemed to spot something ahead in the sweep of Zarrin's flashlight. "The cave's right there, in that northern face of the rock."

He led the way on again, while continuing to speak. "My sons have taken on the task of checking the cave once a month since they were teenagers, just as my father ceded the duty to me. The limestone in these parts did a remarkable job of preserving even the wooden barrels, except for those lost to time, the contents evaporating harmlessly I imagine." Bajão looked toward Kosh, who'd drawn even with the group. "You're going to get your money's worth, Colonel."

Kosh's eyes strayed toward Zarrin. "I always do."

Bajão moved his beefy hands to a rock pile and hoisted the entire connected stack aside, clearing the entrance to the cave. Kosh shoved his way past him, sweeping his flashlight about.

"Is this some kind of joke, Gypsy?"

Bajão followed the colonel's gaze about the empty, dusty darkness within.

Zarrin remained behind them, not needing to see. "I warned you, Matias."

Bajão's face reddened as he twisted his gaze for his sons. "You lied to me! *Lied!*" He lurched forward across the rock and slapped one of his sons across the face. "How long have the barrels been missing, how long?"

"Four months," the son answered, cowering.

"Don't blame them, Matias," said Zarrin, "blame Fernán Andrade."

"Andrade?"

"He's the only other man who knew where the barrels were hidden. He sold you out to the Americans who learned of their existence and followed their trail just as I did, likely just like you did, Colonel."

Exhaustion mixed with disappointment on Kosh's expression, making it look as if the air had been sucked out of his round face. "And what of us, Zarrin, you and me?"

"We can both walk away from this and live, Colonel."

"No, we can't."

"Too bad," Zarrin said, sweeping her bound hands, with fingers interlaced, sideways and up.

The blow took his hulking bodyguard on her right under the chin. Spun him around and exposed the pistol wedged into his belt. Needing their hands to negotiate the precarious climb here had precluded the men from having their weapons drawn and ready, and now that would cost them.

Zarrin stripped the pistol from the stunned man's belt, even as Kosh's other bodyguard was drawing his.

"Shoot her!" Kosh blared. "Kill her!"

And the second man started firing.

CHAPTER 82

Gibraltar

Zarrin leaped off the narrow path into a crevice below, bending at the knees to cushion the impact on the uneven footing. The thick mist welcomed her, engulfed her. Zarrin crouched in the moment before impact, feeling her left ankle turn when she hit a jagged patch of rock. Her right leg took most of her weight, nearly buckling, which would have spilled her off down a much deeper slope. Gun held in her clasped hands, she managed to hold her balance, wavering briefly but regaining all her footing in time to slam her shoulders against the cold face ahead of the gunshots.

They poured down in a constant rain briefly, pistol shots alternating with the din of echoing blasts from the shotguns of Bajão's sons. The latter sprayed flecks and shards of the famed rock into Zarrin, the feeling that of being stuck with pins alternating with the harsher sting of what felt like shrapnel fragments unleashed by a blast. They no doubt expected her to fire back,

JON LAND

but she didn't, knowing they couldn't see her from the ridge and not wanting to betray her own position.

"Maybe she's dead," Zarrin heard one of Kosh's men say in Farsi.

"It's not deep enough," Kosh replied. "Go down there. Bring her back," he followed in Spanish, addressing Bajão's sons.

They grunted their disapproval, but their father ordered them on. And Zarrin heard the clatter of their steps circling slightly back to descend after her.

The enemy separated into two camps now, her odds changed considerably for the better. Zarrin held the pistol between her teeth and used her bound hands to claw against the rock face on the side of the crevice to climb upward. Again using the fog, the thick rolling mist washed in from the sea to collect in thick pockets across the rock. She stayed within it, following its course when it stole sight of what lay before her, knowing it collected thickest at the lowermost points. Follow it and she'd never lose track of the jutting peaks, narrow ridges, and crisscrossing paths that made up the Rock of Gibraltar.

Zarrin heard a heavy thud, followed by a gasp and the clang of metal against rock, as one of Bajão's sons slipped and fell with his shotgun separated from him in the process. Swearing followed, the two brothers berating each other in a language she didn't recognize.

Zarrin would save them for last.

Instinct dictated her next move, as she entered the fog and the flow, became one with the precarious, jagged sprawl of the Rock of Gibraltar the same way she melded with the music of whatever concerto she might be performing. That instinct brought her through the fog in a loop, doubling back toward the ridge leading to the cave and finding herself on an even narrower path that swept around it the long way.

Zarrin felt her heels flirting with the air as she followed that path, face and torso pressed against the rock face. The mist continued to swirl about her, its icelike coating left everywhere in its wake. This side of the peak offered no barrier to the wind lifting off the sea either. It slammed into Zarrin, seeming to blow in all directions at the same time as it whistled across the jagged rock.

She knew she was drawing close when she heard voices, the words muffled. She ended up above the cave opening, looking down on Bajão calling to his sons while Kosh and his men looked on, their backs to her. Zarrin changed the intent of her plan then and there, taking the pistol from her mouth in her bound hands and righting it downward. But she slipped on a piece of sheer rock at the last moment, first tumbled and then slid the rest of the way to the same ridge to which Bajão had brought them.

Holding fast to the pistol the whole time so, though jarred, she was still able to sight and fire on Kosh's two men before her slide had come to a halt. They barely had time to turn, her bullets finding them in the very moment their eyes found her. She kept firing until the shots punched them backwards over the side where they disappeared into the mist.

"Tell your sons to stay where they are, Bajão, or they die too."

Too late. Bajão's sons had already returned to the ridge along an easier slope to manage. They opened up with their shotguns, the rounds echoing in the cold night air, too far from Zarrin to manage anything but a lucky shot. She ignored the spray of dust and chipped rock and rotated her fire between them, her bullets carving a path through the mist. Both brothers went down, vanishing into the mist as well.

"*Noooooooooo!*" Bajão cried out, losing his footing and cracking his skull on the protruding edge of the rock as he started to go after them.

Zarrin swung back toward Kosh, the tiny man with the

basketball-shaped head holding a pistol salvaged from one of his dead bodyguards in a trembling hand.

"You've got one shot left!" he yelled to her. "I counted!"

"One's all I need, Colonel. Drop your gun and you get to live."

Kosh seemed to be thinking of doing just that, then fired instead.

And missed.

Zarrin fired.

CHAPTER 83

Blountstown, Florida

McCracken and Wareagle went straight to Jeremiah's Rule property from West Virginia. But the reverend was nowhere to be found. None of his security was about and a hand-scrawled sign duct-taped to the front door of his church read SERVICES CANCELLED.

His boxy, modular home looked painted onto the scene, surrounded by hastily installed shrubs, fruit trees, and flower gardens planted within fresh mulch that had dried to the texture of clay from lack of irrigation. From this angle, Blaine saw that the windows looked slanted, as if the land had not been properly leveled prior to the house being pieced together.

"Belgrade told me there's something underneath it, Indian."

"Death lives down there, Blainey," Wareagle said stiffening. "And something else, too."

McCracken and Wareagle broke into the house from the back, finding nothing of interest initially.

"Over here, Blainey," Wareagle called from an area of the floor where he'd found a hatchway concealed beneath a throw carpet.

McCracken checked the hatch carefully for booby traps before lifting it open to reveal a ladder. He descended into the basement, more like a root cellar, that Belgrade's satellite reconnaissance had turned up, following the path of illumination shone by Wareagle's flashlight.

The stench assaulted him just a few rungs down. He passed it off initially as must, mold, and ground spoiled by the construction atop it. But the smell worsened, growing more acrid by the time he reached the bottom to sweep his own flashlight about.

The basement, which looked as if had been dug out after the house had been built, was circular and small, no more than thirty feet in diameter. The walls were formed of dark earth, the ceiling held up by hastily and unevenly placed wooden beams. He followed the stench to the far earthen wall before which what looked like a small stage had been erected.

Drawing closer, McCracken saw it was a makeshift church altar complete with a plywood cross nailed together hastily and standing crooked. The dried gray bones of a body, a corpse pulled from a violated grave, rested upon the stage-like altar, perfectly reassembled with all pieces intact. All that was missing was the flesh and blood. Its size suggested a child, ten or eleven probably, but the remains accounted for only a small measure of the stench.

Because a second set of mud-riddled bones, considerably more decayed than the first, had been placed at the foot of the plywood altar. The bones looked to have been pried haphazardly from the earth and reassembled in the same fashion as the first, only with some pieces missing in this case. Those bones, small and likely belonging to a smaller and younger child, rested on a cheap swatch of moldy carpet that reminded Blaine of the kind found in aged cars. The carpet was sodden with cool moist earth, indicating this older set of bones had been brought here very recently, almost surely within the past day.

He and Johnny must've just missed finding Rule on the premises before he fled.

"Indian," he called up to Wareagle.

And that's when he felt them coming, attacking from everywhere at once. Stench-riddled creatures raking at him with talons, jaws snapping below eyes wide with madness.

CHAPTER 84

Blountstown, Florida

Women! McCracken realized, as he fought them off. Not creatures or monsters at all. Desperate, pleading for help in barely audible rasps and cries, hands outstretched to latch onto him so he might carry them from their prison.

Half naked, reeking of their own waste, their eyes wild and terrified. He pushed them aside, realizing even in that terrible moment they must be Rule's prisoners, held down here as further testament to his madness.

Six of them, Blaine counted, six . . .

The light from the flashlight alone forced one off him with filthy hands raised to shield her eyes. Blaine twisted it from her to the others, using its spill to hold the women back.

"Please," he said, trying to sound calm. "Let me help you. I'm here to help you."

McCracken couldn't imagine how long they'd been down here shrouded in darkness; varying durations almost surely, all of them long enough to turn the sudden wash of illumination into a weapon for the women's light-deprived eyes. And he caught splotchy still images in the flashlight's reach, so horrifying that he wondered if they were tricks or illusions of his own mind.

One woman was missing a hand.

The empty eye socket of another was crusted over.

A third had dark blood oozing from her mouth. She opened it to scream and McCracken saw her tongue was gone.

He backed up toward the ladder, making sure he'd missed none in his count. An anonymous call would alert the proper authorities to the Reverend Jeremiah Rule's personal chamber of horrors, Blaine thought as his flashlight froze on one last sight that stole a heartbeat and froze his breath.

He climbed faster than he'd ever climbed before, Wareagle helping to pull him up through the hatch and then sealing it quick.

"How bad, Blainey?"

"Worse, Indian," McCracken said, struggling to steady his breathing, "worse than we ever imagined."

PART FIVE:
THE TENTH CIRCLE

CHAPTER 85

Washington, DC

"I'm in the air now," Zarrin told McCracken, speaking almost too softly to hear. "Talking to you from the lavatory."

McCracken and Wareagle had administered basic first aid to Rule's female prisoners prior to leaving his property. They'd suffered horribly at his hand, their wounds just one indication of his sadistic madness. Blaine and Johnny had no choice but to leave the women in the basement after bringing down water and placing the flashlights at strategic points to keep the darkness from consuming them again. They departed only after placing an anonymous call to 9-1-1 to get rescue personnel to the house.

"The Indian and I are walking across the grounds of the Armed Forces Retirement place to meet up with my old friend H. J. Belgrade again," McCracken told Zarrin.

"Another old friend of yours."

"Only kind I've got. Should be able to report this whole thing is buttoned up, after we've spoken to him."

"Are they going to cancel the speech?"

"That's the hope, but short of that a full-scale roundup of the Rock Machine motorcycle gang should do the trick. Them and the Reverend Jeremiah Rule."

"Be careful, McCracken. The man's insane, and he's got the White Death now."

"Belgrade's also arranging for a dragnet for the whole region in search of the barrels."

"All this from a retirement home?"

"Nobody ever retires in this business. You know that."

They approached the figure of H. J. Belgrade feeding invisible pigeons again from his bag of bread crumbs, his eyes aimed downward, focused intently with a smile on the birds that weren't there.

"Very convincing, H. J.," McCracken greeted. "Almost had me fooled."

Belgrade didn't look up.

"It's us," McCracken continued.

Belgrade finally regarded them, breaking out into a wider grin. "You come to sing with me?"

"No need, Hank. There's no one else watching."

"It gets lonely here sometimes. No one to sing with. But now you're here, two friends to sing with me." His eyes met McCracken's, nothing in them but emptiness. "Come on, let's start." Then, tossing more bread crumbs in rhythm with the tune, he started. *"The wheels on the bus go round and round, round and round, round and round. The wheels on the bus go round and round, all through the town."*

"Hank?"

Belgrade's gaze stayed downward, seeming to forget Blaine and Johnny were even there. *"The wipers on the bus go* Swish,

swish, swish. Swish, swish, swish. Swish, swish, swish. *The wipers on the bus go* Swish, swish, swish *all through the town.*"

"Oh shit," said McCracken, texting Zarrin.

She called him back from the airplane lavatory again.

"I won't ask."

"Don't bother. We're on our own."

"How many in the opposition?"

"We've got to figure this motorcycle gang numbers at least a couple dozen. I've got Captain Seven checking their backgrounds, but I'm guessing plenty will have military experience, demolitions and explosives included. They already tried this once, Zarrin, so motivation won't be an issue. And Rule knows everything he needs to know about the White Death."

"Not good."

"That was my first thought too."

"What was your second?"

"We could use some more guns."

"What about all those old friends of yours?"

"I could use some new ones, Zarrin."

"Tall order right now."

"Maybe not. Call our mutual friend Colonel al-Asi," McCracken told her. "Remind him that he owes me a favor."

CHAPTER 86

Washington, DC

"You call this a motorcycle gang?" Captain Seven said, speaking into his computer through which he'd answered McCracken's call. "More like Anarchists Anonymous. Man, this bunch could use the calming influence of some medical weed in one big way."

"How bad, Captain?"

"Well, sixteen of the original twenty-eight went to federal prison on domestic terrorism and treason charges. Ended up getting released because the Feds messed up the test that connected them to the explosives. Your tax dollars at work, Mac-Nuts."

"Did you say *twenty-eight*?"

"More than five times that number are active in their drug enterprises on the East Coast so you can throw them into the mix too. But it's the composition of the original twenty-eight that'll really make your day. Six marines, five light infantry, seven special ops, and five former army reservists. All with active service and almost all well known among militia, separatist, or insurrection-based movements. Oh, and throw in some white supremacists just for good measure."

"The crazies have been recruiting heavily from ex-military for years now."

"By all accounts, nobody needed to recruit these guys. They *are* the crazies, MacNuts."

"Comforting thought. Where can we find them?"

"With a psychic or maybe a Ouija board. As of maybe twenty-four hours ago, all of them dropped off the grid. I'm checking into the additional members in their ranks now, but you can look forward to having these two dozen or so to deal with for starters."

"Thanks, Captain," McCracken told him, "you made my day."

"I haven't even finished my first bowl yet you've kept me so busy. I'm gonna take a bud break and get back at it."

"I want to hear as soon as you find anything else that may help the cause."

"You'll be the first to know."

"These guys have the means to drive a wrecking ball through the heart of this country, and there's not a damn person left in Washington we can call for help. Find me something actionable, Captain, something I can use to stop them before the president steps up to the podium to give his State of the Union speech tonight."

"Anything else, MacNuts?"

"Yeah. Jeremiah Rule's phone number."

CHAPTER 87

Washington, DC

Jeremiah Rule stood on the shore of the McMillan Reservoir, smelling the air and enjoying the quiet. He kept to the shadows cast by the nearby trees just a block away from the Bryant Street Pumping Station that was responsible for feeding Washington with a vast portion of its water supply. The reservoir bordered the campus of Howard University to the west and the rolling fields adjacent to McMillan Drive to the east, casting it as a pseudo-oasis amid the more cluttered swatch of government buildings a mere mile or so away.

A great calm had fallen over him since he'd arrived in Washington less than an hour before, growing greater with each passing moment as time ticked down to the remaking of a nation that needed to learn from death and hopelessness as he had learned. It was a blessed mission for which he'd been chosen, Rule realizing with vast satisfaction his entire life, the good and the bad, had been leading up to this moment.

I have never lost faith in you, Rule said in his head. *Through all the trials and tribulations, I have persevered waiting for my true purpose to be revealed. I thank you, oh Lord, for casting those who served that purpose before me. I see your hand in that message, oh Lord, and know now that I take your word as my own and will strive to see the mission you have bequeathed to me succeed. It's all so clear at last, all the signs you have sent me, and I look forward to your next message with all my heart and soul.*

Rule's phone rang, startling him.

CHAPTER 88

Washington, DC

"Bless me, Father, for I have sinned," Blaine McCracken greeted. "It's been a really long time, really long, since my last confession."

"How'd you get this number, friend?"

"Don't you want to hear my confession, Father?"

"It's *Reverend* and you still haven't answered my question."

"I've killed a lot of men in my time, but I have nothing to confess in that regard because they were all bad men and many of them were trying to do likewise to me. But I'd like to confess I'm about to kill again."

"Who is the unfortunate victim?"

"You, Reverend. Unless you come clean and do some confessing to me."

Rule wanted to end the call but something stopped him. The voice wasn't familiar at all, yet he felt he knew this man, that they were somehow acquainted.

"Do I know you, friend?"

"Not personally. But I know you well enough to know you intend to carry out the rest of Colonel Turwell's plan. You've got the barrels and your own private army now in the form of that motorcycle gang."

"*Who* are you?"

"The man who took Turwell and Robert Carroll off the map. And now I'm coming for you, unless you have a change of heart."

"I am doing the work of the Lord, friend. Only He can stop me."

"That what you call trying to destroy a country, getting millions and millions of innocent Muslims killed in the retaliatory strike that'll undoubtedly follow? But I'm guessing it wouldn't bother you one bit if the whole Muslim world got nuked."

"My entire purpose."

"Yours now instead of God's?"

"I do this to serve Him and His word. We are one in the same, a unified voice against sin."

"A true pillar of faith, aren't you?"

"I try, friend."

"Then what about the bones of those two boys you've got displayed in your basement, Reverend, not to mention the six women? You made them mutilate themselves, didn't you? The one who was missing a hand, what'd she do exactly to deserve that? Or the one who sliced off her own nipple? My guess is they'd done nothing to merit what you did to them, but it allowed you to keep them prisoners, didn't it? Made them too terrified and dependent to even think of escaping. That's why you didn't need to chain them. You chose victims who had nowhere else to go, who were desperate to belong to *anything*. Then you beat and raped them into submission."

"That is between me and God, friend," Rule said stiffly. "And you will be punished for your transgressions by powers far higher than me."

"One of the women's starting to show, Reverend," Blaine told him, revealing the last sight he'd glimpsed in Rule's basement. "Did you impregnate all of them, or just rape the others for fun?"

"Your words hold no meaning to me."

"But what do you think all your faithful, your flock, would think of you being a child murderer and a rapist?"

"We all have our choices. The women made theirs and I made mine."

"Now it's my turn and I choose to stop you in your tracks. Treat you with the same compassion you treated those women. So tell me, Reverend, was fathering their children your way of bringing children into the world to replace those boys you murdered?"

"Those deaths were part of His plan," Rule stammered, suddenly defensive.

"And was molesting them part of that plan too? Did you have divine permission to partake in that particular practice?"

"I did nothing of the kind," Rule said, without raising his voice.

"So no matter how all this turns out, you won't care if I let the world in on your little secret. Let them judge the obvious for themselves. That this tenth circle of hell you're opening is for rapists and child molesters. How's that for an epitaph?"

"Except there's no grave to put it on, is there?"

"Not yet, anyway."

And McCracken heard a click as Jeremiah Rule terminated the call.

CHAPTER 89

Washington, DC

McCracken pocketed the phone and looked toward Wareagle.

"My powers of persuasion must be lacking."

"Do you recall the legend of the renegade Sioux warrior undone by his blind ambition and delusion?"

"Not off the top of my head, Indian."

"He ravaged the countryside, killing as many from neighboring tribesmen as he could because he believed he was absorbing the soul of each victim, growing that much stronger with every kill. He believed this would eventually render him invincible and immortal. Until one day, he caught his own reflection in a pool of still water. Unable to accept the fact the earth had birthed another as powerful as he was, the warrior attacked his own reflection and ended up killing himself. Reverend Rule is no different."

"But unlikely to kill himself before the president's speech tonight, leaving the heavy lifting to us."

"You're surprised?"

"Not for one second."

"You knew it would end that way, just as I did."

"Because it always does, Indian. Doesn't mean I welcome it, though."

Wareagle stood straighter, seeming to rise even taller than normal. "Go back to the day you came to get me in South Dakota so we could return to the Hellfire."

"Okay."

"I was working on a statue I knew I'd never see finished, Blainey. Pounding away one day, only to return to the next with nothing looking any different. The progress was there, but I couldn't see it and so it wasn't."

McCracken shook his head and sighed. "I really wish the spirits could learn to speak simple English. Just once."

"It's why we welcome these opportunities," Wareagle told him, "long for them even. Because we're able to see the result, and don't have to see what would've happened without our intervention. We don't just do it because we're the only ones who care; we do it because we're the only ones who can."

"Can we this time?" McCracken posed tentatively.

"Even the spirits don't have that answer, Blainey."

"Then we better hope we find it somewhere else before the State of the Union goes to hell, Indian."

CHAPTER 90

Washington, DC

"Reverend?"

For an instant, just an instant, Rule thought it was the voice of God speaking to him, reassuring him, lending reason to the moment. The man on the other end of the line had found his hideaway, the spiritual retreat to which he banished his dark places. To an actual pit instead of a metaphorical one. The women would never bear his children now, but he realized it didn't matter, because that gift he'd intended to bestow upon the world had been replaced by another much greater one.

To be unleashed here. Tonight.

"Reverend?" the voice repeated.

Rule realized a fresh shadow had fallen over him and turned to find Boyd Fowler standing just to his side, dressed all in black above his army boots, flak jacket worn under his shirt making his torso look even more huge.

"Who were you talking to?" the big man asked him.

Rule realized he was still holding his phone. "A man without faith who will fall with all the others."

"I need to ask you something, Reverend, and I need you to promise me you'll say yes."

"You were delivered onto me for a purpose that leaves me in your debt, Boyd. So you have my solemn promise. Take it as the word of the Almighty."

"This thing we're about to do . . ."

"God's work, Boyd. We're about to fulfill His divine plan."

"That's the point. I've never been much when it came to religion or church, was never even baptized. And such things tend to plague a man at a time like this."

"What can I do to relieve your pain?"

"Can you baptize me here and now, before it's time for us to do the deed?"

Rule looked toward the waters of the reservoir, frigid in the chill January wind with waves of cold seeming to ripple on the surface.

"It would be my greatest pleasure to do so, Boyd."

The big man stripped off his shirt and shed his flak jacket right after it. He was down to his skivvies in seconds, revealing a strangely symmetrical mix of tattoos and heavy muscle. Rule left his clothes on, believing somehow it would keep him warmer when he stepped into the frigid water, still cloaked by the shadows cast by the tree cover. He welcomed this blessing as a distraction and another moment bringing him closer to God even as the time of his greatest service approached.

A steep bank led down into the reservoir, not much footing between the end of the drop and the start of the water. The pumping station, contained in a stately brick shell, rose a block to the south and was mostly automated these days, maintaining only a skeletal staff that had been told by their supervisor not to come in today for security reasons related to the State of the Union. And, likewise, its location and relatively innocuous purpose rendered it immune from Secret Service scrutiny as well. Nothing that would deter Jeremiah Rule from completing his holy mission with the help of Boyd Fowler and the Rock Machine.

"You ready, Reverend?" Fowler asked, his massive form looming over him on the rise overlooking the McMillan Reservoir.

"I am, Boyd. I am indeed."

CHAPTER 91

Washington, DC

"It's five o'clock, Captain. State of the Union speech is four hours away," McCracken said into his phone. "I hope you've got some answers."

"I do indeed, my man. But you're not gonna like them, not at all. I have gone through an entire quarter ounce of primo weed since last we spoke, and I still get numb to what I think I've figured out."

"Stop toking and start talking."

"Sorry about that, MacNuts," Captain Seven said between coughs. "Like I told you before, nobody ever figured out what the Rock Machine's plan was for attacking the Capitol Building, but I think I've got on a notion. On a clear day, you can see the answers. Must've been cloudy up until now because I've been focusing on the Rock Machine members that stood trial, not the ones who didn't."

"Why bother?"

"My thinking exactly, but that doesn't make it right. See, when I widened my searched a bit, I came up with the fact that a Rock Machine member who was never charged has built himself a career as a city worker with Washington's Department of Public Works—specifically, supervisor of the pumping station on Bryant Street down by the McMillan Reservoir."

"Don't tell me—the facility that supplies the Capitol Building its water."

"Okay, I won't tell you."

"This doesn't sound good, Captain."

"It gets worse, lots worse. How much you know about the manufacture of methamphetamines, MacNuts?"

"It's on my to-do list."

"Then let me spare you part of the trouble. Care to hazard a guess as to the prime solvent used in the cleanup process?"

"I thought you were sparing me the trouble."

"Liquid Freon."

"Oh shit . . ."

"Yup, it makes a great cleaning agent, but it's also what powers air-conditioning units. You see where I'm going with this?"

"I'd rather just listen to the expert."

"How do pipes burst, MacNuts?"

"They freeze."

"And *voilà*! Rule's motorcycle gang stooges first pump liquid Freon into the line. Freon doesn't work its magic until it reaches the end of the line in the pipes that supply water to the Capitol through piping that runs exposed along the length of the tunnel that connects the House of Representatives to the building. The Freon freezes the pipes pretty much on contact but they won't burst until pressure is brought back up again."

"Which will happen as soon as they flood the pipes with the White Death," McCracken surmised.

"Mixed with water refilling the line. The pipes burst and

release the already formed gas and everyone within a square mile of the Capitol, and maybe a whole lot more than that, is exposed—meaning dead, asphyxiated—within minutes. Colonel Turwell's original plan made infiltrating the Capitol itself a necessity, but now the Reverend Rule can wipe out virtually the entire United States government from around three miles away."

"Maybe he's doing us a favor. No way we could have found a way into the Capitol, but that pumping station is something else entirely."

"Might be just what we need, MacNuts."

"What we really need is the cavalry," McCracken said, checking his phone to see if there was a message from Zarrin yet.

CHAPTER 92

Washington, DC

Jeremiah Rule's feet were already chilled when he dropped into the waist-deep water of the McMillan Reservoir before it deepened just a few more yards out. The sky had shed the sun, the night moonless, which made the descent a dreadful experience done in fits and starts down the slick bank.

"Easy there, Reverend," he heard Boyd Fowler say, "I've got you."

The giant did indeed, hand braced over Rule's shoulder to guide him every step of the way and keep him from falling, while showing no ill effects from entering the frigid water himself. He beamed with a child's excitement and expectation, his slight trembling that of a man about to truly meet the Lord for the first time. To distract himself from the cold's utter seizure of his mind and senses, even his breath locking in his chest, Rule focused on the wondrous matter at hand, the miracle he was about to bestow on the world in keeping with the word of the Lord.

The pumping facility that would forge his miracle was deceptively simple in design, in keeping with its singular purpose of sucking water from this reservoir fed by the Potomac, running it through various stages of cleansing and treatment, and then sending millions of gallons on their way through its respective city grid. That grid included the U.S. Capitol Building, somewhere between two and three miles away.

Rule stretched his hands upward and laid them on Boyd Fowler's massive shoulders on the downward slope of his trapezius muscles.

"Heavenly Father, in your love you have called us to know you, led us to trust you, and bound our life with yours."

Rule paused to pray silently, but his mind jerked him back inside the pumping station where it was warm and dry and cluttered with piping that looked like giant steel snakes coiled about the walls and floor. There were massive tanks too, strung together by labyrinths of pipes leading from one to the other. A sophisticated network of interconnected catwalks rose like a spiderweb over the entire assemblage of steel and PVC, of levers and switches, of manifolds and circulators, of mounted controllers and system pressure gauges, of easy bleed and backup systems.

"Surround this man, and yet still child of God, with your love. Protect him from evil."

Here, Rule moved his numb, throbbing hands to Boyd Fowler's bald skull, easing his whole frame downward under their force. The moments passed with more thoughts of the Bryant Street facility's layout and contents. An entire floor comprised of little more than piping rising from underground, strung in serpentine fashion across the floor and climbing the walls, controlled by a combination of manual toggle switches, automated relays flashing green and old-fashioned crank wheels with rust showing through their color-keyed paint. Heavy steel ductwork and manifolds seemed to hang free in the air, like some outer-space spider responsible for weaving the web-like network of catwalks that allowed ready to access to all from above. The piping shared a uniform shade of easy blue, not dark enough to be navy but not light either.

"Fill him with the Holy Spirit and receive him into the family of our church," Rule continued, Boyd Fowler's head now sinking with the rest of him below the surface of the McMillan Reservoir, "that he may walk with us in the way of Christ, and grow in the knowledge of your love."

Inside the facility, before he'd come out here to pray, Rule had witnessed Fowler's men working on one of the pumps and the assemblage of piping running in and out of it. Connecting the white, plastic drums they'd brought with them via thick, rubber hosing joined by wide, copper line to the assemblage that supplied the facility's northern grid, which included the Capitol. Nearby, the fifty-five-gallon barrels Fowler's men and trucks had hauled away from the mountain filled out the floor near another network of piping that began the actual process of pumping drinking water to a large portion of the city. Rule had seen a bypass being readied so the pipes would carry the contents of those barrels north for the Capitol, instead of the purified water gestating in the holding tanks that towered over the scene.

Rule saw the bubbles flutter to the surface of the McMillan Reservoir as Fowler let out his breath. "May this child of the Lord know your power and your glory, your wisdom and your grace. And I ask you, oh Lord, to welcome him into your house as one of the true faithful in your ways who will keep your word now and forever."

With that, Rule lifted Boyd Fowler's head and torso from

the river as if it weighed nothing at all, as if he was a child in body as well as spirit. Their eyes met and held, Fowler's as happy and celebratory as any the reverend had ever seen, the man still shaking not in the slightest, just blowing water from his mouth and nose with his breath.

"Praise the Lord, Boyd! Praise the Lord, so you may know His glory! It's a true miracle, a true miracle!"

"Today's full of them, Reverend."

"And the biggest one is yet to come," Rule told him, thinking of how the country would look when tomorrow dawned.

CHAPTER 93

Washington, DC

Zarrin's flight landed at Dulles just about the same time as the flight from Detroit carrying the five security operatives Colonel Nabril al-Asi had brought with him to the United States from Palestine did. She knew them all, both from experience and reputation. All members of his private security force trained by Mossad, all having journeyed here when the dream of peace was replaced by calls for the heads of the old guard that had raised so many false hopes. They'd fought alongside the Sayeret, the Israeli Special Forces, on any number of raids and pretty much matched them, as well as their American counterparts, in their precision, training, and experience.

While waiting to meet up with the five men about to return to the violence that had ruled their lives for so long, Zarrin pictured what was happening beyond in the city right now. For starters, air traffic over Washington was about to be shut down. Only US Air Force fighter jets based at Air Combat

Command in Langley, Virginia, would be flying along with Predator drones almost certain to be on station. Beneath their sweep, fifteen hundred Capitol Police officers would be either posted or on patrol in and around the Capitol—this after a redundant triple-check of the entire building, including under every seat in the chamber, was made for any and all conceivable explosives. National Guardsmen would cover the street areas outside the sweep of either the Capitol Police or Secret Service who would also be securing every potential sniper's nest atop buildings or trees. Agents and their Capitol Police counterparts had been on high-security patrol since yesterday, knowing full well trained operatives may well have chosen to hunker down that long in advance to avoid detection closer to an actual planned attack.

The House wing of the Capitol Building, meanwhile, would have already been shut down at this hour, no admittance whatsoever allowed until the entry doors were opened. Similarly, the plaza on the east side of the Capitol would now have been closed to all unauthorized persons, and all streets adjoining the building would have been barricaded with Jersey barriers, including main thoroughfares, like Independence and Constitution Avenues. All this combined to create a daunting task to even conceive of a means to stage an attack during the State of the Union address. But, as McCracken told it, the Reverend Jeremiah Rule had found the ideal work-around, something no one could ever possibly have conceived.

Not unless they too had solved the interconnected mysteries of the lost Roanoke Colony and, now, the *Mary Celeste*.

Zarrin recognized Colonel al-Asi's operatives as they approached together, looking at first glance much more like polished family men than the hardened killers they had once been. But as they drew closer she saw the familiar bent in their eyes, their wariness and fluid movements, and knew they were actually both now, able to shift nimbly from one pursuit to the other.

How long had it been since they'd seen action? Zarrin wondered, certain that al-Asi would have insured they remained sharp and ready, never knowing where the next war might take them or when it would come.

And it had come today—here, far away from the Middle East, that world sure to be rocked dramatically as well if these men were unable to help change the outcome.

She took her phone out to call McCracken.

CHAPTER 94

Washington, DC

"You thank the good colonel for me?" McCracken asked Zarrin after laying everything out for her, including where to pick up the weaponry Sal Belamo had arranged for the force dispatched by Nabril al-Asi.

"I did. Several times. He said you'd be hearing from him. When the time is right."

"And the need. Ironic, isn't it? That five Palestinian special-ops soldiers might be the best chance we've got to stop the United States government from falling tonight."

"Don't forget a Palestinian assassin."

"How are your hands, Zarrin?"

She'd already been gazing down at them when McCracken posed the question. They were fine. For now. "Steady as a rock."

"As in Gibraltar?"

"Hopefully. So what's our play?"

"Captain Seven's still running some overlays and satellite

recon, but the logistics don't favor us. Secret Service owns the high ground everywhere, so that takes employing Sal and his sniper rifle—to change the odds in a big hurry—off the table."

"You knew it wouldn't be easy."

"We're going to be up against upwards of thirty well-armed, well-trained gunmen with a proven history for wanting to see the government fall."

"Maybe your justice system should have dispensed a more appropriate punishment."

"You mean like stoning them in the public square, Zarrin?"

"You tell me."

"Right now, I'm all for it."

"Better late than never."

Sal Belamo was waiting in the suite he'd reserved at the Carlyle just a mile from the Bryant Street Pumping Station when McCracken and Wareagle arrived—promptly at six o'clock as planned.

"Hey, boss," he said, wrapped in a hotel bathrobe. "I figured I might as well make myself comfortable. Already took a trip up to the roof. Secret Service has drones in the air, if you can believe that shit."

"Predators?"

Belamo nodded. "Latest generation. So we can forget about using anything even approaching the high ground."

"I already have. Question being what does that leave us with?"

Belamo stuffed both his hands in the pockets of his hotel bathrobe. "Well, gotta figure they'll launch the attack after the president's on the podium. That gives us three hours to figure out something. Jeez, boss, what about a call to DC Metro, something about suspicious activity at the reservoir. Dump the whole mess in their lap—and the Secret Service's, too."

"The Indian and I thought about that. Problem is we'd be risking the gang turning this into a suicide mission by dumping the barrels into the McMillan Reservoir itself or launching the attack ahead of schedule. Lots and lots of people would still die, Sal, almost all the country's elected representatives just for starters. No, we can't trust this to SWAT or somebody knocking on the door on the pretext of selling Girl Scout cookies. This is our game."

His phone beeped.

"Zarrin and her team are on their way up," he told Belamo and Wareagle.

CHAPTER 95

Washington, DC

An eerie quiet and calm had fallen over the pumping station. From his position on the catwalk looking down over the scene, Jeremiah Rule couldn't help but wonder if this was the way God viewed man. The big figures, even the still-beaming Boyd Fowler, looked so much smaller and less significant from even this modest distance above them.

Then again, he knew he must have appeared of comparably small scope to anyone looking up his way. Rule didn't own a watch, hated to open his cell phone to regard the hour. He was a firm believer that things happened in their own time, just like his blessedly fated visit to Fowler's home in the trailer park. He saw the cosmic rationale behind that now, beating that boy to death in a similar place all those years ago setting the stage for something much more important. Just as the boy Jimmy's accidental death in Black House had started the process. All were events ordained by powers he was just beginning to comprehend.

Rule found himself missing the boy's ghost, figured Jimmy had finally found peace after being laid before the altar in the reverend's basement. God really did work in mysterious ways.

"I won't let you down, Jimmy," he said softly, poised upon the catwalk. "I'll make sure you were sacrificed for a much greater cause."

Mysterious ways indeed.

"The hour is almost upon us," he said loud enough for all to hear below him, before he realized what he was doing. "The hour of wondrous glory and purpose as few men have ever known in their hearts and minds."

They were all looking up at him now, the black-garbed army assembled by Boyd Fowler to fulfill a singular purpose Rule had brought to bear. Looking to him the way he looked to God for guidance and reassurance. The building's dull light swallowed their expressions, making them look faceless. Little more than figures painted in black onto the world, dark against dark, lacking form and substance in the shadows cast by the high overhead bulbs. As if they had risen up for this purpose and this purpose alone, after which the ground would suck them back in. Specters, phantoms, warriors of God under his command about to do his bidding, which was the Lord's bidding as well.

"Let us pray," Rule said, bowing his head so that all those beneath him would follow. "Dear Lord, we ask for your blessing upon this blessed mission we undertake in your name. We pray for the strength we need to see it through and the solace your wisdom provides. Dear Lord, we know the actions we shall undertake tonight are in your name to fulfill your divine purpose. We thank you, oh Lord, for finding us worthy of your grace and vow not to sway from our mission or our commitment. Our faith in you is absolute and we ask that you preserve those who so serve you." Rule stopped, eyes squeezed shut now. "Amen," he finished.

"Amen," came the chorus of voices from beneath him, followed by a voice bellowing, "Let's waste the fuckers!"

"Amen!" came a fresh roar, even louder.

"Give 'em what's coming to 'em!"

"Finish what we started!"

"Bring it all down!"

"Fuck yeah!"

Followed by a brief respite of silence in which a tinny voice sounded through an unseen television speaker.

"Mister Speaker," announced the sergeant-at-arms three miles away in the Capitol Building, "the president of the United States!"

Thunderous applause followed, but Rule's mind quickly drowned it out, even as he saw Boyd Fowler touch his earpiece.

"We got a homeless guy rapping on the fence outside. Need to get rid of him. Team Tango, go to work," the newly baptized Fowler ordered.

And with that, the Reverend Jeremiah Rule watched four of the armed figures beneath him move for the door.

"Go with God," he said softly, making the sign of the Holy Trinity in the air, while beneath him Boyd Fowler moved toward the man at the controls for the pumping apparatus.

"Freeze the pipes," Fowler instructed just loud enough for Rule to hear.

CHAPTER 96

Washington, DC

The old homeless man, dressed in bulky layers of cloth and wool carrying the stench of alcohol, had a bent nose and flattened ears that stood out from a face cloaked by a watch cap hung low to provide warmth to his head.

"Come on, boys, help a fella out, will ya? Just some change for a coffee, maybe a meal."

Three members of the Rock Machine gang approached from the other side of the fence, a fourth hanging back between it and the door.

"Come on," whined the homeless man, "I used to ride too, you know. *Vroom, vroom, vroom!*"

The man in the middle of the three stuck a one-dollar bill through the chain link that was snatched up immediately by a hand cloaked in a half glove. The homeless man unrolled the bill, eyeing it derisively.

"Come on, boys, you can do better than that."

The other two men joined the third up even with the fence. And that's when all of them saw the silenced pistol in the homeless man's hand.

Pfffffft . . . Pffffffft . . . Pffffffft . . .

Then sighting in on the fourth before that man's own pistol cleared his belt.

Pffffffft . . .

"Go, boss," Sal Belamo said into his wrist-mounted microphone, "go!"

"I don't see another way this can play out," McCracken had said back in the hotel suite. "No way to be subtle beyond the entry point, but the logistics give us a window to work with."

"Indeed, they do," Captain Seven said from his railroad-car home, before a fit of coughing from a just-consumed bong hit overcame him. "You're gonna have twelve minutes between the time the Freon is set loose and the White Death follows."

"They'll freeze the pipes on the president's entrance," McCracken advanced.

"How can you be so sure of that?" Zarrin asked him.

"Because they'll be too eager and excited not to. No reason to wait, in any regard. So that's when our clock starts ticking."

"Just remember something," picked up Captain Seven's now-hoarse voice. "Once they let the White Death loose in those pipes, all bets are off. Game over."

"Then we'll have to find a way to play the game on our terms," said McCracken.

"I recently went to Andrews Air Force Base and welcomed home some of our last troops to serve in Afghanistan. Together, we offered a final, proud salute to the colors under which more than a million of our fellow citizens fought—and several thousand gave their lives. We gather

tonight knowing that this generation of heroes has made the United States safer and more respected around the world. For the first time in over a decade, there are no Americans fighting in Iraq or Afghanistan. Osama bin Laden is a memory and many of Al Qaeda's top lieutenants have joined him. The Afghan people have taken responsibility for their own security, and the United States has never been safer or more secure, both at home and abroad."

Boyd Fowler heard the beginning of the presidential speech in a low din over the television several of his men were gathered around. There was little else to do at this point, other than wait for the Freon now surging through the network of piping that led straight to the Capitol Building to work its magic. The estimated time for that to happen, according to the gang member who served as a shift supervisor here, was twelve minutes, leaving nine more before he could send the deadly contents of the barrels jetting down the line. They'd already been poured into a sealed holding tank to mix with the water stored within it. A simple flip of a toggle switch was all it would take to send the contents on their way, jetting through underground piping straight to the Capitol Building to wreak their deathly havoc once the frozen pipes burst.

Fowler looked up to see Reverend Rule hands clasping the catwalk's handrails, eyes aimed down at the television broadcasting the State of the Union speech to follow the remaking of history. Fowler found his own gaze drawn there, unable to resist picturing the sight on screen when the deadly poisonous air flooded the Capitol and laid waste to all.

The president would fall.

The government would fall.

The country would fall.

All glorious. And inevitable.

Until he heard the distinct crackle of automated gunfire as windows shattered.

CHAPTER 97

Washington, DC

McCracken and Wareagle led three of the Palestinian commandos in the first wave of the attack, adding their fire to Sal Belamo's as soon as he'd dropped the four Rock Machine gang members who'd emerged from inside the building. The element of surprise was theirs only until they burst through the gate, angled themselves before the front casement windows, and opened fire.

And that's when time froze, nothing but the staccato bursts of sound and glimpses of movement registering with him at all.

Time changed, places changed, but not battle, one exactly like the last and the next. Context, location, and purpose always distinct, while sense and mind-set remained the same.

And McCracken took to this one, just as he'd taken to all the others. Nothing was forgotten, each piece of every other battle he'd ever fought leaving an indelible mark. There was the sense of the assault rifle vibrating slightly as it clacked off rounds, warm against his hands, steady in his grasp. The sight of the muzzle flash, the strange metallic smell of air baked by the heat of the expended shells and his own kinetic energy. The world reduced to its most basic and simple objects. There was the gun, his targets, the glass and wall between them, and nothing else. Welcome and comfortable in its familiarity with all thinking suspended and only instinct left to command him.

He felt himself moving, return fire heating up before him, the hisses of air telling McCracken how close it was coming. He let instinct continue to steer him, aware of Johnny Wareagle launching himself airborne and crashing through the remnants of a shot-out window. Wareagle hit the floor shooting, spraying fire toward the motorcycle gang members diving, crawling, or rushing for cover amid the clutter of piping, pumps, manifolds, and baffles.

McCracken followed Johnny through the same chasm, everything slowing down before him. The assault rifle seemed weightless in his grasp now and he felt himself firing before his feet had even touched down, slamming a fresh magazine home as soon as they did. He'd done this so often, it was easy to be swept away in the memories, to lose track of the reality of the moment and the surreal nature of it. His ears took the brunt of the initial assault, as he darted between piping and steel stanchions for cover. Continuing to sweep his eyes and weapon about the whole time, keenly aware the tide could turn at any moment given the opposition's still superior numbers.

And it seemed to be doing just that, with gunfire pouring at him from seemingly everywhere at once. McCracken slammed his shoulders against a manifold, unable to spin out in either direction for the time being with the concentrated fire clanging against the steel and ricocheting with ear-numbing *pings*. The bullets continued to drum against the steel, Blaine feeling the vibrations at the core of his bones and being. The assault rifle wobbled in his grip and he concentrated on keeping his breathing steady, so he'd be ready.

Ready when the smoker grenades rolled across the floor past him.

Zarrin and her team had managed to successfully breach the building's rear at last. The smokers ignited with a *poof!*—spreading thick noxious vapor across the floor, adding to the chaos now safe for Blaine to enter with a deft twist to the right, assault rifle leveled.

"Ladies and gentlemen, the state of our Union is strong and getting stronger. And we've come too far to turn back now. As long as I'm President, I will work with anyone in this chamber to build on this momentum. But I intend to fight obstruction with action, and I will oppose any effort to return to the very same policies that brought on the economic crisis we've pulled ourselves from in the first place. No, we will not go back to an economy weakened by outsourcing, bad debt, and phony financial profits. Tonight, thanks to the grit and determination of the American people, there is much progress to report. After a decade of grinding war, our brave men and women in uniform are coming home. After years of grueling recession, our businesses have created over seven million new jobs. We buy more American cars than we have in ten years, and less foreign oil than we have in twenty. Our housing market is healing, our stock market is rebounding, and consumers, patients, and homeowners enjoy stronger protections than ever before. Together, we have cleared away the rubble of crisis, and can say with renewed confidence that the future is bright."

Boyd Fowler's ears were ringing. He'd been in gunfights before, in war as well as battles against rival biker gangs, but never anything like this. It was constant, it was incessant, and it seemed to go on forever as it was muddled by the smoke that was thick everywhere, dominating the air. It obscured his vision and took him out of touch with his own positioning on the cluttered facility floor where a misstep could cause disaster in its own right.

The smoke distorted his sense of direction, stole the easy sight of the switching station that would send the contents of the tank containing the barrels that the Rock Machine had trucked from West Virginia flowing up the line. The deadly vapors on course to kill, to asphyxiate everyone they came into contact with once the Capitol's underground frozen pipes burst under the pressure. He only wished he could be there to see it, the Rock Machine's grand plan at last realized, their name to remain known for all time.

Fowler couldn't help but wonder how many the gas might claim collaterally beyond the Capitol. There was no way to be sure, given so many variables like wind, temperature, and how much of the deadly cloud would actually seep out of the building with virtually all the US government left dead in its wake.

Ten thousand?

A hundred thousand?

A million?

No matter. He was making history here; in fact, he was rewriting it. Let time judge him, as it would the Reverend Rule. He was at peace with his decisions. A good Christian, now that he'd been baptized.

Fowler felt his body heating up at last, no longer chilled to his very core as he had been since that baptism Rule had performed in the McMillan Reservoir. Shapes and movement whirled around him, muzzle flashes cutting through the noxious smoke that was already thinning in the sprawling confines of the facility. He sighted in on a black-garbed figure wearing a gas mask and wielding an assault rifle, fired a bust from his

M-16, and watched the man spin like a top, bloody spray blown from the impact points.

But the dissipating smoke also revealed Rock Machine members strewn everywhere, cut down in the initial assault fueled by surprise in tandem with the enemy's incredibly accurate shooting for a firefight. These were clearly trained professionals for whom battle was nothing new, formidable opponents at the very least. But now the advantage was the Rock Machine's again, the gang's numbers, their superior weaponry, and time still on their side.

That certainty filled Fowler as fresh fire sounded from the breached rear of the building, and he swung that way with rifle already spitting bullets.

CHAPTER 98

Washington, DC

Zarrin flexed the stiffness from her hands, fought with her legs to give her all they could. Her body had been severely overtaxed these past few days, well beyond the capacity of the medication to moderate her symptoms. McCracken was right; a firefight like this required an entirely different skill set and mind-set, both of which had long grown foreign to her. She had been involved in her share of shootouts and gunfights, more than her share, but not against a force of this size, purpose, and training for a very long time. An assassin's work was simple by comparison, seldom meeting any resistance, with escape being the paramount concern as opposed to survival. That gave her more respect for Blaine McCracken, the man having lived in this world for so many years.

Zarrin clacked off shots from her Heckler & Koch HK45 compact pistol with its slim-line grip and ten-shot magazine. It was smaller in length and height than the company's standard model or any .45 caliber pistol. It also weighed considerably less while still offering the legendary .45 stopping power. Zarrin was not a fast draw or fast shot, but she'd trained herself to be deadly accurate, the precision involved not unlike that needed for playing the piano.

She'd led two of al-Asi's commandos on a breach of the backside of the building, catching the enemy gunmen in a classic cross fire to regain the advantage briefly lost once the Rock Machine members had found cover amid the cluttered floor. The pumping station looked like the main deck of an oil rig to her, even as she clacked off shots at targets she'd zeroed in deliberate fashion. Four downed in her first magazine, two more with her halfway through the second.

That's when the fingers on Zarrin's right hand spasmed and locked, quivery and trembling now. She looked for the cover she'd need to steady herself and will the strength back into her hands. But there was nothing offering enough of it nearby, so Zarrin focused on a set of steel stairs leading to the catwalk swirling above and moved for that instead.

"It is our unfinished task to make sure that this government works on behalf of the many, and not just the few; that it encourages free enterprise, rewards individual initiative, and opens the doors of opportunity to every child across this great nation. The American people don't expect government to solve every problem. They don't expect those of us in this chamber to agree on every issue. But they do expect us to put the nation's interests before party. They do expect us to forge reasonable compromise where we can. For they know that America moves forward only when we do so together; and that the responsibility of improving this union remains the task of us all."

The clock continued to count down in McCracken's head, the time drawing ever nearer to the moment when the White Death would be released into the system to rupture the soon-to-be-frozen pipes supplying the Capitol Building with water. He tried not to think beyond that, every resulting picture conjured by his mind being too devastating to even consider.

He continued to clack off single shots from his assault rifle, mixed in occasionally with a three-shot burst. The smokers had ultimately done as much harm as good by rendering it impossible for him to distinguish the controls for the feeder line holding the White Death.

Captain Seven hadn't been able to produce a schematic of the facility for McCracken to memorize, as was his custom in preparation for such scenarios. The captain had, though, come up with a map of the exact route of piping from this facility all the way to the Capitol that Blaine had committed to memory instead. A path strangely zigzagging in nature thanks to the high water table and shale deposits that determined much of the route for the engineers who'd designed, or upgraded, the system.

Keeping a mental count in his head was difficult since he still had no firm grasp of the enemy's actual number. Regardless, keeping track of the level and intensity of each side's gunfire was far more important in determining the tide of the battle and its eventual victor anyway. His vast experience, far too much, had imbued him with an instinctive sense of place in relation to control of territory from a square foot to mile. And right now that instinct told him his forces were winning the day and, thus, hopefully forestalling the Rock Machine's efforts to pump the White Death into Washington's water system.

The lack of high-ground fire from the catwalk above told him Sal Belamo had been unable to claim that strategic point as originally planned. Through the thinning smoke, though, he saw Zarrin clamoring upward, even as he glimpsed the shape of Jeremiah Rule leaning over a railing with eyes closed and hands clasped in a position of prayer.

*　　*　　*

"Those of us who've been sent here to serve can learn a thing or two from the service of our troops. When you put on that uniform, it doesn't matter if you're black or white; Asian, Latino, Native American; conservative, liberal; rich, poor; gay, straight. When you're marching into battle, you look out for the person next to you, or the mission fails. When you're in the thick of the fight, you rise or fall as one unit, serving one nation, leaving no one behind."

Boyd Fowler darted from one position of cover to another, trying to chart a path to the single lever that would transfer flow of outgoing water from one line to another. A routine procedure undertaken to rotate the city's water supply among three separate tanks of purified, treated water sucked in from the McMillan Reservoir.

One of those tanks now held the contents of the barrels salvaged from the West Virginia mountain facility where they otherwise would have done no more than collect dust for decades. Organizing the transport process had been incredibly challenging in such a limited time frame, managed only thanks to his access to trained drivers, trucks, and the proper equipment. Add to that the crucial element of already having a man in place here at this facility to fulfill the reverend's grand plan, and Fowler couldn't help but wonder if there really was a higher power at work.

He finally got enough of his bearings back to chart a clear path from his current position to the control lever he needed to throw in just minutes now, barely two according to his watch counting down the time since they'd released the liquid Freon. Fowler fired an automatic burst high and purposefully off target to gauge the response. A single enemy gunman lurched out, having honed in on his position, and Fowler gunned him down with the rest of his magazine, pulverizing the man with bullets and enjoying the site of misty blood froth erupting from each wound on impact.

He was snapping a fresh magazine into place when a fellow gang member on his right went down, followed by one of his left. The angle told him the fire had come from above and he twisted to see the smaller shape of a woman poised on the catwalk, sighting down with a pistol like she was some methodical Olympic target shooter.

Jeremiah Rule watched Boyd Fowler fire a burst upward, but it missed, clanging off steel, and was returned instantly by a single shot from the woman that would've nailed him had not some sense of danger, some cosmic warning, sent him sprawling to the floor.

Higher power indeed, the reverend thought, guiding them even now.

His eyes followed Fowler crawling across the floor, propelling himself along on his elbows to reach a nearby set of stairs that would take him up to the catwalk as well. The giant seemingly rendered indestructible, now that God was on his side.

"Amen," Rule said out loud.

CHAPTER 99

Washington, DC

McCracken could barely hear a thing, his eardrums singed by the constant cacophony of gunfire intensified by the confined space. He could not remember a time or a battle where it had strummed more incessantly, and that forced him to rely more on his eyes.

The problem was those eyes showed him only two of the five men sent by Colonel al-Asi still standing against what looked to be far more downed members of the Rock Machine; as many as eighteen, Blaine thought. They still had more guns, but their reduced number allowed Johnny Wareagle to whirl unimpeded about the facility in phantom-like fashion. Appearing from the smoke out of nowhere behind or alongside one of the enemy whose fire ceased immediately as he dropped from the battle.

The strategy at this point was simple: Eliminate all of the enemy, and there would be no one to release the White Death into the Capitol's water supply. Until that was the case, it was a

397

matter of keeping members of the Rock Machine too concerned with staying alive to try reaching the feeder controls that would flush the White Death into the system.

McCracken whirled, one way and then the other, from a vast pump to an intricate coupling of piping for cover. His next twist brought him out into the open, though with far fewer guns to threaten his advance. His hearing returned in fluttery fashion, his ears giving up more to him as his eyes continued to sweep about in eerie rhythm with his assault rifle, locking on a shape coming up behind a crouching Zarrin.

Her fingers fought her but she won. Again. She felt the pain, welcoming it since it was much preferable to stiffness.

Steady, sight, fire. . . . Steady, sight, fire. . . .

Tchaikovsky's Concerto no. 1 sounded in her head, the very same concerto she'd played in Istanbul, approaching its crescendo as three more motorcycle gang members dropped to her bullets. Zarrin paused again to snap another fresh magazine into her Heckler & Koch, the music only she could hear settling her mind and holding her to rhythm not at all unlike working the ivory keys.

And then she felt a shape that smelled like grass and standing water and unwashed hair and clothes pounce upon her and wrap itself around her like a snake.

"We should follow the example of a police officer named Brian Murphy. When a gunman opened fire on a Sikh temple in Wisconsin, and Brian was the first to arrive, he did not consider his own safety. He fought back until help arrived, and ordered his fellow officers to protect the safety of the Americans worshiping inside, even as he lay bleeding from twelve bullet wounds. When asked how he did that, Brian said, 'That's just the way we're made.' That's just the way we're made. We may do different

jobs, and wear different uniforms, and hold different views than the person beside us. But as Americans, we all share the same proud title."

"Die, die now!" Rule screamed at the woman, as he tried to choke her. "Die in the name of God!"

But the woman wouldn't die. In the next instant, she had regained her feet, jerking him backward and forcing the reverend up against the opposite side of the catwalk. He felt the steel rail slam his kidneys, nearly stripping him of breath. Still, Rule wouldn't let go, content to hold on for as long as it took him to kill this whore who had come amid the opposition. Her gun was gone. He'd heard it rattle to the catwalk and believed his own foot had kicked it down to the floor in the struggle. That left them equals.

Briefly.

Because she lurched forward, the motion much too fast for the lumbering Rule to compensate for with a shift of his weight. His next conscious thought was that he was airborne, staring at the heavens, which in this case was a ridged, heavily insulated ceiling. Then he realized he was falling, his time in the air strangely slow and drawn out until the floor came up and caught him.

Zarrin knew it was the reverend, the maker of all this madness. The constant echoing din of gunfire kept her from hearing the thud of his body's impact with the floor below. She wondered if an even worse fate had befallen him, perhaps impaled or badly gored by one of the many steel assemblages that sprouted everywhere through the building.

She glanced downward and saw the reverend's body canted on an empty stretch of floor, shoulders and head having dropped into a sunken pit housing a series of auxiliary pumps. Zarrin couldn't tell if he was alive or dead. Just pulled herself back to her feet to find the biggest man she'd ever seen, bald with ink seeming to leak down his face and scalp, standing there.

The giant leveled a submachine gun toward her, an instant away from firing when the equally large shape of McCracken's longtime Native American protector, Johnny Wareagle, pounced on him from behind.

Rule regained enough of his senses to realize where he was in the pumping station, his fall having left him just a few feet away from the lever that, once thrown, would mean the end of a nation bred by weakness and concession to be replaced by one blessed by a God who was no stranger to blood. Blood had been so much His method, so often His means to a desired end. This, here and now, tonight, was no different than the many battles fought at God's hand and in His name with His blessing. The blood of some needed to be spilled, the lives of others snuffed out, so that His word could be heard in a country that had too often turned a deaf ear.

In that moment of clarity and realization for Jeremiah Rule, all pain vanished. All thoughts of death and failure vanished too, because the Lord had seen fit to bestow upon him one last gift before He took Rule home to His kingdom and much-deserved salvation. The women who would have brought his likeness into the world were gone. The bones of the boys they would've replaced, lives he'd taken by lives he'd bequeathed, were gone.

But none of that mattered anymore. Only one thing did:

The tenth circle . . . His to unleash, his own fate to bring to fruition.

The reverend knew his body was broken, even as he felt the final miracle he needed building inside him. A searing heat that chased away his pain and held his shattered bones together.

Maybe he was already dead, his final act to take place in the midst of his own resurrection. Rule felt himself climbing back to his feet, warm blood soaking through his clothes, its slow oozing turning his vision blurry and world wobbly before him.

But he was moving.

Walking. Past the remains of the boys he'd killed and women he'd turned to his service from their own sins.

To bring the tenth circle of Hell upon the world.

Reaching for the lever suddenly and miraculously within his grasp, having appeared magically before him, as something hotter still stitched up his spine and stole the rest of his pain away.

McCracken fired on full auto, watching Jeremiah Rule's body arch, twist, and spasm as his magazine clicked empty.

But Rule didn't die. He somehow righted himself, walked on, and reached out for a lever mounted at eye level with the controls for the one of the facility's pumps. He yanked it downward while McCracken snapped a fresh magazine home, sighting forward again to find the reverend sliding down the steel and the White Death now jetting toward the Capitol Building.

The sight of the reverend falling stole Boyd Fowler's attention away. The man who had baptized him, restored purpose to his life, had fallen in the battle, but, incredibly, not before he managed to throw the switch that Fowler himself couldn't reach.

Doing God's work, completing the mission the Lord had given him. The mere thought of that gave Fowler the chills.

He looked back toward the woman, his finger finding the trigger just as hands draped from behind him jerked the barrel upward and forced his fire harmlessly into the ceiling. He twisted, finding himself face-to-face and eye-to-eye with a man every bit as big as he was, a fucking Indian with coal-black hair tinted with gray and pulled back in a ponytail.

*   *   *

"Boss!" an out-of-breath Sal Belamo called out from near the door when McCracken reached it.

"I know, Sal. Captain, can you hear me?" Blaine said into the Bluetooth device somehow still clipped to his ear.

"Yup, along with the third World War raging there. Mac-Nuts, you are a walking commercial for gun control."

"The White Death's been released into the system."

"Fuck . . ."

"How do we stop it?"

"You can't. It's a gravity-fed system. Once in the pipes, you can kiss it good-bye. Game over."

CHAPTER 100

Washington, DC

"Not what I wanted to hear," McCracken told Captain Seven over the lessening sounds of gunfire.

"Sorry."

"Give me a time."

"Five and a half minutes before it reaches the frozen pipes and they blow under the pressure, six if you're lucky."

"I'm not."

"Then say five until the secretary of agriculture is running the government. You better come up with something fast."

McCracken's eyes strayed across the floor. "I think I just did."

Wareagle and Boyd Fowler locked hands on the assault rifle, struggling for control of it as they twisted and turned about the narrow catwalk, slamming up against the safety rail from one side to the other and back again and exchanging positions in the process.

Fowler tried to bend Johnny backward over it, tried to position the rifle's stock so he could press it into Wareagle's throat and choke him there and then. But Johnny reversed position again, driving the butt of the weapon up on an angle that smacked it under Fowler's chin.

The bald man's head shot backward enough for Wareagle to jam the rifle stock into his windpipe, choking off his air. The man's eyes bulged and his face reddened, then purpled. It should have been over there, and would have been with any other man Johnny had ever faced. But Fowler maintained the presence of mind to clamp both hands on either side of the rifle and push up while Johnny continued to put pressure downward.

And the rifle began to move, slowly until Fowler mounted a powerful surge upward, Wareagle countering with the last thing the biker would ever think he'd do in response.

He let the gun go, so it flew from both their grasps and clattered along the catwalk before coming to a skidding halt. The momentum carried Fowler slightly past Wareagle, leaving Johnny with an advantage he seized by slamming the biker with a series of powerful blows to the ribs and skull. So muscular he seemed to be infused with steel, his bald head with the consistency of a boulder. Fowler lashed blows back at him that Wareagle deftly avoided or blocked until the biker came in fast, and bit into his cheek when Johnny's boot caught in the catwalk grating.

"We are citizens. It's a word that doesn't just describe our nationality or legal status. It describes the way we're made. It describes what we believe. It captures the enduring idea that this country only works when we accept certain obligations to one another and to future generations; that our rights are wrapped up in the rights of others; and that well into our third century as a nation,

it remains the task of us all, as citizens of these United States, to be the authors of the next great chapter in our American story."

Sal Belamo thrust open the front doors, allowing McCracken to jet out them atop an Athena ProStreet chopper, painted with orange flames over black with a seat so low it seemed to be touching the street. He'd already witnessed the last of the Palestinian commandos shot down, keenly aware that both Zarrin and Wareagle were currently continuing the battle from atop the catwalk, with Sal about to play one final card.

Having memorized the twisting route the water system followed from here to the Capitol, Blaine knew there was no chance he could reach the building ahead of the White Death.

But he could come close, close enough.

Maybe.

Zarrin watched McCracken roar out of the building atop the chopper, finding herself amazed even in these circumstances and conditions by the man's grit, by his refusal to quit or concede under any circumstances.

No wonder he'd survived so long.

She'd been watching the battle between Boyd Fowler and Johnny Wareagle from the catwalk floor, had actually flinched when Fowler bit into Wareagle's cheek and refused to let the bite go.

She focused on the assault rifle that had come to a rest a mere ten feet from her and pushed herself toward it, her legs heavy and slow, as if both were asleep. She managed to get the rifle into her hands, was raising it to her shoulder to sight in on the big biker, when her fingers stiffened and locked, and the weapon dropped from her grasp.

McCracken took all the Athena ProStreet would give him as he swung off Second Street Northwest onto North Capitol Street heading in the same direction atop a machine putting out almost a 125 pounds of torque and capable of speeds well in excess of a hundred miles per hour. His plan was to ride the chopper straight to the Capitol, tracing the underground route of the pipes that fed water to the building, pipes that currently pulsed with a deadly toxin that would kill everyone attending the State of the Union address within moments of exposure. His trek was about to become a treacherous path around buildings as well as along sidewalks and down one-way streets, in line with the piping beneath him.

"You there, Captain?" he said into his Bluetooth earpiece.

"Ready and waiting. What's that noise, MacNuts?"

"Chopper I'm riding."

"I won't even ask."

"Don't. There's no time. Let me do the talking." McCracken risked a glance upward for no good reason at all. "There are drones in the sky here, Captain. Good old Predators. Any chance you can hack into the network controlling them so we can fire a couple of missiles?"

"Sure, if you give me an hour."

"Since we've got less than five minutes, just answer me this: How fast are the contents of those pipes moving?"

"Depends on the metric weight of the liquid death but forty, maybe forty-five miles per hour would be a fair estimate."

McCracken glanced down at the chopper's speedometer, which read sixty-five. "Good enough. All right, Captain, here's what I need you to do—"

Before Blaine could continue, though, another voice broke into the line.

"Jesus Christ, McCracken," barked H. J. Belgrade, "please tell me you're there."

"H. J., you are a sound for sore ears. Literally."

"Well, I wake up expecting to see Elmer Fudd on the television and there's the president instead. Then I remembered our little talk. Took me a while to put things into context."

"You need to make a phone call," McCracken told him, "and you need to make it fast."

Johnny felt the blast more than heard it, he and Boyd Fowler still locked up and exchanging hammer-like blows when the explosives Sal Belamo had wired around the exterior of the building erupted in a frenzy of ruptured glass, brick, slate, and plaster.

The surviving bikers had just trained their attention upward when the waves of glass and debris slammed into them, turning flesh and bone into pincushions, the force of the blast substantial enough to actually tear off limbs and heads. The shock wave also separated a section of the catwalk from its brackets, sending it swinging in a semicircle northward over a tank containing the sludge filtered from the McMillan Reservoir water before it entered Washington's system.

Wareagle and Boyd Fowler literally dangled over that tank as they continued their dance of death.

"All right," Belgrade's voice returned less than a minute after breaking to move to another call, "we got Predators on your bubble but they need a fire point. Wouldn't happen to have a laser designator in your pocket, would you, son?"

"No," McCracken said, thinking fast, "but maybe something just as good."

McCracken veered onto the sidewalk at Louisiana Avenue and then hurdled back into stalled traffic with the police now giving chase as he approached New Jersey Avenue. He snatched a road flare from the emergency kit beneath the rear of his seat and twisted the top off with his teeth, the bright chemical flame firing to life.

"Tell Predator Control to fire on a road flare."

"Son, did you say—"

"Yes, just tell them to aim for the flame. That's my twenty and the White Death's twenty inside the pipes I'm running even with. Captain, tell me I've got this right."

"As rain, MacNuts. Carbonic acid needs oxygen to spread. But the blast, if it comes, will suck that oxygen out of the air so all the city's gonna be left with is one massive sanitation problem for a while."

"I think they can live with that. H. J.?"

"Right here, Elmer."

"Make the call," McCracken said, with the National Mall, Reflecting Pool, and Grotto just ahead of him, the majestic Capitol Dome coming into sight.

"No way you can both escape the blast radius and light up the target, son," Belgrade warned, "no way."

CHAPTER 101

Washington, DC

The catwalk bounced over the tank of collected sludge, vibrating madly. The two giants ignored the precarious balance, their blows thrown even harder, incredible in their force and their intensity. Fowler had the advantage as far as pure strength, thanks to his layers of muscle. But that muscle had the dual effect of slowing him ever so slightly in comparison to Wareagle's gliding, lithe moves. So far the narrow confines hadn't allowed him to take advantage of his quickness, though he could tell the mere volume of blows thrown by the biker was exhausting him.

But Fowler fought with the conviction that God was on his side. He and the Reverend Rule had found each other for a reason, his baptism earlier today in no way a coincidence.

Because he had been saved.

And now, no matter what, God would save him, extend the helping hand he needed to prevail and see this fight to its finish.

The sludge beneath them atop the wobbly catwalk smelled like the refuse from clogged drain taps, wafting through the air even as its surface frothed and bubbled. Frustrated by the diminishing effects of his blows, Fowler bellowed and launched himself forward, intending to topple the big man off the catwalk. He'd fought plenty of men in his time, but never one who could match him in size and strength. The ponytailed Indian before him seemed more ghost than man, a test to see if Boyd was worthy of His good graces. All well and good because he knew in his heart he would.

Problem was the Indian had anticipated his attack perfectly and had positioned himself with the separated end of the catwalk at his back to ready himself for it. Their collective weight so close to the edge bent the catwalk downward at a sharp angle toward the bubbling sludge tank. Fowler grabbed the handrail to keep from sliding into it, realizing too late that Wareagle had grabbed nothing at all.

Johnny crashed into him, extending his hands at the last possible instant and using Fowler's own momentum to topple him over the handrail while all his attention was turned to the precarious lean of the catwalk's far end.

Fowler managed to grab hold with a single arm, his huge eyes full of defeat and resignation.

Wareagle extended a hand downward, expecting the biker to reach up and take it.

Fowler looked up, but continued to let himself dangle. Because the hand of God would find him instead. The hand of God would save him. He had never been more certain of any thing in his life, even as his other hand began to slip off the steel.

Even as he fell, believing himself saved as the sludge swallowed him.

"Each time I look at that flag, I'm reminded that our destiny is stitched together like those fifty stars and those thirteen stripes. No one built this country on his own. This nation is great because

we built it together. This nation is great because we worked as a team. This nation is great because we get one another's backs. And if we hold fast to that truth, in this moment of trial, there is no challenge too great, no mission too hard. As long as we are joined in common purpose, as long as we maintain our common resolve, our journey moves forward, and our future is hopeful, and the state of our Union will always be strong."

"President's still talking," McCracken heard Belgrade say in his ear.

"I can hear the applause off your television."

"Then hear this: We got Predators on station, zeroed on your twenty. Just say the word."

McCracken yanked the pull string of the emergency flare off with his teeth, feeling the flame burst singe him before he got the flare extended overhead.

"Word."

"Fire and forget, son. Get ready to get your ass out of there. I'm giving you a standing O just like you're the president. Listen to me clapping."

McCracken didn't veer the chopper off until he heard the sizzle of the Predator-fired missiles streaking downward on his location, zeroing on the flare he has holding. Then he tossed it straight up in the air and banked the chopper sharply left, coughing divots of grass and dirt behind him.

The Althena ProStreet boasted six right-mounted gears and he used all of them in tearing away, kicking up more dirt and grass with the chopper's front wheel lifting briefly off the ground before the bike lurched into what felt like light speed. Accelerating so fast that Blaine's breath was gone even before the dual blast from the Predators hit with nary a gap.

Impact was dizzying. He tensed for it, thought he was ready, but then he was flying through a night momentarily stripped of air. McCracken had stolen a space shuttle once, had done all

411

his training in the ship's initial launch, learning the nature of g-forces the hard way.

That's what this felt like. He churned through the air in what seemed to be slow motion, barely aware of the huge flame burst that had blown a hole in the National Mall and eviscerated everything that lay beneath it.

Including the White Death and the pipes carrying it, lost in a black smoke cloud that blew outward before it seemed to be sucked back into the chasm.

Impact felt cushiony, even when his shoulder crunched and crackled as he rolled across the hard earth, beneath the flight of the bike that continued to soar on. He came to a rest in direct line with the emergency road flare he'd used to mark the target, which flamed out at the same time he felt his hold on consciousness ebbing.

"Thank you, God bless you, and God bless the United States of America."

McCracken heard those words intermixed with applause and his name being yelled by H. J. Belgrade as the cold and darkness finally found him in their grasps.

EPILOGUE:
FOUND

Washington, DC: one week later

McCracken sat alongside H. J. Belgrade on the park bench on the grounds of the city's Armed Forces Retirement Home, tossing bread crumbs to the flock of pigeons that had magically appeared. He used his left hand since his right was still held in a sling.

"Not sure they're gonna let me stay here much longer, son," Belgrade said suddenly, tossing a handful of his own.

"You cause too much a ruckus?"

"Nah. They say I'm a nuisance to the environment." Belgrade tossed another handful of feed, as more pigeons fluttered to the ground. "They said they never had a bird problem 'til I came along."

"Bird problem?"

"That's what they call it."

"Meaning they have no idea what you pulled off from within their walls."

"Nobody does, except the people who need to. Thanks to

415

them, you're not a wanted man anymore, son. And all that video footage featuring you won't be showing up on any network that doesn't want its air to go dead. It's also mysteriously vanished off the Internet."

"They're welcome to use it after I'm dead, H. J."

"Which I don't reckon is coming anytime soon."

"What's the cover story they're going with?"

"Oh, you're gonna love this. An exploding pipe."

"You mean they're telling the truth for once."

Belgrade looked over at him, seeming to forget the bag of bread crumbs on his lap or the clutter of pigeons now brushing up against both their legs. "Know what's good about this mess, son? There's nothing to clean up like there usually is. Rule's dead, the bikers are dead, and the conspiracy's low-life planners have mysteriously vanished."

"This mess, yes," McCracken acknowledged, "but what about the next one? Looks like we got a whole new generation of enemies who grew up pulling toy prizes out of cereal boxes and have now figured out all the corners and potholes along the information superhighway. Gives us both all the more reason to stick around until the younger guys figure all this shit out. We stopped the tenth circle, sure, but what about the eleventh, twelfth—you do the math, H. J."

"Just when I was hoping to retire."

"Me too."

The two men looked at each other, breaking out into smiles, then laughter, at the same time.

Belgrade gazed about him, taking a big breath of chilled early February air. "Know what else? I believe I could do without this place."

"You do have some bad moments, old friend," McCracken reminded.

"Don't we all?"

*   *   *

McCracken was waiting when Zarrin emerged from George-town University Hospital, her eyes widening in surprise at his presence.

"What'd the doctors say?"

"I'll be lucky to able to hold a water pistol from now on."

"And the piano?"

She shrugged. "There'll be good days and not so good ones."

"What's Colonel al-Asi have to say about that?"

"He offered me a job."

"What kind of job?"

"He didn't say, which says everything." Zarrin saw McCrack-en's gaze turn evasive and thrust a finger at him. "You spoke to him yourself, didn't you?"

"He asked for a reference."

"I'm guessing it was something else."

"He offered me a job too."

"What kind of job?"

"He didn't say." McCracken hesitated, trying to keep his expression flat. "Without those men he sent us, this country would still be picking up the pieces."

"And don't think he doesn't know that."

McCracken smiled slightly until his gaze darted to her hands. "I'd like to see you play again, Zarrin."

"I'll make sure to let you know, so you can enjoy the show."

"Wouldn't miss it for the world," McCracken told her.

"After all," she said, coming up short of a smile, "what else do we have?"

"I was just thinking," Blaine was saying, having finally reached Andrew Ericson's father, Matthew, with the news that Andrew was fine and safe now as well.

"About what?"

"The first time I saw you. At rugby practice at the Reading School."

"What do you remember most?"

"All that hair bouncing around."

Matthew laughed. "Just a memory now."

"Andrew looks just like you."

"Poor kid."

"I can make all the arrangements for his trip home from my end," Blaine told him.

"Believe I'll make the trip over to retrieve him personally. That should give us some time to get together, catch up."

"I'd like that. How was Afghanistan?"

"Is that where I was? All the countries seem the same after a while." He paused, the silence exaggerated by the suddenly static-filled line. "I don't know how to thank you, Blaine."

"Not necessary."

"Because it's family."

"As close as I've got, anyway."

"We need to make sure that's close enough. But we never learn, do we?"

"I think I did this time."

"What's the next holiday?"

"Easter, Passover, something like that."

"You available to join the kid and me?"

"I just might be," said McCracken.

It was two weeks later, his sling finally shed and his beard nearly regrown, when Blaine joined Johnny Wareagle in the Black Hills of South Dakota where Wareagle had resumed work on the granite carving of Chief Crazy Horse in the mountain face. This time, McCracken had his own tools ready, but he still worked with a safety harness while Johnny, the stitches still in place where Boyd Fowler had taken a bite out of his cheek, stood out on the ledge tempting the wind and elements.

"Know my problem with all this, Indian?"

"What?"

"Can't change the past. It's already chiseled in stone without adding our efforts to the mix," Blaine said, gazing up at the scope of the carving before starting in with his tools.

"Maybe we're no better at changing the present," Wareagle told him.

"Because no matter how many times we get the call, the phone keeps ringing."

Johnny regarded Crazy Horse as best he could from this angle. "From where we stand, you wouldn't even know this was a face."

"You mentioned that before."

"But with every bit of chiseling we do," Wareagle continued, his heels teetering precariously on the edge, "no matter how small, it takes on more shape. Incrementally."

"Small victories, sure. You're saying it's the same thing with the present."

"Am I? Because it's the future we're really fighting for." Wareagle looked up, focusing on Crazy Horse as if McCracken wasn't there at all. "But no matter where we stand, we can't really see that future because it's unfinished. It's up to us to shape the contours and create clarity, just like we're doing here."

"Only with an assault rifle instead of a chisel."

"Whatever it takes, Blainey."

McCracken raised his hammer into position, imitating Johnny's motion on the sheer rock face before them waiting to join the rest of the sculpture. "Guess that'll do for now, Indian . . ."

Tap, tap, tap . . .

". . . and we'll see if tomorrow brings anything different."

*   *   *

The area around the actual location of the Roanoke Colony was evacuated out to a two-mile radius. The explosive charges set around the site of the encampment were of the shaped variety to assure a total collapse of not only the well that had contained the contaminated water, but also the surrounding ground structure. That was the only way to assure that all traces of the carbonic acid spawned from ancient volcanic activity would be safely entombed. The explosions were set off by remote detonation, the blast wave creating an earthquake-like rumble that was felt for miles beyond the quarantined area.

Hours later, all residents were allowed to return to their homes after ground tests picked up no trace whatsoever of what had wiped out the colonists in 1590, and had very nearly claimed far more victims than that just a few weeks earlier.

The White Death was no more.

ABOUT THE AUTHOR

Jon Land has written twenty-nine novels. His first series titles were the Blaine McCracken novels, and he is also the author of the Ben and Danielle series and the Jared Kimberlain series. The first three books in his Caitlin Strong series—*Strong Enough to Die* (2009), *Strong Justice* (2010), and *Strong at the Break* (2011)—have all garnered critical praise with *Strong Justice* being named a Top Thriller of the Year by *Library Journal* and runner-up for Best Novel of the Year by the New England Book Festival. Land lives in Providence.

THE BLAINE McCRACKEN NOVELS

FROM OPEN ROAD MEDIA

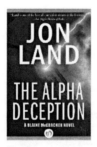
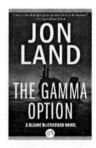

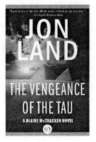

Available wherever ebooks are sold

OPEN ROAD
INTEGRATED MEDIA

Open Road Integrated Media is a digital publisher and multimedia content company. Open Road creates connections between authors and their audiences by marketing its ebooks through a new proprietary online platform, which uses premium video content and social media.

Videos, Archival Documents, and New Releases

Sign up for the Open Road Media newsletter and get news delivered straight to your inbox.

Sign up now at
www.openroadmedia.com/newsletters